T0087988

Verdict on Crimson Fields

ALSO BY M. C. PLANCK

Sword of the Bright Lady (World of Prime, Book 1)

Gold Throne in Shadow (World of Prime, Book 2)

Judgment at Verdant Court (World of Prime, Book 3)

VERDICT ON CRIMSON FIELDS

WORLD OF PRIME BOOK FOUR

M. C. PLANCK

an imprint of **Prometheus Books**
Amherst, NY

Published 2018 by Pyr, an imprint of Prometheus Books

Cover illustration © Gene Mollica
Cover design by Liz Mills
Cover design © Prometheus Books

This is a work of fiction. Characters, organizations, products, locales, and events portrayed in this novel are either products of the author's imagination or used fictitiously.

Inquiries should be addressed to
Pyr
59 John Glenn Drive
Amherst, New York 14228
VOICE: 716-691-0133
FAX: 716-691-0137
WWW.PYRSF.COM

22 21 20 19 18   5 4 3 2 1

Library of Congress Cataloging-in-Publication Data

Names: Planck, M. C., author.
Title: Verdict on Crimson Fields / by M. C. Planck.
Description: Amherst, NY : Pyr, an imprint of Prometheus Books, 2018. | Series: World of prime ; book 4
Identifiers: LCCN 2017057253 (print) | LCCN 2017059056 (ebook) | ISBN 9781633884380 (ebook) | ISBN 9781633884373 (paperback)
Subjects: | BISAC: FICTION / Fantasy / Epic. | FICTION / Fantasy / General. | GSAFD: Fantasy fiction.
Classification: LCC PR9616.4.P56 (ebook) | LCC PR9616.4.P56 V47 2018 (print) | DDC 823/.92—dc23
LC record available at https://lccn.loc.gov/2017057253

Printed in the United States of America

CONTENTS

1

ONWARD FREEZING SOLDIERS

His army crawled over the distant ground below, a trail of brown and black ants on a white tablecloth, flecked in green where the snow had fallen from the fir trees. Christopher floated a thousand feet above, his beard frosting over in the icy wind. He was freezing pointlessly; the forest stretched out for miles ahead, undulating over hills he could not see behind and valleys he could not peer into, and hiding gods knew what under sheltering branches. The wagons meant the column had to pick a winding path, seeking out younger under-growth that could be cut or trampled, or follow frozen stream beds and the occasional wind-swept plain. Their progress was slow, and well-heralded by the ring of axe on wood, the creak of wagons, the clod of hooves, and the curses of cold men. His army advertised its presence with every step. Meanwhile, the enemy had revealed not so much as a stubby green toe.

Christopher's army had fought this enemy once, and won, from inside a crude wooden fort, defeating horrors from pint-sized canni-bals to regenerating magical giants. But that was before the dragon.

The Roman general Varus had lost three legions like this, marching off into hostile wilderness to put down border-raiding bar-barians. Fifteen thousand well-trained men, the products of one of the greatest military machines in history, armed with the best technology the world had to offer at the time, had walked into the woods and dis-appeared. Christopher's three regiments numbered less than a thou-sand, but they had black-powder rifles and cannons where the enemy had only swords, priestesses that could heal a fatal injury with a word, and a commander who could fly. That gave him certain advantages over Varus.

On the other hand, there was still the matter of the dragon.

He could see an obstruction in the line, the stream of men swelling into a knot. The competence of his scouts ruled out impassable terrain. The absence of gunfire ruled out contact with the enemy. But in this dark and quiet forest any encounter must be assumed to include danger.

Christopher put his gloved hands over his face to block the wind and swooped down to where the trouble lay. It was very much like riding a fast but invisible escalator, though without a handrail. Christopher hardly noticed anymore. A fall from even this height was unlikely to kill him.

Inside the forest his aeronautical ability was more trouble than it was worth. Plowing through the snow threatened to tip him forward into a face-plant, while rising above it exposed him to branches and an endless storm of pine needles frozen into painful pricks. Reluctantly he put his foot on the ground and let the spell expire. He immediately regretted the decision, sinking up to his knees in cold powder. He looked around hopefully but had lost track of his horse somewhere else in the column. Not that it mattered. Riding the huge beast would just put his face in the branches again.

He trudged through the slush, turned brown from boots and hooves. His armor clinked and rattled while his men made room for him to pass. Some of their faces were as green as the pine needles, young men freshly drafted and barely trained. Others were like hardwood left out in the sun for too long. Most of them were teenagers; all of them were too young. Even the hardened veterans were not yet middle-aged. Christopher, at forty-two, was the oldest man in the army.

Or was he forty-three now? It was hard to remember. His birthday did not exist in their calendar.

The crowd thickened; the men ahead of him were no longer moving forward. They stepped aside to let him through, giving him plenty of room in case he had to draw his sword. And, of course, getting as far away as possible in case something pounced. The army carried a fortune in supplies, metal, and horseflesh, and in the bodies of the men themselves, but all of it was a fraction of the wealth bound into Christopher's head. The souls of thousands of sentient beings had purchased his exalted powers, bleeding out on his blade—or far more often, torn to bits by bullets and shrapnel—before their heads went into the boiling pots. Out came the fine purple dust called tael, lives reduced to arcane currency for a brief few moments before it all went into his own head. Where the only way it would come out again was in another kettle.

Or in the belly of a beast. Presumably the dragon would eschew boiling and simply eat him, head and all.

In this case his army had foundered not upon an immense, fire-breathing lizard but a pair of youths. A semicircle of young men barely into their first beards, half of them kneeling, with the other half standing behind them, faced a boy and girl surely no older than themselves. The men leveled their rifles at the couple, steady and quiet, waiting for orders. Christopher's advance was halted only when his chief subaltern and best friend blocked him at the edge of the line with an extended hand thrust backward. Karl did not turn around, continuing to watch forward.

On either side of the crowd men wrestled with two-inch cannons, bringing a pair to bear. Once they were in place, Karl dropped his hand.

Christopher stepped forward, a foot or so in front of his men though still behind the ends of their barrels, and studied the conundrum. Both of the young people were beautiful, with an uncanny sharpness to their features. The girl's short hair was white, despite the youthfulness of her face; she was of moderate height and slender build. The boy's long flowing locks were a dark and pleasing shade of green, though he seemed not yet fully grown into his shape.

They were dressed in simple leathers, wholly inadequate to the cold, but they showed no discernable discomfort. The girl wore a bow slung over her back and leaned on a stone-bladed spear planted butt-first in the snow. The young man was unarmed. This marked him as the more dangerous of the two.

They also had pointed ears and violet eyes, identifying them both as elves, which was a promise that talking with them would be at best aggravating, and at worst expensive.

"Lord Vicar Christopher, I presume?" The girl's voice was light, until one listened to it long enough. Christopher heard the force of personality behind her bland words. He had some experience of pretty young things that were not quite what they seemed.

"I am a Prophet now," he answered. "If that matters."

"Not particularly," she said, with a delicate, disarming shrug. "If your rank is still described by a title, you are no match for what lies ahead."

Privately he agreed; what little he knew of dragons—and it was shamefully little, mostly a few old tales from troubadours and the evidence of the burnt-out husk of a castle that had once housed the Lord Duke Nordland and his famous squadron of blue knights—seemed to indicate the wisdom of her position. He and his army had been ordered forward, to avenge the Duke and destroy the threat, but Christopher was pretty sure his true goal was to measure the strength of the monster by how quickly he died. The King, who could also fly, and who also had legions of knights and priests and even a few wizards, was as clueless as anyone else about this foe. Before his royal personage put himself and by extension the entire realm in danger, someone else needed to go find out just what it was they were fighting.

Christopher, despite being the fulcrum of that unpleasant argument, agreed. It did make sound tactical sense. He had stalled only long enough to recruit his third regiment and arm them with the latest devices from his foundry. Then he had marched forward to do his duty.

"I'm not facing it alone," he said. With a wave of his hand he encompassed the silent men around him.

The boy frowned.

"Your lore has faded badly," the girl said, "if you think common men can stand against dragons."

"There are more things in Heaven and Earth, my lady, than are dreamt of in your philosophy," Christopher replied with a diplomatic smile.

"Unless I am very much mistaken," she replied, "neither of those planes is accessible to you. And no amount of rhetorical badinage will impress a dragon."

Christopher sighed. Quoting Shakespeare only made you sound smart when the people you were talking to knew what you were talking about. He tapped the soldier next to him and asked for a round from the man's ammunition box.

"I'm going to take this," he said, holding the bullet up where the girl could see, "and shove it through the dragon's body and out the other side. Then I'm going to do it about a thousand more times. Will that kill a dragon?"

"How will you get close enough to do any shoving?" the boy asked. His voice was like the girl's, high and sweet.

"I'm going to do it from a thousand feet away."

Christopher was being slightly disingenuous. The real plan involved cannons loaded with grapeshot. Dragons had wings, or so he had been told. Their flight, unlike his, was not entirely magical. The gunners would shred the dragon's wings until it was brought to ground, and then hammer it with eight-pound round shot until it was hamburger. Meanwhile, the rifles would keep the dragon's goblin allies at bay, as they had before.

The girl shook her head in dismay. "You underestimate the difficulty at every stage."

"That's okay," he said. "People underestimate me all the time, too." It was a veritable cottage industry in the Kingdom.

"Are you so wedded to this prize that reason cannot sway you?" the boy asked. "Does only greed drive you forward, or is there some other path you might be persuaded to take?"

Christopher frowned back. "That dragon burned an entire county. It leads a horde of goblins that are intent on eating everyone I know. I have been ordered by the King to destroy the threat and preserve the realm. This objective accords with my own desire not to be eaten. So, no, it is not greed that drives me; but unless you have some other suggestion I'm going to have to be moving along."

"No greed at all?" the boy asked, ever so slyly, and Christopher had to bite his tongue.

"Not entirely." He had taken a huge loan from the Saint for his last rank, which would probably require the tael of a dragon to pay back.

"You can destroy the goblins," the girl said helpfully. "We have no interest in them."

"That's quite generous of you," Christopher said. "But unless you're offering to kill the dragon for me, I don't see how it helps."

The boy spoke sharply. "Not kill. Never kill. But I will undertake to drive it away, and guarantee your realm a thousand years of protection from its return."

The boy was standing there, hardly more than sixteen, with empty hands, promising absurdities.

"And what surety do we have?" Ser Gregor asked.

Christopher looked over his shoulder. The blue knight-turned-priest had joined the party, moving quietly despite wearing the same style of heavy scaled armor that Christopher wore. Ser Cannan was with him, wearing the third suit that marked the three of them out as distinctive targets in the sea of brown greatcoats. The enemy would aim for them first; a fair trade, since they were the hardest to kill.

Cannan had his sword drawn and resting on his shoulder, looking almost draconic in his shaggy hair and scales. Christopher glanced at the man he had promised a miracle and stopped feeling superior to the boy.

"My word," said the boy, "and hers. Though hers alone should be good enough for you."

"Her word?" Gregor said. "When we don't even know her name? What binds us beyond a stray meeting in the woods?"

"We are not entirely strangers, Ser Gregor," the girl said. "We are linked through the Lady Kalani. Your lord's liegewoman, your instrument in taming the ulvenmen, and your ally through affiliation."

"And what is she to you?" Gregor said. "Companion, cousin, countryman?"

"Stronger bonds than those drove me out into the snow to find you." The girl laughed, deep and genuine. "Kalani is my daughter."

2

INTO THE ARMS OF THE DEAD

Gregor got the column moving again. Somebody brought up Christopher's horse, and he clambered into the saddle. The branches would have to be endured; walking through the snow in heavy metal armor was not a good use of his strength.

This did not apply to his guests. They strolled alongside the column, through the unbroken snow, and left no tracks. It was disconcerting, so he stopped paying attention to it. In any case, the two of them were perfectly at ease carrying on a conversation, despite the fact he towered over them.

"I don't know if I can accept your offer," he told the boy. "The King was not happy with my last elf-based compromise."

"Your king is your problem," the boy said. "Dragons are mine, and you would be wise to leave them to me."

"Gently, Lucien," the girl said. "The law is on his side in this. Vercingtrox initiated this conflict."

Christopher had become used to exhausting himself with questions, since everything about this strange world had to be explained to him. In this case, however, his exasperation was superseded by amusement. Lalania, his minstrel, political advisor, and history teacher, rode beside him on a coal-black courser, looking like she had eaten a bug. All he had done was quirk a questioning eyebrow at her. He did it a couple of more times, just for fun.

"No, Christopher, I do not know anything about dragon-law," she finally admitted.

"Actually, it is elf-law," the girl said helpfully. "Dragons only have one rule, and it does not apply to non-dragons."

Lalania gritted her teeth. Christopher winked again.

"Ask D'Kan," she muttered. "He's the elf expert."

She was being spiteful. D'Kan knew horses, and hunting, and all the things young men always find fascinating. What he knew about history would fit in a thimble. His grasp of the elven language was worse.

"Nonetheless I advise you to accept my help," Lucien said. The boy wouldn't let it go.

"Ser—Lucien, is it?" Christopher said, "I promise you I will give your offer due consideration. Until then you are welcome to accompany us and offer whatever advice you think will help."

"Ser is not required," the girl said. "Just Lucien. And you may call me Alaine. We do not use titles, but if it makes you more comfortable you may assign whatever terms you like."

If he hadn't already taken them seriously, that would have done the trick. Only people with truly advanced ranks forwent titles, just as only celebrities on the A-list went by a single name.

"Then perhaps you should tell me what I need to know," Christopher said. For all his professed concern, Lucien had not revealed much information.

"We cannot aid you against the goblins," Alaine explained. "Neither in offense or defense. To do so would be to bind ourselves to the same terms Vercingtrox is bound."

"You would watch us torn to pieces by monsters and do nothing?" Lalania asked. She hadn't liked the first elf they had met. This meeting didn't seem likely to improve her estimation of the race.

"Of course not," Alaine said. "I could never watch such a terrible act. I would run away first."

Lalania had a fire in her eyes that was about to explode, so Christopher decided to jump in. "That seems . . . unfriendly," he said. "The end result for us would be the same, whether you saw it or not."

"Is it not always thus?" Alaine said. "You are not the only ones fighting goblins today. You are not even the only ones facing a dragon.

Yet there is only one of me. I cannot aid them all, and therefore they must perish, whether I watch or no. Meanwhile greater threats work their way across the face of Prime, and I have appointments to keep. This is the point of elf-law, after all: to keep us on the path instead of wandering in the weeds."

"You make no exemption for friendship?" Lalania said. "You ride under our protection, eat at our fire, serve the same Bright gods we do, and yet we gain naught from it?"

"In sheer point of fact, we do not require your protection, we have not shared victual with you, and we do not serve your gods."

Christopher took a closer look at the elf. What he had taken for fashionable slimness was instead fitness; the girl's muscles were dense and well-defined, without a spare ounce, the body of a hardened warrior. She was also apparently a hard case.

"Nonetheless," Christopher said, "you are welcome to both our food and shelter."

"Graciously offered," Alaine said, "and thus accepted. Yet do not forget we are bound by our law."

"And who enforces this law?" Christopher asked, trying to imagine what power could impose itself on people so cavalier that they would stroll through goblin-infested woods without a care.

"Why, I do," Alaine said. "That is my function."

Christopher started to speak, but then stopped himself. His time on this planet was having an effect. He was getting better at thinking things through before he said them.

In this case it was significant that Alaine had said "I," rather than "we." Christopher finally grasped the fact that Alaine was protecting him from Lucien as much as she was protecting Vercingtrox. In hindsight, it might have been wiser to just let the army shoot them both. Too late for that, though.

"At least you gave us a name for our foe," Christopher said. "Lala, can we use that to scry on him?"

"It," Lucien said. "The correct term in your language is 'it.'"

Now he could add pedantry to the list of elven crimes.

"The name will be of no use to you," Alaine said. "It is not a true name, merely a term of convenience among us here."

Christopher thought about asking if Alaine and Lucien were their real names, but once you phrased the question like that, it kind of answered itself.

He fished about for some safer topic of conversation. "So, you said Kalani was your daughter?"

"Indeed she is," Alaine said. "Tell me, Lord Prophet, do you have any children?"

"Call me Christopher," he said automatically. "And no." He stopped short then, caught up in misery. It had been three years since he had seen his wife. They had been of an age where starting a family was either to occur very, very soon or not at all. The decision, never consciously addressed, had never been in doubt. If he had not fallen through an invisible portal his problems would be diapers and sleeping schedules, not dragons and surly kings.

Now the window was closing, every day, and he was here on a distant planet playing soldier instead of sharing her life as a husband and father.

Alaine noticed his sudden shortness. She finished her little joke, trapped as she was in the middle of it, but the tone of her voice was compassionate.

"I have but one, yet she is vexation for a thousand lifetimes."

Christopher found himself genuinely interested in what could trouble this serene creature. "How so?" he asked.

Alaine frowned wryly as she answered. "Common sense washes over her like rain off a duck. Patience is a word she understands only as a pejorative for every position I hold dear or counsel I offer."

The Lady Kalani was vexing, Christopher had to agree, but lack of patience was not a charge he would have lain against her. She had volunteered to babysit a horde of dog-men for a dozen generations or more, all in the hopes of raising them to some semblance of civilization.

"If you don't mind my saying so," Christopher said, "You hardly seem old enough to have a grown child."

"By what basis could you possibly judge my age?" Alaine asked. "Surely you would not apply a human standard."

"No, of course not," Christopher said hastily. "That would be silly. I just meant you look the same age as Kalani."

"Only by human appearances," Lucien said. "You just said it would be silly to apply human standards, and now you're doing it. Did you mean to be silly?"

"Lucien." Alaine touched the boy's arm gently. "We talked about this."

"Forgive me," the boy apologized. "Human social interactions are not my forte. Yet you deserve better; I shall strive harder."

"I was being silly," Christopher said with a sigh. Not being able to lie was sometimes a burden. "Not intentionally. But in the absence of any other cue, naturally I'm going to fall back on what tools I have. And both of you look like very convincing sixteen-year-olds."

"Thank you," Lucien said, with every appearance of genuine gratitude.

"Elves do not experience physiological aging," Alaine said. "There is no external cue."

Christopher narrowed his eyes. "You mean . . . never?"

"Never is a very long time." She shrugged ambiguously, clearly uninterested in continuing the discussion.

Christopher decided to take advantage of her desire to change the subject. "I had some questions I didn't get to ask Kalani. Perhaps you could answer them."

"This is hardly the time or place," Lalania interjected. "Nor are they likely to have answers that please you."

That was what she always said. In the many long weeks since she had watched him try—and fail—to go home, she had avoided every conversation about where his home was. It was information she did not want in her head, just in case anyone dangerous wanted it out. Like, for instance, the King.

"Indeed, this is not the time or place for most questions," Alaine said. "Unless your question was, 'Am I riding into a goblin ambush?' It would be a wildly appropriate time to ask that particular question."

A plethora of responses suggested themselves to Christopher, but he chose none of them. Instead he kicked his horse into a gallop and shouted. "To arms! Ambush!"

Men up and down the line took up the cry as the column came to a halt, rifles bristling out to either side like porcupine quills.

Alaine put her fingers to her mouth and whistled, sharp and piercing. Royal turned underneath Christopher, ignoring the reins, and wheeled in a tight circle. Christopher was too busy ducking branches to argue with the horse, but he spared a glare for the elf as they thundered past. These elven women took far too many liberties with his mount.

From the rear of the column, where he was now heading in a churning flurry of snow, came the sound of gunfire. Royal decided a bush was not worth going around and went through it, throwing up so much debris that Christopher was blinded. By the time he got his eyes clear enough to see, they were in the middle of the battle.

Armored human-sized figures fought with swords and bows against rifles. Surprisingly, they were winning. Christopher witnessed one shot straight through the chest at point-blank range with no obvious effect. The creature did not even shrug. It swung its curved scimitar in a vicious arc, knocking a soldier to the ground in a spray of blood. Then it stepped over the fallen man, moving toward the column with implacable determination. Half a dozen other creatures followed, while behind them a dozen more fired repeatedly from short recurve bows.

Christopher drew his sword, panic rising in his throat. He had always carried an unconscious fear that the arbitrary and irrational rules of this world would change one day, leaving his weapons useless. Now the fear was made real, and he did not know what to do.

His men were less reflective. They operated out of habit and training, and not just his. Karl had taught them that high-ranked heroes would require more than one bullet. Consequently they loaded and fired steadily, even as the swordsmen cut into their ranks. Then one of them threw a grenade at the line of archers.

When his vision cleared from the blast, Christopher could see two things immediately. First, the explosion had been less effective than expected; only three archers had been destroyed. Second, and far more important, the blast had shredded the white full-body sheathing that camouflaged the creatures. Underneath Christopher could see naked bone, unencumbered by flesh.

He raised the sword high and shouted in Celestial. He had faced animated skeletons before, as a lowly first-rank, and his power had been sufficient to drive them back. Now he was somewhat more potent. A wave of invisible light washed out from him, and the skeletons caught in its wake popped like rotten mushrooms.

The remaining few took no notice of this event. Christopher trotted his horse closer and repeated the exercise. Two soldiers who had been wrestling with one of the monsters, trying to hold it down while a third applied a burning torch to it, fell into the snow at its sudden collapse.

Christopher dismounted and went to heal the wounded. One of the priestesses was already at work making sure no one died from blood loss, going from man to man and binding their wounds with a word, though leaving them unconscious in the snow. He walked behind her, poking each man gently with his sword and speaking in Celestial. The men opened their eyes and clambered to their feet as he passed.

"You should not spend your power so freely," the priestess chided him over her shoulder. She was tending to a boy who was still awake, though white-faced and red-shirted from an arrow through the shoulder.

"I need answers more than I need spells," he said, inventing a justification for his largesse on the spot. He raised his voice. "Listen up, all of you. Did the rifles take down any of them?"

The men looked at him blankly. He realized that was not a helpful question to have asked, especially if the answer was "No." To cover his mistake he turned back out to the side of the road, where Royal waited. Cannan was also there, his faithful shadow having caught up at last.

"This one, I think." Cannan said when Christopher got close. The red knight kicked a still figure with his boot.

Christopher bent down and pulled the cloth from its face. A wonderful bit of disguise, in that the cloth had no holes for eyes, nose, or mouth. Underneath, the skull was shattered from force rather than magic. Christopher took a more careful assessment and counted three bullet holes, besides the one through the top of the head.

He found another whose spine and hips had been shot out. So the bullets could destroy the skeletons, if they happened to find solid bone. Most shots just snapped a rib or two to no effect. These things would be easier to kill with a sledgehammer than a gun.

A soldier had come over to join them. Sergeant Kennet, one of his youngest and most able subalterns. "Any tactical advice, sir?"

"Aim for the head, I guess?" That was fairly sound advice for dealing with any foe, so Christopher repeated it with more conviction. "Aim for the head. You just need to break enough bone that the enchantment loses its grip."

Kennet saluted and went to share this wisdom with the rest of the army.

D'Kan finally appeared, riding his handsome tan courser. The young Ranger gazed down at the battlefield with displeasure. Dismounting, he paced backward from one of the bodies, to where its tracks began in a pile of lumpy snow.

"Clever," D'Kan grunted. "They simply ordered the creatures to lie still and let the snow bury them. Without breath or heat, they could have lain here for weeks, waiting for us."

"What matter?" Cannan said with a shrug. "They lost two dozen for the price of a few spells. We lost not even a single man."

A blow that did not kill instantly was unlikely to kill at all, as long as you had a healing spell close at hand.

"They gained much, though," D'Kan retorted. "They have observed your sky-fire in action, they know that Christopher is a priest of considerable rank, and they have witnessed that he will charge helter-skelter into battle to defend a few wagons."

"Eh," Christopher said. "They already knew most of that. I fought these guys before, remember. Although . . . they didn't have skeletons then."

"They didn't have a dragon either, I presume," D'Kan said.

"No," Christopher mused, "just trolls." That was why he had so many torches in an army equipped with magical light-stones.

"If they had put a troll under that snow, you would have paid a higher price," Cannan admitted.

"And they would have paid as well," D'Kan answered, instantly taking the opposing position to Cannan, an act he did so consistently it had lost all its charm. "Trolls yield actual treasure, instead of the paltry grains you can recycle from those broken things. In any case, if the goblins can discipline a troll to lie in ambush for a week without trying to eat something, we'd best turn around now."

"Go ahead, if you like," Cannan said. "We'll manage without you, somehow."

Christopher ignored their sniping, kneeling above an inert form and casting the smallest of spells, an orison mostly intended for teaching purposes—though even it would stop a man from bleeding to death. He was rewarded with a single grain of tael. It was hardly worth the effort.

"Can you boil these skulls?" Christopher asked.

"Only magic can harvest magic," D'Kan answered. The Ranger had a few minor spells of his own, so he walked among several corpses, bending down to tap them on the head. "This is all I can do today, my lord." The boy always turned formal when the conversation turned to tael. He handed Christopher three more tiny purple grains.

Christopher scratched his beard. "Get Gregor. And Lala, Disa, and Torme. But not the priestesses." Their orisons would save a life. They were too valuable to spend on treasure hunting.

"You would summon all of your magic to a single spot, for the sake of a few coins?" Surprisingly, it was Cannan making this argument.

"Not just that. They need to see this." Two of those people were priests of some rank themselves. If Christopher had known what he faced, he might have ended the battle earlier.

"Then let us wait here for all of them to assemble," Cannan said, "rather than walking them one by one through this net. Just in case another, larger snare is waiting for a suitable target."

"In that case," Christopher said to D'Kan, "fetch the elves as well."

3

DUBIOUS ALLIES

Gregor nodded approvingly at the twice-dead corpses.

"Something for you to do, my dear," he said to his wife, the priestess Disa. "We'll make a warrior of you yet. Imagine how you'll feel when an entire battle line collapses because you waved your hand."

The woman in question shook her head. "I fear I do not command the same authority as our Lord Prophet."

"You can at least drive them off," Christopher said. "For that matter, so can you, Gregor." The man had a single rank of priest, but that was enough for constructs of this lowly nature. "Send them away while the soldiers reload."

Curate Torme, the commander of the third regiment, was himself a fifth-rank priest. He had dismounted to inspect the corpses, looking slightly wistful at having missed the action and somewhat uncertain as to what the outcome would have been. Christopher sympathized. Like his own, the man's promotion had been sudden, going from first to fifth rank in a few days, a haste-driven necessity. Christopher had needed a man of rank to officer the new regiment, and Torme had been the only choice. But now the man was unsure of his powers, having skipped all the intervening stages where he would have normally practiced and honed them. It seemed to be a feature of the Church of Marcius, as Christopher's career advance had been equally rapid. On the other hand, it was unwise to draw conclusions from such a small sample. They were the only three priests of Marcius in the whole Kingdom. Disa and the other priestesses served the Bright Lady, goddess of Light and Healing. Marcius was a White god, a consort of the Bright Lady and dedicated to all that was good and pure; but he was also a war god, forever with a sword in his hand. The contradiction was not as obvious as it would seem, here on this world where everything ate everything and where even the power for good came from consuming souls.

There was another way in which Torme and Christopher were similar. Both had come from different worlds than the men in the army. Christopher from Earth and Torme from a county ruled by the iron shadow of the Gold Throne, lands as dark and fearful as the sewers of history could provide.

"Is this a tactic you've see before?" Christopher asked. What he really meant was *Is this something the Gold Apostle would do against me?* but even here in the snow he was unwilling to speak so openly.

"No one sends soul-trapped against the priests of the Gold Throne," Torme answered. "They would seize them and send them back. Where we command these creatures to destruction, the Dark simply commands their obedience."

"Still," Gregor said, "they did some damage. A few hundred of these would make excellent shock troops. While we dealt with the mosquito's sting, their principals would move into position. And if the ploy came to naught—it costs them little."

"Agreed," Torme said. "Sergeant Kennet's plan—to let them advance to close range and then aim for the skull—seems sound."

Christopher was watching Alaine and Lucien. The boy was sniffing as if some hidden thing smelled rotten. Christopher assumed the scent of black powder still hung in the air. He had become so inured to it he hardly noticed it anymore.

"Alchemy?" Alaine asked. Christopher detected a welter of concerns in that solitary word. His ability to read people's emotions seemed to be advancing with his rank. An interesting fact that he did not ask Lalania about, despite his intense curiosity. His self-discipline was also advancing, though that might be merely a result of constant exercise.

"Chemistry," he told the elf. "There is no magic involved."

The crease of her eyes told him she found that even more concerning.

"Didn't Kalani tell you about it?" he asked.

"I confess I have not spoken directly with her in some time," Alaine said.

He grinned. "You want me to let her know you're here? Say hi or something? I could do that for you." He had a spell that would let him reach out to anyone he knew, at any distance, but that wasn't why he was grinning. He was grinning because he knew what Alaine was going to say next.

"That's not necessary," she said. "Or even, to be honest, helpful."

He finally had a lever to apply to the elf. One word to her daughter, and the mother would no doubt get an earful. A pitiful bit of leverage, but he was comforted to have it.

Karl apparently felt he had waited long enough for the regimental commanders to get to the point, and, since they hadn't, he would. "We can expect no more easy marches. The enemy has ranged us and will contest our every move now."

Christopher sighed. "Unfortunately we have not ranged them. I still haven't seen so much as chicken coop, let alone a village or town. I'm not even sure we're going the right direction. It would be embarrassing if we just marched past them and froze to death in the snow."

"You need not worry on that score," Alaine said. "Vercingtrox will come to you, should you miss him."

"Then we should fortify and wait," Christopher said. It was the tactic they had used against the ulvenmen, to great effect.

Gregor shook his head. "You saw what they did to Castle Nordland. Lala's wooden fort would pop like a maiden on her . . ." He trailed off, swallowing the rest of his crude soldier's joke. Sometimes it was hard to remember there were women present, since there were only eight of them in the entire army. Nine now, if one counted the elf. Christopher was not inclined to count her.

"Marching around in the snow and stumbling over traps hardly seems wiser," Christopher argued. "What we need is to know where the capital is. Then we can force the issue, perhaps on our terms." He turned to look at Alaine expectantly.

"I told you," she said. "We cannot aid you directly. I can only say that if you turn anymore westward, you will trespass on troglodyte territory, and Lucien and I will have to leave you. The last time we went there, I couldn't get the stench off for weeks."

As he had suspected, the elf was willing to skirt the law as much as the letter would allow her. Warning him about the ambush had made that clear. What was not so obvious was whether or not her assistance would be helpful to his cause or hers. Whatever that was.

They made camp early, the men still jittery from the encounter with the skeletons. They were solid, brave men, but killing ulvenmen did not require special instructions. Just shooting was good enough. That this first brief battle had resulted in a lecture on tactics was disconcerting. What other tricks would the goblins throw at them?

"They can go invisible," Christopher said, sitting in front of a fire and eating porridge. Army life had inverted their normal diet. They ate hot, fresh bread in the morning, after the bakery wagons had cooked all night, while the dull sludge of porridge was hastily boiled at the evening meal, with dried meat or salted pork thrown in to bolster it. Christopher suspected Lalania used magic to make her meals more palatable. He didn't ask, though. She couldn't do it for the whole army, and thus by extension she could not do it for him. He still said a prayer over his food, but it was only to render it safe from poison. His magic left the lumps and cardboard flavor intact.

Alaine and Lucien accepted bowls as well. The girl gave no apparent sign of noticing how poorly his troops cooked. The boy seemed to think the bowl was an interesting specimen, in the same way a scientist might be fascinated by a hideous, deadly spider.

"So could the ulvenmen," Gregor said, picking up the thread of his conversation. No doubt the topic was on everyone's mind. "And they could do soul-trapped. But the shaman was smart enough to put all of his power in one big creature, where it could withstand your chant."

"They can also regenerate," Christopher added. "At least, the trolls. And they had a flying giant. It did something else—went intangible, so bullets couldn't hurt it. Oh, I forgot. The giant can freeze stuff." He stopped, haunted by a terrible image. Karl, white and stiff, turned into a meat popsicle by frightful magic.

Alaine looked at Christopher curiously. "If your bullets could not harm an ogre magi, what makes you think they would harm a dragon?"

"Magic," he answered. "Disa, you can do the weapon blessing. So can Gregor, and Torme. Keep it in mind, as many copies as you can." He'd used the same spell on grenades and ghosts. It had an excellent track record of introducing the supernatural to the power of physics.

"Unlikely to be required," Lucien interjected, "since I will be dealing with the dragon."

"Do it all the same," Christopher said to his fellow priests. "What if more of those blue giants show up?"

"I take it you prevailed in this earlier battle," Alaine said. "Defeating an ogre magi is no small accomplishment. Indeed, I would hesitate to engage one. May I ask what rank you were at the time?"

"Just first," Christopher said. He turned back to the rest of group, waving his spoon for emphasis. "The blue giant had a bunch of trolls and a couple hundred goblins. And all those damn wolves—remember those, Karl? I'd hate to meet those guys in this snow."

"Excuse me," Alaine said. "Do you intend me to conclude that you won against such foes as a mere first-rank?"

"I told you," Christopher said. "I wasn't alone." He'd tried to tell Lord Nordland that at the time, and failed. Nordland had retreated and Christopher's army had gained the victory and the credit. And the spoils—that battle had made Christopher both rich and powerful, though it felt trivial now, after thousands of dead ulvenmen and a reanimated *Tyrannosaurs Rex*.

"Your chemistry seems quite effective," Alaine said, though her tone suggested she did not believe him. He'd tried to tell Nordland the same thing, and failed at that too.

"It is," he said. "It is that effective. And it's even better now." Then his biggest guns had been a handful of two-inch cannon. He had a few new toys in his baggage train. The elf boy would need to get used to the stench of powder, if he planned on staying.

"All of this through craft alone, without magic?" Alaine was finally giving the topic the attention it deserved. If only he could get her to knock some sense into the rest of the peerage of the Kingdom.

"A little magic," he conceded. The rifle breeches needed the arcane powers of a master smith, and his sulfur was refined by witches. But this was apprentice-level magic, below even the first rank. In any case, it hardly mattered. "Given a little time, I won't even need that." His machinists were getting better, and the Bardic College could probably teach Fae and her girls how to make sulfur without spells.

"This is most . . . interesting." Alaine didn't seem happy with the word; based on her frown, he suspected she meant to choose "disturbing" or even "frightening." It was kind of the reaction he expected from high-ranks, when they learned that their supernatural powers weren't so dominating. Or necessary.

"You stick around, you can see for yourself." More words he had tried to say to Nordland. "Assuming we can find some goblins."

"I trust to that," Alaine said. "And I shall, thank you. You must understand, at my age, one sees little that is truly new. I could not in good faith walk away from this without investigating it."

That was as close to a promise that she would lead them to the goblin capital as he was going to get. Christopher sat back, contented.

"I would know more about the disposition of their forces," Karl said. "The abominations are your business, but there will still be a battle of flesh and blood between men and goblins without rank. How many soldiers do we face? Do they favor cavalry or infantry? Do they build trebuchets or other engines of war?"

"I cannot answer you, Goodman," Alaine said, "because I do not know. An encounter with goblins is perpetually surprising; the race prides itself on inventiveness and trickery, at least where pain and suffering are concerned. Indeed, I would have expected to find your chemistry among them."

"Damn," Christopher said. "That would be bad." Now that he thought about it, the goblins had adapted to his tactics quickly last time, despite the fact that the battle had only raged for a single day and night. They would not be like the ulvenmen, trusting to strength and courage alone. And if they learned his secrets—guns in the hands of goblins was enough to give him nightmares while still awake.

"So it would," Alaine said. "So it would."

4

RIVER OF SAND AND FOG

Over the next few days, the army stumbled over three more snow-covered skeletal ambushes. The traps were impossible to detect and difficult for the men to contend with despite Kennet's instructions, though they melted instantly in the face of the high-ranking priests. Disa was not at all pleased with her new role as defender of the column, even though she rode in the middle with Gregor. Christopher was at the head, leaving Torme to take the rear.

Karl was equally unhappy. "We are breaking the first and second rule of war."

Christopher screwed his face up in confusion. He was about to argue that they were fighting automatons, not soldiers, so there could be no prisoners and thus no rules, but sense reasserted itself in time. There was no Geneva convention here. Instead he quirked an eyebrow.

"We are splitting our ranks," Karl explained, "and worse, we are becoming predictable."

Cannan growled his agreement. "Gregor and Disa should always be by your side. Sooner or later you will rush to a knot of skeletons, only to find it backed by trolls and ogres."

"They poke us until our response becomes automatic and complacent. Then they lure you into a battle on their terms," Karl said.

"Ah, but I am doing the luring," Christopher said. "We haven't used a cannon yet. When those trolls and ogres show up, it will be my trap they are falling into."

Karl frowned, and Christopher sighed as he watched the young man talk himself into believing. People paid far too much deference to Christopher's rank, as if they thought the god Marcius whispered in his ear at every turn.

"Actually, that's a terrible plan," Christopher said. "They already know about cannons, at least the small ones. They won't be surprised." The bigger guns took too long to bring to bear, designed for set-piece battles, not hit-and-run tactics under the cover of trees. "So I am open to suggestions."

Gunfire interrupted their conversation. Christopher and Gregor charged off to deal with the threat, a terrifying ride into unknown danger that left his heart pounding even after all the skeletons succumbed to his invisible radiance.

Once again there was no hammer behind the needle, but Christopher felt the pain of the blow all the same. One of his men had taken an unlucky arrow to the face and died instantly. All of the profit they had made from breaking skeletons would be wiped out by the cost of a single revival spell, and then some. The goblins were now winning on points.

Christopher looked down at the still forms of the enemy. It would drain his casters of their minor spells to harvest the tiny grains of tael, spells that could save a life in the heat of battle. When D'Kan arrived and prepared to dismount, Christopher shook his head.

"Don't waste the power. We're not going to win this war a coin at a time."

Instead, Christopher swung off of his horse to stand over the dead man. He took a lump of purple from the silver vial around his neck and placed it on the corpse's chest. This would be the first time he had performed the revival spell; it felt like there should be ceremony to mark the occasion. In its place, a handful of common soldiers watched silently, their breath coming out in soft white clouds, while the rest of the column trudged by, the drivers glancing askance and wide-eyed, the hardened soldiers pretending indifference.

He drew his sword and spoke in Celestial, eschewing the long build-up Faren had used when preparing a village for a miracle and its possible failure. Many of the soldiers watching had already been revived, though they would have woken up in the Cathedral under the Saint's gentle hand. They were used to miracles now, while their profession demanded they be prepared for tragedy. He did not need to speak of those things to them. Christopher tapped the body with his blade on each shoulder and then the head, like a ritual of knighthood. The purple stone, worth ten pounds of gold, sank into the man's flesh and disappeared forever.

Christopher tried not let his annoyance creep into his voice. "Get up. We're not done yet."

He felt if he were talking into a narrow doorway that opened on some vast space. The soldier was surrounded by a shimmering light that gradually revealed a carpet of soft green grass. Sunlight dappled the soldier's face as he smiled, staring off to the side at something Christopher could not see.

The soldier turned his face to look at him in bemusement, but did not speak. Christopher did not blame him. Wherever that place was, it looked a lot nicer than the real world.

"You owe me two more years," Christopher said. "Honor demands it. So get up and get back into line."

"Is my mother still there?" the boy asked, and Christopher was reminded how young he was.

"Yes," Christopher answered confidently, assuming that nothing could have happened in the last two minutes to make him a liar.

The mist faded, returning the boy to a bloody body lying in the snow. The boy opened his eyes and gasped. From his perspective, it was the instant after he had seen the arrow flying toward his face. Christopher knew from experience that the boy would not remember the conversation they had just had or what he had been gazing at or the sun-drenched meadow.

The boy looked around wildly, jerking his head and pawing at his face with both hands.

"Soldier, I gave you an order," Christopher barked.

The sound brought the boy back to focus. He glanced at Christopher, seeing him for the first time, and scrambled to his feet.

Christopher pointed to the rifle lying in the snow. The young soldier blushed and snatched it from the ground. He trembled for a moment, until finally training reasserted itself. Then he stood erect and saluted.

"Find a wagon to ride. Tell your sergeant you are excused from duty for the next twenty-four hours." The boy swayed where he stood. "Dismissed," Christopher said, and watched him stagger back to the column. Christopher turned away to the forest, where he could drop the mask of hardened commander. It hurt his face worse than the cold.

"Still looking for suggestions," he said to Cannan, standing by his side.

"I have none you will like," the knight replied. "By tradition the answer is easy. These pinpricks would not even register against high-ranks. They exist only to foil the mundane. That you spend your power protecting your commoners must no doubt mystify the goblins. They will wonder why you even brought an army, if you have to babysit it at every step."

"Well, that's something," Christopher said. "As long as we keep them guessing."

Cannan shook his head. "Their patience for your jest will only last so long. We will not like the one they tell in return."

The next day dawned cold and clear. The empty sky pressed on Christopher with a sense of dread. All jokes depended on timing; if the goblins were half as competent as their reputation, today would deliver their punchline. Watching the army rouse itself to the smell of fresh bread and frying meat, Christopher gave an impulsive order.

"Extra bacon," he told the cooks. Karl glanced at him but did not argue. Perhaps he could feel it too.

A dozen attacks by skeletal forces reinforced his judgment. Several of the ambushes were clearly hurried, the snow over their forms shallow and obviously placed by hand, instead of the vastly superior technique of letting natural snowfall cover them. The mood of the army tightened like a bowstring in the cold. The scouts fell back, driven from the field by the threat of soul-trapped abominations. Christopher found himself at the leading edge of the column, with only a dozen cavalrymen, Cannan, and D'Kan in front of him. Late in the day they rode down a small slope under thick trees and spilled out onto a frozen river plain, several hundred yards wide, flat and clear, and found an army waiting on the other side.

Cautiously, Christopher's group picked their way forward halfway to the river, claiming enough ground for their own army to fall into battle line behind them, but still far enough that they could flee from archery or a sudden charge.

A handful of cavalry raced up to support them. Gregor and Karl, with twenty more horsemen. The column began splashing out to either side, like a stream breaking upon a rock.

Gregor stood in the saddle to peer out at the enemy. "Quite a welcoming party. But what are they waiting for?"

"Better to ask, why are they waiting in daylight?" D'Kan asked. "They can see through the night like a man sees the day. Why not fall upon us when we are sleeping?"

"They wish to contest our advance," Karl answered. "Fording a river puts us at greater disadvantage than a fortified night camp. The men will be easy targets in shallow water."

Gregor seemed to mull over Karl's words. Christopher was surprised to see the older man deferring to Karl's military wisdom, until Cannan provided an explanation.

"An uncommon concern," he told Christopher. "Traditionally speaking, we high-ranks would ride downstream, cross the river unopposed, come up behind them, and kill their high-ranks. The enemy commoners would disperse in panic, and we would send our own commoners out to hunt them down one by one."

With a shock, Christopher realized that Karl had more experience with mundane armies than any of his other commanders. Even Torme had been a knight; he would have fought rank-to-rank, with little regard for the lives or capabilities of the commoners. All of their hopes rested on Christopher's stratagems and Karl's tactics.

Against courageous but unsophisticated savages that had been enough, but the patient discipline of the enemy across the river was like a thousand red flags waving in wind. A metaphor made apt by the fact that there were actual red banners snapping in the icy breeze. The goblin forces were drawn up into a dozen squares facing the river, with each block of a hundred flying a red pennant on a long pole. The groups were separated by a few yards of clear space. The pattern jogged something in Christopher's memory.

"I can answer one of your questions, Karl. The goblins favor pikes."

"I don't see any weapons," Gregor said. "Just shields."

"They know we have horsemen," Karl said. "An empty plain, a frozen river, and a shield wall. It practically begs for a cavalry charge."

"And then the pikes come up out of the snow." Christopher grimaced. He'd seen it in a movie once. He could only assume it would be uglier in real life.

"While skeletons come up out of the ice behind," D'Kan said. "They could hide an entire regiment in that river. They could have left them there since last spring."

"I, for one, am bloody sick of surprises in the snow," Gregor said. "Maybe we should come back in summer."

"There are better things to do with warm weather," D'Kan said. "But why quibble? I will scout out a path upstream. We will flank them and destroy their commanders. By the time we are finished taking heads this rabble will have melted away."

"You'll find no ford upstream," Cannan said. "The river will run fast in those hills."

Cannan had probably said that just to argue with D'Kan, but there were hills sprouting up to the north. The closest had a sharp cliff face cut into it, the exposed gray rock a dull contrast to the whiteness of the rest of the world. Both Christopher and Karl stared at the bluff.

"How far does a trebuchet shoot?" Christopher asked his second-in-command.

"A thousand feet at most. I would think that ridge too far. But if you held the defense, you would hide cannons up there. Do we trust the goblins not to make their own surprises?"

"If they had siege engines, they would have used them against us last time." Although the goblins had been in a hurry then, so perhaps that was not a sound inference. Something about the ridge made Christopher uneasy. At one point he almost thought he saw a shimmer in the air. "But just in case, make sure a few field guns are aimed at it."

"As long as we are worrying about invisible threats, take another look at their battle line. Where are their reserves?" Karl gestured across the river, where the enemy army apparently was backed by a still, silent forest. The tree line bothered Christopher. It looked entirely too innocent, literally picture-perfect.

Gunfire erupted behind them, startling Christopher. In their previous encounter the goblins had flanked him with invisible trolls. For that matter, despite their very professional-looking army, they might not be with the modern program: for all he knew their high-ranks were stalking up behind him for the traditional coup de grace. He turned his horse around, a task made difficult as Royal was eager to have at the enemy in front of them. By the time he finished, he could see Torme coming out of the woods and waving a dismissive hand. It had merely been another skeleton ambush.

"Karl," he said, "put the two-inchers in our own reserves, facing backward. We can hold the front with just the big guns." The long range would give them time to aim.

"Agreed," Karl said, and rode off to change the orders.

"D'Kan," Christopher said, interrupting some poorly argued point about the different freezing rates of deep and shallow rivers, "take the scouts to the rear. If their ranks are coming after us, we need to know before they get here."

"I'd best get to my regiment, too," Gregor said. Torme was already taking up his place on the left flank. The priests needed to be close enough to stop the skeletons wherever they appeared. This meant Christopher was left alone in the center, with only Cannan as a ranked companion.

And Lalania and the elves. Now that the column was turning into a line, they had rejoined him. Lalania was looking miserable, her great brown coat belted against the cold with the sleeves hanging empty. Her arms were pulled inside and bunched up against her chest. The elves were looking entirely too casual for people in thin leather clothes.

"Lala," he said. "I don't trust the ice on that river. If we need to cross it, I'll want a bridge."

Lucien objected. "A single note from that harp will draw all of Vercingtrox's greed upon her."

She hadn't taken it out of its case since the elves had arrived. Lucien had sniffed it out anyway. Christopher realized there was an advantage to be had from that.

"Good. When it comes for her, we'll light it up."

Lalania did not look pleased with her status as bait. Alaine and Lucien looked almost as dubious.

Christopher turned to the elven boy. "The artillery is loaded with grapeshot. We'll take out the dragon's wings and bring it to ground. If it survives that, you'll have twenty seconds before the gunners reload with round shot. Convince it to surrender in time and I'll try to find a way to keep it alive."

"Unacceptable," Lucien said, and skipped ahead, running toward the river line alone.

"Get back here before you get yourself killed," Christopher barked, but the elf was not one of his soldiers. Lucien ignored the order and kept running along the top of the unbroken snow. Christopher wasted a moment debating whether or not he actually cared. Alaine didn't seem to be worried, standing by idly.

"Don't you think you should call him back?" he said to Alaine.

"No," she said. "I don't."

Christopher frowned at her. "What the Dark is he doing?"

"I imagine he intends to provoke Vercingtrox before your artillery is prepared."

"Dark," Christopher swore. "Cannan, we've got to stop him." He kicked Royal into a gallop and leaned into the saddle.

Except he didn't go anywhere. Royal responded to the command by throwing his head back. Christopher got a face-full of horse hair and narrowly missed a bloody nose.

Cannan was having no better luck with his mount. A mere cavalry horse, it withstood his anger timidly instead of fighting back, but it remained equally motionless.

The knight drew his sword and glared at Alaine. Christopher followed his attention and saw that the elf was holding one hand up in denial.

"If the goblins interfere, then I will allow you to do as you please. Until then, you must yield the center stage."

Christopher was of half a mind to turn the red knight loose on her. Not just out of jealousy that his horse kept choosing her over him, but also because his entire battle plan depended on those cannons being ready, and they were still being unlimbered. The decision was taken out of his hands by events.

Almost to the river's edge, Lucien stopped and faced the bluff to the north. He called out in a language that Christopher had never heard before, but was nonetheless clearly not meant to be delivered by a high, piping elven voice. The syllables were too sharp for that, cut steel rasping on glass.

Both armies paused, their attention caught by the obvious challenge. Christopher was surprised that the goblins weren't raining arrows down on the boy, until he saw his own men had stopped wrestling with their cannons and were staring like country bumpkins themselves. He opened his mouth to order them back to work, and paused himself, weighed down by a blanket of expectation. Something shimmered in the air in front of the bluff, large and moving fast, sweeping down on them like a hard winter wind.

Lucien spread his hands in a wrestler's pose. In the air above him a monster became visible by rapid degrees, like a snake crawling out from underneath an invisible blanket. First its head, horned and plated in shades of scarlet and burgundy, a long snout over a gaping maw of ivory saw-edged teeth, on a sinuous neck that went on forever. Claws grasped forward, inset with glittering rubies. Then wings, vast and wide, and a body that stretched far too far before the rear claws appeared, tapering into a thick tail with broad flat plates like the tailfins of an aircraft. The beast loomed over Lucien for an instant, a freight train suspended in the air on wings a hundred feet across, and vomited a river of red flame.

The elf disappeared in a cloud of steam as the snow boiled. The dragon flew on, so much faster than Christopher had expected, far too fast for anything mortal. Its tail skimmed over the cloud left in its wake as it banked its wings and turned, barely a hundred feet off the ground.

Christopher rose in the saddle, driven by panic. The guns were not ready, could never be ready for such speed and proximity. The flame would turn his soldiers into ash that would blow away in the wind, sending them beyond even the Saint's reach. He tried to shout orders but the creature spoke first.

A wave of sound spread out from the dragon, the rumble of the thunderhead, the roar of the cataract, the grinding of the earthquake. Men were washed away, fleeing it like foam before an incoming tide. They ran mindlessly, shattered, wild-eyed and sobbing, dropping everything in their hands, scrambling over each other. The horses bolted with them, keening in fear. The world moved underneath him; Royal, rearing and screaming a challenge. Then Christopher fell off the back of the destrier and it joined the flight, its flashing hooves barely missing him as it sped away.

He scrambled to his feet. A man ran past. Christopher caught him by the jacket. One of his mercenary officers, so hardened he had told jokes while standing in a sea of fangs, and this in their very first battle, when death had been their assured fate and Christopher's power untested. The man bit at Christopher's hands, trying to get free, and pissed himself.

A hand on his shoulder; Alaine. "Let him go," she said, so he did. The man raced away, his legs moving in jerks.

The elf stood unarmed. She had lain down her weapons at some point. Around them the flood of men and horses thinned. Behind them came the dragon, a ship of destruction sailing on the wind. He stared up at its approach and fumbled for his sword.

Alaine blocked him, her hands grasping his.

"Give it no reason to see you as a threat."

He pulled his hands away from her. Even now his brain calculated. He began walking toward the nearest cannon, long purposeful strides that pretended to ignore the approaching monster. In the distance, he could see one lone brown-coated figure standing its ground. At first he thought it was a soldier, but when the man turned to face him he saw the sword hilt that marked a priest of War. Curate Torme stopped watching the men fleeing around him and watched Christopher. Then he, too, began to walk toward a gun.

Alaine skipped to catch up to Christopher and restrained him with a hand on his shoulder. He almost killed her in that instant, the *iaijutsu* pattern of draw and strike flashing through his mind. Instead he spun to face this alien creature, staring at her as the shadow of doom swept to him over the deserted battlefield.

"Are you friend or foe?" he said, in what might be his last words. His hands went to his sword.

"Neither," she said. "Today that is good enough. Stay your hand and observe."

Something moved across the river. Around the edges of the mist Christopher could see the goblin horde picking itself up to advance. The backdrop of trees rippled and then faded into a different set of trees, but this one with streams of wolf-riders and armored cavalry threading through the gaps in the pike squares, squads of armor-plated ogres close behind. They would charge across the frozen river and hunt his fleeing men like rats. Not that they needed to. Without a baggage train his men would freeze to death in the night, and the goblins could harvest them at their leisure. His entire army was destroyed, his prize weapons merely loot for the enemy, and now he and Torme would die one after another by fire.

There was no thought of fighting the beast. Even if he could reach it, a meter of steel would only annoy it.

He looked across the field again. Torme was standing in front of a cannon, wielding a ramrod. The man was going to operate an entire artillery section single-handedly. The least Christopher could do was buy him some time. He still had a flight spell in his head. Glancing again at the goblin army, he calculated how long he had before they caught him on the ground. He wanted to find some grenades before he went into the air. The enemy army, however, seemed stalled. The dragon had also tempered its charge, craning its neck to peer at the river.

Out of the fading cloud glided a shape. The goblin army faltered; the red dragon roared, frustration obvious regardless of language.

Rising up out of the mist, massive wings beating down, another dragon appeared.

This one was green, where the other was red, and bright, where the other was dark. Its scales were the color of fresh grass with emeralds sprinkled like dew. It moved its head and spat fire in a line up and down the river. Ice turned into steam and billowed up impossibly high, shrouding the river in a wall of fog. The new dragon and the goblin army were lost to sight but not sound. Christopher could hear the ice breaking up, the rush of water, the jingle of metal and cries of distress. At least until the red dragon beat its wings, furiously fighting for altitude to take it above the rising fog. The deafening windstorm came from almost directly above his head. The creature's belly was open and as inviting as a bomber bay. It might be his best chance. He opened his mouth to speak the spell of flight.

"Are you so determined to throw your life away?" Alaine asked, interrupting him with a finger to his lips. "Lucien prepared for this. Your assistance will be both futile and fatal."

Above the wall of fog rose the other dragon, upstream and crossing back to this side. The red tacked, trying to head it off; the green dipped and banked, sliding under it. The two great beasts clawed their way into the sky, hurtling roars and invective at each other that did nothing to deter their chess game of position and altitude. Twisting and wheeling they moved, a complex dance, and then the red folded his wings and dropped, claws outstretched in a stooping dive. The green rolled underneath, narrowly dodging the grasp of the red, and latched onto its back as it passed. Their tails intertwined, a gesture whose intimacy was spoiled when the green bit into the red's neck just above the shoulder. The red responded with a gout of flame, washing over itself as much as the green. Even Christopher could tell this was an act of desperation. Both dragons were untouched by the fire. Then their wings collided, bashing into each other like squabbling children, and the dragons fell into the cloud of fog.

Christopher heard the impact and felt the spray from the splash on his face when they crashed into the river. Sound rumbled out of the cloud, like a subwoofer unhooked from any sensible input. Lightning flashed, three quick flares that lit up the fog like stage lights.

Silence.

Christopher reminded himself to breathe. The moment stretched on. Wind began to tear at the cloud. His heart thudded when he saw a shape rising out of it. In the white shroud, it took a moment to see the color—red. The dragon climbed heavily in the air, above the cloud. He heard a great cheer from the goblins. He took a step back, involuntarily.

The dragon ignored them all, terrified priest and celebratory goblin army, continuing to climb. It began to dwindle, picking up speed, flying away into the distance. The goblin cheers strangled and died. A figure came walking up to Christopher and Alaine out of the mist.

Lucien approached to within a dozen feet. There was a distance in his eyes and Christopher wondered how he had ever thought of the boy as young. The elf inclined his head in acknowledgment.

"I appreciate your forbearance. I have kept my part of our bargain; the creature you know as Vercingtrox will not trouble your realm again."

"Now see to your men," Alaine said. "Be gentle with them; there but for the grace of rank go thee."

"You might have told me," Christopher said, and Lucien's eyes flashed, hard as gemstones.

"Yet I didn't."

"Nor did I," Alaine said, making it placation instead of challenge. "Come, we must find your men before nightfall. The goblins will not trouble you in the light of day, now that they do not have wings to shade beneath."

He left Torme to hold the field alone. The man was already loading a second gun.

5

PICKING UP THE PIECES

The snow was as greedy as mud, grasping at men and horses, slowing their flight. Christopher found them one by one, some sobbing, some shivering dully in the cold. None of them would meet his eyes. Their empty hands twitched. He had trained them so long and so hard to the rifle that they could load one in their sleep, and yet they had cast them away without a thought, the better to flee.

"Magic," he said for the hundredth time. "A spell. It's done. Get back to your post." None of them did. Instead, they followed him like a cloud, at a distance but unwilling to move out of sight or sound.

Hooves pounded. Cannan came riding up on a lathered horse with wild rolling eyes. He slid out of the saddle in front of Christopher and stared at him, challenging.

"You cannot blame me," the red knight said. "I have not failed my duty."

"Of course not," Christopher said. "It was just a Dark-damned spell. Nobody is to blame." He raised his voice. "Do you hear? Even Cannan ran. There is no shame."

"You say that," Cannan said, "but it was not you who fled like a child in the dark." His voice was low, his words gruff and jagged. Cannan had waded through pools of darkness that Christopher had feared to dip a toe in. To see the man reduced like this was unbearable.

"They put me to sleep," Christopher said. "In the castle, the first time. They snapped their fingers and I fell into their hands like a rag doll. It's just magic. It doesn't mean—anything." He trembled under the lash of his rage. That such a power existed, to turn men into puppets in their own skin, fought with the glory of raising the dead and threatened to lose.

Cannan stepped around him and shouted at the crowd of soldiers.

"What the Dark are you moping about? Did you think you could stand where I could not? You are dogs, no better than me. Get your fellow curs and get back to your posts."

The men stiffened. One of them had the courage to speak. "But what of the dragon?"

Alaine appeared from somewhere in the trees. "The dragon is gone. Flight in the face of its aura is no cowardice. But to return to your posts afterward would be true courage."

"Well, then," Cannan said. "Are you mice or men?"

"Men," a few affirmed, hesitantly.

"I can't hear you," Cannan roared.

"Men!" they shouted back, stung to pride.

"Again!"

"MEN!"

Other voices joined them, filtering out of the trees. Christopher's army began to solidify around the heart of sound. He found an officer, young Kennet, stumbling into the growing circle.

"I am sorry, my lord," the boy begged.

"Dark take that," Christopher said. "Never apologize for this again. That's a Darking order. Now: where is Karl?"

Kennet shook his head.

Christopher made up some more orders. "Take the first regiment back to the front." He knew there was still a front, because Torme hadn't fired any cannons yet. "Set up a battle line. Send anyone from the second regiment to secure the baggage train. Send the third regiment out to fetch stragglers."

"First regiment, to me!" Kennet shouted. The words inflated him. His shoulders stopped sagging as men fell in behind his march.

"Karl!" Christopher shouted. Other men began to shout out their regiment and platoon designations. The chaos felt good. It was action, throwing off the smothering blanket of fear. It was also wildly undisciplined and a broadcast to the enemy of their position and unreadiness. That hardly mattered. The goblins could roll up his whole army with a single squad right now if they were so inclined. Presumably they were having the same issues on their side, however. This battle would go to whoever recovered fastest.

The thought spurred him and he finally cast the flight spell. He rose up through the trees and skimmed along their tops, shouting for Karl. When his throat went hoarse from the cold, he used a minor spell to heal it.

He was attracted to the sound of gunfire. He recognized it as a pistol shot. It led him to a clearing, where Lalania stood with one hand on a man's shoulder. Karl.

"Don't land," she barked, when he zoomed in close. "Keep the spell up. You have to find my Light-blasted horse."

"Karl," he said, watching the young man worriedly. "It was just magic. Like—" He paused. He had almost referred to the mind control Karl had suffered at the hands of the witch Fae, but Lalania's presence stopped him. Only afterward did he think it might not have been the most helpful example, or even particularly analogous.

"I never realized something could hurt worse than dying," Karl said. The honesty of it was biting. "But not you."

"No," Christopher said, guiltily. "Or Torme."

"Then we have to conclude Gregor was also unaffected," Lalania said. "What about Cannan?"

"He was . . . affected. But I haven't seen Gregor. He wasn't on the battlefield after."

"We can assume it was because he was chasing after Disa," Lalania said. "Nothing under fifth rank seems to have stood against the dragon. What of the elves?"

Christopher was impressed that she was so functional after the experience until he saw her trembling hands. She was acting a role. The real Lalania was a helpless girl lost in a dark forest. So the real Lalania would be banished from the stage, at least for now.

He did what he could to help her, by playing along. "Alaine didn't so much as blink. Lucien turned himself into a dragon and chased the other one off."

"I should have guessed," Lalania said. "He could have Darking told us."

"That's what I said," Christopher agreed.

"You have to find my horse," Lalania repeated.

"And mine." Royal was out there, somewhere. Possibly injured in his mad dash. Christopher needed to find him and heal him. He could stop the horse from dying, even repair a broken leg, but he couldn't revive it. Even if the spell would work on a horse—a fact he was completely uncertain of—he could never justify such an expenditure of tael.

"Dark take your horse," Lalania snapped. "You can buy another one. Mine has the lyre."

"Okay," he said, hovering up.

"Watch the time," she called to him. "Don't let the spell fail while you're too far away to walk back."

"Okay," he called back. He managed to keep the "mom" to a mutter.

He rose above the treetops again, revealing his location to anyone else in the air. If one of those flying blue giants came after him now, they could catch him alone. On the other hand, he had a head full of spells and his tael was undepleted. It might be a fair fight. Presumably that was disincentive enough; he certainly wouldn't go flying over the enemy army just to pick an even-sided battle.

Whenever he saw motion below, he dipped under the trees. His men took heart as he hovered over them, picking themselves up and saluting. He sent them forward to join the army and went further south himself. Eventually he found the tracks of horses, and at the end of them, an entire herd.

Royal and Balance, the two great destriers, stood guard over a clearing containing several hundred cavalry and draft horses. The animals were pawing the snow, looking for grass underneath. They looked up at his approach, equating his arrival with oats and barley. The fear had dissipated and they were simply horses again.

He landed next to Royal, letting the horse push against him with his forehead to demand a scratch behind the ears. Lalania was wrong. He could never buy another horse like this.

Balance, Gregor's warhorse, watched from at a respectful distance. Christopher concentrated on a memory of Gregor's face.

"Found Balance and most of the horses. Three miles south, the last clearing. Send teamsters. Any trouble from the front?"

"I have not found the front yet," the image replied. "But I do not hear gunfire. I'll come to you soon."

The connection broke. Christopher was left to stew in the snow, waiting. He spent the time looking over the horses to see if any were injured. A few were scratched by branches, but he saw nothing serious. The fear spell did its damage on the inside, and the horses were too simple to suffer from it. Running away didn't bother them, especially when it was the sensible thing to do.

After half an hour he had company. Lucien rode up on Lalania's horse, trailing a small herd himself. The elf joined him in helping the horses, undoing bridles that had tangled and righting saddles that had slipped. They exchanged no words. The elf seemed wholly absorbed in the animals' plight.

Finally he heard the whistles of his men calling out to their horses. A crowd of soldiers descended on the clearing, led by Gregor and Disa.

The young woman was pale and subdued. Gregor was different as well, and Christopher realized it was tightly contained anger. He decided an open and frank approach was best.

"Did the spell affect you?" he asked the blue knight.

"No," Gregor said. "I left the field to run after my wife. I should not have done that."

"Of course you should," Christopher said. "What if something happened to her?"

"She is fourth rank," Gregor answered. "She was not going to stumble in the snow and break a leg. But we might have all died if the goblins had attacked and I had not been at your side."

"Gregor," Christopher said. "If I had seen you on the battlefield, I would have ordered you to find Disa. She's the most valuable person in the army after myself."

Gregor's face softened. The rationalization worked because it was true. Gregor and Torme were higher rank and led regiments, but Disa was a priestess of the Bright Lady. She had more healing power than the two men put together.

"In any case," Christopher said, "the goblins weren't going to attack. They still had to recover from what Lucien did to them."

"Lucien did nothing to them," the elf said, stepping out from behind a horse he was checking. "They chose to retreat on their own."

A jolt shot through Christopher. He'd assumed the enemy were in as bad of a shape as he was. Instead, they were intact and no doubt preparing more surprises.

The elf stepped in closer and lowered his voice. "As for me, I can only remain in your company as long as my identity is not widely known. Only your high-ranks saw me, and they have wit enough to keep it to themselves, I assume."

"Then what I am supposed to tell them?" Christopher said. His army had fled from a dragon. How could he tell them not to fear its return if he couldn't tell them why it left?

"Whatever you like," Lucien said. "You can even tell them the truth. But if you do, I will have to leave. And I would be interested in staying a bit longer."

Christopher would be interested in it, too. As dubious an ally as the elf might be, having a dragon in your pocket was too much of a good thing to give up.

"Okay. I'll think of something. But you have to tell me this much: can Alaine turn into a dragon? Or her daughter?"

"No," Lucien said. "Alaine can transform into neither a dragon nor her daughter. Nor can anyone. Even the gods themselves cannot transform into dragons."

Christopher stood open-mouthed, trying to grasp the implications.

"Though there are a number of entities that could transform into Kalani, or at least the seeming of her," Lucien mused.

"But you are . . ." Christopher started.

". . . a dragon that can turn into an elf," Lucien finished for him. "Which is precisely why my identity must remain secret. As a dragon I have far too many foes to be larking around in the woods where anyone can find me."

"So . . . you're not Kalani's father?"

Lucien looked at him as if he were the village idiot. "No, of course not."

"In my defense," Christopher said, "you did not exactly make your relationship clear."

"And you applied a human template," Lucien answered. "It seems to be a persistent failing of yours."

"We'll keep your secret," Gregor said. "You might try keeping a civil tongue when you talk to our lord."

"Is that what an elf would do?" Lucien asked, with apparently sincere curiosity.

"Based on my experience so far, probably not," Christopher conceded. "But you should ask Alaine if you want to know how to impersonate an elf."

"She is not perhaps the sterling example," Lucien demurred, but then turned his attention back to the horse, walking away with it while watching its right front hoof.

"If they're all like that," Gregor grumbled, "I can see why nobody likes them."

"The elves serve the White," Disa said. "They have served since the dawn of time. But they do not worship the Bright Lady. They serve in their own fashion, which I confess I do not entirely understand. Though perhaps Lalania knows more."

"Are you okay?" Christopher asked, looking into her eyes.

"I am . . . well enough. The memory of utter terror lays no charge against my identity, as it must against your soldiers. No one expects me to stand in the face of certain death."

"I think Cannan fixed that for me," Christopher said. "He ran, too. Nobody can think less of themselves for running when Cannan did."

"And he will let you tell them this?" Gregor asked.

"He told them himself."

Gregor gave an ironic chuckle. "Of course he did. Pater Sven warned me. Your changes won't stop with our armor and weapons."

"But all for the better," Disa said earnestly.

"I don't know what you two are talking about," Christopher objected.

"Yes, you do," Gregor said. "We are iron in your forge. You are making us into a weapon the likes of which this world has never seen. I suppose in due time we will understand why."

They turned away to deal with the horses and men, leaving Christopher alone with his unvoiced arguments. He had no grand plan; he was just trying to survive long enough to go home. But that wasn't strictly true anymore. He could go home right now if he wanted to. Cast a fifth-rank spell, take a single step, and travel from this world to his. Take his horse and all the gold he could carry. The only cost was that he couldn't come back.

And why should that matter? What did he need to come back for? Only to fulfill the promises he had made. The tael he had borrowed from the Saint; the wife he would revive for Cannan; the revolution for Karl. Promises that had dripped from his lips so easily, comforting balm for the wounded around him, purchased at the price of a few words.

He needed to stop making promises. He considered promising himself exactly that but decided not to. Not only because of the irony but also because he knew the promises he made to himself were the only ones he felt he could break.

He addressed his troops on the river plain from horseback, under a darkening sky. The army had straggled back in, all men and animals accounted for. The terror had left them as soon as they had left the battlefield. Only inertia had carried them further, and the snow had absorbed that. Even most of their equipment was accounted for, having been dropped or abandoned on the spot rather than strewn throughout the forest.

The one thing that had gone missing was their morale. He had marched that morning at the head of an army of steel tempered in fire, men who had in many cases stood and fought until overwhelmed by monsters, suffered through their life's blood being torn out by fangs and claws—and then, revived in the Cathedral, marched out to face it all again.

Now they stood before him in shambles, their pride revealed as a bit of cloth that could be torn off by powers beyond reckoning. Alaine's words were his only guide to salvaging them.

"While you were gone," he shouted, "We had a little conversation with the dragon. He kindly agreed to take his nasty tricks and leave."

The men shuffled nervously. A few managed to raise a weak grin.

"As you know, everything under fifth rank ran. Including my horse. And Ser Cannan."

They were quiet now, utterly silent.

"And as you can see everyone came back. Now look across that river. What do you *not* see? You do not see goblins. They weren't chased off by a dragon's aura. But they left the battlefield all the same. And they didn't come back."

He paused, letting them look for themselves.

"So tell me: where does courage lie?"

"Here!" Gregor shouted, a lonely voice.

"I can't hear you," Christopher said, and was greeted by the roar of a thousand throats in return. Even Royal threw his head back and bugled a neigh of challenge.

He waited for them to quiet on their own. They stood straighter now, but Christopher could see the exhaustion in their eyes.

"I think tonight we deserve to sleep indoors," he announced. "Lala, if you please."

She strummed the lyre, summoning a thin white mist. Axes lifted themselves out of the tool wagons, streaming to the edge of the forest to fell trees with superhuman speed. The fallen trees floated onto the plain, flying saws trimming them en route. After half an hour, a wooden fort stood, with ten-foot high walls of tree trunks and fresh-sawn lumber walkways. Inside were storage sheds, stalls for the horses, crude barracks for the men with rough timber roofs that would keep out the snow, and a long hall they could pretend was a kitchen. The wood was green, so it would not stand against a siege engine, but at least it would not burst into flame at the first excuse.

Dragon fire had burned stone in Nordland, but there was no longer a dragon here to fear. Christopher could fall back on the tactics that had won him all his previous battles. Assuming he still had an army. Alaine had tried to warn him, the last in a long line of Cassandras who had told him mortal flesh could never replace the power of rank. In the morning he would find out if they were right. His army would be challenged by their first retreat, or broken by it.

6

MIDNIGHT DANCE

He woke to the sound of axes, the sun well above the horizon. Karl had let him sleep in.

In his absence the young man had taken command, sending the men outside the safety of the fort to work. Standing on the wall, Christopher watched trees fall, this time by human hands. For now they only piled them up near the river. Christopher would have to put his engineer's hat back on and design a bridge.

Armed squads watched the laborers in the woods, while inside the fort gun crews winched their cannon to the firing platforms. The camp displayed the appearance of perfect order.

Alaine and Lucien were watching one of the gun crews with considerable interest. It occurred to Christopher that they had not yet seen a cannon in action. He joined them at the bottom of the wall.

"Delay is not wise," Alaine said. "You should never give goblins time to ponder. They only think of something worse."

"This is how we fight," Christopher said. "One step at a time."

"An admirable strategy," Lucien said, "if only for its novelty. Yet it would seem to require incredible resilience."

"My men are still here," Christopher said, surprised by the harshness in his voice. "I think that proves their mettle."

Lucien took no offense. "So it would seem. Yet you cannot linger all the same."

The elf was right. The army's supplies would not hold out that long. On the other hand, did they need to? The dragon was gone. He could summon the King and the realm's armies now.

"I need to find the capital first," he said, thinking out loud. "Then I think I will have discharged the King's command. He can take it after that."

Alaine looked at him dubiously. "You would surrender the tael from your victory so easily?"

"What victory?" Christopher said. They hadn't killed a single goblin yet.

"You have decapitated the snake. Without the dragon, the goblins will be leaderless and unfocused. For a time, they will be easy prey."

"Then the King will be pleased," Christopher said, "and I can go back to my real job."

"I understand little of local politics," Lucien said, "but even I can see that your optimism is unwarranted. One would almost describe it as willful stupidity."

Christopher frowned, but Alaine answered for him with a wistful smile. "A resilient ignorance would seem to be your race's greatest asset." She put her arm through Lucien's and led him away, looking for all appearances like a pair of young lovers.

Arrogance would seem to be the elven race's chief asset. With a harrumph Christopher went looking for his scout officer. He wanted to know what was on the other side of that river.

Later that afternoon he held a command conference. His regimental leaders, Gregor and Torme; his general staff, Major Karl and Charles the quartermaster; and his retinue, Cannan, D'Kan, Lalania, and Disa.

Charles's report confirmed what he already knew. The food would hold out only another two weeks, and that was short rations for the horses. Christopher had brought more wagons than any other lord would have, but his were filled with powder and shot.

The scouts had not gone over the river after all. Gregor had sent them behind, to verify their rear was safe. He was ready to build a road and send for the King. "The terms of our charge are fulfilled. Let us build a road to the Kingdom and summon the peers before we are knee-deep in monsters this time."

Sound advice, given that they had done it the other way around with the ulvenmen.

D'Kan disagreed. "To send for aid now would be an embarrassment. We have not struck even a single blow against the enemy. Let us at least try our blades before we cry for help."

Christopher bit his tongue. Yesterday's debacle was sliding down the memory hole rather faster and more completely than he had intended. While he was trying to frame some kind of diplomatic reminder, Torme nodded his head.

"I find myself moved by Ser D'Kan's words. We marched heedlessly into this woods; to pause now would be to admit fear."

"Not entirely heedless," Lalania objected. "We had the safety of the lyre at my fingertips. A protection we shall not have again for another week."

"Nonetheless, the boy is right," Cannan grunted. "Let your men sleep in this fort again and they will never have the heart to leave it."

It was insane to let his strategic decisions be decided by emotion. Yet they would be. The men could not be allowed to think of themselves as afraid. They might start to believe it.

"We can delay at least one day to build a bridge," Christopher said. "Nobody wants to go wading in this weather. We'll advance after that."

Two mornings later the army decamped before dawn, filing out of the gates by the flicker of light-stones. Once again Christopher was abandoning a perfectly good fort on goblin lands. He wondered if they appreciated the things he kept building for them. The new bridge, in particular, seemed like the sort of improvement he should be paid for.

As the sun rose so did the men's spirits. They were marching into the enemy's heartland without opposition. Even the skeleton attacks had ceased.

By noon they found their first evidence of civilization, such as it was. A dozen long, low buildings, made from dirt walls and roofed in straw, were laid out with a precision that contradicted their crude nature. The village rested in the midst of snow-covered fields, utterly empty. The men fired the buildings, burning the straw roofs until they collapsed. Walking through the ruins, Christopher found himself slightly mystified. The buildings were deserted, without so much as a grain of wheat or broken pot left behind. Yet the village showed clear signs of having been inhabited only days ago. The stench of an open sewage pit attested to that.

The buildings had no windows and only a single door three feet high at the front. They were more like barns than houses.

"Hobgoblins," Christopher guessed when D'Kan came to report on the tracks running through and around the village. The diminutive creatures were a separate species than their goblin masters. He had verified this with the Ranger; he wanted no more terrible surprises like the ulvenmen had given him, when he had mistaken their children for warriors of a different race. Not that it had mattered. The pups had fought as ferociously as the adults, expecting and receiving no quarter. Never knowing the truth would have been a mercy. But he was not allowed to choose ignorance simply because it was more comfortable.

"Correct," the Ranger said. "Half a thousand, at least. The goblins evacuated them within hours of our crossing the river."

"So fast," Christopher mused. He wasn't sure he could move peasants out of the way of an invasion that quickly.

"They will do the same within ten miles of our march. Leaving us not a scrap of tael to gain."

"Probably poisoned the wells, too," Christopher said.

"Undoubtedly," the Ranger agreed. "Fortunately we need not care." Christopher's army drank out of a magic bottle that created a fast flowing stream on demand. They didn't even have to melt snow. "But do warn the men. Anything that looks edible or valuable is merely a trap."

"Burning the villages is waste of time, then."

"Not from their perspective." D'Kan shrugged. "The smoke plainly marks our advance."

Christopher was pretty sure the goblins knew exactly where his men were, anyway. A thousand soldiers and several hundred horses were hard to hide. They passed through two more villages in the next six miles and he let the men burn everything in their path. Their suspicious hostility was rewarded at the third village, when a squad of skeletons burst out of the flames, wielding curved swords. Torme put the monsters down before they did any harm. The point was made, though. Nothing could be ignored, no detail could be overlooked. While the sun was still well above the horizon, Christopher picked a snow-clad field at random and called a halt.

Half the army pitched tents while the other half demolished the nearest copse of trees. The ground was too cold to dig trenches, so they settled for building a fence of crude stakes around the camp. Light-stones sat on high poles in the midst of the stakes, giving the men a few dozen yards of clear firing. The cannons were loaded with grape-shot and placed at regular intervals along the edges.

Christopher sent them to bed before the sun. Half the men in their tents for half the night, and then they would switch. Six hours sleep was the best they could hope for. The goblins could see in the dark, so everyone expected a night attack. The darkness would shrink the range of his guns to almost nothing, robbing him of his best advantage. In its place he made sure there were plenty of grenades.

And his latest surprise. Long tubes welded together like organ pipes, though no one here knew what an organ was, held black-powder rockets. Their range was a few hundred feet, with an accuracy barely any finer, and it took hours to reload them, but all twenty tubes could be fired from a single fuse, and each rocket exploded on impact with the power of three grenades. He was counting on their shock and awe to break up cavalry charges or disperse enemy archers. They fired in an arc, like mortars, so they could be set up behind the lines, pre-aimed to strike at a fixed distance away, two per side of his square camp.

He had hoped to use them against the dragon, sending a cloud of missiles into its flight path. He had not expected it to be so fast or invisible or capable of forcing his men to flee. So many plans swept away because a dragon had flexed its wings and wielded a power he did not even know existed. The depth of his ignorance gnawed at him. Alaine was probably right; if he had any idea what came next, he'd be too afraid to continue.

The goblins, perhaps driven by their own unwarranted optimism, struck in an utterly conventional manner at the unsurprising hour of midnight. Arrows rained down on the camp, provoking more curses than actual damage. All of his men wore chainmail now, and the high angle robbed the missiles of most of their force. The men in the tents were somewhat protected by the tough canvas roofs, though it was an unpleasant awakening to be sure. While they roused themselves and dressed for battle, the other half knelt at the perimeter, waiting for something to shoot at.

After the third wave of arrows, Christopher's gunners got a bearing on the enemy's direction. They swapped out the charge on one of the five-inch guns for an explosive round, angled it for howitzer fire, and returned the gesture. Tents flapped under the pressure of the shot, and off in the distance flame blossomed and faded. The men cheered. The shot was probably as ineffective as the goblin's arrows, but that didn't matter. The point was that this exchange was merely prelude. Nothing would be settled by it.

Lights flickered in the darkness. A wave of flaming arrows launched into the sky. This would be more problematic. While the powder wagons were supposed to be covered with wet hides, there was always a chance of an explosion. Also, the tents would burn. On the other hand, the archers necessarily gave away their position, and Christopher's gunners were well trained. They responded instantly with the two-inch guns, which already had explosive rounds loaded, and the rest of the five-inchers, whose grapeshot had a range of six hundred feet. By the time the flaming arrows landed, the goblin archers could be seen dispersing in the flash of explosions.

The battle was soon to be joined in earnest, so Christopher drew his sword and began to pray. The strength spell for himself, Cannan, Gregor, and Torme, the only swordsmen in this army of rifles. Lalania had her pistol and D'Kan had taken to using a carbine. He had gained some new spells with his rank, including a much improved version of the weapon blessing that lasted hours instead of seconds, and also his flight spell lasted longer. He cast them both. For the next hour and a half he would be a threshing machine with wings. Royal whickered from the center of the camp, clearly annoyed at being left out of the action. Christopher was sympathetic. Riding astride the big warhorse made him feel like a hero; flying around with a drawn sword just felt silly. His men loved it, though, cheering as he swooped over their heads to the side of the camp firing at the archers.

The enemy archers were not dispersing; they were charging. He arrived just as they swept out of the dark, utterly silent, rushing forward without a battle cry, even their footsteps audible only from the crunching of snow. Belatedly the riflemen began to fire, with distressingly little effect.

Christopher recognized this trick. He raised his sword and chanted. The enemy fell before him, collapsing into piles of dry bone. There were hundreds of the creatures. Undaunted, Christopher sent wave after wave of power into them, floating above the battlefield and glowing like a streetlamp. In his zeal he allowed himself to drift in front of the wall of stakes, a mistake he recognized only when he fell from the sky and crashed into the ground.

The light on his sword went out, the weight of his armor pulled down with its customary force, all of his magic undone in an instant. As he scrambled to his feet, darkness leached at him from the edge of his vision, a black cloud closing in around him. He felt his will battered and struck by invisible blows, one after the other, until it broke, leaving him paralyzed, unable to make any volitional movement, standing alone in front of his army while bullets whistled past. He wasted precious seconds struggling against the bonds before he remembered that, as a priest of Travel, he had a limited immunity to this kind of nonsense. He shrugged off the effect and raised his sword again, chanting to ward off the skeletons, but the two large figures charging at him ignored the feeble light. Only instinct saved him, as he stepped back and lowered his blade.

The lead monster ran into his sword. The creature slid up the blade, grabbing at him with fierce claws, gibbering spittle from a mouth full of fangs. He ducked a swipe at his head and twisted the blade. The troll howled in pain and pushed forward anyway. The other one caught him by the shoulder, hooking its claws into the scales of his armor. It windmilled the other hand around to deliver a terrible blow at his face.

Christopher stepped back and away, the troll's grip slipping off him as easily as the paralyzing magic had been pushed aside. The troll's blow took him in the arm like a sledgehammer. If not for his tael, bones would have shattered.

Both creatures lunged forward, trying to grapple him and pull him close, where their fearsome mouths could bite and the claws on their feet could rend. Their grasp slipped off his divine protection like he was greased. He batted at them with his sword, inflicting deep cuts, but the trolls hardly seemed to care. Already the wound he had given the first one was closing.

A bullet screamed past his head. His men were trained to unleash fire and damnation on trolls, in the form of grenades and cannon. The grenades he might survive, but a five-inch gun would tear him apart at this range, tael or no. He could not turn and run to the lines because the trolls would club him to pieces from behind. They were faster on the ground than he was in his armor. His protection against their grasp and paralyzing spell would expire soon. And he couldn't cast another spell; pausing for even an instant would get his face chewed off.

He felt movement behind him, though he could not spare a glance, dancing back again from another lunge. Then Cannan rushed past him, plowing into a huge troll and knocking it back half a dozen yards. A knot of men flowed around Christopher, their carbines barking.

Cannan slashed madly at the creatures. Parts of them came off and flew through the air. Both trolls ignored the bullets tearing into their flesh, concentrating on battering Cannan. Christopher shouted at him, trying to get the knight to fall back. His voice was drowned out by the guns. The situation was hardly any better than it had been a moment ago, except now a dozen men would die with him.

Christopher readied a spell, one of the new ones he had gained with his last rank. He held it, trying to find an angle that wouldn't blast Cannan along with the trolls. One of the creatures smacked the knight in the head, spinning him like a top. Cannan fell to the ground and rolled, ending up at the feet of the squad. He stared up at Christopher with wild eyes, then sank back to the ground unconscious.

The trolls tried to follow. Christopher unleashed his spell. The air above the trolls split, white light spilling out to illuminate a circular area twenty feet across, immediately followed by a roaring gout of flame forty feet high.

As the burnt and smoking husks of the trolls fell apart, Christopher bent to touch Cannan and pour healing power into him. The knight instantly climbed to his feet, sword in hand and ready, though Christopher could tell from the look in his eyes that he had no idea where he was or what was going on. Fortunately Cannan's default setting was combat.

"Fall back," Christopher said, and the group of men retreated step by step, reloading their carbines as they went. He didn't look behind until he felt one of the stakes prod him in the back. Then all the men broke and ran, slipping through the lines of their own men, to the safety of the camp.

Only then did the fear the find him, as his divine right of travel faded away. Fortunately the spell that had dogged him had gone without his noticing. He stood in front of a tent and tried to control the trembling.

Lalania was there. She touched him, searching his face, relieved when he stared back at her.

"A poor exchange," she said. "So many spells for a pair of trolls."

"I shouldn't have gone out there," Christopher said. "They were waiting for me."

Cannan spun back to the front. "Cannons! Fire now!" he barked at the gun crews, and they responded. Consequently, it was a moment before Lalania could continue her discussion.

While the guns reloaded she massaged her ears. "It is what any other lord would have done."

"They tried to paralyze me. If it had worked—" He stopped. The consequence was too terrible to speak. The trolls would have torn him apart like a piñata and eaten the bits.

"Why didn't it?" she asked.

"Marcius," he said.

She nodded in understanding. "Is there any left?"

"Not today."

The girl frowned. "Dark take it. Their principals are out there, right now. Such effectiveness against your rank demands rank of their own. We could take their heads and end this. But you dare not challenge them again without defenses."

"Faster!" Cannan shouted at the gun crews. He was firing at random, hoping to get lucky. It didn't seem like a good use of ammunition to Christopher. As he tried to issue a counterorder, the other side of the camp erupted in a wall of sound, as every weapon fired at once.

He was already running through the camp before he made the conscious decision to go. Lalania ran beside him with the lyre in her hands, while Cannan lagged behind, moving with the steps of the utterly exhausted.

The army's horses were quartered in the center, tied to picket stakes. They were roiling like water on the boil, whinnying in fear and panic. Lalania stopped and looked around wildly. She had only two ranks. Being trapped in the midst of a stampede would be fatal. With an apologetic glance at him, she struck up a tune on the lyre.

The horses quieted, an expanding circle of calm carried by her sweet voice and the chords of the lyre. Christopher left her there. They would need those horses tomorrow.

On the other side of the square the din began to resolve into distinct sounds. The crack of rifles, the boom of grenades, the screams of men, the high, terrible keening of the trolls. A shaggy horse charged at him, bearing a veritable giant of a goblin on its back. The horse was the equal of Royal or Balance, and the rider was at least seven feet tall, swinging a spiked bowling ball on the end of a long chain. Mesmerized by the spinning ball, Christopher swayed left and right, seeking a way to cope with its approach.

A soldier stepped out from behind a tent and leveled his rifle, too slowly. The ball swung around and the soldier went down like a bowling pin. Christopher could see his soldier was already dead. Disgusted, he stopped trying to dodge and met the charge with a lunge.

The monster had not expected that. Christopher's sword slipped under the massive shield, glanced off the saddle, and caught in the creature's groin, sliding all the way through as the body fell off the horse and knocked him to the ground. He struggled under the dead weight of the corpse while the shaggy horse pranced into a turn and came back to stomp on his head.

Royal intercepted, smashing into the beast's side. His horse had apparently followed him out from the herd. Christopher stopped trying to crawl out from under the corpse and hugged it like a shield instead. Hooves flashed around him, churning up mud in great clods, as the two destriers reared and fought. Then, suddenly, there was quiet, the horses fleeing in opposite directions.

Just as Christopher pushed the huge goblin corpse up, it crashed down again. A troll leered at him from on top. The weight was immense, putting him in danger of suffocating under the pressure. The troll casually tore the head off of the corpse and began eating it, gore and blood and chunks of brain matter spilling over Christopher's face.

He couldn't shout. He couldn't even breathe. The troll finished its gruesome snack, tossing the cracked skull aside. Christopher prepared to call down the tower of flame on top of himself with the last of his breath, wondering if he had enough tael left to survive it.

Someone whistled. The troll looked up, its eyes going wide, and it leapt forward. Christopher craned his neck in time to see the monster eagerly bounding toward Alaine. She frowned, shaking her head, as if to dissuade the troll from such a poorly chosen course of action. At the last minute she moved aside like a dancer, the spear rising and lashing out to catch the troll in the face.

The troll went down. Alaine leaned on the haft of the spear and twisted it into the ground before letting go and stepping back. The troll flopped like an ugly fish, pinned by the spear through its brain, unable to regenerate the nerve endings necessary to control its body. Alaine hooked her thumbs together and spread out her fingers. A sheet of flame leapt from her hands; the troll jerked and went still. She stepped forward and retrieved her slightly smoking spear.

She looked at Christopher and shrugged. "It attacked me," she said. "You saw that." The elf smiled apologetically and walked away, disappearing into the night.

Cannan finally arrived and helped Christopher out from under the headless body. He spent a few minor spells restoring his tael and one major spell restoring his sword's magic. Then he waded into the fight, Cannan at his back. The next time a goblin knight charged him, he stepped to the side and cut the legs out from under the horse. Cannan beheaded the rider before it could stand. The animal lay on the ground, gushing a fountain of blood and snapping its teeth at Christopher until he put it out of its misery.

The goblins had made an impressive attempt. At some point the sky lit up with rockets. In the brief glare it became clear the attack was only one-sided. The skeletal archers had been a feint, abandoned once the enemy cavalry had charged home on the far side. Men drained from the other sides of the camp, pushing back against the churning madness. The tall goblins were no more fierce than ulvenmen, though better armored. But armor didn't matter anymore; their breastplates could not turn a bullet. Their shaggy black horses were almost worse, attacking with a savage fury that was out of place for herbivores. The green trolls fought eagerly but unintelligently, never seeming to grasp that stopping to feed would earn them a face-full of grenades. White-coated wolves and small hobgoblins raced through the swirling men and horses, biting and stabbing, and losing. There simply weren't enough of them. Christopher's men formed squares and lines, each rank firing and retiring to reload. Reinforcements arrived in good order. The enemy was expelled.

On the edge of the camp, Christopher recognized the fatal flaw in their plan. The goblin infantry and armored ogres had also maintained good order, advancing in pike squares behind the impetuous charge of the knights and wolf riders. Cannon and rockets had torn their tight formations apart. They would have been better served to simply charge into the fray as a mob of individual targets.

The remnants of the goblin cavalry streamed out into the darkness, fleeing. Gregor appeared beside Christopher, breathing heavily.

"Do we follow?" the blue knight asked.

"Dark no," Christopher said. Their high-ranks were still out there. He was not going to go blundering around in the night looking for them.

The men reformed the edges of the camp, carrying their wounded into tents where priestesses prayed over them. The prayers turned to sobs when they ran out of magic. Christopher and Torme went to help with what they had left.

The sun came up on his shattered camp, revealing the true extent of the destruction. Outside the camp was—nothing. The goblins had spirited their dead away in the middle of the night. Other than footprints in the snow, there was no evidence that they had ever been there, not even bloodstains. Goblins bled clear ichor that dried into jelly, invisible against the ground.

Their only winnings from the battle were those who died inside their camp. Whatever fatalities his artillery had inflicted had only enriched the goblin rulers. Christopher watched the enemy heads boiling in the kettles and wondered if they would yield enough to repair the damage.

7

HARD MATH

They laid their dead out in the square. The cold served them now, protecting the corpses from decay and insect depredation. But with each additional body Christopher's spirit was stretched by the limits of mathematics.

He had only nine days to raise a dead body, and he could only raise one a day. There was a spell to break the rule—with magic there always seemed to be a way to break the rules—but only he and Torme could cast that spell. If he robbed himself of all other magic, he could keep ninety men indefinitely on the border between merely dead and dead beyond reach, and Torme another twenty. These were hard limits imposed by rank; no amount of effort or desire would budge them. They could only ask for so much divine power before the tap shut off. That was the one rule that could not be broken.

The equations meant that if he had suffered more than one hundred and nineteen dead, someone would necessarily be deprived of a second chance of life. It would be up to him to choose who.

Sending men into battle was something he had come to terms with. They each stood the same chance, and he shared their fate. Choosing afterward who deserved to live or die was a wholly different matter.

It was worse than that, of course. He was in the middle of a war. Last night's battle had consumed all of his resources. The goblins would not let him sit and recover for an entire season. Nor would the King.

So he stood and counted the bodies as they piled up, stewing in despair.

Disa, despite her rank, could not help because of the peculiari-
ties of her service to the Bright Lady. Her healing power was greater,
and she had saved far more lives the night before than all of his other
priests put together, but now she stood next to him biting her lip.

"My lord," she said, with a small curtsey. The formality pained
him, because he knew it meant she had only hard words to follow. "We
require your instruction."

Christopher grimaced. "It seems unlikely there is anything about
healing you can learn from me." He hated being in the healing tents
without magic, reduced to mere bandages.

"Not the art, but the practice," she said. "Our spells renewed at
dawn. Though we expect to lose no more patients, we still have men
grievously wounded. Shall we spend our magic now, to restore them
to fighting strength and spare them pain—or shall we save it against
the heat of battle?"

One well-timed spell could stop a man from bleeding out, even
if it did not put him back on his feet. On the other hand, it could be
argued that the more men he had standing in the first place, the less
wounded he would take. Disa had already made her preference clear:
she could not bear to leave men to suffer while she still held the power
to heal. Christopher couldn't bear it either, but he had no choice. Strategic doctrine allotted no value to mercy.

"Save your magic until the end of the day."

"As you command," she answered, and curtsied more deeply, a
rebuke so forceful it felt like he'd been slapped. Undeserved, as she
understood as well as he did. No one would die. Anyone who took a
turn for the worse could be healed. But if the goblins attacked again,
the healing magic would mean far less deaths.

On the other hand, if the goblins stayed away, the men would have
borne their suffering for nothing. They would have permanent scars to
remind them, marks that spoke to the world that their lord had been
too poor in magic to heal them instantly. Which, given their lord

was a Prophet, was embarrassing. It didn't make Disa or the White Church look good, either.

She wasn't angry at him. She was angry at math. Well, so was he. Another body laid out on the ground, and he gritted his teeth to block the snarl creeping up his throat.

Disa left, to be replaced by Karl. For once the young man bore good news, in the form of a purple stone. "Despite the goblin's meanness, we have made a good harvest. The tall ones were the equivalent of second-ranks."

The body count reached ninety-seven. Christopher swore.

Karl ignored his outburst. "I recommend that we camp the day, heal our wounded tonight, and march tomorrow with fresh magic."

"We can't do this again," Christopher said. "Gods, Karl, we'll be stretched to the limit preserving just this lot. We can't handle more corpses."

Karl looked at him with a hint of doubt. "We know now that the Saint is not so limited. His reach extends for years, not days. The price is high, but the goblins have not yet begun to pay."

Christopher was startled. Of course he knew that. How had he forgotten? He had unconsciously come to think of himself as on his own. The Saint seemed so far away, like an old high-school friend left behind, never to be seen again.

The forest must be affecting him. He shook it off and took the lump of tael from Karl. "Form a roster. First to be raised are scouts." He needed them most, and they needed the morale boost, having the most dangerous job in the army. "If the number goes over a hundred and twenty, we'll have to pick one to wait out the campaign."

"Not only one," Karl said. "You will need your magic for other causes soon enough. In any case, most of these men will not be revived until after our campaign ends. We shall be back in the Kingdom in another twenty days."

Ninety-eight bodies. Christopher could bear the pressure no

longer. He recognized the latest corpse: Sergeant Kennet, a young man unhealthily addicted to heroics.

"Start the roster tomorrow," Christopher said, and strode over to the body. The camp paused while he cast the revivification spell, holding their collective breaths, as any man must in the presence of miracles. The private vision hardly had time to form. Kennet all but leaped out of it, coughing as he sat up, groping for his rifle out of reflex.

"Welcome back," Christopher said.

Kennet was more practical. "How long?"

"Last night," Christopher said. "You've missed nothing of consequence. You're relieved of duty for the day. Go to your tent and rest. We'll not march until tomorrow."

The boy sagged back onto the ground, exhausted. Coming back from the dead was a trying experience, as Christopher well knew.

"Yes, sir," Kennet said, saluting weakly.

The gesture hurt even more than Disa's curtsy, because there was no anger behind it. These men spent their lives merely because he asked them to, let him gamble with their bodies and their futures. And when they were miraculously restored, given a second or third chance at life, they threw their chips back into the pot without questioning.

It was a ridiculous burden for any man to carry. He wandered away to find a place to hide, but the open sky pressed down on him. He found himself standing in the cavalry yard, looking for his horse. Last he remembered, Royal had been in a battle royale with one of the goblin's warhorses.

He found the destrier dozing on the edge of the herd. It woke long enough to acknowledge him with a snuffle, and then went back to sleep. He looked over the beast, but saw no wounds or scars. Someone had spent healing power on the animal, in a camp full of wounded and suffering men.

The elves were nearby, Lucien sitting on a stump while Alaine fooled around with his long green hair. Christopher walked over to them, accusation in his stance. He was tired of lines that could not be crossed and scribbling in the margins.

Lucien looked guilty, at least. Alaine was unperturbed, as always.

"I think it is time you made your intentions clear," Christopher said.

Alaine smiled, like a debutante denying her latest flirtation. "Be careful what you ask for."

"I like horses," Lucien said, looking at the ground.

Christopher pressed. "Did you know the goblins would attack?"

"Didn't you?" Alaine answered.

"And next? Is this the worst they can do?" In this world, warfare was rarely attrition and strategy. Instead, generals led with their best strike first, gambling everything on total victory or utter defeat.

Alaine looked at him almost tenderly. "There is always worse."

"Tell me," he demanded.

She returned to braiding Lucien's hair. "I am not an oracle. I can only tell you that your enemies will become more inventive as they become more desperate. Would you not do the same?"

He knew she was hiding something. He also knew she would not lie. Between the two, he strongly suspected that she had already told him what he wanted to know, and he was just too dense to understand it. He changed tack, seeking an opening into her inscrutable truths. "Have you seen enough of my chemistry yet?"

"It is remarkable," she answered. "It might even, with the gods' own luck, kill an unprepared dragon. You can imagine how intriguing that is."

"We are not your enemy," Lucien said. "Yet you would arm our enemies against us?"

"I'm not giving guns to the goblins," Christopher objected.

Lucien stared at him earnestly. "I referred to your king."

Alaine did not let Christopher question that comment. "You gave guns to ulvenmen. The goblins are notorious thieves; might not they steal the secrets you share so freely?"

"Then help me defeat them."

She sighed. "A goblin kingdom here or there hardly matters. I speak of the future, after you have lived your span of years. What then of the world you leave behind?"

Christopher smiled grimly. "I will leave a Kingdom that respects the rights of common men. I imagine the goblins will be equally happy to constrain their feudal lords." For that matter, serving the same notice to the dragons and the menagerie of supernatural beasties that ran this world would be equally admirable.

Alaine laughed at him, a peal of genuine amusement. "No one has spoken so kindly of goblins in ten thousand years, at least."

"He is generous," Lucien said to her. Almost shyly, as if he knew it might not count for enough.

Alaine spoke with authority, though her eyes and fingers were on the boy's braids. "I do as much as I can, always and everywhere. I am, in the end, constrained by forces I despair. Yet I promise you, in my place you would do no more. And no less."

Christopher fumed silently at this wholly ambiguous and useless answer. She sighed and patted the boy's head, finished with her efforts, though Christopher felt she was not satisfied with the result. "I will look around. Perhaps some direction is in order; there is no need to let the affair drag on while you blunder through the forest. If nothing else, the squirrels will appreciate an end to the disturbances."

"Thank you," Christopher said, trying to mean it.

"Do not," she answered sharply. "Never thank an elf. Our actions are not motivated by the gratitude of anyone who could give it." She walked away, so quickly and silently that she seemed to vanish.

"Is she always like that?" he asked Lucien.

"I cannot say for certain," the boy said. "I have only known her for a few centuries."

"What?" Christopher said, startled again. No matter how many times they told him they weren't human, he forgot. Watching them eat porridge and dry their moccasins by the fire was simply too normal. "How old are you, anyway?"

Lucien cocked his head in puzzlement. "I do not know how to answer you. Shall I count the years I slept in my egg? Shall I count the forms I wore before this one? In my own terms I would describe myself as middle-aged. But if it is history you are after, speak to Alaine. I do not know how old she is—she would not tell me, even if I were mad enough to ask—but surely you can see she bears the mark of great time."

Christopher chose to reduce the scope of his inquiry. "Has she always been like that for as long as you have known her?"

The boy chose his words with care, delivering them with the hint of a sly smile. "In the presence of others—yes."

Another sunrise found him out of his bed and already in armor. The army had slumbered through the day and most of the night, groaning fitfully. Now the priestesses discharged their power into the wounded. Christopher and Torme could spare their smallest spells, the scraps that slipped through the all-consuming need to preserve bodies, and Gregor had his first-rank magic to contribute. By dawn the army was whole and hale again, save for ninety-seven corpses resting in wagons. Kneeling before the first rays of sunlight, the priestesses prayed for refreshment while the army packed.

"Can you imagine having to rise at daybreak every bloody day?" Gregor joked, preparing to join them.

"I hadn't thought of that," Christopher said. Marcius's sacred hour came whenever it was convenient. One of the benefits of serving a war god, who understood that religious duties had to bend to practical considerations.

"I did," Torme admitted. "Though of course it was the least of my considerations."

"Of course," Gregor laughed, and the three men lowered themselves onto a tent flap stretched across the ground. Christopher assumed a lotus position, feet folded up over his knees. Torme made an attempt to imitate him before giving up, as he always did, and joining Gregor in kneeling. It didn't matter; Marcius didn't care about details like that. Christopher wasn't actually entirely clear on what Marcius did consider important. He didn't know what would happen if he tried to lie. The opportunity had never come up. Despite all his trials, there had never been a time when lying felt justifiable.

Yet he had killed—so many deaths. Not only monsters, though it was unfair to call either the ulvenmen or the goblins monstrous. They were people, no matter how alien. He had killed men, too, bad men by all accounts but human all the same. He had tried very hard to kill a woman as well, and still regretted his failure.

In the midst of this sea of blood it was difficult to understand what made him White. As he prayed, the hallucinatory animated suit of armor that served as his conduit to Marcius appeared and offered him his daily selection of spells. Apparently the god, at least, still found him worthy.

8

UNFINISHED CONVERSATIONS

They passed a dozen more empty villages, following a trail of subtle hints from Alaine. On the second day after the night battle, the goblins attacked his column on the march. A score of eight-foot-tall ogres clad in good iron, a dozen trolls, and the remains of their cavalry struck at the rear, having run fast and long to evade his scouts and fall on their flank unawares.

Unsupported by magic, outnumbered by guns, the enemy fell in a hail of hot lead. A few smashed wagons and twenty dead was a small price to pay for a resounding victory. Having learned his lesson, Christopher did his fighting from horseback and surrounded by cavalrymen. Consequently he arrived on the scene only when it was effectively over.

He let the men finish off the trolls with grenades. Every spell he cast would be one less body he could preserve. With the additional casualties he was now four fatalities away from his self-imposed limit. Not that anyone else was counting.

The act reeked of desperation. The huge creatures were rich sources of tael, as if each one was of moderate rank. The variety bewildered Christopher. Even the goblin knights seemed a different species than the foot soldiers, impossibly tall, and the trolls were obviously supernatural: no ordinary flesh could regrow that fast. More to the point, the ogres were brown and without magic, which was quite foreign to his experience of the obese, powerful creatures.

"Where are the flying blue ones?" he asked, not expecting an answer.

Lucien provided one anyway. "Vercingtrox probably ate them.

They were too powerful to trust, yet not strong enough to be of use. As your previous encounter demonstrated."

"So their entire battle plan was the river? That was it?"

Alaine shook her head gently. "You discount what just occurred. Against steel and magic this would have been a dangerous lunge. As it is, they failed only because they did not bring enough flame. Had they set fire to your chemistry, you would have been forced to retreat."

The attacking cavalry had deployed torches, but as they were the least hardy of the enemy, they had all died before they had inflicted much damage. It was still disheartening. The goblins were learning quickly. Every attack probed a new weakness.

Charles delivered the harvest, a fat purple plum. Christopher was now back in the black; the tael he had taken would pay for the revival all of his men and leave him with pocket change.

"This cost them," he said.

"To double purpose," Alaine said. "You have harvested their nobility. They can hope you will take your winnings and be satisfied."

Christopher frowned at her. "That's only one purpose. What's the other?"

She shrugged her shoulders delicately. "They have also cleared the field for new leadership. The remains of the old order are broken under your heel. Now they are free to find a new strategy. And so have they adapted for millennia; so they infest every corner of the great expanse of Prime. Where there is a way, a goblin will find it, provided only that it is dark, cruel, and profitable."

"You don't think much of them, I gather," Christopher said.

"On the contrary. I have the highest respect for their tenacity. Of all our mortal foes they are perhaps the greatest. You, on the other hand, underestimate them at your peril."

"It doesn't matter what I think," Christopher said. "I'm going to locate their capital and then send for the King."

Alaine smiled ambiguously. Christopher dismounted and went to inspect the wagons. The same low-rank magic that could heal men could, for him, also repair. He bound a shattered axle back together with a word. In half an hour the column was moving again.

After a quiet night, the army advanced with caution. It was obvious that they were close. The density of the fields and the age of the villages told them that. But the silence was disconcerting. They had heard not so much as a cock crow or a chicken cluck. The goblins took all of their livestock with them.

Thus it was a shock when they followed a wagon track out of a forest and found themselves staring at a walled city lying a thousand yards away, surrounded by empty fields. The city itself made no sound. No figures moved on its walls nor stood guard before the closed gates.

"Are they even there? Will we find the whole city deserted?" Gregor asked, peering across the plain from horseback.

"More likely we will find it neck-deep in hobgoblins," D'Kan said. "They must have put them all somewhere."

Christopher was focused on the walls. They were fifteen feet high and made of stone. Against an ordinary attack, such as the King's armies could deploy, they would be quite formidable. He did not want to leave any room for criticism on this task.

"Prepare for a siege," he ordered. "And let's open those gates for the King."

Camping in front of a hostile city was unnerving. The fact that the city took no notice of them was somehow worse. They placed their stakes with care and forced a shallow trench through the frozen earth. As twilight approached, Christopher decided a show of bravado would do everyone good, rather than waiting for morning. He ordered two of the five-inch cannon to fire on the gates.

The artillerymen, enthusiastic to finally have a stationary target, chained the cannons to the ground and double-loaded the powder. The guns belched flame and smoke a dozen yards, sending a wave of sound rolling across the snowy fields. One shot smashed into the gate, throwing splinters into the air as it punched through. The other went high, sailing over the wall and disappearing into the town. The gun crews cursed, adjusted their aim, and reloaded. Within moments the gates collapsed under the assault, falling from their hinges into a pile of shattered lumber.

The army cheered. The sun went down. Christopher set out the usual pickets and went to his tent. He raised another dead soldier and preserved the next lot, saving only one higher-rank spell to call home with. He could afford one spell, as he had one less corpse to preserve now.

He focused on an image of the Cardinal, waiting to be acknowledged. When the Cardinal's eyes met his, he delivered his message.

"We have dispensed with the dragon, found the capital, and opened the gates. I consider our task to be complete; send the King and peers."

The memory of the Cardinal's voice sounded in his head.

"You never make any sense. If I, who know you like the back of my hand, am confused, consider how mystified the realm must be."

Acerbic, but he expected no less from the old man. He unhooked his scabbard and was about to set it aside when the tent flap burst open. Cannan, always by his side, leapt to his feet and drew his sword.

"My lord," said a white-faced private from the open doorway. "You must come."

Christopher bit back a curse. He did not want to waste the breath. As he ran out into the camp and toward the front lines, guns began to fire. The camp roused itself, soldiers staggering out of tents and into his way. He pushed past them, aware that he had virtually no magic left. Cannan dogged close behind, naked blade on his shoulder, his eyes scanning left and right.

They arrived just in time to witness the rockets roaring overhead, bank after bank of them, all fired at once in a panic. The fields before them seemed to be alive, shadows roiling and shifting, revealed by the rocket's red glare to be a sea of hobgoblins that stretched as far as the eye could see. The entire world was blanketed in the creatures, moving cheek to jowl, an unbroken carpet of menace flowing toward them.

The cannons roared, mowing down whole swathes. The rifles fired and fired again, every shot tearing through two or three of the small creatures. Out on the plains the rockets landed, throwing up flame and mud and flesh, leaving gaping holes in the living carpet. Fresh ranks moved forward, closed the gaps as if they had never been.

Mercifully the terror became occluded by the thickening gun smoke. The cannons fired on, unimpeded. They hardly needed to aim. Brave men stood and threw grenades at a measured pace, while others shot the green bodies that filled the trenches and piled up on the stakes.

Christopher found his commanders, Torme and Gregor, swords in hand, with faces drawn as tight as steel. Lalania stood next to them, holding the silent lyre with silent tears streaming down her face. Disa stood behind them, a dagger gripped in trembling hands.

"We cannot hold," Gregor said. "Do you understand? They will crawl over us like ants, until we smother under the corpses."

"They have sent their slaves against us," Torme said. "A sea of hungry mouths. We came to harvest, and they will drown us in the wheat stalks. Not even the Gold Throne would stoop to use its treasure as a weapon."

"You must fly," Disa said. "Take our fingers or no. You at least must escape."

"To what end?" Christopher said. All he held dear in this world was here, in this camp. If he left it behind, he would lose everything. He would be poor and discredited and alone, and sooner or later the Gold Apostle would come for him. The Saint and the Cardinal would look away, because they would have to.

"Save the lyre," Lalania said, holding it forth. "Save yourself."

He shook his head in denial. "They will break. We will hold until the bodies form a wall, and then we will fight from on top of that. Sooner or later the hobgoblins will lose their nerve and flee."

Cannan grinned, his white teeth flashing in the flickering light. "Unwarranted optimism, indeed." The big man strode purposefully to the front line, claiming a ten-foot section from the soldiers. He whirled his sword once over his head in preparation, and then waited for the enemy to reach him.

"As plans go, it is not your best," Gregor declared. "Next time, more rockets." He went to join Cannan, taking a position on his right, shifting more soldiers down the line. Several short green forms stumbled out of the smoke; Cannan sliced through three of them in one stroke. Gregor stabbed the last one, almost negligently. Disa went to stand behind her husband, looking at the ground.

"Use your flight to engage their principals when they appear," Torme instructed. "Break them and the hobgoblins will follow." The priest drew his sword and went to the line, on Gregor's right. Christopher did not bother to tell him he had no spells left.

"I am going to bury the lyre," Lalania half-sobbed. "It is of no use to us today, and if all comes to worst—perhaps it will go unfound."

"Lala," he said, but she turned away and fled.

Karl was somewhere in the camp, fighting. He could tell because the cannons continued to fire at a measured rate. Panic had not yet set in. He could not understand why. In the gap held by the swordsmen, hobgoblins were now appearing in uncountable numbers. The swordsmen cut them to pieces, bodies and parts of bodies spilling in front of them. The ones behind climbed over their dead to lunge and snap at the men, fighting with claw and teeth and unquenchable hate.

Several made it through the screen of rifle fire. Two men went down screaming under their biting, clawing attack. Christopher rushed to the scene. His sword was too clumsy to use in a wrestling match, so he threw himself into the line and slashed at the next wave to hold it back. Behind him other soldiers stopped to stab at the little horrors with bayonets. In front of him the child-sized creatures kept coming. No feint or threat mattered; they hardly bothered to dodge. He struck down creature after creature. More came.

The wounded soldiers returned to the line, bleeding but standing. Their rifles were bayoneted now, and they used them like spears. Behind them a corporal reloaded his carbine. More screams from down the line. Christopher ran to help.

Once he had restored order, he stepped back to look for the next breach. It occurred to him he could no longer see the wooden stakes. The line was receding, falling back in on itself. The space they occupied would contract until they stood shoulder to shoulder. And then it would fail, when they were too tired to lift their arms. Thousands of hobgoblins had already died, perhaps tens of thousands, but one by one the cannons fell silent as their positions were swallowed by the slow tide. He saw Kennet and Charles firing spare rockets by hand. Apparently the supply of grenades was already exhausted.

In the dark and smoke there was nothing to do but fight for the moment. No thought could be spared for what came next, which was surely a mercy. The men did not run away, because stabbing goblins was easier than running. There was nowhere to run to anyway. Without tents and wagons and supplies the men would simply die in the frozen forest. So they stood and fought and measured their lifespan in inches of ground lost.

He turned around and found the elves standing behind him. They looked like a vacationing couple delaying a long overdue departure to say a sentimental goodbye.

"Do something," he growled at them.

"I am," Alaine said with sympathy. "Though it is not what you wish, it is still what you want."

More ambiguous words. He stared at her, angry beyond measure. She shook her head sadly.

"Would it not be better for your secrets to die here, rather than tainting our entire world? Prime has stood in balance for all of time, the Light against the Dark. Yet we have a plan for victory, a careful strategy that stretches over a million years, tipping the scales mote by mote. You are a wild card, a roll of the dice, and none can say who would profit greater at the end of it. We will not risk the certain for the possible."

He found words to hurt her with. "It's too late. People in the Kingdom know how to make guns. They won't just forget."

"No," she admitted. "They will not just forget. Your ignominious failure will kill the interest of men, but darker things than you know live in your realm, and they will not just *forget*. I will have to make them. If it is any consolation to you, my chances of surviving such an operation are middling. I will have to call on my fellows, and some of us will almost certainly die the true death, beyond all magic. Such is the nature of your hidden enemy, our true foe. The ones we have fought since the dawn of creation; the ones we dare not let learn any of your clever tricks."

"I can still fly," he said. "I can go back and start over." A lie, but not even the Saint would hold it against him. "Would you cut me down to stop me?"

She shrugged. "Your life or death is incidental. All that is required is your failure, so that men will look away. And that only to spare me pain; I could not bear to make them . . . forget, as I must the others."

"There is another option," Lucien said. "I can carry one more. I will take you to safety, if you pledge never again to dabble in chemistry. You can still live out your life doing good works. Surely that is worth something."

"If I wanted safety," Christopher said, "I would have kept a spell to go home with." Instead he had raised a dead man, who would merely die again in a few minutes.

"Not to your Kingdom," Lucien said. "The enemy would never

cease stalking you there. I can take you far away, where none know what danger sleeps in your head, though it means you will never see your family again."

"The Kingdom is not my home," Christopher said, despair liberating his tongue. "And it was never within your power to return me to my wife. So you both can just go f—"

A shuddering explosion cut off his words. Someone had set fire to a caisson. The explosion had torn a hole in the slowly collapsing line. Snarling with disgust, Christopher stalked away.

"Take Lalania," he called over his shoulder. "Take her to safety, wherever you think that is. Take her against her will if you have to." Then there was no more time for talk. He stabbed and sliced at the swollen knot of green flesh that poured over the smoking crater.

Behind him he felt the presence of the dragon, filling the sky, its wings spread wide, appearing from nothing in mid–down beat. The wind knocked him to the ground, swept the hobgoblins away like leaves. Lucien, making his grand exit.

Except he did not depart. Instead, he roared, the nerve-wracking bass rumble rippling over the ground. Christopher and his men collapsed before it, shuddering in awe. The hobgoblins shattered before it, shrieks ripped from tens of thousands of throats, the first sounds they had made other than the occasional grunt or wheeze while dying.

Christopher scrambled to his feet, disoriented. He watched the enemy disappear into the wall of smoke. His men slowly stood, too unbelieving to celebrate. The gunfire had ceased instantly, the reversal complete. The hobgoblins fled in hooting terror while his camp lay in utter silence. Christopher looked back to where Lucien stood, an elf again after his momentary transformation. Alaine was watching the boy with an inscrutable expression that nonetheless communicated severe disappointment.

"I wasn't finished talking," Lucien said. "Never turn your back on a dragon before they are finished talking."

"Very well," Christopher said, shaking only a little. "What else did you want to say?"

"Now that it comes to it," Lucien said, "I've quite forgotten."

9

JAWS OF VICTORY

Gregor recovered first. Within moments, he had ordered the cavalry to mount and led them thundering through the wall of smoke, their light-stones bobbing and winking in the haze. They claimed the plain, protecting their treasure. The goblins would not spirit their dead away tonight. Karl limped through the camp, nursing a painful but not dangerous bite on the leg, organizing harvesting parties from the least wounded and sending them out to collect heads.

Christopher stood in the center of his camp and considered the fortunes of war. Moments ago defeat had been crawling over corpses to claim him. Now his men rushed to collect the spoils of victory.

There were shockingly few casualties. The nature of the battle had been all or nothing, the men standing all but untouched until the final moment when they would have died en masse. Not that casualties mattered. The wealth they had just won would pay the Saint's fees a thousand times over.

Assuming they were allowed to keep it. Unable to summon any diplomacy while surrounded by the wounded and the dead, Christopher spoke directly. "How much of this do I owe you?"

Lucien looked away and whistled. Alaine, her voice locked into a careful neutrality, answered for him.

"None. Your men did the killing. Lucien has merely balanced the scales: a roar for a roar."

Christopher really wanted all that tael. It represented fantastic wealth and power, two things he desperately needed. Nonetheless honesty demanded its due. "I think he is entitled to more than that."

"I do not," Alaine said. "If I let you pay him, it will look like a bribe. Worse, Lucien may be persuaded to stay. And this we must not do. The goblins only attacked because they hoped your dragon had departed with the defeat of theirs. There is no concealing our presence now. We must leave soon."

"I do not deny the attraction. I could put that tael to many uses, all of them good," Lucien agreed. "Yet her arguments are sound."

"How long?" Christopher asked.

"A few days at most. You may think to carry the pretense for longer, but I do not suggest doing so. Whatever chooses to come to hunt a dragon will squash you without noticing. Better that Lucien be seen to leave."

A few days to put his army back together and prepare for whatever the goblins came up with next. At least the lyre would be ready then. Ten foot walls might have stopped that horde from overrunning them. Though he wasn't sure. His army did not have enough bullets to destroy an entire civilization.

"Okay. I appreciate it."

"You give thanks too early," Alaine said. "The goblins will hunker behind their walls. They have more provision for siege than you. I suggest retreat."

Unpromising advice, after such a victory.

"Their walls won't last a day against my cannon."

"And then what? A slaughter, house to house, through the streets? Your men are poorly equipped for that kind of warfare, either materially or mentally."

True enough. But the King's army was suited for the task, both because they wore heavier armor and because they were not led by a man who found murdering women and children to be shameful. Of course Alaine already knew that.

"You want me to turn the city over to the King. Just another kind of failure."

She smiled sadly. "Nothing I told you before has changed."

"Perhaps it has," Lucien demurred. "What did you mean when you said the Kingdom was not your home?"

Alaine glanced at Lucien, as sharp as broken glass, then turned the same look on Christopher. He realized he had been indiscreet. While he was trying to decide what to say next, a cavalryman rode up and snapped out a message.

"Colonel, Ser Gregor needs you at once."

"If you will excuse me," he said to elves, relieved to have an excuse to run away from the conversation he had been trying to spark since he had met them.

He found his horse and let it carry him out into the night, Cannan following on his own mount. Their guide led them to where a knot of cavalry stood with steaming nostrils and uneasy feet. The horses did not like walking on the carpet of broken bodies.

"What is it?" he asked when he joined them, but the answer was self-evident. A goblin knelt before them, stark naked and shivering in the cold, his empty hands clasped before him as if in prayer, or perhaps being offered for binding. This was the sign of surrender on this world, where open hands could be misinterpreted as a spell being cast.

Gregor stood to the side, sword drawn and prepared to strike, his attention focused on the kneeling goblin. Sergeant Kennet stood in the saddle, his horse disciplined to perfect stillness, and stared down the barrel of his carbine at the creature. The other men kept their carbines pointing out, in case this goblin was merely a diversion.

Kennet spoke without moving his head. "He asked to speak to our leader. We sent a rider for the Lady Minstrel to divine him for magic but she has not yet arrived."

Cannan dismounted and drew his sword in the same motion. He took up a position exactly opposite to Gregor, where he could block the goblin's advance with a simple sidestep.

Christopher couldn't help himself. He felt sorry for the poor thing. Most of it was a dark green, but its legs were turning blue. Other than the yellowed fangs and the huge multipointed ears and the vertical irises like cat's eyes and the odd shape—the goblin's chest was more tubular than a man's, round at the shoulders where a man would be broad—the creature looked almost human, and unquestionably cold.

"Let's assume I am the leader of this army," Christopher said. "What did you want to talk about?"

The goblin looked up at him, clearly considering its options. Which were, at the moment, very few. It spoke in a sibilant hiss, enunciating its words with a careful distinction that seemed to discomfort it, uttering the last words Christopher had ever expected to hear.

"We wish to surrender." It opened its hands in supplication, revealing a purple ball the size of a tangerine, a king's ransom in tael.

Christopher stared at it, at a loss for words. The goblin spoke on, with a growing sense of urgency.

"You have defeated us thrice. You slew Prince Ooodlibn at Calibon Ridge; you have dispatched the Dragon; you have foiled Duke Olerooen's last and final strategy, at ruinous cost to our nation. We bow to your superiority; we offer you all our treasure and wealth; we accept whatever terms you place upon us, asking only for the bare minimum—the survival of our people, as servants and slaves of your fearsome power."

What possible answer could he give, other than the obvious?

"Alright. Okay. Whatever. Somebody give him something to wear. It's freezing out here."

Cannan growled in opposition. "This is not wisdom."

"What choice do I have?" Christopher asked, hoping somebody would give him one.

Gregor lowered his sword. "Do not look to me. I can only say I wholeheartedly agree with both of you. So much so, that I have dropped my guard hoping for a surprise attack, because then the decision would be out of our hands."

Christopher looked around but could see no other avenues in the starlight shining down on a field of broken and blasted tiny corpses. He wanted to ask Lalania what to do, but she would only tell him what he already knew: the King would not approve, the problems would be insurmountable, and the whole thing would just end in a huge bloody mess.

"Give him a coat before he freezes to death," Christopher said. "Send him back to the camp and we'll talk terms."

"Oh munificent lord," the goblin said, "the spell will expire soon and my speech will desert me. I beg you grant me leave to return to the city and carry this most excellent news. We will not repair the gates; you may enter the city without opposition, and the people will pile their gold and silver before you."

It felt like a trap, invisible jaws of serrated steel clamping around him.

"Sure. We'll wait till daylight, though."

Cannan sighed and took a hand off of the haft of his sword. He held it out, palm up. After a glance at Christopher, the goblin carefully handed Cannan the ball of tael.

"Okay," Christopher said. "Go on before you get frostbite. Remember, we'd rather you didn't surrender, so if you give me even half an excuse, I'll level your whole city the same way I destroyed your gates."

"Yes, oh munificent lord. You will find no fault with us; our pathetic race is adept at serving those of true greatness."

The world's worst humble-brag, and curiously passive-aggressive for a creature that had just surrendered to an alien being. On the other hand, Christopher knew he was nowhere near as imposing as the dragon had been. For one thing, he wouldn't eat any of them.

The goblin ducked its head and shuffled away, hopping and skipping with a jittering gait that was either nervous exhaustion or glee.

Christopher reminded himself not to apply a human template, as Lucien would say.

"Well, let's go tell everybody the war is over," he said.

"You'll have to do the talking," Gregor said. "I don't think I can lie that well."

Lalania was, predictably, aghast. More disconcerting was Alaine's reaction. The elf bit her lip in pain.

"What would you have done?" he asked her.

"I would never have put myself in this position in the first place," she answered. "No goblin would ever attempt to surrender to an elf. They all know better; a reputation we have carefully cultivated precisely to avoid this quagmire."

"They are clever," Torme said. "Even in the act of submission they seek to divide us."

"Indeed, and you can be assured their envoy has made a full report. Their assassins now know who to stalk, and their spell-casters know who to target. They know the style of your armor, the shape of your face, the horse you ride. Please tell me you did not introduce yourself by name, at least."

Christopher coughed. Fortunately the conversation had not gone on long enough for him to toss out his usual admonishment of "call me Christopher."

"You can't tell me you would have killed the whole lot of them," he said. This did not seem consistent with the blinding white aura that Alaine gave off every time he looked at her with magic sight.

"I lack the power to slaughter a city of squirrels, let alone goblins. Yet I would never have accepted a surrender. Either I would have retreated myself or pressed them until they fled. Now they are yours, and you are responsible for their fate."

Christopher eyed her speculatively. Alaine guessed what he was thinking, because she responded definitively.

"Absolutely not. You cannot foist this off on me as you foisted the ulvenmen on my daughter. Nor can you burden her with this. For all her stubbornness, she is no fool; she knows when foul cannot be remade into fair. There is no redemption for the goblin race."

He was startled. "You're condemning an entire species? Every single individual is irredeemably evil?"

"Yes," Alaine said earnestly. "You do not understand. For millennia the goblins have carefully sorted their hatchlings, under the divine guidance of their priests. Those that possess even a shred of Bright are destroyed. Whatever potential for goodness that may have once existed is gone now. The goblins have deliberately bred it out."

"I'm not sure that's . . . possible," Christopher said. It didn't seem like sound genetic theory to him.

"You watched an elf turn into a dragon, and yet you dispute the limits of possibility?" Alaine was as close to incredulous as he could imagine that world-wise woman to be.

She had a point. He could not even begin to understand the change in mass. The dragon must have weighed tons, while the elf was barely a hundred and twenty pounds. Turning back into the smaller form should have released enough energy to vaporize half the planet.

"Maybe we should tell them we changed our minds," Gregor said.

"And then what?" Lalania said. "Walk away and leave them here? The King will hang us all for treason. Let them flee? The King will sue us for his share of the lost spoils, and then hang us for treason."

"You could turn them over to the King," Alaine suggested.

Christopher frowned at her, tired of this unceasing argument. "And he would simply slaughter the lot of them, promises be damned."

"Already it starts." Alaine looked truly distressed. "Your morality will be a chain that binds you, until you are slave instead of master. Can you not see that however distasteful it is now, your options will only grow worse? Can you not understand: this is what they *do*. They find a crack, a weakness, a mere consistency, and exploit it. This is how they dealt with the ogres and the dragon; this is how the goblin race survives. They employed flattery and greed in its turn, and now those creatures of power are dead, but the goblins remain. They will do the same to you."

"It doesn't matter," Lalania said. "The King wants Christopher destroyed as much as the goblins do. He will never let Christopher out of this vise."

"I fear it is true," Torme said. "The King will not send the army to relieve you. You won too easily; he will force you to finish the task on your own. He sent us up here to bleed and die, and we have not done nearly enough of that to appease him. The only way to avoid disobedience is to deliver the tael from every goblin to his court, and even then he will only assign you a greater and more impossible task."

There was a general silence at this depressing analysis.

"Also," Torme added after a moment, "this looks like a massive trap. The King will assume you have gone over to the enemy and made a deal with the dragon, to lure him into an ambush."

"The King already thinks I control the dragon," Christopher said. "I was planning on sending the head back as proof that it was dead. I guess that's not going to work now." He stared at Lucien. "If you have any brilliant ideas, now's the time."

Lucien shook his head. "You would not like my suggestion."

"Why are we wracking our heads over this?" Cannan said. "The goblins are the clever ones. Make them come up with a plan that doesn't involve all of them dying. Squeeze enough tael out of them, and the King will look the other way. As he has done so far. There is plenty more where this came from." He handed Christopher the ball of tael.

"And there is still the battlefield to harvest," Karl said. "Let us make the goblins bleed in our stead. It is not as if they are innocent; they have a county to pay for."

The goblins had destroyed Nordland, burning the town and slaughtering all of its people. The Lord Duke and his lovely wife, his Ranger captain and troop of knights, thousands of peasants and craftsmen, all murdered to feed the monsters' appetite for tael. And other things. Christopher had not forgotten that. He had chosen to overlook it, for the same reason he had overlooked equally horrific crimes by the ulvenmen. It was their way, after all. They had not been immoral by their own standards.

Yet those same standards entitled Christopher to a terrible retribution, as the goblins would be the first to admit. Cannan was right. The only way out of this box was a steady supply of tax to the King. The goblins were masters of both greed and manipulation. Let them come up with a way to buy off the wrath of the King.

"Any advice the goblins give you will only benefit them," Alaine warned.

"I don't care," Christopher said. "I just need to keep all these balls in the air for a while longer." A steady stream of tael was his goal, too.

"And then what?" Alaine asked, penetrating him with a look.

"Then—we'll see," Christopher said. It was the least dishonest answer he could make.

10

THE LION'S MOUTH

Passing through the shattered gates into the silent and alien city took immense courage. Fortunately Royal supplied it all. Christopher merely had to sit on the horse's back without falling off.

He was surrounded by rank, Torme and Gregor on either side, D'Kan and Cannan immediately in front, and Lalania and Disa behind. All were mounted and armed in their usual fashion, save for Disa. They had convinced the poor woman to wear chainmail for a change. She looked wildly unhappy in it, and Christopher sympathized, remembering the first time Karl had won that argument with him. She carried no weapon, however; her only role in any battle would be healing. Lucien and Alaine rode behind the two young women, the boy carrying the spear and the girl with her bow in hand.

The party had been preceded by a platoon of cavalry and was followed by another. They had provided the necessary courage on their own, a feat that still impressed Christopher.

The city did not fare well in the light of day. At a distance it had appeared sophisticated, with multistory houses and broad streets. Up close the houses were demented. Roofs peaked at odd angles, and many of the walls were not entirely perpendicular to the ground, inset with windows of random sizes and with extremely narrow and uninviting doors that had no visible handles or knockers. Only half the buildings were painted, in dull shades of blue and brown; but all of them were dirty, layered in grime and grease so uniform it seemed intentional. The main street was paved conventionally enough, though. The horseshoes rang on the cobblestones, as clearly unwelcome as the army but without rebuke. Every window remained shuttered, every door barred.

Christopher had been expecting a pile of loot, or a negotiating committee, or at least a surprise attack. He almost knocked on a door at random, just to see what would happen.

Instead he followed the main street, winding and turning as it led inexorably to the vast stone keep in the center of the town. The building was not as tall or as fanciful as the great castle in Kingsrock, being merely a huge square block with shallow crenellations that made it look more like a warehouse than a fortification. When they got closer, Christopher could see the arrow slits cut into the upper walls, cleverly disguised to blend into the wall with an artistry the engineers of the Kingdom apparently lacked.

The keep was surrounded by a hundred feet of open ground, the city abruptly stopping on a knife's edge, and a moat that might have doubled as a sewer given how badly it smelled. At their approach the drawbridge began lowering itself. By the time his party reached the moat, it was down, and the portcullis behind it began rising.

And still they had seen not a single living thing.

The mouth of the fort opened into a high stone hall, unlit, and black as night where the slanting morning sun did not reach. The lead cavalry platoon had taken up a position to the right, waiting for the following one to occupy the left. Now three brave men of the first cavalry platoon urged their horses in front of Christopher's group and onto the wooden bridge. Just looking at the maw of darkness made Christopher want to turn tail and run; he could not imagine what possessed those young men to advance.

Cannan spoke. "Hold."

The men stopped fighting their horses, which promptly backed off the bridge.

The red knight turned in the saddle to look at Christopher. "It's a trap."

The entire mission, from the day they had marched out of the Kingdom, had been one long extended trap. A little more detail was called for.

"What kind?" Christopher asked. There were so many he could think of: a floor that dropped into a spiked pit, a ceiling that collapsed heavy stone, hidden spigots spouting boiling oil—and that was before considering simple ambush or magic.

Cannan shrugged his shoulders. "Only one way to find out." He swung off his horse and stepped onto the bridge.

Now Lucien spoke up. "Wait . . ." He stood in the saddle, sniffing, his face darkening. He moved his hand in a spell-casting motion, clearly annoyed at having to resort to mortal means while in a mortal form. Peering through the ring made by his thumb and finger, he nodded, his suspicions confirmed.

"Did you say you owed me a favor?" he asked Christopher.

Christopher was about to categorically deny it, but Lucien didn't wait for an answer.

"The keep lies under a powerful enchantment, a dark scar on the face of the world. Your men are rightly afraid to enter; it will slay them instantly."

"Right," Christopher said, tugging on his horse's reins. "Back to the cannons."

"That will not help," Lucien said. "Reduce the stones to dust and the enchantment will remain, to trap unwary innocents."

"What do you want me to do about it?" Christopher asked. He was trying to get Royal to back up, where the big horse could turn around, but since Balance wasn't retreating Royal didn't want to go.

"I want you to go in there, find the source of the taint, and remove it."

Christopher stopped arguing with the horse to focus all of his attention on arguing with the elf.

"I have no idea how to do that, even if I were stupid enough to try. Why don't you do it?"

Lucien grimaced. "I would not voluntarily place myself inside a keep, where stone walls would pin my wings. It would be a risk of . . . phenomenal proportions." As an afterthought he added, "Also, it is beyond my ability to undo this spell."

"I don't think I can do anything you can't do." Christopher didn't know what rank of magic the dragon could use, but it was safe to assume it was more than his.

"You are a priest. While you cannot destroy this enchantment by arcane methods, you could sanctify the ground that it rests upon, negating its Dark affiliation and thus unbinding the spell."

"I can?" Christopher asked. This was news to him.

Lucien seemed to think he was negotiating a price. "While it will cost more tael than it yields, I shall make good the difference, out of a desire to see the world cleansed. Remember, this serves your own interests. You cannot rule where you dare not step."

"Or," Christopher said, "we could knock the place down by cannon fire, and then build a wall around it."

"That would just make it harder to find the center of the spell. And in due time your wall would fall, but the taint would remain."

"So you want me to walk in there, find the heart of that darkness, get down on my knees, and pray over it?" Christopher shook his head as Lucien nodded his agreement.

"Yes. Although I don't know if kneeling is necessary. You must take that up with your Patron."

"You're overlooking the bit about how anybody that walks in there dies."

"Not you," Alaine said. "Obviously not you. At your rank you would have to be quite decrepit to fall to this level of assault."

He cocked his head at her.

"Yes," she said, "I can enter as well. Probably anyone of fifth rank or so will survive the attempt. You must take enough force with you to dissuade the goblin's greed, yet you must leave enough outside to maintain their fear."

"I don't even know how to do this sanctify thing."

"I can assist you," Torme said. "The act requires an entire day and night of continuous prayer, so it is normally done by several priests whenever possible."

"Then I can enter as well," Gregor said.

"To what end?" Lalania said. "Neither you nor Disa can sanctify. Nor would it be wisdom to send all three of you. The army would cease to be viewed as a threat if it had no ranked commanders left."

Gregor frowned, but Christopher agreed with the bard. "If something does happen, you two are the best suited to either help us or save the army. Or, hopefully, both."

"I will accompany you as well," Alaine said.

"Don't the goblins hate you more than they hate me?" Christopher asked.

"They do," she admitted, "but they fear Lucien more than they fear your army. They may or may not believe that he will seek vengeance on your behalf, but they will not doubt his fury on mine."

"It is true," Lucien said boldly. "I would tear down this building block by block and drown it in a lake of fire, whatever the risk, should the elf known as Alaine not return whole and sound from within."

It sounded like a promise, not a threat. A very ritualistic and formal promise.

Christopher shook his head. He'd been this close to wriggling out of the goblin's surrender, and Lucien had gone and cocked it up. With friends like these, who needed morality?

"What do I take?" he asked with a sigh, giving up on the idea of getting out of it.

"Food," Alaine said. "You will not care for their fare. I would bring water as well, all of your weapons, and a healthy dose of suspicion and paranoia."

Torme was already rooting through saddlebags. The cavalry troop took the hint and began to throw a kit together, contributing water

skins and rations. Cannan helped Alaine and Torme gather the supplies, stuffing three packs with far more than three people would need.
In a distressingly short amount of time, the expedition was ready to
go. There was no point in delaying. They could not be any more ready
than they were now, and Lucien was already on borrowed time.

Alaine went first, shouldering her spear and borrowed pack to step
across the threshold into the hallway. There were audible gasps from
the watching crowd as black shadows ran over her body like writhing
leeches. Her lip trembled in a snarl, and then the shapes faded away.

"Do you need healing?" Disa asked.

"It would not go amiss," Alaine responded, extending her hand
outside the keep. Disa touched it and cast a spell. Then, eyes slightly
wide, she cast another.

"Dark take it," Christopher growled, and forced himself to step
over the barrier.

The pain was immediate and intense. For a terrifying moment
he thought it would burn through his tael and into his flesh. The
shadows retreated before that, leaving him half depleted.

He stuck his hand outside and let Disa replenish him.

With grim determination Torme stepped inside. He started to
follow the shadows to his knees, blood running out of his nose. Christopher caught him and cast a healing spell. Torme steadied himself
and put his hand out to let Disa finish the job.

"Be ready," Cannan said, and before anyone could stop him, the
red knight howled in rage and leapt over the barrier.

Christopher stepped closer, to heal, and Cannan caught him by
the throat, his eyes wild. Yet some discipline held; his fingers did
not tighten, and after the first healing spell, the red knight sagged in
relief and put his hand out for Disa.

"I am depleted," the priestess announced, after burning through a
number of smaller spells, "so please, no more guests."

"Like I would let him walk into this den of deceit without my counsel," Lalania said. She screwed her face up in determination and briskly stepped into the keep.

Christopher moved to stop her; she was only second rank. The shadows would definitely kill her. But much to his surprise, they did not appear.

Gregor frowned at her. "This is not wise," he said.

"I am no longer yours to censure," she responded, somewhat more acerbically than the situation demanded.

"How can I tell, when it has exactly the same effect as always?" Gregor said, but then thought better of continuing the argument. He put his arm around Disa instead. "We'll give you until sundown tomorrow. Then we'll start shelling, and dig your bodies out of the rubble later."

A credible threat. No one would be digging the goblins out to revive them.

"Take care," Lucien said, his eyes glimmering.

"You are in more danger than I," Alaine told him. "Do not forget that."

Torme was tying a handkerchief to his head. Christopher thought it was an odd fashion choice, until he realized there was a light-stone contained in the sash. Now Torme had both hands free for his sword.

"That's a good idea," Christopher said.

"Painting a target on your head is never a good idea," Cannan said. He was doing the same thing, however. "Just carry yours. We will need your magic before we will need your sword."

Lalania had her pistol in one hand, a light-stone in the other, and the lyre slung over her back. Alaine merely shrugged when he looked at her.

"It is not dark enough to discomfort me," the elf said. "Though your light pleases our guide none too much."

At the edge of the flickering light a goblin knelt, shielding its eyes. This one was dressed in a rich purple gown and a tight bonnet with golden trim.

"About time," Christopher said.

The creature bowed low and hissed at length, sibilant vowels that Christopher struggled to hear. Just as he was about to interrupt and demand a translator, Alaine answered the creature in the same language, and it stopped abruptly.

"Save your spells for their ranks," she said. "This is merely a footman."

"What was all of that?" he asked.

"It was detailing its many faults and flaws, in an attempt to stave off your criticism of any future failures."

"What did you tell it?"

"That you could not understand, and I did not care."

The creature stood and began hobbling down the hallway. Christopher looked behind to the sunlit entrance one last time, where Gregor stood holding Disa, and Lucien stood alone. With an act of will he forced himself to follow his party into darkness.

11

THE BELLY OF THE BEAST

The goblins were no taller than men, but their castle was built to a different scale. The vaulted ceilings loomed over twelve-foot-tall arched doors. A few times he saw light reflect off of metal on the walls, only to wink out immediately. Eventually he realized that there were arrow slits cut into the top half of the corridor, with goblins behind them. He could hear nothing save for the steps of his people, though.

After three turns, two halls, and four sets of doors they came to a chamber. Christopher recognized it as living quarters and balked.

"We're not here to sleep," he said to Alaine. "Tell it to wake up the boss."

She hissed at the footman, who hissed back in clear agitation.

"It assures us to do so would lead to its certain death, and begs you to reconsider."

Christopher frowned. "Kindly explain that I am the ruler here now, and I make the rules. The only certain death is displeasing me."

Alaine did not seem to wholly believe him, but she translated with a minimum of smirk. The goblin was not at all convinced. The two had a brief argument, which ended when the goblin signaled surrender with a strange mixture of relief and dread.

"I have forged a compromise. While the ogre lords slumber, we will accept a tour of your new demesne. With particular and immediate focus on the altar. Given that you will require twenty-four hours, I suggest we start that task first."

Christopher could not fault her strategy, though he would have liked a chance to comment on it first.

The goblin led them through more vaulted halls until they came to a large, octagonal room with a huge round dais made of gold. Christopher boggled; gold was measured in fractions of tael, but in this quantity it hardly mattered. The walls of the room were festooned with hideous, ugly statues of precious metal and inset with glittering gemstones. Other than that, the room was empty, without benches or chairs on the naked stone floor. He had at least expected carpets. Every goblin Christopher had seen here spent a lot of time kneeling.

Their guide went one better, flinging himself on the floor completely prostrate. The room did not seem to justify such a reaction— it was no more foreboding than the darkness and sense of evil that pervaded the rest of the castle—until Christopher reflected on what the altar was for. It was big enough to sacrifice an ox.

Lalania wandered over to the nearest wall. She held her light-stone close to a small grotesque statue made in silver. From here it looked like some kind of demented frog. She was focused on the gemstone eyes, tapping at one with her fingernail. Before Christopher could frame an objection, she produced a dagger and popped the gemstone free.

Holding it next to her light-stone, she spoke with undisguised disgust. "Fake."

Christopher turned his head to look at Alaine. Unsurprisingly, she was not surprised.

"Dark take it," Cannan said, with the closest to genuine disappointment Christopher had ever heard out of him, "that means the table is fake too."

"Then this whole room is a fake," Torme said. "The Emperor enjoys a good jest at the expense of his victims, but not to his face. Whatever ceremony takes place here is merely performance, not divine."

Alaine still displayed no sense of surprise. Christopher let annoyance creep into his voice. "You might have told us."

"To what end?" she said. "The goblins were always going to bring you here first, regardless of what you did or said. Might as well let you learn their nature firsthand."

A clanging ring echoed around the room. Cannan had attacked the table with his dagger. Christopher started to object, but Cannan was hammering at the butt of his dagger with a mailed fist and the echoes drowned out the words. Instead Christopher stepped over to upbraid the goblin, struggling to think of a way to credibly frighten the creature without doing something as distasteful and clichéd as administering a beating, but it was watching Cannan and trembling.

He let the man finish his investigation. After a moment Cannan stopped and inspected his work, bending his face close to the gleaming metal and the scratch he had carved in it.

"Gold leaf," Cannan announced. "Stone underneath. But it's thick; there's a dozen pounds of gold lying on this table, if we had time to peel it off."

"What about that statue?" Christopher asked, pointing at random.

Lalania, clever as always, caught on to the game.

"This one?" she said, negligently tipping a statue out of its nook and letting it crash to the ground.

The goblin flinched.

"Or these?" she said, knocking two smaller ones down with a wave of her hand. They clattered and rang on the floor while the goblin covered its head with its hands, displaying abject terror at their blasphemy.

"I think we've made the point," Christopher said. "Tell it we want to see the real one."

Alaine hissed at the goblin, which underwent a startling transformation. It sat up, all semblance of groveling vanished, the performance dropped the instant it was no longer useful. The sense of intelligence in the yellow eyes startled Christopher; how could he have missed it before?

"It's not the same one," Alaine explained, sensing his confusion.

"They switched after the chamber. The second set of double doors. If you recall, our guide was out of sight for a fraction of a heartbeat."

Lalania hissed something herself, but only in frustration. Christopher knew she would be angry at not having caught it.

"Can you speak our language?" Christopher asked.

It hissed an answer, which was clearly a "No" since he couldn't understand it.

Alaine translated for it, communicating its disdain and challenge with the tone of her voice. "If I could, I would tell you that you would not dare to disrespect the Emperor on his own ground."

"I intend to do more than that," Christopher said. "This is the first term of your surrender. You cannot maintain sanctified ground to Dark gods."

"Then how shall we practice our religion?"

Christopher shrugged and let himself sound annoyed. "Not my problem. You want to return to your old ways, pack your bags and go where I can't see you." He knew it was a safe threat. If there was any possibility of retreat the goblins would have run out the back while his army lounged around in their front yard.

"Would you dishonor your god, if we came to your keep and knocked you to your knees?"

He struggled with an answer, but Cannan spoke first, responding to Alaine's translation while staring coolly at the goblin.

"You would not give us the chance. You would cook and eat us on our own altar, laughing all the while."

"Not eat. Humans have no taste; I would rather eat bread," it said with disgust, as if ranking below grain on the flavor scale was a grievous insult.

Christopher was suddenly stung with a sickening revelation. "How the Dark do you even know what people taste like?"

Alaine stood silently; after a moment she said, "Do you really want me to translate that?"

"No," he said with a heavy sigh. "I suppose not."

Torme offered a suggestion. "Tell it we intend to challenge the Emperor with magic. If it truly believes in the Emperor's power, it need not fear the outcome."

Alaine obviously thought the idea was sound, because she spoke to the goblin. Christopher wanted to discuss the whole concept of challenging a god, but the goblin snarled, displaying large yellow fangs. It stood, smoothly and fluidly, and stalked from the room.

This time they passed through only one hall before the goblin stopped at a seemingly random spot and pressed on the wall. A door opened, short enough that all of them had to duck their head to enter, and narrow enough that Cannan had to turn sideways. Inside was a thin passageway that immediately struck Christopher as different. It had the sense of being lived in, instead of the staged quality of everything else they had seen. It was warmer, stank of what he assumed was goblin sweat, and the floor was covered with well-worn carpets.

Now they passed small wooden doors, some of which Christopher could see closing at their approach. At one point the hall broadened into an impromptu room, as if there had simply been some space left over. Half a dozen goblins sat at stilled spinning wheels, their heads bowed and eyes closed.

"Are these their women?" Christopher whispered to Alaine.

"I would not care to guess. It is difficult to determine gender without a close inspection."

"I didn't know that," he said, surprised.

"Do you know *anything* about goblin biology?" she asked.

Stung, he made up some facts off the top of his head. "They eat. They are born, grow old, and die. They care for their children and work to better their future. And when pricked, do they not bleed?"

"Some of that is even true," she conceded. "Though they are hatched, not born. How they care for their spawn would horrify you. And the future they work for is for themselves only, at the expense of all other futures, ever."

He decided to stop while he was behind. If pressed, she might elaborate on the horrifying parts. Behind him he heard the spinning wheels start up again, whispering quietly. His party's footfalls, the clanking of their armor, even their breathing, felt gauche in this castle of silence.

They went up stairs, curving in tight circles, and then down others, turning the opposite direction. Eventually Christopher realized they were being led in circles. They could have traversed the entire building several times by now. Just as he was about to be annoyed enough to say something, their guide stopped in front of a plain wooden door.

On first glance the door was no different than any of the others. A closer inspection revealed subtle clues. This door was clean and whole, untouched by dirt and without nicks, dents, or signs of wear. Their guide made no move to open it.

"Do you think it's trapped?" Christopher asked.

"Bear. Woods. Et cetera. Yes, of course it's trapped, you idiot," Lalania said. "I don't need magic to know that, though I would need to use a spell to find out what kind it is."

"Or we could just ask," Christopher said, glaring at the goblin.

Alaine hissed, and the goblin responded with astonishing contemptuousness.

"Does your god's power fail already? Then you must turn back. Nothing but a goblin can pass through that door without dying, by the grace of the Emperor. Do not ask us to undo it, for we cannot."

"Well, whoever put it there can," Christopher said. "Get him down here."

"You do not listen. Our priests cannot remove this spell; the Emperor would never allow it. Their spell would fail and earn them nothing but penance and contempt."

"Does it really work like that?" Christopher asked Torme. His own god, Marcius, was remarkably remote and had never commented on his use of magic. Nor was it possible to imagine the animated holo-gram he received his spells from having any opinion on his actions, let alone interfering with a spell as it was being cast.

"I cannot say," Torme answered, "having not studied theology when I served the Gold. Though it is true that the priests often spoke of various difficulties, I could not help but notice they always seemed to align with whatever outcome the priests desired."

"That doesn't mean they're not real," Christopher grumbled. It was precisely the kind of bureaucratic machinations he would have implemented, if he were interested in that kind of power. "Fine, we'll do it the hard way."

Cannan stepped forward. Christopher had to grab his shoulder to stop him.

"Not that hard," he said. "Lalania, put up a detection spell. If you can see something, I'll try to dispel it."

She held her circled finger and thumb to her eye. He finally real-ized why it looked so familiar; it was like the farewell in the old TV series *The Prisoner*. "Be seeing you," he muttered, but no one else thought it was funny.

After a moment she uttered a low whistle. "Yes, I see some-thing, and I wouldn't touch it with a ten foot pole for all the gold in Kingsrock."

Christopher had done this before, breaking magical traps in a wiz-ard's bedroom. Though he would use the same spell, he was consider-ably more powerful now. In this particular case success would appear to be necessary.

You owe me this one, Christopher thought to his distant patron. He went through the motions and said the words in Celestial, to no visible effect, as always.

Lalania glanced through her fingers and smiled in triumph. "Tell that creature the Light always defeats the Dark."

"I'd rather not lie," Alaine said.

Cannan forcibly stepped forward and shoved on the door. It rattled but did not move. Christopher was about to ask their guide for a key when Cannan raised a booted foot and kicked the door in. It flew open with a crash, falling off the hinges.

"Tell it strength always wins," Cannan said, and strode into the room, his sword in both hands.

Torme followed, while Christopher made sure the goblin went in next, before he and the women entered. Not that it would matter. The goblins would pretty clearly sacrifice their guide without hesitation if betrayal were on their minds.

The truth of this room leached at him. The altar was plain stone, in an irregular shape, covered in black stains. The room was smaller than the one upstairs, with a low ceiling, and the heat of their bodies warmed the floor and walls, activating a foul smell that he desperately tried not to identify. Their light-stones flickered more than usual. The light itself seemed to recoil from the stone in the middle of the room.

"I trust we have found the true source of the taint," Christopher said to Alaine.

"I think so. Though it seems suspicious that they only tried to kill you once."

"They would not see it that way," Torme said. "To them his death would have been his own fault."

"I wouldn't have died. Cannan would have, and then I would have made them pay to raise him."

"Would you?" Alaine asked. "If they brought you a gaggle of laborers to harvest, would you have lain to with your sword?"

Christopher had faced this before, though Gregor had wielded the axe and Faren had passed the judgments. Still, his actions had been the fulcrum of that bloody morning, and they were not among the things that kept him up at nights. "No. But I would have found well-dressed fellows like this one, and started with them."

Alaine appeared to be satisfied with this answer. The goblin had been watching her closely, and seemed to understand what her attitude signified. He shuffled back a half-step, trying to shrink into obscurity.

"Is this a fellow? Look, ask him—her—it—whatever, for a name. Next time they try a substitution, we can at least catch them in a lie. And I think they understand: I am willing to kill for a lie."

The elf's attitude returned to dubious, but she hissed away.

"This most unworthy creature is called Liang Chia. I am male and of only miniscule influence. The priests chose me to be your guide because my death would not diminish anyone."

Lalania stepped closer and smiled sweetly. "Then maybe you ought to try and keep us happy. It seems likely your best bet for making it through this affair alive. And just imagine how your stature will rise, when the priests who sent you to die see you at the right hand of the new lord of the keep."

"They will kill me when you leave. Or if they suspect me of disloyalty at any instant."

"And we might choose to revive you."

This last bit seemed to be pandering too blatant even for the goblin. He bared his fangs in what Christopher realized was a nervous laugh.

Lalania responded. "Tell him, my lord, how many common men you have payed to revive in your own army."

He wasn't sure. Despite the expense, he'd lost count a long time ago.

"I will say it is common practice," Torme answered for him. "I swear it by my color."

Apparently even the goblins knew the priests of the White did not lie. The creature licked its lips with a tubular blue tongue.

"When Krellyan told me to make friends and allies, I don't think this is what he meant," Christopher objected.

"It does no harm to speak in terms they understand," Lalania said.

True enough, but the way she was acting still made him uncomfortable.

Torme had already dismissed the issue. He had opened his pack and was laying out supplies on the altar, in what Christopher found to be an impressive display of pragmatism.

"There is some preparatory work to do," Torme explained. "And then we must pray. We can take shifts, but you must pray at least one minute longer than I, else your rank will be eclipsed by mine."

Another thing Christopher hadn't known, but he kept his ignorance to himself this time. Not that it mattered. None of his people would be fooled, and the elf probably didn't care.

12

TREATY NEGOTIATIONS

Absent sunlight, and therefore a sundial, there was no way to tell the passage of hours. Given that they had to time this to the minute, that was a problem. Alaine cut their discussion short by offering to keep track of it for them. Christopher accepted, because he was going to be sitting and chanting for half a day. It felt like the least she could do.

He took the first shift, for six hours. Torme would take the second, doing a brutal twelve hours in one go while Christopher got some rest; then Christopher would finish for six hours and a minute more. It seemed unfair, but the younger man asserted that it was both usual practice and wise. Lalania had gone out with the goblin while he and Torme drew patterns on the floor with chalk. She returned with a large, comfortable red velvet cushion. He almost kissed her for that.

Sitting on the floor mumbling the same phrase over and over again would have felt silly, except that he could feel the effect of the power flowing through him. It was like washing a particularly dirty car with a weak hose. Cannan had put the door back up and sat with his back against it, holding it in place. The rest of the party had gone away, to get some rest of their own.

The time passed more quickly than he had feared. He was so focused that he missed Torme's entrance. The first he knew of it, Cannan was helping him to his feet while Torme took his place on the cushion.

It took him a minute to recover. His legs were unsteady and his mind felt narrow. It was hard to remember there was a world outside of this close, dark chamber.

Alaine offered to stay and guard Torme. Christopher wanted Cannan to do it, but the big man just shook his head. He would not leave Christopher's side in a place like this. The two of them followed Lalania and the goblin through the narrow halls back to their original sleeping chamber. The trip was much shorter this time. Lalania had clearly been working on Liang Chia to successful effect.

The room contained a massive bed, covered in more red velvet. He threw himself down, reflecting that luxury was clearly relative. The mattress felt like bales of hay. He was about to peel the covers back and check when Lalania sat down next to him.

"Do not get too comfortable," she said. "It is now night outside, and the castle is waking up. Our guide tells me the ogre lords will host a feast in your honor, which you must attend, though I recommend only pretending to eat. After that you must perform diplomacy. You have a peace treaty to work out."

"Arg," he said. "I need to clear my head first. And I'm starving."

"I can address those needs," she said, rifling through a pack. While he lounged around, feeling guilty, she assembled a plate of food: hard bread, salted meat, and dried vegetables. Then, before he could stop her, she cast a spell over it.

The aroma wafting off the plate silenced his objections. He wolfed it down, startled by how much difference her magic made. Halfway through he caught a bad case of the giggles, unable to suppress the image of the bard strutting through a reality TV cooking show. She could make shoe leather taste like filet mignon.

When he was done she produced a bowl of water, washed his face, and combed his hair. It was so refreshing that he overlooked the intimacy of the act.

Until he couldn't. She paused, kneeling on the bed next to where he sat, hovering over him, warm and soft where her body leaned against his. It was far too comfortable, and here in the circle of dim light that held out the darkness, he did not have the strength to push her away. Her face was inches from his while her fingers lightly stroked his chest.

"Send your guard dog out. A few moments of privacy and I will set your mind at ease."

The explicit offer broke the spell. He caught her hand in his.

"I can't."

"Can you not? The greatest test of your life waits outside this door. The ogres will seek to deceive you, and, if that fails, they may well choose to kill you. Battle will be joined with either words or swords, and who can say which will prove more deadly? This may well be your last few minutes of life. How shall you choose to spend them?" She leaned in, whispering, until her golden hair tickled his face and her lips touched his ear.

He raised his other hand behind her back, to try and pull her away; she bent her head and kissed his neck with such naked hunger that he was paralyzed for a long moment.

"You promised," he finally said.

She sat back, teeth bared.

"Would you hold me to such a poor bargain? Even the Gold would not chain a dog within sight of a bone and leave it to starve."

"Yes, they would." Foolishly, he tried to argue with logic, as if that had any purchase here.

"They would only respect the beast that broke its chain and took what it needed. And I need this . . ." She leaned in to kiss him again.

He brought his hand up and intercepted her face.

"Lala," he said, trying to sound angry.

"You ask so much of me," she said, her eyes glistening. "I ask so little in return. Is it wrong that I should be paid in coin I can spend?"

The character of her words rang false. Not because they were untrue—there was no questioning their urgent veracity—but because they did not sound like the Lalania he had spent so long with. They did, however, remind him of her conversation on the road in Feldspar, when she had presented the case for the Black in utterly convincing terms. The Lalania that could walk into this keep without feeding the shadows was not quite the same Lalania he was used to. Apparently her acting was so polished it had supernatural implications.

And he dared not challenge her. To break character, here and now, would be fatal.

"Not here," he said. "Not now. I would never take that from you for mere convenience. When we are back in Burseberry, safe and sound in our fortress, then you can ask for a change in terms, and I will give you whatever you tell me you deserve."

She pressed forward, pushing against his restraining hand. He could feel her trembling.

"You swear it. By the White," she whispered fiercely.

"I do," he said, biting his lip to say no more. The forcefulness of her seduction did not bother him. She could hold a gun to his head without either of them fearing it would actually kill him.

But her desperate longing burned him raw. He understood it, felt it, lived it every day. The urgency of it was a continuous ache; seeing it in reflection was unbearable.

She sensed that he felt her vulnerability and tore herself away, standing on the floor in one smooth, leonine motion. His hands followed her of their own accord, only falling when she was out of reach.

Cannan stood at the door, watching them as impassively as a telephone pole.

Christopher's head was clear now, sparked awake from the hours of droning slumber.

"You should eat," he said to Cannan.

"I already have. Lalania brought me food while you prayed. Just as well it was then; I would not take it from her now."

"We have made our peace," Christopher said to him. "Don't worry about her. The last thing we can afford is to doubt each other."

The bard and the knight stared at each other for a long, tense moment. An entire conversation might have passed between them. In the end, much to Christopher's surprise, Cannan looked away first.

"As you command," he said to Christopher.

The tinkle of a bell came from outside the chamber door. Their goblin guide, summoning them to dinner.

Christopher stood, wading through the desires and promises that littered the floor like broken glass. Time now for others to watch their dreams shattered.

13

DINNER AND A SHOW

The goblin led them through the halls with poorly disguised glee. Christopher didn't know if it was because the creature thought it would soon get its revenge on its fellows, or because he was leading them into a trap. Since both paths led to the same thing from Christopher's point of view—a lot of dead goblins—he tried not to care.

Their guide threw open the last set of double doors with gusto. The revealed vision froze Christopher in his tracks. A banquet hall, with richly dressed nobles sitting at the high table, jugglers capering in the center of the room, while servants threaded in and out, feeding a disconsolate and rowdy crowd on the main floor.

Except that the guests and entertainers and servants were all goblins, tubular and green and fanged, jostling each other in almost complete silence, with bared teeth and the occasional dagger. The nobles were ogres, and even in the dim light of Cannan's light-stone they were filthy, covered in bits of food and drink, a continuous stream of debris spilling from their large, misshapen mouths, which were inset in bulbous heads, each of which was missing one or more of the usual attributes, such as ears, eyes, or noses. Half a dozen sat at the table, towering over their cringing goblin servants, dealing out buffets and slaps, and by sheer deduction Christopher determined that all but one of them were female.

The male sat in the center, lording it over the room, waving a large silver goblet with homicidal negligence. Two horns stuck up from his bald head, which was slathered in blue paint that had dried and cracked on a huge swollen jaw. Only a child would have confused the filthy brown ogre with the flying blue giant he had fought before.

It roared unintelligibly. In the quiet of the room the sound was magnified. Christopher almost took a step back. Instead, he cast his translation spell.

"I apologize . . . Ser Ogre, but could you please repeat that."

The ogre leapt to his feet and bellowed, striking its chest with the goblet and spilling dark wine everywhere. "I prince! You say prince! Prince!"

"My apologies," Christopher said. He could not stop himself from speaking normally, even while it was obvious the creature in front of him was barely sentient. "You are the ruler here?"

"Prince! You say prince!" It stared at Christopher without outrage.

"Prince," Christopher said, because it seemed the only way to stop the creature from charging across the room and attacking him.

The monster sat down and laughed, bobbing its head like a broken doll. "More!" it demanded, thrusting out the cup. A goblin filled it from a jug and then hid behind the monster's chair.

"You should not show so much deference," Cannan said in a low voice.

Of course not. Christopher had been momentarily dismayed by the grotesquery. Summoning back his courage, he strode forward through the empty space, the entertainers having scampered away with the first roar. "I am here to negotiate a treaty. Failure to do so will resume hostilities, forcing me to bring this castle down on your head with powerful magic."

"You drink," the Prince said, thrusting the cup at him, splashing wine across the table. "Drink good!" It was impossible to determine if it was an offer or a command. The ogre ladies batted their eyes and smiled wide, toothy grins. With a shock Christopher realized they were trying to flirt with him.

He had reached the table, or as close as he dared, given the splash radius of the wine. His face barely cleared the surface of the five-foot-tall table. Silver serving trays containing whole roast pigs rose higher than his head. He felt small and ridiculous. Perhaps the flight spell was called for. Hovering in mid-air would no doubt be more impressive.

Before he could cast, a goblin sidled up to him, cringing. With round eyes it silently begged him to take the silver cup it carried. He took it without thinking, but merely holding on to it was a trial; the stench of the foul wine almost gagged him. He held the cup away from his face and spoke to the ogre. "We need to settle a few things first."

"Me prince," the ogre said. "Me pay tax. Dragon tax too much. You tax less."

"It is not that simple," Christopher said.

"Me prince!" The ogre jabbed at his head with a fat finger; one of the horns fell off.

There was no way this idiotic creature could manage a cave-in, let alone a castle.

"This is absurd," Christopher said, putting the glass on the table. "Who is really in charge here?"

"Me prince!" it roared, pounding the table so hard the roasted meats fell off their trays. With revulsion Christopher realized they were not pigs, but hobgoblins, bound and trussed and roasted whole.

He reached for his sword.

Goblins appeared from behind each of the ogres' chairs, holding golden goblets. One slipped out from under the table to offer a similar goblet to him. This wine smelled far sweeter, and the ogre-prince was mollified.

"Drink good," the ogre said, encouragingly. The goblin at Christopher's feet implored him with its eyes. He could not tell if it was the same one or not. Reflexively he raised the goblet to his lips. Behind him Cannan and Lalania both stepped forward with haste, but he was not that stupid. He did not drink.

The ogres did, draining their goblets in a single go, guzzling down the sweet wine. They set down the empty vessels, giggling at each other like naughty children with an unexpected treat.

The ogre thrust out his goblet. "More!" he demanded. One of the ogre ladies rolled her eyes and fell off her chair, out of sight. The two next to her looked down with mild curiosity. The rest of the ogres did not seem to notice.

Grunting incoherently, the ogre stood on unsteady feet. Another ogre lady fainted forward, her face splashing into her plate of gnawed bones. Two more crumpled from their chairs, landing on the stone floor with wet, sticky thumps.

The ogre thrust out his hand at Christopher. Strangely, it did not feel like a threat. Perhaps it was a plea for help, or even a warning. Regardless, the creature fell onto the table like a dead tree. The last ogre lady had stopped moving. Now she sat slumped in her chair, her eyes open and unblinking.

The corpses' bowels released in a chorus of gurgles and foul smells. Christopher put the golden goblet on the table next to where the silver one had spilled and struggled against the urge to throw up. He took two steps back and turned to face the room, his hand on his sword.

"For the last time. Who is really in charge here?"

From behind him came a sibilant whisper. He spun again to face the table, battling dizziness and disgust. The goblin who had handed him the wine bowed at his feet, though dressed now in rich velvet robes with the sparkle of gold thread running liberally throughout.

"You are, my lord," it said.

Splitting hairs with these creatures would drive him to murder. "I know you have a high-rank priest." The original emissary had been under a translation spell. For that matter, the legions of undead had to have come from somewhere. And there was the ease with which they had undone his spells and paralyzed him in the first battle. "Get him, her, or it out here right now."

The goblin swept its arm out in another, more elaborate bow. "I am at your service."

Christopher stared at it, suspicious. In the human tongue he asked Lalania, "It says it's the boss. Do you think it's telling the truth?"

"A simple test," Cannan answered for her, and ran the creature through with his massive sword.

Christopher, caught by surprise, could only gape.

Cannan stepped back, letting the goblin slide off his blade. It lay in a heap, but after a moment of stillness it peered up at Christopher with one yellow eye.

"Permission to cast," it whispered.

"What did it say?" Lalania interjected, before Christopher could answer.

"It wants to cast a spell," he said.

"Then, for Light's sake, ask it what spell it intends before you agree."

That would seem obvious; it wanted to heal itself. But in this environment the obvious would always be a trap. "Cannan, stand it up," he ordered instead.

The red knight grabbed the creature by the shoulder with one hand and lifted it to its feet. Its robes were cut, glistening with dampness from colorless ichor. Cannan twitched the robes open with his free hand. The flesh underneath was whole.

"You do not need healing," Christopher said. Keeping its tael diminished was a good idea, in case the negotiations turned to violence. "But you can cast the translation spell on yourself."

The goblin nodded but did nothing else.

"Let me rephrase," Christopher said. "I order you to cast the translation spell on yourself."

"As you command," the goblin said, and muttered in a different language. Surprisingly, Christopher recognized it as the same language the Yellow priest Joadan used to cast spells. Perhaps more surprisingly, his translation spell did not translate the words.

"Let's start over," Christopher said, when it was done praying. "I am the Lord Prophet Christopher." He stopped, the phrase sounding utterly foreign once he said it out loud.

"And we are his companions," Lalania said, picking up for him. "You need not know our names or ranks. Yet we need know yours. State your title, position, and common name, unambiguously."

"I am Chia Laing, Eldest of the Servants of the Emperor, a rank equal to your Lord Prophet," it said in human speech. "I have served Him, my people, and my masters faithfully. I will serve you as well, for the sake of my religion and my race."

"You just poisoned your prince," Christopher said. "I don't want to be served like that."

"That creature was no true prince, as its easy death has proven. The dragon took over and ate the royal court after you defeated the true prince. The dragon kept only the mundane ogres as soldiers, and yet they still bullied us, with the depredations of the dragon on top of that. Now we are liberated. Pray do not judge us for the terrible things we did while ruled by ogre magi and dragon; we are weak in the face of such strength, unlike your most formidable self."

"Do not believe a word of it," Lalania said.

"I speak only blunt fact," the goblin said.

"And yet every fact leads away from the truth," she countered.

"Here is a blunt fact," Christopher said. "The King wants all of you dead. The only way I can think of to change his mind is tax. Huge, glowing piles of it. Gold, silver, and above all tael need to leave this place by the wagon load."

"And how shall we live?" the goblin asked. "Beggar our merchants if you must, but how shall we protect ourselves from creatures of the Wild without tael?"

"You just complained about ogres and dragons, so pretty clearly your tael wasn't protecting you in the first place," Christopher said.

"To be ruled is always the fate of goblins." It bowed its head again, either in sorrow or surrender. "Yet there are lesser creatures that prey upon us. Without the strength of our knights, even wolves will take our hatchlings from the nest."

"Where are the knights?" Christopher asked, looking around. He didn't see any of the seven-foot-tall goblins in the hall.

"In your pocket," the goblin murmured. "You have already slain them all."

"Then where are their females?"

"There are no females," the goblin said, looking at him with surprise. "Why would there be female goblin knights?"

"Then where do they come from?" Christopher asked, confused.

"I think," Lalania said, "they are made."

"Correct, of course," the goblin confirmed. "We select an egg before hatching and imbue it with tael. The result is a large, powerful, and loyal knight. As they served us, they will serve you."

"No. Just no." Christopher was too disgusted to continue the topic. "You'll have to make do with ordinary soldiers. If anything bigger shows up . . . somebody else will have to deal with it." Although he couldn't think of who that somebody else would be, other than himself.

"It's where princes come from, too," Lalania said. "You could have turned that ogre into a prince, if you wanted to."

"We lack the tael, having already given you what we could spare."

"That's not the point. The point is, you weren't conquered by ogre magi. You found a band of ogres and turned them into magi, to do your fighting for you. And the minute they stopped being useful, you poisoned them. As you will do to Christopher, as soon as it seems profitable." She picked up the golden cup they had given Christopher. "Here," she said to the goblin, "prove me wrong. Drink this."

The goblin demurred with a sly smile. "As I said, it is our nature. Yet if your master is stronger than any other, he need not fear our disloyalty."

"It's not me you need to fear," Christopher said. "It's the King. He wants you all dead."

"And you do not?" it asked him.

"No," Christopher said. "I just wish you'd go away where I never have to see you again. But I guess that's not an option."

"It is not," the goblin confirmed. "We would be consumed like mice in the Wild. So we will serve you as long as you protect us from this genocidal King, and any other dangers that threaten our very existence."

The way it said that caught Christopher's attention.

"Is there a threat at the moment? I mean, other than my army."

"There is," the goblin agreed. "Though I believed you were already resolving it. You destroyed an astonishing number of hobgoblins in only one day. At that rate you could exterminate them in only a few weeks more."

"I thought they were your peasants," Christopher said.

"They were. Yet ruling over a sea of those demented creatures is a delicate act. Without our principals we would not likely be able to maintain dominance; now that you have broken our last and most desperate attack, our authority is completely demolished. We must hunker behind the city walls until you clear the countryside. Then we will scrabble in the dirt like chickens, and try not to starve."

"Let me get this straight," Christopher said. "You want me to kill how many hobgoblins?"

"Our last estimate was a hundred thousand, but I am uncertain how many you have already slain. Absent our control, they will begin to feed on each other, but that leads to tael-empowered hobgoblins, which only makes things worse."

"Not coincidentally, the death of all those multitudes will pay a magnificent bounty to the King," Lalania said.

"It would seem serendipitous," the goblin agreed.

Christopher had come in here to negotiate a surrender and extract a tax. Instead, he was being sent out into the field to do the goblin's dirty work. "Send your own troops," he said.

"If you insist, I shall; but I tell you now, we will fail. Our soldiers will be overrun and consumed. You will lose their tael to the hobgoblins, which will again be empowered as a result. Perhaps I need to state the obvious: while the hobgoblins hate you, as they do all living things, they now hate us with a fury that transcends what little reason they possess."

"Not unjustly," Lalania said, waving her hand at the table with its horrible bounty.

The goblin bowed its head. "They cannot distinguish between ourselves and our overlords, whose appetites were insatiable."

"I can't butcher an entire country," Christopher objected.

"Then the terms of our surrender would seem negated," the goblin snapped. For the first time Christopher felt naked menace behind the words. "If you cannot defeat the hobgoblins, kindly withdraw and allow us to promote knights until we can defend ourselves. Else you offer us a choice of deaths. And if I must state the obvious again: we will not choose starvation."

"We need to ask Alaine what to do," Christopher said.

Lalania laughed, a little bit wickedly. "She will only parade her I-told-you-so's. Before our spells elapse, we must settle the further terms beyond this immediate problem. How shall goblins live next to a kingdom of men?"

"I can control my own," the goblin said with authority. "I can promise no raids, crimes, or provocations. Can you control your people?"

An embarrassing question that Christopher did not want to answer, since the answer was no.

"We need a simple, clear treaty," Christopher said. "You get the city, and the farmland around it. Any goblin that leaves that territory is subject to death. No humans will enter your lands, on pain of death, except my soldiers and envoys. You have to contain your population; if you breed beyond the farmland's ability to feed you, I will let you starve. You cannot maintain sanctified ground or promote any priests above the rank of Curate. Nor can you promote any other profession, or make non-goblin creatures like ogre magi and knights."

"Or hobgoblins," Lalania said. To Christopher's inquiring look, she said, "Where do you think they come from? The same process as the knights, though with different effect."

"Only the original generation," the goblin said. "After that they breed on their own."

"Why would you do that?" Christopher asked, boggled.

The goblin shrugged, annoyed at having to explain the obvious again. "Hobgoblins yield little tael, but they mature quickly and breed with abandon. You humans prefer to banish your own kind to the fields, to labor in the dirt and to feed your great lords with their too-early deaths, and yet somehow we are the wicked ones?"

Christopher found himself wondering when the translation spell would expire. Sadly, he was high rank now, so it would last for hours more. Certainly far longer than his patience.

"The tael in excess of what you need to maintain priests that can heal and cure disease will go to the King. All of it. Should you violate this treaty, it will be a declaration of war. The King will demand your destruction. There will be no second chances, no renegotiating. However, I reserve the right to change the terms as I see necessary. Do you agree to this?"

"It would seem rather one-sided. Do you consider it fair?" The goblin's jibe was somewhat undercut by the obvious admiration in its tone. Apparently sharp practice was one thing they respected.

"Whether or not it's fair is irrelevant. It's the best I can do. You have to agree, on behalf of all your people, and hold them to it."

"And you will agree, on behalf of your people, and hold them to it?"

"As best as I can," Christopher said. "Don't bother to object. It's the best you'll get."

"Very well," the goblin said. "On behalf of my people, I accept your terms. Let us live in peace for as long as you can keep it." It took the golden goblet from Lalania's hand. "To fate, ever changing," it declared, and drained the goblet in one long drink. Afterward it bowed, green lips pulled over yellow fangs in a sly smile, obviously unharmed by the experience.

"That goes into the treasure wagon," Cannan said, taking the golden goblet. "The silver one, too."

14

CLEAR AND PRESENT DANGER

Following their guide back to their chamber, they passed a goblin mopping the floor. Christopher still had the translation spell active, so he stopped and asked the goblin for its name.

The creature threw itself to the floor and hissed, "I am Chaing Lia, most unworthy to address your supreme self."

"All of their names seem to sound the same," Christopher told Lalania.

"No doubt by design," she said. "It would not surprise me if they all have different names tomorrow."

When he put the question to their guide, Liang Chia, the goblin objected. "We are not elves. We keep our names, as we keep our word, even when it does not profit us."

"And what rank are you?" Christopher asked.

The goblin bared his teeth. It looked like a smile, but Christopher was beginning to realize that for the goblins it was an expression of hatred, anger, pride, or triumph. Assuming there was any difference in those states for them.

"I am third rank in the service of the Emperor."

"I though you said no one would miss you if you died," Christopher said. "A third-rank is too valuable to waste."

"My mentor was destroyed by one of your mysterious spells in the midnight battle," the goblin replied. "Hence I, and several others, became unaffiliated with any faction. The others foolishly groveled until they found new masters. I chose to wait for better opportunities, and now I serve you."

CLEAR AND PRESENT DANGER   131

"How many factions are there?" Christopher asked.

"Eleven, not counting the Eldest, who is above faction."

"So there's only one Prophet-rank?"

The goblin bared his teeth again. Christopher had extracted a fact they would rather not have him know. He had done more than that, as he explained to Lalania in human speech. "I'm betting the faction leaders are fifth rank. That's a bucketful of Curates, which explains why there were so many skeletons."

"More priests than this population needs," she said. "Announce that only ten factions can exist. They'll murder the excess for you, and we can use the tael."

He chose to overlook her bloodthirstiness. Or ichor-thirstiness, in this case. Speaking in goblin again, he interrogated their guide as they walked. "What other ranked professions are here? I command you to answer fully, truthfully, with only relevant information, to this and all future questions."

Liang Chia nodded in appreciation of his exactness. "The secret police, who serve the priests. I do not know how many or what ranks they hold; suffice to say that if three goblins meet in a closet, they assume the priests will hear what they say. Occasionally a trouble-maker is found in his bed with a second mouth where his throat used to be, and all know that justice has been done."

So here the Invisible Guild worked for the government.

"We have no arcane disciples. The ogre magi would not tolerate the competition. For the warrior class we had knights and ogres, which you have slain. The guild-masters have their petty craft guilds, without which our tools would fail and our hatchlings would starve. Other than that we are as we came from the egg."

Luckily for Christopher, the dragon had already pared this society down to the bone. Now he just had to keep it there, while keeping the King from uprooting it altogether. He had essentially commuted their death sentence to life imprisonment, which seemed harsh. On the other hand, they were murderers a thousand times over.

"I think they're right," he told Lalania. "They can't deal with those hobgoblins."

"And how shall we?" she said. "I doubt your soldiers can reload as fast as they breed."

"Aye," Cannan grunted. "Your rifles are adept at destroying large targets. Against hordes of rats they are both overkill and yet not lethal enough."

"Rats," Christopher said. "A plague of rats. I need an exterminator."

"A thousand exterminators with ten thousand rat terriers would not be enough," Lalania said. "Yet Kingsrock houses at most a dozen."

"Brave little dogs," Cannan mused. "They go into the tunnels and bolt-holes despite being outnumbered. I tried to buy one but Jeger would have none of it."

Christopher laughed at the image of the little black winged cat hissing its disapproval at a yapping dog, as it had so many times toward him.

Then he remembered both of them were dead, the kittenhawk and its owner. He bit his lip, and no more was said until their guide left them in their chamber. He sat on the bed and pulled his boots off.

"Don't I have an army of dogs?" he said, dropping the last boot onto the floor.

Cannan nodded, brought back to the present and by appearances grateful for it. "You do indeed. Their axes would be ideal for this work."

"And they might do it for sport, which is well, because you cannot afford to pay them," Lalania said, sitting on the far side of the bed.

"The terms of our treaty are simple enough that I can explain it to the ulvenmen," Christopher said. "They can kill any goblin they find outside the city."

Lalania smiled at him in a way he found discomforting. It was pride for his cleverness, without a trace of concern for his callousness. "You would solve one problem with the other," she said. "If either revolts against your rule, the other will destroy it to curry your favor."

"Sharp practice that would do a Yellow proud," Cannan said.

The words stung.

"You must rest," Lalania said. "You have many hours of prayer ahead of you, and if you miss a single syllable, you will have to do it all over again. I will return to Alaine and wait." She pulled a pair of pillows and the quilt off the bed. "The floor is cold and hard," she explained.

Christopher laid down on the bed, fully dressed, and placed his sword next to him. A poor bed-partner, he reflected, and yet the best he could hope for. It would not entice him with unwise desires. Even after all this time, he did not find its methods attractive.

Cannan saw Lalania out, and then slumped against the door. The red knight took his light-stone headband off and stuffed it in his pocket. The room turned pitch black, lacking any window or crack for starlight to trickle through. The total absence of visual feedback was disorienting.

He began composing a message to Kalani, trying to fit everything into a few words. The nature of the treaty he wanted enforced, the terms of payment he could afford. Mostly he worried about how she could possibly move an army of ulvenmen from the south to the north of the Kingdom without causing a war. Such logistical details were comfortably abstract, and he forgot the darkness long enough to fall asleep.

He sat up with a start, reaching for his sword. Lalania stood by the side of the bed, still as a statue, unwilling to provoke him further. The room was lit again, thanks to Cannan and Lalania's light-stones.

"It is time," she said.

While he put his boots on she made a breakfast for the two men out of the backpack, using her magic to make it edible.

"You must still pray over it," Lalania told him. "They won't try to kill you outright, but there are any number of mind-altering substances that could subtly affect you. They have had hours to insert them into our supplies."

"Cannan slept in front of the door all night."

"That would not stop the Invisible Guild, let alone a goblin in his own castle," Lalania said. "If this room doesn't have at least three secret entrances, I'll eat my lyre."

He muttered an orison over his plate, then had to do it again when Cannan switched plates with him.

Walking through the castle with Lalania as a guide was a different experience. The goblins did not hide now, so they encountered many working servants and even a small squad of chainmail clad soldiers with halberds. All of the goblins went to one knee and stared at the ground while they passed. The translation spell had expired, so Christopher could not interrogate them, but he didn't really want to.

Alaine was sitting nonchalantly on the altar while Torme knelt on the cushion in front of it, mumbling. Christopher picked up the pillows lying against the wall. The cushion was not entirely adequate. He was about to replace Torme when Alaine spoke up.

"Before you begin, I would like a few words with you."

"Do we have time?" he asked.

"We do. I have erred on the side of caution."

"How are you timing it, anyway?" If she had the magical equivalent of a watch, he wanted one.

"I have been counting my heartbeats," she said.

And he had thought praying was tedious. "What about when you slept?"

"I have not slept since we entered. Do not concern yourself. A few days without rest will do me no harm."

He dropped the pillows with a sigh. "Okay, then. What do you want to talk about?"

"I am uncertain whether you wish to discuss it in front of your companions. Yet this room is the only place that is safe from listening ears."

"Is that why you came in with us?" Christopher said, half-joking. "Just to find a private room?"

"Yes," she said seriously. "While the ground is sanctified, none can scry us. If you would be so kind as to cast your translation spell, I will speak in one of my more obscure tongues. Thus we may talk freely, or as freely as one dares on this plane."

He could cast the translation one more time, though if it did not last through his shift of prayer he would not be able to talk to the goblins again today. That was a pleasant incentive, so he quickly ran through the words of the spell.

Alaine smiled, a professional kind of smile that was approving without being particularly friendly, and spoke in a language with grating syllables he had never heard before. "I recommend sending the bard away. Though I am certain she does not speak this language, she might well memorize the sound of our speech for later translation."

"She can do that?" Christopher said, surprised. The spell automatically transformed his words into the last language he had heard, so he had to consciously switch to common speech to address Lalania. "Lala, can you ask them for a chair? If I sit on the floor for another six hours, I won't be able to walk."

"You don't have to lie," she said. "I know the elf wants me gone."

He frowned at her. "I really would like a chair."

"Of course, my lord," she said with a bow, and left the room. At least she didn't slam the door behind her, but only because it was still leaning against the wall.

"You understand why she acts this way, yes?" Alaine asked him.

He turned back around to face the other difficult woman in his life at the moment.

"I think so. Something about the sanctification, and why the shadows didn't attack her."

"She pretends to an affiliation she does not hold. Few professions are capable of this; fewer still are willing. Should she spend too long in this guise, she runs the risk of forgetting it was merely a false face."

Lalania took far too many risks for Christopher's taste. A complaint he shared with Gregor.

"I tell you this," Alaine continued, "so that you understand. There is a war, has always been a war, across all worlds and time. All of us are soldiers in battle, even those who never touch a weapon. And we are not always aware of what side we are on. Alliances shift and ebb in the currents of the moment, the exigencies of the day. What seems fair may become foul, or otherwise; yet the final victory is as stark and unambiguous as it is possible to be."

"What is this final victory?" Christopher asked. He didn't really care for the sound of the phrase.

"Justice for all, even those who have died and those who do not yet live." She said it with the kind of apologetic reserve that meant she knew it was an inadequate answer.

"I swore that oath when I became a priest," Christopher said, frowning at her. "I didn't know then what it meant, and I don't know now. But of course you already know that. And you're not going to enlighten me."

"It is not within my responsibility or my capacity to do so," she said. "But now perhaps you understand my position. I cannot pretend to be overly concerned with the fate of one small human kingdom, let alone a single priest, even when they are on my side. But the fate of an entire plane demands my attention."

"What plane do you think I threaten?" he asked. He had only defeated the goblins with the dragon's help. Putting whole planets under his feet was farfetched.

"Your own," she said.

He stared at her. "Why would I . . ."

"You would not, intentionally. Or more accurately: the person you are at this moment would not. Yet affiliation is not immutable, as the bard has shown you."

"She didn't need to," Christopher said. "I already knew that. Cannan got taken over by a ring that made him kill his wife and burn her corpse. I think the ring was meant for me."

Alaine nodded sadly. "It will not be the last trap they lay. I commiserate; to be a specific target of the Dark is no pleasant thing, as I have known all my life. Yet if I am to risk myself on your behalf, I must have more than pity. Lucien suspects you are from the ancestral plane of Man. Is this true?"

So many times he had wanted to say that, to talk about what it meant. Now that it was here, all he could do was nod silently.

"Then the danger is beyond reckoning. Do you understand why?"

He did now. He was the only person who could open a gate to Earth. He wanted to do that for the best of reasons: to bring over technology, and to go home to his wife. But if he fell under the control of the *hjerne-spica*, he would want it for the worst of reasons.

"There's something you don't understand," he said to the elf. "These rifles of mine are toys. My army wouldn't last a day against real soldiers. And more," he went on, before she could object, "so much more. We can talk around the world with a device so cheap even peasants own one. We have machines that fly, and fight, and dig trenches, and everything else."

"Yet against magic it would all be for naught. And I know your world does not have magic."

"That's right," Christopher said. "There's no tael there. So there's no reason for the *hjerne-spica* to invade."

"When you open a gate that goes both ways," she explained, her voice weary with its own hardness, "that will change. Magic will flow into your home; your land will become accessible to any who can walk the planes. Your people will be bound to tael with their next breath. While they are ripe, yet before they can learn our ways and promote their own defenses, the enemy will sweep in and devour the feast. We know this because it has happened before. Whole planes are now clad in shadow, their people raised like beasts to feed nightmares."

Christopher could not speak.

"Do you see why your death might be the best possible outcome?" Alaine asked him. "Now, before you gain the rank necessary to find your way home, trailing doom in your wake?"

He struggled to put words together. "You're only seeing the bad side. We can help, too. We've fought evil before."

"With toys? Are your machines proof against darkness?"

"Not our machines. Our knowledge. There are libraries there that contain things you can't imagine."

"Such as?"

He reached for the most exotic knowledge he could muster. "We know how stars make light."

She smiled wryly. "I cannot imagine how that would matter. Yet I am a soldier, not an academic. No doubt the spell-casters would find such trivia fascinating. Perhaps even useful."

When he started to argue, she held up her hands in surrender. "You have won, for now. I will support you as much as I am able, which will be less than you expect. But understand: if you go over to the enemy, either by choice or accident, I will extirpate you and all who know your secrets. I tell you this not because I seek your permission but because I demand your acquiescence."

She wanted him to be a partner in his own judgment, to condemn his future self to death for crimes he had not yet committed.

He answered the only way he could. "Of course," he said. "I agree."

15

WHISTLE TO THE STARS

After such terrible conversation, the simple act of prayer felt like relief. His despair was reduced to the fear that he might fall asleep in the comfortable chair Lalania had produced. Time passed effortlessly, marked only by the distinct sense that the altar in front of him was growing infinitesimally less dark with each mumble.

Suddenly Alaine stood before him, her expression unmistakable. It was time.

He rose up and spoke the phrase for the last time, relief and hope in his voice. Then he collapsed back into the chair, dizzy with the unexpected motion. His people were all there, Cannan and Torme with their swords drawn.

Torme strode forward and cast a detection spell. He studied the altar carefully for a dozen heartbeats, each one of which Christopher felt pounding in his chest.

"Well done, my lord." Torme, normally discreet to a fault, did not try to hide the satisfaction in his voice.

There was no other effect. Christopher had expected fireworks, or the roof crashing down around their ears, or at least a howl of agony from the collective throats of the goblin priesthood.

"How shall we know for certain?" Lalania asked.

"If you do not trust my divination," Torme answered, "we can leave the area and reenter. The absence of shadows will confirm it."

"There are far easier tests," Alaine said.

"And immediate." Lalania squared her shoulders. "We need to know now; if we have failed, they may not let us in to try again."

Christopher was going to argue the point, but Lalania closed her eyes and drew a deep breath. Her face softened, losing the hard cast it had worn for the last day and night. Reflexively he leapt forward to catch her, readying a healing spell.

No shadows appeared. She opened her eyes in his arms, unscathed. The old Lalania, the one he was used to. He hugged her close, hanging his head over her shoulder, because it was the only way he could stop himself from kissing her.

"Welcome back," he whispered.

"I was always here," she answered plainly, and then, whispering, "I always will be."

"Or you could have tried to summon a creature," Alaine sighed. "But I suppose such a simple test lacked sufficient drama."

Christopher let go of Lalania and stood back. "So: now what?"

"Now we can leave," Alaine answered in her place. "If the goblins are truly reduced to a Prophet as their highest rank, they cannot renew the spell. Nor could they afford to, if you keep a tight leash on their tael. Your army can enter their fortress at will, which presumably will allow you to intimidate them into some semblance of obedience. Of course they will scheme constantly to undermine and ultimately destroy you, either physically or spiritually, but so much you already knew."

"We can't go home yet," Christopher objected. "We still have the hobgoblins to deal with."

"By 'we,' I meant Lucien and myself," Alaine said. "The hobgoblins are your problem. Should you fail such a trivial task, my work will be done for me."

"Your loyalty is remarkable." Lalania smiled with false sweetness. She might be his old Lalania again, but she still didn't care for the elf.

Alaine ignored the jibe, addressing Lalania with only helpfulness. "You may wish to learn the goblin tongue, as many creatures of the Dark use it for a common language. Goblins are almost as ubiquitous as humans."

"I have already made a start," Lalania confessed. She turned to the goblin lurking in the doorway and hissed.

The goblin hissed back, clearly correcting her. Only when she hissed to his satisfaction did he bare his teeth and run off.

"Impertinence seems to be in their nature," Lalania muttered.

"It is," Alaine confirmed. "Goblins only have two manners: overweening pride and abject groveling."

"What about scheming?" Cannan asked with distaste.

"They are always scheming."

"Then we need exacting terms," Christopher said. "A limit on their ranks; only one Prophet, and no higher." He could not, in good conscience, deny them the ability to revive their own dead. "Alaine, how many priests of Curate rank do they need to contain outbreaks of disease?"

"For the population of this city, two would suffice."

"That's a lot less than they already have," Christopher mused.

"There is a simple solution," Cannan suggested. His sword was resting on his shoulder. "Which has the added advantage of being profitable."

"As much as I dislike it," Torme admitted, "Ser has a point. Their priesthood will be nothing but trouble. Fewer numbers would breed fewer plots."

"How would we adjudicate who should live and who should die?" Christopher asked.

"Kill all the existing Curates, and promote new ones," Lalania said. "Liang Chia would appreciate that. He might even be loyal for a season or two."

"And how do we do that?" Christopher demanded. "Stalk through this castle, looking in every nook and cranny, stabbing goblins until we find ones that don't die from a single blow, and then killing them anyway? We can't order them to turn themselves over to be killed: no one would obey such a command. We can't demand the other goblins turn them over: they'll close their eyes while the Curates hide and then tell us, quite honestly, they don't know where they are."

Alaine nodded her head in satisfaction. "I believe you are beginning to understand."

He understood more than she thought. Earth politics were so much more sophisticated than the crude rule of sword and spell. Ironically, the only place he'd seen real duplicity was from the White Church, with its program of plausible deniability.

Their guide, Liang Chia, returned, bowing low in the doorway before presenting the Eldest.

"Can you tell the Eldest to cast the translation spell on itself?" Christopher asked Lalania. He was thankfully out of those spells for the day.

"Herself," Lalania said. "Not that it matters." She hissed at the goblin, who played dumb only as long as it was amusing to do so. Once Lalania stamped her foot, the Eldest bared her teeth and chanted her spell.

"I have modifications to the terms," Christopher explained. "You may keep the ranks you have now, but you may not replace them above the following limits: one priest of Prophet rank, four of Curate, no more than a dozen of lower ranks. No more than a score of your secret police may have ranks, and none of them above third. All other aspects of our treaty remain in place. I will contact you on a regular basis and demand an honest answer as to whether you have kept these terms. If you fail, I will execute you and pick a new leader to take your place. Is this clear?"

"As clear as the night at the bottom of the well," the Eldest intoned.

Christopher grit his teeth. "I require a direct and unambiguous answer that is not cloaked in metaphor."

The goblin laughed at him. "Yes, Lord Prophet, your emendations are clear."

"Don't forget the gold," Cannan said.

"Right. Every piece of gold, no matter how small, must be collected and delivered to the city gates within the next three days. You will continue to turn over any gold that is discovered. Failure will bring the same consequences."

"Of course, my Lord Prophet," the goblin answered, bowing in deference. "Though as our protector and lord, may I ask how we shall manage our commerce without coin?"

"Use paper," Christopher said. "When you confiscate someone's gold, give them an equal amount of paper. Let them trade in that. As long as you don't make more paper than you had gold, you should be fine."

"What an astounding idea," the Eldest said. "Drollery recommends it, if nothing else."

"Or use silver. Or carved seashells. I don't care. I just need to be able to tell the King he won't find more gold here if he comes looking. It's the only chance we have of stopping him."

"You play the angel, shielding us from the demon if only we cooperate. As if we were stupid enough to believe you had our best interests at heart." The goblin did not conceal the disdain in her voice.

"I don't like it any more than you do," Christopher said. "If you want to go back to trying to kill each other, just say so."

"No," she said, baring her teeth again, "it is too late for that. I have just made a down-payment on a clutch of eggs."

If it was a joke, he didn't understand it. If it wasn't, he didn't want to understand it.

"I'm going to send for reinforcements to deal with the hobgoblins. It might take a while, but I don't want you to panic when you see the woods full of ulvenmen."

The Eldest hissed. "You would replace our plague of rats with rabid dogs. Ulvenmen are barely more sentient than hobgoblins."

Christopher started to argue, but Lalania stopped him. "You need not explain your decisions. The Eldest does not actually care; she only seeks to lure you into confusion."

"The bard is right," Alaine said. "It would ease my mind and my task if you would listen to her more often."

Lalania did not seem happy with the praise. Christopher was beginning to miss her constant battle with Disa. At least that wasn't about him.

"Can we go? I would like to get out of this place sooner rather than later."

"I apologize that our hospitality is inadequate," the Eldest intoned. He had forgotten she could understand him.

He decided to follow Lalania's lead. "Next time I have to come in here, I'm going to knock out some skylights and let a little light into the place. So it's in your best interest to make sure I don't have to come back."

"On that we can surely agree," the Eldest said, bowing her head to hide her wide smile.

"This way," Lalania said, and they all followed her with relief.

The bard led them directly to the main gate, with only one short backtrack after a wrong turn. Christopher was hopelessly lost and gave up even pretending to learn the route after the first two minutes.

Now, standing on the drawbridge in the noonday sun, he took a deep breath of fresh air. Even the stench of the moat was preferable to the closeness of that lightless, windowless keep. Then again, no. The stench really was remarkable. A platoon of cavalry was waiting for him at the other end of the bridge and he hurried over to join them, where the sweat of horseflesh seemed sweet compared to the alternative.

A cavalryman was ready to ride ahead with a message. The platoon sergeant saluted Christopher and asked, "What word shall we send to Ser Gregor?"

It would have been wise to have come up with a password, so that Gregor would know it was the real Christopher who had come out of the keep, but then he realized it wasn't necessary this time. To his right Lucien was embracing Alaine with a fervor that matched his apparent youthfulness.

"Everything's fine. Tell him everything's fine, and we'll be home in time for lunch."

The horseman galloped off. Other men were saddling spare horses, one for each of them. Christopher saw the sergeant frowning as he counted the new additions to his troop.

"What is it?" Christopher asked the man in a low voice, while pretending to fiddle with a saddle.

"We are short a horse, Colonel. We did not realize Ser Lucien was with you."

"He wasn't," Christopher said. "He was probably hanging around out here while invisible."

The sergeant was taken aback, which Christopher found satisfying. His men needed to remember that magic was always lurking, making even simple things complicated.

Like his bargain with Lalania. Now that he was outside, in the comfort of daylight, all of his self-control had evaporated. He felt reckless and desperate. Action was the only safe response. He swung into the saddle of the cavalry horse and threw out a clipped command. "Ride on, Sergeant."

Half the troop led the way, the other half bringing up the rear, in a long column two abreast. Cannan rode beside him, Lalania and the elves behind. The two elves shared a horse. Lucien seemed to be whispering sweet nothings in Alaine's ears, which was a sight so incongruous with the steely lecture she had given him in the keep that it made Christopher dizzy. He caught Lalania's eye, but she quickly looked away.

They rode through the town, silent as always, and then through the fields outside. Gregor had been busy. A dozen huge pyres consumed small corpses, a feast for crows interrupted as the black birds circled and cawed their complaints. Parties of men with wheelbarrows and pitchforks were gathering more. Hard labor, but then his troops were almost all farmhands. They were used to it.

"Welcome back," Ser Gregor said, when they entered the main camp. Disa stood by his side and Christopher suddenly could take no more.

"Lala will fill you in on the details," he told Gregor while dismounting. "I need to send a message to Lady Kalani. Please see that I am not disturbed." Then he marched into his tent and pulled the door flap closed behind him.

A few seconds later the tent opened. Cannan stepped inside, staring at him warily.

"I'm okay," Christopher said. The man spent far too much time in Christopher's company for pretense. "It's just Lala. I need . . . a break."

Cannan gave a short, single nod that spoke volumes. He understood, in a way perhaps no one else could. The red knight stepped back outside, and Christopher sank back onto his bunk and focused on something else.

What could he pay Kalani? Not in tael. He needed that for the King, and in any case she had no need of it for her charges. And how could she move an army of ulvenmen through the Kingdom and still have any left by the time she reached the other side?

There wasn't time to work out the details. He needed help now, and he had only one spell to spare before he had to return to the preservation of his dead. He called her face to mind.

"I need ulvenmen to clear the goblin forest of hobgoblins. How many can you send, and how fast can they travel? Also, met your mom."

The answer came quickly.

"I beg you do not judge us all by her example. Elves are no more monolithic in their nature than humans. Give us ten days."

The limited communication of the spell left much to be desired. Trapped between asking for clarification and condemning a soldier to the Saint's expensive mercy, he chose to wait until tomorrow. Kalani wouldn't have time to cause any trouble by then.

He went outside to speak to Alaine, slightly curious about Kalani's emphasis. Was she trying to say that not all elves were as murderously judgmental as her mother? But he did not believe that. Alaine's promise was exactly the sort of thing he would do in her place.

The two elves were not around. Christopher sent a soldier to the horse pens, where Lucien could often be found, but there was no trace of them. After another hour of searching the camp, he was forced to conclude that they had finally taken their leave.

"A bit sudden," Gregor complained, standing at the fire in front of Christopher's tent.

"It is in keeping with their nature," Torme explained. "They would not have you know the hour of their departure or their destination."

Gregor snorted. "As they say, 'the greater the wizard, the greater the fear.' I guess that counts for dragons too."

It was true. The Lord Wizard of Carrhill was a paranoid recluse, who only left his tower disguised as an undead monster.

"Now what do we do?" Gregor asked.

"Kalani said she needed ten days. So we've got to hold out until then."

"Lala can build a fort soon, by my reckoning." Gregor looked around. "Where is that woman? Don't tell me she left with the elves."

Twin emotions sprung to life in Christopher, desperate relief and bitter jealousy, entwined like red and green dragons in airborne battle.

Cannan stilled them both. "She has retired to her tent. The time in the keep has tired her."

"As it did us all," Christopher said, and changed the subject. "I need a plan for feeding an unknown number of ulvenmen, before those ten days elapse."

"Ever since I joined your army," Gregor said, "I seem to do more planning than fighting. It's almost as if the weapon of a general is a pen, not a sword."

"Not all generals," Torme answered. "Only the successful ones."

16

VISITORS IN THE NIGHT

Lalania kept herself scarce for the rest of the day. Christopher was finally forced to seek her out. Standing in front of her tent as the sun went down was the last place he wanted to be. But he had questions that required answers.

He rapped on the tent pole. After a moment she pulled the leather flap back, staring up at him with ambiguous eyes.

"I need to know when the lyre will be ready," he said.

"It is at your service now. You need but whisper to me, and I will bend all my skill upon your desires."

Deep breaths while he tried to gather himself. "We want a wall. Around the fields, to keep the hobgoblins out and the goblins in."

She stepped closer to him, her face almost in his shoulder, her eyes looking down, as if she could not bear to face the answer to her question. "And what do *you* want?"

Christopher closed his eyes. "I cannot do this alone," he said, the final words of a long silent argument in his head. Of their own accord, without his permission, his arms reached out for her.

She caught his hands in hers and stopped him. He opened his eyes to see her shaking her head in despair.

"I did not sign up for this," she whispered. "There is a reason I did not pledge to a higher color. You offer me everything I ask for and charge only the price of guilt. A currency I can barely identify, let alone pay. My soul is not carved in stone."

"Neither is mine." Death and horror shrouded him; monsters and immortals stood at every juncture in naked threat; in his dreams he swam through seas of blood. It had been a very long time since he had felt normal human contact, the touch of intimacy that made life worth living, the balm of Gilead that raveled up the torn flesh of the heart. He gripped her hands, their fingers intertwined. "I cannot do this alone," he said again.

"And you shall not," she answered, her eyes glistening. "Let it not be said that I failed my test. Let me not be the rung of the ladder that breaks beneath your feet. I release you from your promise. I will not renegotiate the terms of my surrender after all. I will abide. In due time . . . yet I will abide."

She stepped back, her gaze cast low. She let go of his hands and turned away, drawing the tent flap closed. Leaving him outside, in the dark, alone. He stood, paralyzed by weakness, drawing long ragged breaths.

Not alone. Cannan emerged from the shadows. The big man could move quietly when he chose.

"You ask much of yourself," the red knight said.

"I did not ask for any of this."

"And yet, here we all are. Caught in your current like leaves in a stream. With no more knowledge of where we are going than the leaves."

"Does it help to know that I don't know, either?"

Cannan answered with a ghost of a smile on his lips. "Somewhat. Somewhat."

Christopher turned around. "We all need a break. I'm going to my tent to get drunk. It might be our last chance for a while. The goblins don't know the dragon is gone yet, and the hobgoblins are scattered and leaderless. I release you, too, for the night. You cannot stand guard unceasingly. No one can."

The red knight cocked his head in a motion that might signify agreement or acknowledgement or simply no desire to argue. Christopher went back to his tent and wallowed in wine and self-pity until sheer disgust drove him to sleep.

In the morning his head ached. He accepted it as penance and kept his spells for his men. Lalania, escorted by clouds of cavalry, rode around the perimeter of the fields. The lyre raised a wall in her wake, the labor of weeks accomplished in minutes. There was a limit, though. She only made halfway around before she plucked a single wrong note and the magic stopped.

The men moved their camp to inside the wall, on a patch of ground that had been cleared of corpses. The hobgoblins hid in the woods beyond, only occasionally coming close enough to the camp to be shot. They avoided the fields, which would need plowing soon. The goblins were even more invisible. Their gate stood open, repaired in the night without a sound, but other than that the city seemed as deserted as it always had.

When Christopher contacted Kalani again, the response was comforting, if somewhat obscure.

"We shall skirt human lands under the shadow of night and sorcery. We will arrive tired and hungry. Please see that food is made ready."

Christopher spent most of the day fretting about what the elf could mean. Creeping around the Kingdom with an army of dog-men sounded like the kind of task Hercules would have been assigned. No one else seemed worried, though. Finally D'Kan explained, exasperated with Christopher's questions.

"The Wild is far bigger than you understand. You have no idea what horrors wander blindly past, but a day's walk away. We Rangers are the only ones who would even notice, and we are too wise to needlessly antagonize an army on the march."

Cannan, surprisingly, agreed with the young Ranger. "I have been outside of the Kingdom further than most. Yet twenty miles distance is enough to hide the entire realm. There are no signs of habitation; huntsmen do not stalk through the woods, nor do roads lay paths to distant realms. Your lord's patrols rarely go more than a mile or two beyond the border. Only the ranked go seeking adventure in the Wild, and they are wise enough to cover their tracks."

"So there could be anything out there?" Christopher asked. "Another kingdom. A possible ally. Shouldn't someone check?"

"We did check," D'Kan said, waving in the direction of the silent city, "and we found *this*. Do you really want to find more?"

Christopher ignored the jibe. "We need to know if there are other threats at hand."

"We already knew there were goblins here," D'Kan said. "As for elsewhere, there are always threats at hand." The young Ranger shrugged. "If danger was imminent, the Lord Ranger would inform the King."

"If he thought it wise to do so," Cannan said. "I recall a forest valley on the southern border that had no game and no tracks, yet the grass was cropped as low as a nobleman's garden. No one ever spoke of that."

"What's this?" Christopher asked, intrigued. The Ranger, however, merely glared.

"I don't know," Cannan said. "Niona would not say any more than that we needed to avoid it."

The conversation paused. Cannan was subdued, even more so than usual, D'Kan was too outraged to speak, and Christopher was startled. It was the first time the man had mentioned his dead wife's name.

"You should not speak so," D'Kan finally managed to sputter. "Those are not your secrets to reveal. You have no right—"

Christopher interrupted before the conflict went any further. "Cannan shouldn't, but you should. Why didn't you tell me? You're supposed to be my scout."

The young man transferred the target of his anger to Christopher.

"Had the topic become relevant, I would have advised you. Yet the southern border is as far from here as it is possible to be."

"Advise me now," Christopher snapped back. "Because I asked."

"I cannot," D'Kan said.

They glared at each other for a moment. Christopher became distracted, though, when he realized Cannan was not paying attention to either of them. The red knight was staring into the distance, lost in his own memories.

"I cannot," D'Kan repeated. The anger was gone, replaced by defeat. "Even if our law allowed me to, I have nothing to tell you. Like the Moaning Lands, the area is known to all Rangers and avoided, but no one has told me why. No one ever thought it necessary to explain to a lowly first-rank."

"And elsewhere?"

"The north is bound by troglodytes and goblins, as you already know. There is no prohibition on hunting such mundane creatures, as there was not on the ulvenmen. That leaves east and west, which contain nothing of note for at least a hundred miles. After that I cannot say; perhaps no one can."

Such ignorance was intolerable. "Somebody should do something about that," he mused aloud, wondering how hard it would be to build a dirigible. He had put Fae's magic to refining sulfur; perhaps she could also manufacture silk and hydrogen. Mapping the world out from the safety of the skies seemed a likely proposition.

"I would be," D'Kan said, "save that I am here serving you. It is each generation's task to pierce the veil of the forest and report what they find. A task my instructors assured me would be fresh and new, for the world perpetually reinvents itself. Consider: only a decade ago a report would have described a goblin city here, without a hint of dragon. In another decade it seems likely it will report nothing but ruins."

Christopher opened his mouth to argue. Instead, he bit his tongue.

He knew the Kingdom itself was only a few hundred years old, a fact that the Ranger might or might not know. More to the boy's point, Christopher knew that there was a very real danger that the Kingdom would be reduced to rubble in any given decade. Between the hidden *hjerne-spica* and invading dragons were the threats of civil war and homicidal elves. There were a thousand ways to die in the Wild. Even for kingdoms.

"A depressing thought," he said instead.

D'Kan smiled, looking for a moment like a much older and wiser man. "So do not think it. Enjoy the sun while it shines instead of worrying over inevitable clouds. For instance, we find ourselves on a large, flat clearing, expecting nothing to fight or build for at least ten more days, with a goodly supply of horses and men that need exercise. A lesser man would see boredom; I see a chance to play polo."

Christopher had no rejoinder to this, for he was awestruck by the most unexpected event: Cannan chuckling.

"You will have to teach them the rules," the red knight said, perhaps the first time he had spoken to D'Kan without taunting him.

"I will have to play left-handed, so as not to discourage them from even trying," the Ranger answered. He paused, as if surprised by his own daring, and then continued, almost diffidently. "Perhaps you would captain an opposing team?"

"With Christopher's permission," Cannan said.

"Of course," Christopher agreed. "Sure. Go ahead. Just don't get anybody killed."

"We won't," D'Kan promised. "Well. Probably not."

There were still a few hours of sunlight, so both men left to begin recruiting for the following day. Christopher was too pleased by the change in Cannan to worry about his absence, though it was strange not to be relentlessly shadowed by the big man. There was no breach of duty, however. Christopher could not possible be safer than in the midst of his army camp.

As the sun was setting Karl came to his tent to issue the day's final report.

"One other matter," the young soldier said, after all the boring parts had been gone over. "Likely mere superstition, yet under the circumstances I feel I must report even the least detail."

Christopher wholeheartedly agreed.

"One of the sentries last night saw Cannan drinking in the stables. He had presumably wandered there for solitude."

"I released him from duty last night," Christopher explained. "I think I'm safe enough here, and everybody needs a break sometimes."

Karl shrugged, not willing to argue with Christopher's decisions. "The issue is that the soldier claimed he was not alone."

"I don't know what you mean."

"I mean the obvious. He had a companion while in the stables. The sentry swore he saw no one enter or leave yet glimpsed two people making use of a bale of hay."

"Using it how?" Christopher asked, and immediately changed his mind. "No, don't tell me, I don't want to know. Who was it? Wait, do we even care who it was?" If Cannan had made a tryst with one of the priestesses, that really wasn't Christopher's affair as long as it did not affect the man's dedication to his task. Which he knew perfectly well it would not.

"Ordinarily, no. I would not even report such a thing. But the sentry caught a glimpse. He described waist-long black hair, hanging down in curls and waves."

None of the handful of women in the camp had hair that long. For that matter, none of the men did either.

"The sentry is one of our original recruits," Karl continued. "He remembers the Lady Niona."

Christopher caught his breath.

"As I said before, probably superstition. Men often see what they want to see in the dark. The lady was well-regarded, and Cannan has earned their affection of late. I do not think we are haunted by a ghost, yet it would be remiss of me not to mention the possibility."

"Of course. Thank you. I'll take care of it." Christopher said the words he knew he was supposed to say, though he had no idea what to do about ghosts. Or, for that matter, whether he should do anything. Was it possible to be haunted by a benevolent spirit? Was Cannan's new lease on life a balm from the other side of the veil, or just the bait in a cruel trap?

Given the nature of this world, one would be a fool to discount the latter.

Karl nodded. "That will suffice for the men. Even they are not foolish enough to be frightened of ghosts in the presence of a priest."

Then the young officer left, before Christopher could spoil his sangfroid by admitting his ignorance. The men needed to believe they were safe. Christopher needed them to believe it.

But he also needed advice, so he set out into the camp in search of his bard. For the most part it was quiet, the few men who had duties after dark working by light-stones while their fellows slept. Lalania's tent was empty, so he went by the stable yard, thinking that he should at least check in on Cannan, whom he had not seen since that afternoon. Walking quietly so as not to disturb the sleeping horses, he stepped around a fence post and felt his heart leap into his mouth.

A slim, slender figure was skipping away, a dark gown clutched in front of her, long black hair flowing down her naked back. For an instant Christopher was terrified by the appearance of a woman he knew for certain to be dead and ashes. Yet this world had beaten old, primitive fears out of him by brute force. His hand leapt forward, unbidden, and caught her by the arm.

His fingers touched flesh, warm and soft. The woman spun around, startled, and froze.

Harsh words died in his throat. Lalania stared up at him, her hair golden now, spilling across her shoulders.

"You have no right," she whispered, fiercer than a dragon.

"I—" No words followed.

"He knows," Lalania said, her voice a rasp on iron. "He pretends to be dreaming. I pretend not to care. And for a moment we both are alive again."

Christopher's mouth moved, to no effect.

"You dare not pity us. You have no right." She stood under the glittering light of a hundred thousand stars, challenging him.

"Never," he said, and let her pass.

17

DOGWOOD

They made it through three days of polo practice with only a dozen broken limbs among the horses and men. Then Lalania induced the young priestesses to promise a kiss to the winning team, and things got bloody.

Gregor was gone, leading a resupply column back to the Kingdom, taking Disa with him to deal with any remaining skeletal surprises. Torme and Christopher were still using most of their spells to preserve their dead, so the quantity of injuries piled up until Christopher forced a man to spend a night with a broken arm, waiting on dawn for the daily renewal of spells. After that the men displayed some modicum of caution and the casualty rate stayed within manageable bounds.

The infantry cheered them on with a viciousness that unnerved Christopher, but as Karl was often leading the chants and jeers he kept his doubts to himself. Probably they weren't any worse than hockey fans.

D'Kan and Cannan had become rival warlords, each captaining a dozen teams that battled every afternoon. They rode in every game, wearing out three or four horses a day. Despite the cold and their tael, the two men ended each day dripping with sweat and exhaustion. By some unspoken agreement, Cannan offset the imbalance of their ranks by allowing D'Kan to have first choice of mount. Christopher watched them carefully, worried that the hostilities might exceed the bounds of sportsmanship. The Ranger, always formal to a fault, seemed perpetually on the verge of an outburst; the taciturn red knight spoke less than usual, but when he lashed out a comment or correction to his team, their faces blanched and they leapt to obey.

Both men let their other duties slide. D'Kan had brought the scouts into the game, disrupting their patrols and leaving the camp blind to the wider world. Cannan collapsed in such exhaustion each night that he could hardly be considered guarding the blanket he slept on. Christopher bit his tongue and did not intervene. There was nothing outside the camp but hobgoblins, and no danger inside. And it had occurred to him that it would be better for the men to remember this campaign for the absurdity of a polo tournament under the walls of a goblin city than for the ludicrousness of their victories, both of which had come from the wings of a dragon who had now abandoned them.

There was an end in sight. Somehow the games had been scheduled to conclude the day the lyre would recharge. An excellent ending point for their little holiday, when completing the exterior wall would signal their return to work. Christopher wanted to find out who had planned that and reward them, but he was afraid it might be Lalania. And he did not trust himself to speak to her in private yet.

That ache, too, began to fade in the muddy hoof-churned fields and shouting mobs of men. The experience of the long night in the keep receded. Normalcy, such as it was, crept back into his life, carrying with it an inexpressible sadness that he resolutely ignored.

Thus it was some relief when a gunshot drew Christopher out of his tent in the middle of the night. He went to investigate, accompanied by Torme and a squad of carbineers.

On the edge of the camp, a pair of sentries stood over a dying ulvenman.

"It was trying to sneak in," one explained. The other looked terrified. He was a new boy, and this would be his first reminder that the Wild held worse terrors than goblins.

Christopher privately observed that it would be more correct to assert that it had already snuck in far enough to do some serious damage, if it had wanted to. It was also unarmed, which seemed uncharacteristic for random monsters from the Wild. He bent down and healed the creature with a spell.

It leapt to its feet, causing the sentries to scramble backward so fast they fell over. Fortunately his carbineers were of sturdier stuff. They lifted their guns but held their fire, waiting for a clearer signal.

The ulvenman grinned, pulling back black lips over his long toothy snout and wagging his red tongue back and forth. He was naked save for a thick leather cuirass, which now had a hole through both sides. The ulvenman poked his long clawed fingers in the front and back, and laughed. Then he threw himself at Christopher's feet and growled wildly.

"Is it mad?" asked the youngest sentry, warbling a bit.

"I think it's bragging," Christopher said. "Or asking for something to eat." It was hard to tell. He cast the translation spell, only to discover it was both.

"Wake up our quartermaster," Christopher told his men. "Our allies have arrived, and they're hungry."

Christopher watched the ulvenman wolfing down salted pork with dismay. The creature seemed insatiable. "Enough," he finally said. "Save some for the others."

The ulvenman gave him a dubious glare, stuffed what he was holding into his mouth, and grabbed more with both hands. Then he loped off, chewing like a dog with a too-big bone.

Christopher followed, armored and mounted on Royal with a full platoon of cavalry at his heels. Allies they might be, yet a show of force would not go amiss. Especially if they were all as hungry as his guide.

The woods beyond his wall were infested with dog-men, lolling around under the trees and playing in the snow. The ulvenmen were scraggly and thin, testifying to the difficulty of their journey. Yet they seemed happier than he had ever seen them, wagging their tongues in the circle of light cast by the troop's light-stones. Kalani's governance would appear to be going well. He found her in the midst of a crowd of somewhat less happy ulvenmen, or more accurately, ulvenwomen, surrounded as they were by hundreds of pups, all of whom went into a barking frenzy when they smelled his horses.

One tried to take a bite out of Royal's flank. Only a quick twitch of the reins prevented the warhorse from kicking it for a field goal. The translation spell was still active, so Christopher unfortunately understood what the pups were crying about.

"Tell them," he told Kalani, "that the horses are not dinner."

"You can tell them," she said. "It would be good that they see your authority in action."

Like parents, they quibbled over who would be the disciplinarian. Like usual, Christopher lost the argument.

"The horses are not to eat!" he growled in the ulven speech. The pups howled louder in disappointment. Christopher raised his voice, feeling a bit foolish.

A bark rang out, and the camp went instantly silent. An ulvenman strode in from the dark forest with a confident swagger, draped in metal scales like the ones Christopher wore. He stopped approaching only when Royal flattened his ears and snorted in challenge. The two animals stared at each other a moment, baring their teeth, before Rohkea looked at Christopher.

"You whistled to the stars, god-man, and we have come running. Your enemies are our enemies." He raised his axe above his head and burst into a howl. From the forest around him echoed a thousand howls.

"How many did you bring?" Christopher asked, startled.

"All of them," Kalani said, "or rather, all that matter. You may open the swamp to hunting again."

"But what about when you go back?"

The ulvenman chieftain growled. Kalani gave Christopher a look as fraught with challenge as Rohkea's, and switched to the human tongue. "We are not going back. This is the bargain I have made in your name: the forest for the tael. The tribe will clear the woods of hobgoblins and gift you their souls, for nothing more than the right to live under trees again."

Christopher frowned. He'd thought he was securing two borders; now he had abandoned one and created an inherently unstable flux on the other. "These woods belong to the goblins," he argued.

She was having none of it. "You have confined the goblins to their city. The woods are yours to give away. Knowing that the woods are full of ulvenmen who are permitted to kill goblins on sight will keep them to their bargain."

He tried a different tack. "You're not concerned about cultural contamination? The goblins are hardly an appropriate influence."

Her smile would probably seem condescending to anyone else, but Christopher had Alaine fresh in his memory. The daughter was a softie, comparatively. When he didn't back down, she twitched her nose and conceded the point.

"I had not perhaps considered that fully. Still, the terms of your treaty allow for no trade; I will inoculate the tribe against their influence. Regular stories about their wicked cleverness, and a bounty for the head of any goblin who strays outside the perimeter. There are some existing myths that I can adapt for the next generation."

Stoking racial hatred was not really what he had been looking for. However, there were other, more pressing issues to discuss. "How do you know the details of my treaty?"

For the first time he saw embarrassment on her face. "I was told. The Lady Alaine and her companion accompanied the tribe on its migration. Honesty compels me to admit that it greatly simplified the journey, resulting in far less attrition than I had feared." She hesitated, ever so slightly, over the word "companion," and Christopher had to struggle to prevent a chuckle.

"They did not mention that when they left," he said instead.

"Figures of their stature do not normally share their plans with others." Kalani rushed through the obvious to reach the real heart of her concern. "I beg you, Christopher, do not judge us all by the Lady Alaine. There are divisions among elves, as there are among all peoples; and no one can choose their parents."

This was the second time she had brought the topic up. At least this time his word count was not limited to a short paragraph. "Say something in elvish," he said to her.

"I presume you wish to discuss sensitive issues," she replied. He could tell she had changed languages even while the translation spell made her words perfectly clear.

"I do. Without putting too fine a point on it, your mother threatened to kill me at some future date for possible transgressions. Are you saying other elves might stop her?"

"Oh no," Kalani said. "Her authority in this domain is absolute. Whatever promise she made you will be honored by all of Álfheimr."

"Then what—?"

She interrupted him. "I am not certain I could explain our political disagreement in any coherent sense. Nor am I comfortable discussing it. I merely wanted to note that the Lady Alaine does not represent Álfheimr in all particulars."

Painfully ambiguous, but she had already made the source of her concern clear. Apparently elf girls hooking up with dragon boys was not quite kosher.

Rohkea, standing by with as much patience as any ulvenman was capable of, grabbed his metal-scaled stomach and let it rumble in hunger. He gave Royal another look, and the warhorse bared its teeth.

"Lady Kalani," Christopher said, trying not to be too condescending in turn, "I have much bigger problems to worry about. My experience with elves is limited enough that I will refrain from drawing any conclusions about your people as a whole. Now, tell me how we're going to feed this horde before they eat my horse."

There was no point in chastising her for making so free with his invitation; she had obviously been put up to it by her mother, no doubt as another ploy to cause him to fail. He found himself warming to the girl over their mutual frenemy.

A sentiment that was sorely tested by dawn, as he watched a week's worth of rations for his army disappear down five thousand doggish muzzles. At this rate he couldn't ship food in fast enough, even if he could afford to pay for it all. Kalani's solution was not comforting. She assured him the ulvenmen could live off of hobgoblin flesh until the spring thaw.

The tribe spent the morning resting around campfires while Lalania finished the wall. In the afternoon Christopher stepped out of his tent to issue an order and found his camp deserted. His army was easy to find, though: it sat in midst of a sea of dog-men, watching a polo match. The ulvenmen were, if anything, more excited by the spectacle than the men, although they were quite disappointed to discover that the losing team would not be eaten.

"Not even the horses?" Rohkea queried, translated through Kalani. She diplomatically did not pass on his remarks when the priestesses handed out nothing more than kisses to the victors.

D'Kan's team had won. The young Ranger had scored the winning goal with a wicked curveball that went directly under Cannan's horse. The red knight took the loss well, shaking D'Kan's hand afterward where everyone could see. D'Kan accepted this with a grace Christopher had not known he was capable of. The week of naked aggression had burnt out something in both men.

Later, in a quiet moment, Christopher, against his better judgment, found himself discreetly asking Cannan an impolitic question. "Did you let him?"

The red knight shrugged. "I didn't have to. It was a good shot." Then the knight went back to the keg of ale, where the two teams were gathered around, talking over the glory moments of the last week.

18

DANGEROUS TALK

The men built a fort on the outside of the wall, mostly because Christopher didn't want them to sit around idle. He dispatched the rest of the wagons on another supply run. Food was now in short supply, and he wanted enough to host the King's armies when they arrived. Nothing earned good will with soldiers on campaign like a hot meal.

The ulvenmen fell to their bloody work with a will. D'Kan and the scouts accompanied them, mostly to make sure the full measure of tael found its way back to human hands. This turned out to be unnecessary; the ulvenmen were not thieves. Absent Kalani's firm hand, they would probably turn on the humans and eat them, but they were not about to stoop to accounting shenanigans. Hobgoblin heads poured into the camp, keeping the kettles boiling day and night. Christopher watched his wealth swell to unimaginable proportions by the hour, until he encountered a problem he had never imagined possible: he could not find a place to put it all.

"Cannan, I need advice," he fretted, standing in his tent with a tangerine-sized lump of purple in each hand. So much would never fit in the vial around his neck, and putting the equivalent of a ton of gold in his pocket was wildly unwise.

"Advice that any child could give," the red knight said. "There is only one safe place to store tael: in your head."

Christopher grinned at the jest. "Not in this case. The King would not hesitate to crack my skull open for it."

Cannan stared at him levelly. "The King's share is only a quarter. There is more yet to come."

"Hold on," Christopher objected with some alarm. "That was not the plan. We've got to pay the King off to keep the goblins alive."

The red knight shook his head. "The only thing that will save the goblins is your sword. And only if it is strong enough to dissuade kings. You must take another rank."

Habit summoned an objection to Christopher's lips. Wisdom silenced it unspoken. This was the bargain he had made: fantastic power was the price of all his many promises. Cannan, as bondholder of one of those pledges, was entitled to speak thusly.

"In any case," Cannan added, "you will never buy Treywan's faith. Whatever you pay him, he will always assume you kept the greater portion for yourself. Turn over this wealth and he will only dun you for triple the amount."

Christopher had an objection now. "But if I take another rank, won't that make him jealous?"

"The Gold Apostle is tenth rank. You have precedent."

Something in Cannan's tone was not comforting.

"And then?" Christopher asked. "When I reach the next? And after that?"

A grim smile on the red knight's face. "When you equal his rank, the whole realm cannot help but see it as a challenge. Treywan is no fool. He will not wait for that day to dawn."

Christopher fell back onto his cot, rendered unsteady. He had not expected such political sophistication from the warrior. But of course that was foolish. The machinations of power were as much a part of the hero's education as swordsmanship. More to the point, where had all this strategy been while he was digging this hole?

"Why didn't you point this out earlier?" he asked the red knight.

"Because it did not serve my purpose. Treywan never held my loyalty. Now he is naught more than a stone in my path, to be kicked aside."

"And myself? What of your loyalty to me? For that matter, why didn't Lalania warn me?"

"Because she assumed you already understood. This was ever the only path open to you."

Again objections died stillborn. This was simple truth, so plain it had been written in the sky in the smoke of the first rifle fired on the plane of Prime. A rifle in the hands of Karl Treyeingson, perhaps the one man in the galaxy most capable and eager to end the age of kings.

"You are openly talking rebellion." Unwise words to issue, knowing that they could be spied on at any moment.

Cannan shrugged, dismissing his caution. "The lumps in your hands speak louder than words ever could. One glance at that and the war begins. So best we hide it sooner than later."

The big man stepped forward, looming over Christopher, grabbing both his wrists in a powerful grasp. He growled, as threatening as a tiger. "Claim your destiny, or it will claim your life, and I will not let you die until you have kept your promise."

The fury in Cannan's eyes was not the wildness of rage; it was so much deeper, flame rendered as solid as a mountain. The red knight drove Christopher's hands to his face and crushed them against his mouth, where the tael leaked through and automatic salivation did the rest. Tael was almost impossibly delicious, though it had no taste.

Afterward Cannan stepped back, neither contrite nor defiant. Christopher could not feel violated. He had been in the man's head before, sharing in the memory of acts of unbearable shame and grief. The two men were closer than lovers on the topic of wives and loneliness.

And he had made a promise.

"Karl would demand that I punish such insubordination," Christopher finally said.

Cannan laughed mirthlessly. "Tell him, and tomorrow he will hold you down for me."

More simple truth.

He had to come clean to his council at some point.

Lalania had instituted certain precautions. Their command conferences occurred at a random time each day, in a tent that contained no furniture and was sealed against all outside light. Not enough to foil the most powerful divinations, but against ordinary scrying they could speak reasonably freely.

"You should know that I have gained another rank," he told them.

Their lack of surprise was troubling.

"If my estimates are correct," Lalania said, "you will gain another before the season ends."

"Can we hope for two?" Torme asked.

"Not unless we also reduce the goblin city," D'Kan answered. "The hobgoblins alone will not suffice."

"We're not going to do that," Christopher said hastily.

"A wise choice," Torme agreed. "To do so would reveal our hand. At the moment no one in the Kingdom can guess the true wealth of the hobgoblins, nor the rate at which we harvest. As long as our Brother does not promote others, we can keep this secret." He bowed his head to Christopher. "Forgive me for not using your proper title, but I would advise that we eschew formalities for the time."

Christopher was not in a forgiving mood. "Sooner or later the truth must come out, and then what?"

"Then the obvious," Torme said. "You have won a fantastic victory. You have stuffed your fort with the supplies of war. You have gathered your armies together in your fist. What comes next follows as surely as the thunder follows the lightning."

"No, it doesn't," Christopher objected. "The King rules for more reasons than just his rank. I took a vow of fealty to him. I can't just break that because I want to."

"You will not have to." The man stared earnestly at Christopher with what might have been pity. "He will break it for you. Only the hope that you will perish in these woods, or at least be bled to weakness, has stayed his hand. When he discovers you have gained rank instead, he will strike first."

"How can you know this?" Christopher demanded.

Torme smiled grimly. "Because it is what any would do, in the King's place. Only the bonds of White would hold a greater rank in thrall to a lesser; and even then, it is good that the Saint never equaled Treywan's rank. Nor will he ever, as anyone can see. But you . . ."

"You cannot pretend to the meekness of Saint Krellyan." Lalania shook her head in denial, but it looked like triumph to Christopher. "Even I could not act that part convincingly, given your history. In defiance of all logic and tradition, you gain ranks faster the higher you go, rather than slower. At this rate you will surpass Treywan before he has time to blink."

Christopher kept searching for an out. "So if we gave him enough tael to take another rank, he wouldn't feel threatened. As long as I promote him every time I promote myself, he'll feel secure."

This earned him only hostile stares, until Karl spoke.

"You cannot afford to do so," the unranked soldier said, and Christopher knew it was true. Even if he had the tael—which he did not, as promoting someone to the fourteenth rank would require unimaginable quantities—the cost would be something far greater: Karl's loyalty.

"And in any case," Karl continued, "he would not let you. To accept a rank from your hand would make him your servant in the eyes of all the world. Including his."

"We have some time," Lalania said soothingly. "We may pretend as if nothing has changed, for a while yet. But you must warn your allies of what is to come."

"And how do I do that?" he asked. He could not imagine a conversation with the Saint or the Cardinal that included the word "rebellion."

"Tell them no more than you have told us," she answered. "They will understand. How could they not? My College has failed; war is coming regardless of all our machinations."

"Your machinations are in no small part responsible for it." From their very first meeting, when she had come to warn him of the bloodshed the future held.

"And why not?" Lalania spoke without repentance. "Treywan falls under the Shadow day by day. You stand in the Light. And more importantly, you could actually win. What better chance will we have?"

"You think I can beat the King in a duel? Because I don't." Christopher knew he was, at best, a competent swordsman. That he could outclass the other men in his army—men who had grown up with swords in their hands—was only due to his greater wealth of tael. This would apply in the other direction with Treywan.

"No," Lalania said, smiling sweetly. "You are perhaps the worst duelist I have ever seen claim victory. Yet in war you need not face him alone. We will stand by your side and block his sword with our bodies if we must."

A noble sentiment, but Christopher was too annoyed with their manipulations to let it pass. "Only because I'll revive you again afterward."

Torme nodded agreeably. "I confess the thought has crossed my mind." Then he tilted his head and gave Christopher another earnest stare. "As it will others. Even in your generosity you laid the foundation for revolution. It is almost as if you had planned it all from the beginning."

People were people, no matter how far from Earth he had traveled. When they got it into their heads that a thing was so, nothing could dissuade them. His staff now considered his every action to have been part of a masterful plot; they reinterpreted the past in the light of the present, and concluded that the inevitable future was the result of divine providence. The attitude filtered down to his men, and he found himself in the position he had tried to avoid from the very first time he had issued a military command: no one questioned him anymore.

He would have argued with them, but he could not in good faith. While it was true that he had only accidentally become George Washington, it was also true that he had always assumed that feudalism had to pass away. Simply by acting as if some other way of life was possible, he had made people believe it. And now the strength of their belief would make it possible.

There were still some hard knocks coming, chief among which was that he had no idea what would replace the current government. He was pretty sure there was more to running a democracy than just having elections. The future promised to be disappointing to everyone.

There was also the possibility that this whole mess was just another way for Alaine to get him killed. Or a trap laid by the Gold Apostle or, for that matter, the hidden enemy. Just because he had planned a perfect war didn't mean he would win.

On the other hand, he didn't have a choice. He never had.

Gregor confirmed that when he returned to camp the next day.

"I called on the King, for courtesy's sake," the blue knight reported. "He did not receive me. Instead I issued my report to Ser Morrison. I told them the goblins were defeated, though not yet subdued, which I felt to be true enough. Morrison's reaction was troubling, insomuch as he had none. He took my report without speaking. I expected disbelief or, improbably, congratulations. Instead I received hostility."

"I gained another rank." Christopher said quietly. His heart sank while he watched the blue knight silently work through the implications and quickly come to the same dangerous conclusion everyone else had.

Gregor finally blew out his mustache and stretched hugely, a bear awakening after a long winter. "So it begins," he murmured. With a sharp salute he hustled away, no doubt to share the news with his wife.

Disturbed, Christopher contacted the Cardinal via a spell and told him the same thing. The Cardinal's response was even less comforting: "I have received and understood your message." The form-letter reply one would expect from a lawyer, delivered by a man who did not trust to speak freely even in his own thoughts.

The wagons left again the next morning. Christopher went to ask his quartermaster why.

"Major Karl signed more requisition slips, sir. Should I have questioned them?"

"Of course not," Christopher said. "I was just, uh . . ." Unable to think of a good lie, he turned and walked out of the room.

Days passed, and then weeks. The sun grew warmer, the snow began to melt in open spaces, and the flood of hobgoblin heads began to slow. Christopher consumed the harvest as fast as it came out of the kettles, the better not to let anyone see how much there was. The ulvenmen only occasionally asked for supplies of grain or iron from the camp, ranging far afield for dozens of miles in every direction. The goblins could be seen, but still not heard, in the fields at night, their horses plowing the fields in almost complete silence. The tension grew invisibly, water rushing under the thinning river ice, until it cracked all at once in a frightful shower of shards and freezing spray.

A horse, its rider hidden in a voluminous brown cloak, galloped through the gate of his fort, escorted by a young cavalry scout whose face was a rictus of fear. The newcomer dismounted poorly and leaned against his lathered horse for support. Christopher advanced across the muddy yard with growing trepidation. The stranger could portend nothing but trouble. Why anyone would send a messenger instead of a spell was a mystery, though one that would be answered shortly. He drew in a deep breath and put on his best commander's voice, but he didn't get a chance to use it.

The stranger looked up at his approach. The hood fell away to reveal Cardinal Faren's ancient, weathered face, stained with old tears. Fresh ones washed at the grime as he spoke.

"The Saint is dead. You have destroyed us all."

19

THE HIGHWAYMAN

Christopher slipped in the mud, the once hard-frozen ground having thawed unnoticed into treacherous muck. He went down on one knee and both hands, plunging into the mire, not all of which was as wholesome as dirt.

Faren leaned against his horse, breathing heavily.

Slowly Christopher climbed to his feet. He was in no hurry; as unpleasant as the mud was, it was preferable to speech.

Lalania came running with more haste than dignity, her face bearing an urgent message. She stopped short when she caught sight of the Cardinal, and then turned to Christopher and said simply, "You already know."

Christopher looked for something to wipe his hands on. In the end he used his trousers. They were already filthy from the knee down.

"Let's go inside," he said. He could feel the news spreading like a wave around him as men gazed on the tableau.

Lalania went over to Faren and took his arm. For the moment he was reduced to an old man, trembling in her grasp. To see the Cardinal pared away, leaving only a grief-stricken grandfather, unnerved Christopher more than any talk of war or death.

"Let's go inside," he repeated. The cavalryman was the nearest soldier, so Christopher pointed to him and issued an order. "Summon the general staff." When the man did not immediately respond, Christopher narrowed his eyes. "Now, if you please."

"Sir," the man said, snapping out a salute. He turned his horse and galloped through the camp. Giving an order felt good. It felt like being in control. Christopher picked out another soldier and gave some more. "Bring food and ale to the command tent. And a chair. And have someone see to this horse."

The bard led Faren to their command tent. Christopher followed, the mud sucking at his boots with every step.

Cannan joined them along the way. Even now he was impassive, saying nothing, betraying no emotion with his eyes. Gregor was waiting at the entrance, his face grim. Disa rushed forward to take the Cardinal's other arm, her eyes wet.

Soldiers followed them inside, bearing chairs, tables, and platters of food and drink. Christopher sat down heavily and looked around for a towel or cloth to clean his hands, but this was the army. Such niceties did not rise to the soldier's notice. He wiped the drying clay on a still-clean part of his trousers.

Torme and Karl came in on the heels of the departing soldiers. D'Kan was in the field with the scouts, so Christopher didn't have to make the long-delayed decision as to the young man's official status.

The Cardinal slumped in a chair, his head in his hands. Disa clung to her husband, standing off to one side. Lalania draped herself across another chair and picked lightly at her lyre, simple, single notes floating in the air. Her hair hung loose and unbound. Christopher stared at her.

She shrugged, unapologetic, and set the lyre down. "My lord," she said to the Cardinal, "I do not dismiss your grief; yet we must discuss events sooner than later."

The Cardinal drew in a deep breath. When he looked up his power was restored, but Christopher was not comforted. He had never thought to see hatred in those old eyes. Sarcasm, yes, steel, even judgment and death; but not this.

"I was warned," Faren said. "But I should not have needed warning. The King sent me away on some ludicrous pretext; I indulged him, because we always do. I resolved the matter quickly and turned my carriage for home. Halfway back a man stood in the road, looking for all the world like a common bandit. How droll, I thought, how utterly amusing, that a highwayman should attempt to waylay the carriage of a Cardinal. I confess I may have even smiled.

"'Excuse me, Goodman,' I called through my window. 'But you seem to be occupying the entirety of the road. Perhaps you could step aside and let an old man pass.'

"He stood silently, as if considering his next words. Maybe he was already rethinking his life of crime. An interesting juncture to ponder, and yet, some unknown urgency drove me homeward. 'Come now, my good fellow. Speak your piece and let me pass by.'

"He walked closer, biting his lip and trembling. I thought perhaps he was terrified of issuing his demands; as young as he was, perhaps he had never robbed a carriage before. Impatient, I almost spoke for him—'Stand and deliver!' I muttered under my breath, trying to feed him his next line.

"Yet when he approached my window, I saw not fear but grief in his eyes. He drew his sword and cast it away, as if rejecting the curse of violence. In my hubris I thought I had won a convert solely by my august presence.

"'I know myself to be cruel, and cowardly, and a fool,' he muttered. 'And you have already cast me off. Yet there is a limit to how low one man can stoop. Say what you will of me, but say not that I betrayed the man who saved my mother's life.'

"I had no time to ponder on these curious words, for he looked up and speared me to my soul with his next.

"'They are killing the Saint,' he said. 'And they will kill you when you return.'

"Then he walked off the road, into the fields, as if he had chosen a new direction at random. I sat transfixed, unable to comprehend his words. My driver called down to ask if we should drive on, not having heard. I could not answer. Impossible that those horrible words were true; incomprehensible if they were not.

"I had, as always, a sending prepared. It finally occurred to me to use it. My apprehension fell over its own feet, for the spell failed. There was no longer a target for it to reach."

Cardinal Faren closed his eyes for a moment. When he opened them again they were the eyes of a hawk, searching for prey.

"For the first time in my life, I panicked. I shouted to my driver to make all haste, stopping for nothing on pain of death. Yet a hundred yards on reason crept back into my brain, unbidden. When the carriage rattled past a gorse bush close by the road, I slipped out of the door and tumbled to the road unnoticed. The carriage went on without me, as I suppose the world will eventually. But not today. I crept through the woods like a criminal; I stole a cloak and a horse; armed with nothing but the clothes on my back, I rode for the only weapon that I could imagine. All day and night I have ridden, spending my power to keep the horse alive, to cast aside a lifetime of peace and mercy for blood-thirsty vengeance. And you shall be my instrument."

Disa wept softly in the background. Christopher could only manage a single word. "Who?"

"The King has proscribed the White Church," Lalania answered. "Its lands are forfeit to the crown and its priests ordered to surrender themselves for judgment. A mercenary mob descended upon the Cathedral; the watch only intervened to hold back the crowd. When it was clear no divine force would vaporize those who attacked the building, the King personally led a strike force into the Cathedral. Initial reports assert that both the Saint and Cardinal are missing and presumed dead."

Christopher came up with another word. "When?"

"A day ago. Do not blame us for not warning you sooner. They cast a tight net. Three agents have missed their reporting deadlines. The Skald learned the news only a few minutes ago."

"We have to warn the Vicars," Disa cried, tears spilling down her cheeks. "But I do not know what to say."

"'Tell them only the facts," Faren said. "We are no longer in a position to give them orders. They must each make their own path."

"Dark take that," Christopher countermanded. "Tell them not to surrender for any reason. He'll just kill them."

"They have no choice," Faren said. "Unless they wish to forsake their vow of obedience as I have. I cannot ask that of anyone."

"I can," Christopher snarled. "There's no forsaking going on. The King declared war on us. By the Dark, he'll get a bloody war."

"To do so is to violate every principle of the White Church," Disa said tremulously. "We swore to bind wounds, not cause them; to obey the throne, not battle it. If Treywan has acted within the law, then we must remain within it as well."

"What law?" Christopher demanded.

Lalania apparently thought it was not a rhetorical question. "He charges the White Church with conspiring with nonhumans, arming a foreign enemy, tax evasion, and disobedience of a royal summons, through its agent, the Lord Prophet Christopher, and, by conspiracy and alliance, the entirety of the clergy."

That was wildly unfair. Some of them didn't even like Christopher.

"Those charges are night-soil," Christopher said. "Which is why he stormed the Cathedral instead of holding a trial he knows he can't win. I've already shown up for trial twice now; why wouldn't I show up again?"

"Who would believe you were stupid enough to put your neck in the noose for a third time?" Cannan shrugged. "Only those who know you. The rest of the world will assume you got wise."

"You can tell them whatever you like, since you must cast the spell," Faren said. "I have missed my sacred hour. I cannot renew until the morning."

"There is a greater reason he may instruct them as he chooses," Lalania said. Her eyes were smoldering with a dark triumph as she turned to Christopher. "Though I know the news will grieve you, my dear Lord Apostle, you are now the highest priest of the White in the Kingdom. You have authority over all those bound to your color."

"It's only temporary." Christopher shrank back in his chair. "We'll revive Krellyan, and he'll still outrank me."

Faren barked. After a moment Christopher realized it was supposed to be laughter. "They will not make the same mistake twice. I know not what agent cheated your foes last time and left your empty head on our doorstep, but I know with certainty that this time the Gold Apostle will incinerate every scrap of the Saint's body, and then burn the ashes again. No power in this realm will bring back my sweet lord." Tears ran down Faren's cheeks.

Karl faced Christopher and drew himself up to attention, tipping his head in formal apology. "I should not have doubted you."

Torme nodded in agreement, amazement spreading across his face. "This is why we have worked our fingers to the bone preserving our dead. You foresaw this!"

"No," Christopher sighed. "I didn't." *If I had*, he thought bitterly, *I would have taken Lucien up on his offer.*

"I didn't plan this." He put a hand over his eyes, and then snatched it away in disgust, leaving dried dirt on his face. "If I had, I would have been depending on the power of the Saint." Krellyan had been the only person in the Kingdom who could regenerate missing limbs or restore life to a finger-bone. "We are now in the worst possible position. I am miles away, our counties are defenseless, and our greatest asset is already gone."

"And yet," Gregor said, speaking for the first time, "we are not without assets of our own. We have the best army in the Kingdom, fully provisioned and loyal beyond measure. We have allies both inside and outside the borders. We have the power of the Cardinal. And unless I miss my mark, we will soon have a Saint of our own."

The blue knight lifted his scabbarded sword from his side and held it front of him like a cross as he knelt. "Though it be unnecessary,

I repeat my vows. You are more than my brother in faith, more than my commanding officer, more than my friend and companion. You are the hope of all that is Bright in this realm, and I will spill my blood without measure at your will."

Torme knelt beside, his katana offered hilt-first. "I owe no fealty to any but you, and no gratitude to any but Krellyan. I will follow you to death or victory, as the winds of fate blow."

"You bought my freedom from Krellyan's service," Disa said. "You laid no price on it. So now I swear to you, also without price." She joined her husband on the floor.

Cannan lowered himself to his knees. His grim smile spoke for itself. Christopher tried to crawl away, but the chair blocked him in.

Lalania curtsied, ending in a bow so low she was almost prostrate. "The College of Troubadours has maintained its independence since the beginning. We held no land beyond our campus, solely so that when this day came, we could honestly say we broke no vows of fealty. The Skald speaks through me, for all of my sisters. The final chorus sings; the curtains draw near. We are yours to the bitter end."

Paralyzed by horror, Christopher watched the old Cardinal struggle out of the chair, only to sink to his knees. "I should have let Hobilar kill you. But I coveted a sword of our own, to rattle in the face of our foes. I have been justly punished by Heaven for my vanity. And yet the sword is still before me, sharper than ever. I bend to it now; I accept your authority; I place all of the servants of the Bright Lady under your command and protection, accepting responsibility for breaking their vows to any other; I swear myself to you even beyond my vow to Her."

"I can't," Christopher said, his voice edging on despair. "I can't be all those things you want me to be."

Karl laughed, all the more shocking for its rarity, his victory complete. "You have no choice," he declared. "No one does. No one ever did."

20

CAVALRY TO THE RESCUE

Christopher had to struggle to enter his trance-state. His hands wouldn't stop trembling. It was not a relief when the animated suit of armor appeared before him. He had been secretly hoping that leading a rebellion, subverting the Cardinal from his faith, and getting the Saint killed through his stupidity, had finally been enough for Marcius to renounce him.

Instead, the avatar cheerfully complied with his request to replace several of the preservation spells with sendings. Christopher had been planning to use his spells that night, and then immediately replenish them, leaving his hour of prayer to the last possible minute. The flexibility was an underappreciated boon, one of the nonobvious advantages of serving a war god. This knowledge was not comforting, either. It just meant that other priests had other advantages he didn't know about.

He had been reviving two men every day since his last promotion, so there were only forty dead left. Faren would double that rate, not that it mattered. They didn't have weeks left. They might not have days.

His first spell went to Vicar Rana of Knockford. Never mind his friends there. His army lived and died by its supplies, and the town was the only source of gunpowder in the world.

"The King charges me with treason. Cardinal Faren and I shall dispute the charges with force. Preserve Fae and the powder mill at all costs."

Her reply was as flat as a grinding stone, yet no less disquieting for it. "You and your patron have much to answer for. I look forward to my death, so that I might take my complaints directly to him."

Next was the man most in danger, the Vicar of Samerhaven, whose county lay in the south, bordered by the Gold. The man had a low opinion of Christopher, and at the moment Christopher did not feel he was prepared to argue the point. He stuck to the same text.

The response came quick and sharp. "I will do what is best for my people. If that includes pulling the lever of the trapdoor under your gallows, I will not hesitate."

Well, at least he didn't say anything mean.

Much to Christopher's surprise, the ancient geezer who ran Cannenberry was still alive to take his message. The reply was far gentler, though it included a dismaying coda: "Channel all further contact through my Prelate."

This exhausted his spells of that rank for the day. Yet the need was great; Disa had given him a scroll of sending that she had been hiding in case of emergencies, issued to her seasons ago by a forward-thinking Cardinal suspicious of Christopher's ability to stay out of trouble and alive.

Now that they were all in the soup, all of the cards were coming out on the table. Sadly, there were no more. The Cardinal had brought nothing with him. The White Church was not wealthy that way. On the plus side, it meant that the enemy had gained hardly anything by looting the Cathedral.

Reading the scroll into burning ash, with some difficulty he brought forth the memory of the face of the Vicar of Copperton, a solid, unassuming man whose realm bordered Kingsrock itself. The reply was delivered with sad resignation. "I pray you resolve the issue quickly, for our people's sake. Our defeat will change little, while your rebellion exposes them to grave danger."

Shockingly, the end of the day came, the sun lowering itself to bed with no more hesitation than it had the day before, almost as if it were untroubled by the calamitous events it had shone over. Christopher collapsed into his bed, expecting misery but falling exhausted into unconsciousness instantly.

And thus, awaking again, with no sense of time passing. Karl stood in his tent doorway, armed and armored. "I am taking the cavalry into the field. The hobgoblins must be induced to die at a faster rate. We would be fools to march away from your eleventh rank, if it is as close as Lalania says it must be."

"It is," he admitted, groggy and glaring at the early morning light. By the time he got out of bed, Karl was gone.

It was with some trepidation that he heard hoofbeats in the after-noon. Karl should not have returned so early unless something had gone amiss. He headed toward the fort's gate and discovered the wrong cavalry pouring through his door.

Armored knights in shades of blue filled up the open square, more coming in behind them. Christopher's men looked on, stricken with indecision. He wanted to rage at them for letting the enemy in without a fight, but of course no one had told them that they were the enemy. Christopher had not yet informed his army of his rebellion, still hoping for some diplomatic solution to suggest itself.

Now it was too late. The armored and mounted men were inside the walls, while Christopher's cavalry and carbines were off in the woods. A battle would be ruinous even in victory, which was by no means assured.

The man at the head of all this glittering armor was unmistak-able. Lord Earl Istvar stood in his stirrups, sword in hand, and called down to Christopher.

"Lord Prophet Christopher, you are under arrest, by order of the King. Surrender your sword, your person, your prisoners, and your soldiers."

The challenge splashed over Christopher like ocean spray, washing his misgivings away in instinctive reaction to unconstrained authority. He dug his heels into the mud.

"No, no, what prisoners? And . . . no."

Istvar sat back down in the saddle, though he kept his sword out. "You hold Cardinal Faren against his will and against the summons of the King."

"No one holds me," Faren said, approaching from behind Christopher. "I shall come to the King in due time, but he will not appreciate my deliverance."

"Lord Faren," Istvar said, his commanding voice strained with friendship, "you have ever been loyal beyond question. The King can be made to see this."

"No man or woman has ever been more loyal than Krellyan," Faren shot back, hot and threatening. "Yet he was murdered at his own altar. Tell me, Lord Istvar . . . where were you when this foul deed was done?"

Istvar bristled, controlling his anger with visible effort. After a moment he spoke again, still striving for neutrality. "Far from Kingsrock. I know not the details and would not care to dispute them. At this point I seek only to preserve what may yet be saved."

"Then I thank you," Faren said, without a trace of gratitude. "Yet you have come too late. There are none here left to save."

The Earl seemed taken aback at the despairing words. So was Christopher, for that matter.

A redheaded woman on a fine white palfrey advanced out of the herd of horsemen. "It is as I told you, my lord. The Cardinal has gone over to rebellion." The bard Uma, second-in-command of the College, and Christopher's least annoying poisoner. He would have warned the Earl, but the man looked at her with sufficient suspicion.

"I chose not to heed rumors, for the sake of a good man." He faced Faren again. "Yet you leave me no options."

"There are always options," Faren answered. "Some end in death, but that does not necessarily recommend against them. You know as well as I that there are worse things than dying."

"Oath-breaking is among them," Istvar declared gravely.

Gregor marched up to stand beside Christopher, offering moral and physical support. "Then how much you must hate the King for breaking his. Of what value is a lord who cannot protect his own? Yet the Saint was delivered to his enemies at the point of Treywan's sword."

"You speak treason, Ser," Istvar growled.

"A pox on you!" Faren cried, startling everyone. "You sit and bandy words while a murderer sits on the throne. Do you think he will spare me, despite my innocence? Do you think he will not come for you soon after? Words mean nothing to the Black. The Shadow makes its move against us, and you whine about your paltry oaths!"

Even Christopher could see this was an undiplomatic approach to take with a priest of the Blue. "Lord Earl," he said, before anyone else could speak, "the King's charges are obviously false. Even if they were true of me, they could never have been true of the Saint."

"That is not so clear," Istvar said with some resignation. "Despite your clumsy tongue, your words are poisonously effective. I myself have felt their effect, in our one brief encounter. Who is to say that you did not eventually sway the Saint from common sense? Look at what you have done to the Cardinal."

"He did nothing!" Faren shouted, shaking his fist at the Earl. "It is you, and your obdurate stupidity, that inflames me."

"My Lord Earl," Uma said, soft and soothing. "Grief ever unhinges the mind, and the greater the mind, the greater the fall. Forgive an old man who has lost his second son."

"Your words are no less poisonous," Istvar sighed, while Faren glared hotly at the bard.

Christopher wanted to ask if she was being literal or figurative. Family relations in the White Church carried no special favor; it was entirely possible, though wildly improbable, that Faren had been Krellyan's father all along and no one had bothered to mention it.

Before he could figure out how to introduce the topic, the Earl returned to his. Staring at Christopher with narrowed brow, he spoke with a certain amount of venom of his own. "But are these charges false? I rode through woods infested with ulvenmen; I see a goblin city in the distance still standing and whole; I look about in vain for the corpse of the dragon that murdered my cousin and his people. We keep sending you out to fight our enemies, and you keep making friends with them. One need not be quick of mind to leap to suspicion."

"They surrendered," Christopher said. "What would you have me do?"

Istvar boggled at him. "Why would you accept their surrender? They are goblins. They only seek a pause to prepare further mischief."

"You know, this would have been handy to know beforehand. But nobody thought to tell me."

"Why would anyone think you needed telling?" The Earl had the look of a stern schoolteacher facing down the class clown.

Christopher forced himself to pause and gather his thoughts. "That is not relevant. The goblins and the ulvenmen are no longer a threat. Both depend on me—I mean, the Kingdom—for their survival. We don't have to be at perpetual war."

Istvar shook his head in amazement. "You speak madness with such sincerity that I doubt my own sanity. Yet some things transcend reason. Tell me you have made a pet of the monster that killed my cousin and his wife, and I will ride you down where you stand."

"The dragon escaped," Christopher confessed. "Another one chased it off."

"Now you expect me to believe you consort with dragons." Istvar was no longer amazed. He was just angry. "Your idiotic fantasies have come to an end. You will surrender and your men will slink home, to weather Treywan's wrath as best they can. You will hang for your stupidity, and the rest of us will labor to repair the damage you have done."

"You got your army inside my gates," Christopher said. "But I still think I can beat you. Many of my men will die. But they know they will live again. Can your men say the same?"

Istvar glanced around the camp, where men stood clutching rifles. Some of them had been in this position before, facing down a Blue lord on the eve of battle. They had been soft then, merely boys. Now the faces that stared back at Istvar were the faces of hard men.

The Earl returned his gaze to Christopher. "They will stay dead if you die. And I think I can beat you. So: shall we sacrifice hundreds of men to your vanity and my oath?"

"No," Christopher said. "Ride back out. Return to the King and tell him at least one charge is true: I reject his summons."

"To what end? We shall only meet again on a different battlefield. If you would challenge a King, surely you would not defer to an Earl."

"Then what do you suggest?"

Istvar swung down from his horse, his long straight sword on his shoulder, its edges glinting in the cold sunlight. "I suggest a duel. Nay; I demand it. Prepare to defend yourself."

21

THE DUKE OF EARL

It made a certain kind of sense. If Christopher couldn't defeat the Earl in a duel, he surely couldn't defeat the King.

Of course, Christopher had been telling people all along that he couldn't win that duel. And it seemed absurd that his rebellion against feudalism and the capricious tyranny of the sword should depend for its success upon his personal swordsmanship. Yet these were the rules of this, or any, world; those that would introduce a new art must first master the old.

At least, Christopher reflected, the Earl had not knelt and pledged undying fealty. A good honest hate was refreshing. If nothing else, it gave Christopher an acceptable target for his anger. The Earl was a big boy of a decent rank: he could handle himself in a fight. And he was on the list of people Christopher felt needed taking down a peg or three.

"Will you allow me to prepare, then?" Christopher said.

"I can give you an hour to pray," Istvar answered, "but no more. Though you should not need that. You are at war now; violence can descend at any moment."

A point the Earl was making in the flesh. "I have been healing," Christopher explained, though strictly speaking it was a nonsense answer. He could always trade any prepared spell for a healing. It was the preservation of the dead that consumed his daily prayers.

"I will relieve you on that score," Faren said in a bitter growl. "You must put this jackanapes down."

"Well," Christopher said uncomfortably, "not permanently." Both of them could revive the dead. It would cost the Earl a rank, but he had plenty to spare.

"I must, in good faith, reject your offer." Istvar shook his head with noble dignity. "For you must know that should I win, you will not live again."

The pomposity made Christopher glad they were about to clash swords. Still, he looked with some concern at Faren, who seemed to have taken the descriptor "blood-thirsty" distressingly literally.

"What a fine and pretty honor," Faren snarled at the Earl. "Where was it when you sat in your fine hall, with your pretty maids, while the Iron Throne ground peasants under its heel? When did you ever call out Black Bartholomew for his crimes?"

"It is not that simple," Istvar answered, with strained patience.

"And yet," Faren said with a shrug, "Lord Christopher was here nary a year before he killed the monster for the first, second, and final time."

The Earl finally snapped. "And gaze upon the result. My inaction did not destroy your Church or precipitate civil war."

"If you will excuse me," Christopher said. "I should pray. Brother Faren, will you accompany me?" He wanted some advice, but mostly he wanted to get the old man away from the Earl before he sparked a second duel.

Istvar answered by turning away to deal with his horse. Christopher put his hand on Faren's shoulder and steered him back into the camp.

In his command tent his retinue gathered to discuss tactics.

"Your magic is greater than his," Gregor said. "But although you are higher rank, he holds several ranks of warrior in addition to his priestly ones. In a straight sword fight he will at least be your equal."

Cannan rumbled in his throat. "Flattery is of no value here."

Christopher agreed, and said so. "The man's been wielding a sword since the day he could walk." Never mind the two inches of height and thirty pounds of muscle the Earl had over him. "In a fair fight he'd stomp me silly."

But of course it would not be fair. Christopher sat down to fill his head with magic while the swordsmen prepared his armor.

An hour later he walked out of his tent, draped in metal scales and filled with purpose. It felt like a second chance to argue with the Blue Duke, but this time he could speak a language the nobility could understand.

Istvar was waiting for him in the center of a wide circle marked out in the fields. It was their old polo grounds, the only spot the goblins had not yet plowed. Istvar's men mixed with his indiscriminately. Everyone seemed to assume their champion would prevail and the other side would abide by the result. Christopher hoped it was true, however it went.

"My Prelate shall divine for me," Istvar called across the barren dirt. "The Cardinal may do the same."

As another man in armor approached Christopher, casting a detection to verify that he had no active spells already cast, Faren waved a hand negligently in the Earl's direction. "Spell or no, what does it matter? My Lord Brother will bend your pride over his knee and spank it like a redheaded stepchild."

It was actually kind of heartening. This showmanship was something the old Cardinal Faren would have gloried in.

"As this is a duel of priests, we each shall have a chance to cast one spell before crossing swords," Istvar explained, drawing his sword and holding it before him like an upside-down cross. "Are you prepared?"

"I am," Christopher said, and both men began chanting.

Istvar appeared to be calling for the general favor of his god. Christopher chose to go in a more direct route. He had learned from his duel with Joadan. While sharp blue light sparkled off of Istvar's armor and sword, Christopher enjoined the Marshall of Heaven to send him allies and was rewarded when two very large white buffalo appeared on his side of the circle.

He tried not to be disappointed. Herbivores were not really what

THE DUKE OF EARL   191

he had been expecting. Joadan had summoned a panther, and Christopher had been hoping for lions or something equally majestic, given his higher rank. However, he kept his ire to himself and moved on to his next spell, the energy protection which had saved his life when fighting the ulvenman shaman.

Istvar had also chosen to cast a second spell instead of charging into melee. Christopher couldn't hear the words he was chanting, so he didn't know what the spell was. The buffalo charged, pinning the man with a cage of horns. They weren't trying to hurt him so much as keep him away from Christopher, who moved on to his third spell.

The Earl seemed annoyed by his failure to close, and began slaughtering the animals holding him back. It would have been an ugly scene except the buffalo shed white smoke instead of blood and died in utter silence, disappearing in misty clouds one by one.

Nonetheless, they had bought Christopher the time he needed. His third spell was one that had only recently become available to him, of too short duration for the battlefield but perfect for the situation at hand. He felt himself swell with power, a heady sensation, almost drug-like. For the next minute his priestly ranks would count as warrior ranks when it came to combat. The fight was no longer even remotely fair.

As Istvar charged him without a sound, Christopher realized that the man was surrounded by magical silence. A clever tactic that would have deprived Christopher of all the spells he had just cast, if not for the buffalo's delay. As it was, Christopher gave up the initiative to cast one more spell. The sudden appearance of Istvar's fierce roar told him the dispelling had worked. Istvar now charged him bereft of any magical defenses.

The Earl did not let this dissuade him. His sword smashed into Christopher with such force that his head would have come off if not for tael. Sparks and bits of metal flew as the Earl cut at Christopher like a woodsman at a tree. For his part, Christopher returned the favor. Another lesson he had learned from Joadan: he did not even try to parry the Earl's magic blade with his own mundane steel sword. Instead, he took each of the Earl's blows, and used the opening to return his own, battering the bigger man like a punching bag. Knowing the Earl's rank, he did not hold back. The habits of the last year of relentless violence came easily now.

Eventually, inevitably, the Earl stepped back to cast a healing spell. Christopher could have used the same, but instead he opened the heavens and called down flame. To be certain of striking the Earl, he allowed the spell to strike himself. The world flared red and white while the dirt cooked to the consistency of pottery.

When Christopher could see again, the Earl was staggering backward and desperately casting another healing spell, the bits of his clothing not covered by metal charred and smoking. Istvar's armor was revealed as enchanted by the act of not melting into a puddle. Christopher, protected by his energy ward, was untouched. When he stepped forward to follow the Earl, he left behind two brown footprints in the blackened earth.

"Yield," Christopher said, "or I'll do it again. And there'll be no body left to revive." The flame would have vaporized anything not protected by tael. Istvar's was clearly depleted; a second strike would land on merely mortal flesh.

"You cannot have more magic," the Earl gasped.

For answer, Christopher pointed to a patch of ground thirty feet away and called down a second roaring column, leaving behind a black shiny circle.

He raised his hand to the Earl again. "I gained a rank," he explained. "You should have asked."

For a moment he feared he would have to destroy Istvar. His martial prowess was on a short timer, and without it the Earl might well rally and beat him after all. He had to win before that happened.

At last Istvar sank to one knee. "I yield," he said. "None can hold it against me. I held my oath until certain death. To hold any further would change nothing and would rob the world of a servant for the Bright. So I shall yield, Lord Apostle, to the power of your patron."

Christopher sighed in relief as he dropped his hand and the last dregs of his supernatural strength faded away.

Faren stalked across the field to glare at the Earl. "I hope you have your ransom to hand, or you may yet lose your head. For my Church can no longer afford to buy out fools, and my Lord Brother has great need."

"I have brought a ransom," Istvar said, "if you will have it. My men are bound to the King through me. Now that my oath to him is broken, I offer them to you, if you pledge that your cause will adhere to the strictures of justice."

So it had been a trick. The whole performance, with live steel and killing magic, was merely a ritual to allow the Earl to exchange one oath for another. And to saddle Christopher with more responsibility.

"You can't do that," he tried to argue. "The King will turn on your people back home."

"If I ride out from here without your head, he will anyway. What-ever objections I have to your person and your patron, I cannot fail to see that the future of the Bright will be decided within the year."

If only Duke Nordland had been so far-sighted. And yet Istvar surely did not see to the final end, a future that had no place for swordsmen. As Christopher was trying to find a way to express this truth without unduly alarming the Earl, Faren spoke.

"We shall not be bound by mere justice," the Cardinal announced. "Our remit is larger than that. Yet neither will we ask you to dishonor yourself or your patron."

Istvar gave Faren a careful stare. "You spoke with the Saint's voice, by his decree. I do not know that you speak so for the Apostle."

If Faren was ready to step back into his role as second-in-com-mand, Christopher wasn't about to stop him. There was more than enough weight to be born.

"Gods yes," Christopher exclaimed. "What he said."

22

A FLY ON THE WALL

Faren healed both of them, replenishing first Christopher's and then Istvar's tael. Christopher recognized this as a formal demonstration of both the Cardinal's power and his loyalty, so he let it go without comment. He needed his magic to piece his armor back together anyway. Istvar's would need the same treatment.

When he offered, Istvar declined. "I thank you, my lord, but my camp contains sufficient magic for such needs."

Gregor seemed struck by an idea. "What else does your camp contain, Ser? We need to know so as best to allocate our forces."

Istvar frowned at Gregor. "An intimate question. You can see for yourself that I have brought three score of knights. You may presume my personal retinue is adequate to my rank and assign me duties based on that capacity."

"That's not how it works anymore." Gregor gave the Earl a sympathetic smile. "In Colonel Christopher's army, we all eat from the same pot. And I mean that both figuratively and literally, Ser. Your knights will be served from the same mess as our soldiers, they will sleep in the same tents, and they will obey the same commanders."

The Earl was looking a bit dubious, so Christopher felt it would be profitable to make the point clearly. "That means taking orders from commoners. Major Karl serves as my second-in-command, even over Baron Gregor and Curate Torme. This is a non-negotiable point; if you can't deal with it, you are free to leave."

"What is the purpose of this peculiar doctrine?" Istvar asked. Christopher was impressed with the diplomacy of the question. And, to be honest, grateful for it. The Earl's formality was not always annoying.

"The purpose is that we want to win," Gregor answered. "And Major Karl is our best guide to victory. You have not seen, and thus cannot truly understand, the nature of the army we have raised. I mean no disrespect, Ser. Before I witnessed it myself, I could not understand and would not have believed. There will still be employment for your sword, in minor engagements and scouting missions, but the bulk of the slaughter will be carried out by commoners under the command of commoners."

Istvar's diplomacy had its limits. He was unable to pretend to take Gregor seriously. "You would claim to have inverted the art of war?"

"The world has gone topsy-turvy, and all of us must necessarily hang on by our toes." Cardinal Faren, despite the sorry state of his hair, was his old self again. "This is not the last adjustment you need make. Consider that the Lord Apostle will pay you in gold, not tael, and only enough to survive on. This is no mercenary adventure, and you are not an ally. You serve at his whim solely for the privilege of having a home to go to when this is all over."

The Earl looked back to Christopher with such honest distress that all of his sharp feelings died.

"I'm sorry," he told the nobleman. "It's all true."

"And if my men fall under your command?"

"Then I will revive them. But I will not restore their rank. They can continue to fight as common men." This was such hard news Christopher felt compelled to apologize again. "I'm sorry."

"You offer a poor bargain indeed, barely better than the enemy's. It appears we must surrender either our lives or our privileges."

Faren stared levelly at the Earl. "If you would seek counsel, ask the Saint which is the wiser course. Oh! But you cannot; for he is dead, and the dead have no privileges at all."

Istvar went off to dispose of his men, who did not seem unduly dismayed to find themselves having switched sides in the war. Then again, Istvar probably hadn't told them the new rules yet.

Christopher went back to his command tent and faced a mound of paperwork that represented a mountain of problems. At least the problem of Istvar had required a straightforward response: beat it with a stick until it behaved. If only all solutions were so direct.

But then again, they probably were. "The sooner we march on Kingsrock, the sooner this can all be over," he announced.

"Yesterday you trembled to face the King in personal combat," Lalania said. "Today you strain at the leash. The Earl is barely half the King's rank; the experience will be dissimilar."

"The King has no magic," Christopher said. Treywan was a warrior through and through, without any magical ranks. Not that Christopher held it against him. After today's display, he had been convinced of Lalania's old argument. Splitting ranks did not seem wise. Istvar's weak magic could not make up for the loss of warrior ranks. Gregor would be a dozen times more useful to him as a pure Curate than as a Viscount with a Pater rank.

On the other hand, without those warrior ranks Gregor probably would have failed to keep Christopher alive to this point.

"You are lethally wrong." Lalania leaned to stare at him earnestly. "You watched me snatch the lyre from his vault. Did you think he left his best treasure to molder under dust?"

"I knew it," muttered Gregor.

"Enchanted arms and armor will be the least of your concerns," Torme agreed. "Nor can you discount the spell-mongers that surround the King. Master Sigrath, the Gold Apostle, a dozen lesser priests and wizards will all offer him their services. The battlefield is no duel. He will come before you cloaked in all the power he can command."

"Like what?" Christopher asked, slightly alarmed and deeply annoyed. When he was shirking the fight, they pushed him forward; the minute he leaned in, they pulled him back.

"Like flight," Gregor said. "You should have snatched his boots instead of his harp."

"He can fly?" Christopher looked up at the tent roof, half-expecting Treywan to descend through it in a slashing fury.

"Of course," a different voice answered. Startled, Christopher jerked his head around.

Uma entered the tent. Christopher wondered why he bothered to post sentries.

"How else could he have slain a dragon?" the exceptionally beautiful redhead continued. "A feat, my Lord Apostle, that you apparently failed to equal. An opportunity missed."

"You did not see this dragon," Lalania said, and for a moment her voice trembled at the memory.

"I am well aware." Despite the words, Uma's tone was sympathetic. "As I am aware that the beast the King slew was black. Less than half the size of what you described, with hardly any magic and barely sentient."

"Still," Christopher mused aloud. A creature only as big as a moving van, instead of a locomotive, was nothing to sneeze at. "Pretty impressive."

"It was positively heroic. There is a reason he has held the throne for twenty years. There is a reason no other has dared to challenge him." Uma had no sympathy for Christopher. "He remains a formidable and wily foe. I can only pray that you have a plan of scintillating cleverness to defeat him."

Christopher scratched his beard.

"Our lord can fly as well," Torme said. "Among other things, as you saw today."

"That is not our greatest asset." Gregor put his hands on the map table. "The men are. No mundane army can stand against us. The King cannot rule from Kingsrock alone. If we capture every county seat, he must seek out Christopher. He will fly to us, to a place of our choosing, far from his casters, to do battle on our terms."

"Have you served a different commander than I?" Cannan asked. "Treywan need but poke a child in the shoulder, and Christopher will hurtle himself into battle on the spot."

Gregor sat back and scratched his own beard. "It made more sense when Karl explained it."

"Where is the Major?" Uma asked, with what Christopher found to be an unhealthy level of interest.

"Where we should be," Cannan answered. "Out killing hobgoblins. Doing something useful."

"If that is truly useful, then I suggest putting Lord Istvar's men to the same task. It would be wise to keep them occupied."

It was more than wise, it was brilliant. Killing monsters could only make the new men side with him, while turning over the tael would prepare them for doing the same later. And if one of them should die, he could earn their eternal gratitude by reviving the man.

"I agree," Christopher said. "Can we?"

"They are well-suited to it, though lacking in magic. His retinue contains a Prelate and five Paters, but otherwise his men are knights and a few captains."

"He has many knights," Torme noted, with a little awe. "Are all northern courts so deep?"

"In addition to his own household troops he has brought contingents from every other Blue house. With but a little effort you can turn those lords to your cause. Each of them has a retinue and at least a hundred common soldiers. If such things are still of use to you."

"Aye," Gregor agreed. "I recognized some faces. Their lords would not have given them leave to go if they were not begging to be turned. And we can use their soldiers—it takes surprisingly little time to turn a crossbowman into a rifleman. I can do it in three days, and that's on the march."

"How many rifles do you have?" Uma asked.

Christopher gestured to the papers on the table. "I was reading the production schedules from Knockford when I got . . . distracted."

"Let us hope it is sufficient, for you do not have time to make more. The news is still filtering throughout the Kingdom; soon people will begin to act on it."

Christopher looked at Lalania. "Why are you so quiet? I need your help here." She should be the one to tell him these things.

"My sister speaks for me," Lalania said. "And her news is fresher." She reached out and squeezed his hand, making it all better.

"The help we need is Karl," Gregor declared. "We must protect the White, recruit the Blue, placate the Green, restrain the Gold, and assault the throne all at once. I hardly know where to begin."

"And what of the druids?" Torme asked.

As if on cue, another woman stepped through the tent door. Small and dark-haired, dressed in a simple green gown as if she was popping out to the market, Lady Io strode boldly into his secret command council.

Christopher stood up, framing a set of harsh words for his so-called door guards, but the druidess was already speaking.

"Say nothing of the druids," she said. "We will not intervene, on either side. This is not the Black Harvest; you cannot call on us to fight your internecine battles."

Torme seemed to think the remark was directed at him. "That is not wisdom, Lady. The Iron Throne ever casts its eyes east. They hate the independence of your people second only to their hatred for the White."

"We can defend our own." She spoke directly to Christopher. "As I do now. The terms of your arrangement with my son are complete. The moment you turned to rebellion you released him from his oath. I have come to take him home."

A fair enough argument, though Christopher would miss the boy and his woodcraft. Still, their future battles would be fought on well-mapped lands.

Before he could concede the point, Cannan spoke.

"That is for him to decide."

Lady Io turned a murderously freezing glare on the red knight, her shoulders raising as if her hands had become heavy claws ready to strike. "If you think I will let you steal a second child from my womb, your life is measured in breaths."

Cannan answered without heat, though still implacable. "He is not a child anymore. A man cuts his own path in this world."

"The blind give advice only to the dead," she hissed.

Christopher raised his voice to intervene. "Lady Io. We are all on the same side here. I will release D'Kan, but please do not threaten my staff."

"You are mistaken. We are not on a side." Though she spoke to Christopher, her gaze did not leave Cannan.

Uma raised her hand, seeking to interrupt, though her head was tilted and her attention elsewhere. She looked very much like a person on the phone, about to relay some interesting comment from the party on the other end. The image was so familiar, and yet so foreign in this place, that for a vertiginous moment Christopher thought it must all have been a terribly long and exhausting dream.

Then he saw the misty ball of translucent white surrounding the center tent pole and understood. The Skald was scrying on them and speaking to Uma through the spell.

"Lady Io," Uma said, dropping her hand and putting on a concerned face, "it seems no one informed the Gold of your neutrality. Soldiers from Balenar are even now assaulting the river crossing at Farmark."

Christopher sank back into his chair, the reality sinking in. This was the final straw, the last turn-off to diplomacy receding rapidly in the rearview mirror. Whether Balenar acted with the King's permission or not hardly mattered. The war was on, everywhere. Like a wildfire it would rage, setting castle against castle, raising a flood of corpses that Christopher could never hope to revive.

At that moment he would have welcomed a duel with Treywan, under any terms, just for the chance to stop the madness.

"Why would they do that?" Gregor exclaimed, ruffling through the battle plans on the table with confusion. "How can that possibly help them?"

Lady Io shrugged, unconcerned. "Understanding the acts of madmen is a fool's errand. The blood of their servants will cloud the river, yet by tomorrow the current will have washed the banks clean. All the more reason D'Kan must go home: his bow has targets to seek."

A soldier stepped into the tent, his carbine at parade rest on his shoulder. "Colonel, the Lord Earl is here."

Apparently they found the swordsman less intimidating than the women.

"Of course," Christopher said. "Show him in." The Earl actually had a right to attend.

The other men stood when the Earl entered. Christopher didn't. It wasn't required of him, and he didn't want to give the Earl the wrong idea. For that matter, his men should not have risen. The Earl didn't even have a rank in his army yet.

"My lord," Istvar said. He had changed into non-combat dress, which still meant chainmail and the shiniest boots Christopher had seen in a very long while.

"It's just Colonel, or sir," Christopher told him. "I'll give you a rank so my men will salute you. But you cannot expect them to treat you like a lord. We don't do that here."

"I see you have much to occupy yourself with," Lady Io said, with evident distaste. "Surrender my son and I shall leave you to it."

Uma was whispering to Istvar, presumably filling him in on the latest news from the Kingdom. Christopher couldn't object, as the woman didn't work for him.

"When he returns from the field, I will send him to you." Christopher sighed. "But I will not force him to leave, if he chooses to stay. I need every man I can get."

The boy's mother glared at him, but Istvar tipped his head in sympathy and addressed her. "Lady Io, it is not without precedent. Ser D'Arcy served my cousin for many years, to the mutual benefit of both our people."

The druidess gave Istvar the kind of look that battleships followed up with full broadsides. Christopher was suddenly seized by the intuition that she was angry enough to unleash long pent-up secrets of devastating effect, as if the corrosiveness of the civil war had already infected their camp. Without even a shred of a clue of what that knowledge could be, Christopher found himself rushing to keep it hidden.

"True," he almost shouted. "It's true. I learned a lot from D'Arcy." He was babbling, saying anything to keep Lady Io from talking.

Fortunately Lalania remembered what he paid her for and leapt in to fill the gap.

"He may well be safer with us," the bard said. "The Kingdom is aflame. The roads will not be safe for a young man of dubious allegiance so far from home."

"No Ranger requires roads," Lady Io said contemptuously.

"Yet he still must walk the land. We cannot all fly across the Kingdom in an afternoon." Lalania smiled sadly. "The battle for Farmark will be decided long before he can join it."

"My lady," Istvar continued, oblivious to the danger, "no good man sunders his oath in the Wild. Let the lad stay at least until the Lord Apostle steps a foot back into the Kingdom. And he will travel far more safely behind our line of advance than in front of it, where he might well be mistaken for a spy."

"The entire discussion is premature," Uma announced. "The

Verdant Court will be convened to discuss Balenar's crimes, and your people might yet reach out to us for alliance."

The combined assault worked. For once Lady Io did not immediately respond.

"Corporal," Christopher called out to his doorman, who appeared with suitable alacrity. "See that the Lady Io has accommodations while we wait for Ser D'Kan to return."

With a hostile glare that spared no one, the druidess followed the young soldier out.

In her absence, Christopher breathed a sigh of relief. "Thanks for that timely information," he said to Uma.

She looked back at him disapprovingly. "You cannot rely on us to watch the whole realm. You must scry or message your own people; we do not have enough agents to spare."

He glanced over at the Cardinal, who had remained uncharacteristically silent so far.

"Do not look to me," Faren said. "I will relieve you of the need to look after your dead. The rest must be up to you."

"Hang on," Christopher said. "I think you've got another call," he told Uma, pointing to the ceiling, where another barely visible translucent ball had appeared.

The bard looked up with surprise, quickly hidden under her actor's discipline. Faren frowned, staring at the roof. Gregor looked up and then searched his companion's faces, perhaps trying to determine if they were pulling some kind of prank. The little tell-tales were not easy to spot, even when you knew where to look.

"That is not one of ours," Uma said flatly.

"Ahem," Torme coughed. The rest of the room sat in uncomfortable silence. The tell-tale seemingly noticed, and politely winked out of existence.

"Okay, then," Christopher said after it was gone. "Do we know whose it was?"

"Does it matter?" Uma shrugged. "In the future you must take precautions. Surely Lalania has made this clear."

"She did," Christopher said, defending her. "We just got lazy. It won't happen again."

Lord Istvar massaged his temples with one hand. "This is not the kind of warfare I am used to."

In the distance they heard the sound of horse's hooves. The absence of gunfire told Christopher they were his own troops, returning from their long day in the field.

"We have something more familiar for you, then," Gregor told him. "Tomorrow you can lead your knights into the woods, hunting hobgoblins. We'll even give you the Ranger for a scout. Completely traditional."

"Forgive the impertinence of the question," Istvar said, "but do not our enemies lie further south?"

"They do," Gregor answered, "but our business lies here for a few days yet. And now I am going to stop talking until we are in a safer area."

The conference broke up to the sounds of mess-hall bells summoning men to dinner. As they walked through the darkening camp, Christopher pulled Lalania aside for a private comment.

"What the Dark was that business about D'Arcy?" he asked.

Her eyes deepened, pools of distant sympathy. "The path of true love is not always straight. Those of us caught in its turbulence must make what accommodations we can." With a smile as enigmatic as her words, she walked on.

23

NIGHT-FLIGHT

A man stood in his doorway, calling out in a foreign tongue. Christopher swam up from unconsciousness in a panic.

"Colonel," the corporal repeated. "The Lady Minstrel asks that you come to her tent. Immediately, sir."

Christopher looked around the room, gathering his bearings. Cannan sat on the edge of his own cot, sword already in hand. The big man slept in the same room these days, while the tent was surrounded by a guard of half a dozen soldiers all night.

Christopher threw off the blanket and swung his feet onto the ground. "Of course."

The corporal managed to communicate his disapproval, though the tent was dark and he said not a word. His stance was enough.

"Don't worry," Christopher said. "I'm sure it's just some crisis." On that note Christopher realized it almost certainly was. Lalania had probably received another report from the Skald, and it could only be bad news.

Alert now, he and Cannan put on boots, chainmail, and swords. Cannan finished first and stepped out of the tent. When disaster did not fall, he opened the tent flap and motioned for Christopher to follow.

They walked through the camp, Christopher trying not to yawn where his sentries could see him. There were always men awake and active. Sleep was the first casualty of war.

Cannan proceeded him into Lalania's tent, which seemed to meet with the corporal's approval. Apparently the army still viewed his chastity as their good-luck charm. It was utterly silly and yet also very annoying.

For a brief moment Christopher felt that compact challenged. Lalania was in her night-gown, brushing out her long hair, and Christopher almost forgot there were other people in the room.

Other people being the correct phrasing. A short, slightly paunchy man sat in a chair next to her bed, drinking a glass of wine. The Lord Wizard of Carrhill, outside of his disguise as an undead monster, and far, far outside of his realm.

"What are you doing here?" Christopher asked him, startled.

"The obvious," the wizard replied with a leer. "But why didn't you call me?"

Christopher had not merely forgotten, he had never even considered it. He had run out of spells the first day he'd contacted people, but since then he'd had a chance to renew. While he tried to think of a diplomatic answer, the wizard shrugged.

"I get it. Gotta show some initiative. So here I am. Here being the lady's tent, as it looked a lot easier to sneak into than yours, and I presume you do not wish to announce my presence. Earl Istvar would certainly disapprove."

"The Lord Wizard has news that you should hear," Lalania said, directing the conversation to her own purposes, as she usually did.

"That I do. The Vicar of Samerhaven has decamped, abandoned his castle and taken his most trusted servants and his handful of police away. He left his people instructions to submit to whomever or whatever came next, without resistance or complaint."

The wizard clearly disapproved. Christopher was not happy about it, but he understood. "It's the best he can do. He's trying to put distance between the King's edict and his people."

"He has surrendered his right to rule," the wizard said. "Even now freebooters and criminals despoil his people, robbing and raping. Soon enough they will turn to murder for the treasure in those heads."

Christopher was briefly surprised to see the wizard so concerned about the fate of peasants.

"It is unbearable," the wizard continued. "That tael belongs to the nobility, not mercenary scum. I have certain knowledge that both Earl Donfeld and Baron Longwelt intend to claim the county for themselves. Their armies will march in the morning."

"There is nothing I can do about it from here," Christopher growled helplessly.

"Then you should be glad to see me." The wizard smiled, slightly oleaginously, though that was just his normal smile. "I have no interest in the land; I have plenty of that, thanks to you. But I have an interest in the people. With your endorsement I will offer them a chance to relocate. Life in a march county is not so soft as in your White enclaves, but they will at least be protected by my law and counseled by your Church."

It was a good offer. The only priest in the wizard's city was a priestess of the White—again, thanks to Christopher. The wizard, despite his personal creepiness, was neither cruel nor wicked to his people. And the high stone walls of Carrhill, defended by the rifles he had sold the wizard's captain, would keep them safe.

Despite that, he almost said no. When this was all over he could restore the Vicar to his county. The land would still be there to claim. But the people who fled in fear would not return, and who could blame them? The wizard, his most dubious ally, would permanently gain in wealth and power through the clever stratagem of having earned it.

"Yes, please," Christopher said anyway.

"That was almost too easy." The wizard stared at him calculatingly. Again, though, it was just his normal stare. "So I have to ask: are you going to win?"

"I have to," Christopher answered.

"That's not really the confidence I was looking for," the wizard said dryly.

Here, in the dead of night, sitting on the edge of a spell-casting actress's cot, arguing with a paunchy wizard who would have been an insurance adjuster in any other life, under the steady gaze of a professional swordsman who was the second loneliest person in the world, some long-curing substance finally crystalized.

"Yes," Christopher said.

Lalania stopped brushing her hair.

"Well, then," the wizard said guardedly.

"Every crime, every murder, is on the King." Christopher stated. "When he denounced the Vicar, he robbed him of his power; but he did not offer his own protection. If the Vicar's abandonment invalidates his right to rule, then the King's negligence invalidates his. If the protection of the people is the justification for the crown, then the crown has *failed*."

Lalania put down her brush.

"That sounds like a formal challenge," the wizard observed.

Cannan grunted in agreement. "About time."

The wizard upended his glass. "To victory, then. And justice and peace, or whatever. Don't get mad if I keep playing it low; my position is stronger if my neighbors aren't sure which side I'm on. Just stealing your peasants is noncommittal. Let me know if there's anything else I can do for you."

"Give them reason to keep guessing," Lalania offered. "Do not hesitate to engage their armies. Your men must inflict enough damage to make them fear you."

He bristled. "I trust they fear me now."

"Not really," she said with a sweet smile. "Else they would not strip their garrisons to pillage whilst you are on their doorsteps."

Despite magic and tael, a force of common men in a stone castle was still a potent defense. Cowering behind walls was certainly the option Christopher would have taken, if it were open to him.

"Point taken." The wizard looked from Christopher to Lalania and back. "I'll profit from some heads anyway. Those toys of yours were expensive. Time to see if it was worth it."

He stood up, drawing on a voluminous black cloak. "Now if you'll excuse me, I have a long flight home. I won't be joining you out here again, as I had to burn a scroll to make it this far. The scrying tell-tale was mine this afternoon. In the future I'll try to look in on you exactly at sunset, in case you want to give me a message. Don't count on it, though. It shares a slot with my best invisibility. And I feel like I'm going to be invisible a lot for the foreseeable future."

Christopher stood, something nagging at the back of his mind. Cannan took his time stepping aside when the wizard approached the tent flap, gazing down at the smaller man with intimidating distaste. The wizard winked at him and vanished from sight in the blink of an eye. The tent flap opened itself. Outside, the corporal looked on in surprise.

"Sir?" he asked.

"Never mind," Cannan answered, drawing the flap closed again.

The restored intimacy jogged Christopher's memory. He looked down at Lalania and frowned, suspicion blooming in his mind.

"Stop it, both of you," she sighed. "I make my own choices. If I choose to serve the cause in this manner, you cannot object. There will be plenty of unpleasant duties for you to share in the coming days anyway."

Christopher's anger boiled over. This kind of privilege was the entire target of his revolution. "I'll kill him," he said, only realizing after the words were out that he meant them.

"For what?" she snapped. "Do you think he understands? He sees what I want him to see, and for a moment I saw him as the man who would spare hundreds of peasant girls from cruelty and their men from pain and death. My gratitude was real, for the moment."

"Still," Cannan growled, "it is disrespectful. The wizard must learn his place; he cannot sup at his master's table without an invitation."

"I'm not sure he sees it that way," Lalania said, with a twisted smile.

"Then I will kill him," Cannan answered.

"Only after," Lalania said. "Assuming no one else gets to him first."

Bereft of options, they left her tent with their jealousies intact. Christopher's was the larger, since he was also still jealous of Cannan, which made even less sense. But there it was.

"She is right," Cannan said. "There will be unpleasantness to come. Men will die on our blades. You may even recognize a face or two."

Christopher walked without speaking for a few paces.

"We have killed men before," he reminded the red knight.

"Servants of the Black, criminals one and all." Cannan shook his head. "Soon we will face men whose only crime was feeding their families."

"That was no less true of the ulvenmen," Christopher said. "You don't need to question my resolve. I have learned; I understand now. The faster I kill, the fewer have to die." Like a surgeon who cut off diseased limbs to save the rest of the patient, the sword of a war priest was merciful by virtue of its speed and precision.

They finished the walk back to their tent in silence.

24

NIGHT FIGHT

In the morning he got his bad news from the Skald after all. As Lady Io cornered her son between his horse and her fierce arguments, Uma took Christopher by the arm and led him into the midst of it.

This was a place almost as uncomfortable for him as it was for D'Kan, and the boy was wilting like a shrub in a hundred-year drought. Lady Io turned a truly formidable glare on Christopher, but Uma spoke peremptorily.

"It is worse than you know. Balenar's forces were decimated yesterday, choking the river with their dead."

The druidess drew in a breath, preparing to speak some pithy version of "I told you so," but her advanced rank necessitated a certain amount of wisdom. In the end she stood silently, waiting for the rest of the news, while Christopher bit his lip in dismay.

"In the night," Uma continued, like a glacier inching across the helpless land, "the corpses crawled out of the water, relieved of their flesh and their mortal weaknesses. Arrows do little harm to creatures of bone. Their advance could not be resisted. Farmark Keep stands in flames."

Lady Io shrugged. "The keep is a false lure. The Lord Ranger will have already taken his people into the woods. Those abominations are practically deaf and blind; a child of five can evade them. Meanwhile, the invaders will sleep on beds of nails."

"And yet, my lady, the enemy occupies your lands. They will burn your fields, slaughter your livestock, and children of four or less may not be as safe as you hope."

"All the more reason we must depart at once," the mother said to her son.

"All the more reason he must stay," Uma answered. "The Lord Apostle could cleanse your land with a wave of his hand, were he but there."

"But he is not there," Io replied, with what Christopher felt was quite compelling logic.

"He will never find his way if you take away his guide."

"What use is a guide to a man with no feet?" Lady Io spoke like a bag of daggers upended onto the floor, sharp points flung in every direction. "Your Lord Apostle sits here in the woods, playing with hobgoblins, while the Kingdom devours itself."

"I completely agree," Christopher said. "The sooner you let Ser D'Kan discharge his task, the sooner I can march south."

Uma paused, as if surprised that Christopher had anything useful to add to the conversation.

"Earls and Cardinals flock to you like birds to a grapevine. What need can an Apostle have of one boy's labor?" Lady Io asked.

Christopher looked down at her with a frank expression. "He is going to make me a Saint."

The words hung in the air, pregnant with power.

"You ask much," Lady Io said in a low whisper. "Yet you give little in return. I know you do not promote those who serve you. You would consume the wealth of the world for yourself alone and call this justice?"

"I call it justice," Uma declared. "My Lord Apostle has tamed the spirit of flame and bound it to the hands of common men. The magic is his alone, and so the reward must be also. Those high lords would pick the vine clean and squabble over every grape, leaving nothing but pits for the rest of us; while my lord makes wine for all."

Such an impassioned defense caught Christopher by surprise. He had not realized Uma was on board with the republican part of his revolution, or quite so aware of the revolutionary effect of gunpowder. Of course, the knowledge just marked her out as one of the targets Alaine would have to make "forget," if he failed. He was struck silent by the enormity of it. He had potentially condemned Uma to a doom she knew nothing about. And how many others?

A horn blew in the distance. Istvar's troop, preparing to leave. D'Kan took his bow from its sheath on his horse and handed it to his mother. With deliberate effect, he replaced it with his carbine. The boy swung into the saddle and rode off, without uttering a word.

Lady Io hugged the bow to herself, as if it were a child's teddy bear left behind.

This was the point at which Christopher usually issued an apology of some kind. Instead, he inclined his head in respect and walked away.

Lalania had abandoned him, riding out with Karl so that the bards could have a ready line of communication with the armies in the field. The Skald could contact Christopher directly, if she wanted. Torme was the only one of his command staff left in the camp. Christopher stood behind him, tapping his thumbs together in aggravation, until Torme paused the stream of soldiers that came to ask him for advice, instructions, and orders.

"Is there something I can help you with, Colonel?"

"We should be out there, helping. Collecting tael." Standing around waiting rankled Christopher. The sting of Lady Io's words inflamed his own gnawing guilt.

"It is far too dangerous for you to leave the camp without an escort, and the infantry are too slow to catch hobgoblins on the run. Sir."

Christopher already knew these facts. Torme knew he knew them. Christopher grimaced but stuck to his guns. "Then we need to find some tael we don't have to run to catch."

Torme looked at him carefully. Then he turned his head, to look over his shoulder to where the goblin city squatted in the daylight.

A few minutes later they were riding across the barren field, Cannan and a platoon of infantry marching behind them. Christopher spurred his horse a dozen yards ahead, beckoning to Torme to join him. Cannan watched with careful eyes from astride his mount, but the field was as empty as a beggar's bowl.

"There's something I need to say," Christopher told his fellow priest when they could talk without being overheard.

"To me or the men?" Torme rode a cavalry horse, disciplined and brave, but hardly the equal of Royal, who eyed it sideways in case it got any ideas about pulling ahead.

"The men," Christopher said. "It doesn't really apply to you."

Torme waited patiently, which Christopher found no help at all. Finally he just had to say it.

"The men don't understand. I won't have the power of Saint Krellyan." Not all saints were created equal. Though he would officially gain the title at the eleventh rank, Krellyan had been twelfth, and a priest dedicated to healing. "My reach will still be delimited in days, not years." Nor would he be able to regenerate missing limbs.

"And?" Torme prompted.

"*And* they won't all come back." Christopher tried to speak without bristling. This was no time for Torme to play dumb. "We're all so used to the Saint just raising everybody. The Cardinal and I will be able to revive only five a day, and that's if we're not using other spells. *And* it seems highly likely that our casualties will exceed that pace." Particularly once the high-ranks came to battle. A single moderate level knight could kill a fistful of men before bullets brought him down.

"We are not all used to that," Torme said mildly. "I have served most of my life in an army where the dead stay dead, even if their bodies got up and fought again."

"Okay, I get that," Christopher said, chastised. "But my men don't."

"After you defeat the King, you will have thirteen years to gain sufficient rank to replicate the Saint's power. Your men will trust to that future."

Christopher hadn't thought of it, but it felt dishonest. He was consuming a goblin nation for his next rank. Where would he get the exponentially larger quantities of tael for the two after that?

But then, it was the same problem he already had. He needed to be seventeenth rank to open a gate to Earth that would allow him to go and return. And before he could do that, he would have to sniff out and destroy the hidden enemy that would use that gate to consume Earth.

"That doesn't seem truthful," he said to Torme. "What if I never make it that high?"

Torme looked behind, to where Cannan led the column of men, and spoke softly. "Then Ser Cannan will have served in vain."

He would also need to be seventeenth rank to revive Niona after what Cannan had done to her. Torme's point, of course, was that he wasn't deceiving the men any more than he was deceiving Cannan. And since he'd been doing that for years, what was the point in getting prickly about it now?

Christopher scowled across the dirt field at his fellow priest, but Torme was immune to petty rebuke.

"That's different. I had to make that promise to Cannan to save his life." Nothing less would have convinced the man to live, or the druids to let him.

"Whence the difference, then? For these men are all surely doomed if you fail. The King will hang them for the tael in their heads. To merely speak of rebellion is to justify the profit of the executioner. How much more so, then, for those who actually raise arms against the crown?"

In a world where a skilled craftsman could earn two pounds of gold through a year of labor, or three pounds by simply dying, the economics of criminal justice were, well, criminal.

"I'm never going to revive the enemy," Christopher warned. "Even though you'll probably know some of them."

"No one I knew will expect to be succored by you," Torme answered. "Life under the Gold Throne does not dispose one to presume mercy. And yet: there will be many from other counties who will trust to your good nature to pull them out of the grave after they have forced you to put them there."

Christopher stared at him, half in horror and all in anger.

Torme continued with a shrug. "What is the point of the White, after all, if not to do right by all? You have made war a game. The Greens will oppose you stridently, safe in the assumption that you will forgive them after the fact and heal their injuries to boot."

"But that's absurd. Not the least because—what if I *lose*? If the idiots fighting me actually win, then who do they think will revive their fallen?"

"That thought will not occur to them until their own death is immediately to hand, and then it will be too late."

The world was beginning to thaw. The field had taken on a certain stench, not the least of which was the product of the mass slaughter that had occurred only a few weeks ago. Christopher wrinkled his nose in distaste.

"Such is the folly of men," Torme said. "But it does mean that we cannot follow Major Karl's clever plan. As successful as a war of attrition would be, the cost would be staggering. By the time you convinced the dubious that you were serious, the body count would be so high that your refusal would simply inflame them. Unless your goal is to depopulate the Kingdom, we have little choice but to march arrow-straight to Kingsrock and challenge Treywan on his own terms."

"That strategy does not seem likely to succeed."

Torme smiled blandly at him. "So very little of everything you have ever done seemed likely to succeed. And yet, here we are."

They were indeed here, at the gates of the city. Their conversation had to stop while the men milled around them and the gate slowly opened.

The city stank almost as badly as the field, though with an entirely different kind of odor. Christopher was happy enough to meet the Eldest at the edge of the clearing around the keep, a hundred feet before they would have to cross the odiferous moat.

She bowed low and spoke in the human tongue. "How may I serve you today, most puissant lord?"

He didn't feel right talking down to her from horseback. But then, he'd come out here to browbeat her into surrendering treasure. That was never going to feel right.

"The hobgoblins are mostly reduced," he said. "The ulvenmen will continue to hunt them, so you shouldn't have any trouble, as long as you stay within your walls."

He was going to continue, but she interrupted him.

"Speaking of which: while our fields may suffice to feed us—just barely—we still have need of the forest. You must allow us access, or provide us with sufficient wood to feed our fires and sustain our industry."

It was impressive. He had threatened her with the pain of future visits, and now she was making him sorry he'd come out to see her.

"I'll set up some kind of boundary marker outside the walls. Your people will stay inside of it to cut wood, and only in small groups at a time. Again, if you overcut your timber, you'll have to do without."

"As you command, oh soul of generosity."

He decided he was glad he was still on the horse.

"I'll be marching south soon. The more tael you give me, the sooner I will go."

"And leave us to the mercy and restraint of your rabid wolves? I think I would prefer that you stay, then. Surely we can prove to you that we are more worthy of your sky-fire secrets than they are."

She was definitely winning this engagement. He gave up on subtlety and went for directness.

"I came out here to collect tael. Give me what you've raised so far."

"Of course," the Eldest said. "As luck would have it, we have just made a culling. The proceeds should be arriving now."

Out of the mouth of the castle came a procession of goblins in pairs, each pair carrying a sheet-covered stretcher on their shoulders. What lay under the sheets could not be mistaken.

Christopher glared down at the Eldest.

"As you noted," she explained, "we must maintain a limit on our population. These individuals were judged not worth their keep. But all is not lost. Their bodies go to fertilize the fields. Their flesh will rejoin the goblin race, albeit in somewhat altered form."

She bared her teeth at him. "And you also shall profit, for their souls will serve you until the gods see fit to set them free."

As the parade passed by, the lead pair stopped to hand a ball of tael to the Eldest. During the transfer, they mishandled their stretcher and dropped the corpse onto the ground. It rolled out from under the sheet and stared up at them with sightless eyes, a third hole drilled neatly into its forehead. Christopher could hardly tell one goblin from another, but the identity of this one could be deduced from simple malice. Liang Chia, their erstwhile guide, murdered solely to provoke him.

"That wasn't necessary," he said with a sigh. He had borne the creature no ill will, but neither could he pretend he would do anything about it.

"It was in my estimation," she answered. "And since any error of judgment on my part will likely result in the death of my people, I am disinclined to mercy or rebuke."

"Provoking me can also be an error of judgment."

"How? Should you lash out at me in cruel rage or petty vengeance, your patron would cast you out. And how much would the Emperor reward me for depriving the enemy of a Saint?"

He glared at her. "I thought we were talking about what is best for your people."

"What is good for the Emperor is good for the goblins. Our service to him is rewarded, both here and in the Tiered City. I have no doubts that my place will be high. Indeed, I would go there now, but I hope yet to gain a few floors before I leave this plane of tears."

Torme seemed to think it would be helpful to change the topic. "Haven't the fields been fertilized enough?"

"True," she conceded. "But your lord will not allow us to put these corpses to work, so ash and soil is the best we can do with them. Unless you want to reduce us to cannibalism."

"Well, this has been helpful," Christopher said. "I was feeling conflicted. Now I'm ready to kill something. Anything, really. Anything at all."

She laughed at him, her fangs bared and her head tilted back. "I live to serve, my lord," she said, through gasps of amusement.

Gathering his paltry treasure and shredded dignity, he rode back to camp in silence. The odd thing was, he really was refreshed. The price of obdurate stupidity was death; this was an iron law of the universe. He was merely the cutting edge of that law. As bad as that was, it was better than being on the other side of the equation.

25

FURTHER DEVELOPMENTS

His various cavalry forces did not return that night, or the next. They were bivouacking in the field, pushing to the edges of goblin territory. Consequently he spent the days twiddling his thumbs. It was hard to sit and do nothing while other people were killing or perhaps dying on his account. On the other hand, it wasn't as hard as doing it himself, so he tried to keep his impatience in check.

Istvar finally returned after dark, three days after riding out. He brought Uma with him, and therefore, of course, more bad news.

"Ser Morrison, the King's Captain of Foot, has been rewarded for his loyalty with a county," she told him. "Specifically, the county of Copperton. He marched in yesterday with a detachment of crossbowmen and claimed the town. There was no one to oppose him."

The Earl watched Christopher with apprehension, perhaps worried about how he would take the news.

"That's good," Christopher said. "Morrison can hold it together until we take it back."

"Ser Morrison is not the only one rewarded, though the other appointment is far less public. It seems that Master Sigrath has gained a rank. Or possibly two."

Christopher shrugged.

Torme, perhaps thinking Christopher had forgotten who that was, which was not at all an unlikely assumption, offered an explanation. "Treywan's wizard."

Istvar shook his head, concerned that Christopher wasn't concerned enough. "They work some new magic against you."

"Treywan?" Uma queried.

"There seems little point in using an honorific that we no longer recognize," Torme replied.

"That might be getting ahead of ourselves," Uma said. "And yet this will take us a step closer." She produced another fist-size lump of tael and handed it to Christopher.

He took it and consumed it greedily, while they watched in fascination tinged with disapproval. It was a crass act to do in front of others, especially considering it would have bought any of them a rank or two.

"Where's Karl?" he demanded.

"The Major's horse are lighter than mine," Istvar said. "He ranged faster and further afield, though I believe him to be only a few hours behind me now."

"Was he as successful as you?"

"Assuredly," Istvar answered, his eyes narrowing slightly.

Christopher smiled grimly at them. "Then tomorrow we will work some new magic of our own."

Istvar drew himself up to stand even more erect than normal. "I understand," he said. "My men will be ready to march in the morning." The Earl snapped out a salute, impressive for its precision above and beyond the fact he'd only learned how to do it three days ago, and marched away.

"I am so sick of waiting," Christopher said to Uma, and then sat down to wait for Karl.

The sun rose on chaos, the fort a buzzing hive of activity. Men hurried to and fro, all the more remarkable given how they had lounged around for the previous weeks.

Karl had returned in the middle of the night, as rich as expected, and Christopher had finally gone to bed with strange dreams. Now his army roused itself around him, while he tried to stay out of Torme's way.

"You march early," Uma said to him privately. "Your rank cannot have manifested yet."

"It will tonight. What difference does it make?"

"You will be on the road, and thus exposed, before your powers are fully realized. This is an inflection point. If Treywan intended to strike at you in the field, it would be now. Should you not fortify until it is too late to interrupt the process?"

"How would Treywan even know?"

The bard shrugged. "I assume he has spies in your camp. In addition, of course, to the scrying talents of both Sigrath and the Gold Apostle."

Christopher shook his head. "The man is a coward by nature. He won't strike me here, or anywhere. He'll hide behind stone walls and hope a dragon eats me."

She bit her lip in professional judgment. "Too obvious. You're acting like a person pretending not to know they're being overheard, instead of acting like a person who doesn't know they're being overheard."

"Are we being overheard?"

She made a ring out of her finger and thumb and peered around critically. "Not at the moment. Still, my first-years can do better than that. For a man of your rank, it should be trivial."

Acting was uncomfortably close to lying. For that matter, so was diplomacy. The only saving grace was that strategy was defined by lying; deception was truly the art of war. Therefore he could engage in strategic misdirection without any qualms of conscience.

"As long as we are clear," she continued, "please reassure me that you have a plan for extracting Treywan from his castle that does not rely on your dramatic abilities."

"I do," he answered, and said no more.

After a moment of silence, Uma frowned at him. "You know Lala will just tell me later, right?"

"I do," he said again. Forcing Uma and the Skald to rely on Lalania was a boon, in his book. He wasn't particularly concerned with what it was in their books.

"Men," Uma grunted, in a rare lapse of poise. She immediately took herself elsewhere, which, again, suited Christopher just fine. The woman was prickly, provocative, and literally bad news.

Perhaps in reaction to his defiance, the College relayed their next bit of information through Lalania. It took until the middle of the day to get his army out of the gate. While he was fretting over the delay, she came to him with a smile.

"We have some reports of engagements in Samerhaven. The wizard has made good on his word. His men have been escorting wagons of refugees for days. This morning the brigands finally got tired of squabbling over the scraps, and a few of them made a lunge for a wagonload of women, only to receive a face-full of fire. They left behind at least a dozen dead, one of whom was a knight. Much cursing can be heard in the camps of Longwelt and Donfeld on the topic of wizards and magic."

"I don't get the credit?"

"Not yet. Which is to our benefit; better to let that coin drop at the right time. For now they assume the wizard has armed a few troops with wands. They will not expect all of his men to be equally dangerous."

They would make the same mistake Gregor had made, way back at the beginning. But Christopher was distracted by a new worry.

"He's not just taking the young women, is he?" That was exactly the sort of thing he would expect from a man with the wizard's attitudes.

"Oh, Christopher," Lalania said with a sigh. "Of course not. For all his faults, the wizard thinks with the head on his shoulders. The wagon was full of old women, not that the idiots who attacked guessed that.

Everywhere his men offer horses and seats to the eldest first, solicitous of their age and dignity."

Christopher sucked on his lip. Perhaps he had misjudged the man.

Lalania looked at him and rolled her eyes. "Some of them will no doubt expire of natural causes in the next few days or weeks. The wizard wants to make sure that happens on his land, so he gets the tael."

His judgment had merely been going in the wrong direction.

"Still," she said to his frown, "he does as we asked. The people are spared, though they may not feel so thankful once summer starts in earnest. The mosquitos, at least, will be happy."

Christopher didn't allow himself to be happy until he rode out from the fort, behind his long column of guns and wagons. Istvar's men rode with him, their destriers ambling along with the draft horses. Royal had been wildly excited, issuing challenges left and right. Normally he and Balance were the only warhorses in the camp, and now there were scores of them. The knights spent a fair amount of time keeping their stallions from starting fights, which presumably left them little time to pick fights of their own. Despite the color they wore, they still made a living at the point of a sword, and the law of the land did not allow Istvar to outlaw dueling. Here in the Wild they could count on common sense to keep the nobility together, but once back in the Kingdom it would require careful leadership to keep all their lances pointing in the right direction.

Christopher had an easier time of it, as his men were commoners. Not only was he allowed to forbid them private duels, they also tended to resolve their differences with fists instead of weapons. And more: they took their cue from Karl, and Karl was a model of obedience. The formal codes of honor that Christopher found so restricting were there to keep the knights from killing each other when in large groups. Christopher's army replaced those codes with a code of subservience, which was only possible for commoners, and ironically the exact opposite of what he was fighting for.

And yet, his army would easily beat Istvar's in any fair engagement. It was a paradox he was unwilling to engage at the moment. The immediate effect was that he could leave Karl's cavalry behind to recover for a day or two, and then let them catch up to the column on the march.

He had to say goodbye to Kalani, who did not seem sorry to see him go.

"Your boundary markers are making my task harder," she told him. "It would have been better to force the goblins to buy wood over the wall."

That would have been a terrible solution. The ulvenmen were the least reliable workforce he could imagine. They might get bored with woodcutting and leave the goblins to freeze, regardless of what inducement was offered. Christopher didn't want to argue with her, though.

Torme did. "If we were interested in better, we would be taking goblin and ulvenmen troops with us. That we are in the fight of our lives and yet leave weapons lying on the ground should astound you."

"I am grateful for your forbearance," Kalani said, though the gratitude was not entirely obvious. Nor should it be. Torme's threat was empty. Leading an army of nonhumans into the Kingdom would turn every sword against him, and never mind the difficulty of keeping the goblins and the ulvenmen from killing each other. "But mostly I am grateful for the forest," she continued, and now the emotion was genuine. "The ulvenmen are actually joyful sometimes. You cannot imagine what it is like to see them rolling in the snow, simply playing for once. And for my part, I do not miss that blasted swamp one little bit either."

"Guard our lord's domain well," Torme told her. "Do not burden us with troubles, lest it cause us to stumble and fall."

"And if you fall, through no fault of ours?" she demanded. "What then of us?"

"If I die," Christopher said, "you're on your own. Do whatever is best for you and the ulvenmen."

"Will the Kingdom send more soldiers against us?"

"I don't know," he said honestly. "I mean, there was a goblin kingdom here for years and they never invaded. I don't know why that would change now."

"Both the goblins and ulvenmen had strong leadership for all those years," Kalani pointed out. "They do not now. You have lopped off the heads of their states and made them dependent on your sword for protection. It would be a moral crime to die and leave them defenseless."

Apparently the morality of the act bothered her more than the dying part.

Torme, ever his stalwart defender, spoke for him. "We know our duty. See to it that you know yours."

She did not seem to take offense at that, but with elves it was always hard to know. The most hostile reaction he had ever gotten out of one was by saying "Thank you." They rode away in ambiguous silence, until Christopher finally quirked an eyebrow at Torme.

"Ser Gregor has the right of it," Torme said. "Every moment in an elf's company feels like a rebuke, for acts I have not done or even thought of doing."

"I don't find them quite that bad," Christopher mused.

Torme took a deep breath. "To be fair, my lord, sometimes your presence has a tinge of that as well."

To his stricken look, Torme tried to explain. "It is just that at times you seem to expect us to reach conclusions that are not only unobvious, but nigh invisible."

That made a kind of sense. Christopher was operating off of a profundity of facts that no one else had. He might be clueless about feudal politics or how to shoe a horse, but he had a wealth of common knowledge to draw on. Understanding the message spell, for instance, was for him simply realizing that a few people had cell phones that worked a few minutes a day. He already understood what long-distance communication meant and how it would affect the wider world. He didn't need to revise the assumptions of a lifetime spent where information traveled by foot or hoof.

Which implied, to the extent he found the elves insufferable, they knew something he didn't.

"Fair enough," he said to Torme. "You know I don't mean anything by it. It's just that I grew up in a . . . different place. So some things are obvious to me, and others aren't."

"I know astonishing little about where you grew up," Torme said, "and, judging by how carefully the bard has avoided learning anything about it, I don't want to know. If it please you, my lord, I would prefer to stew about elves in blissful ignorance."

Christopher grinned in sympathy. After all, he wasn't entirely sure he wanted to know whatever the elves were hiding from him. Alaine's track record of happy surprises was nonexistent.

The pleasure of not knowing survived the night and halfway through the next week. Then he stood at a crossroads, with his companions looking to him for answers.

"If we angle east, we can pass through Istvar and collect my infantry and perhaps turn neighboring Tomestaad to our cause," the Earl of Istvar offered.

"South takes us to Romsdaal, and from there to Kingsrock," Torme announced.

"West will bring us to county Camara, which is friendly to the White, a good base to recapture Copperton from, and closest to defend Knockford," Karl said.

"You may find a battle in Romsdaal," Istvar warned. "Count Armand will hold his vows as seriously as I held mine."

"Yet we need not ride to Tomestaad to turn it," Lalania countered. "We can trust the College to deliver that ally."

Karl didn't argue his point. He never did.

Uma was silent, which made Christopher feel a little guilty. On the other hand, having a strategy meeting from horseback in the snow with a dozen people was enough of a pain in the ass that it trumped any other considerations.

It didn't matter, anyway. The decision was already made.

"South. We'll pass Romsdaal town by if we can." They had been good to him, once. He would spare them as much as he could.

Mostly it pained him because it was the obvious route. He would have liked to at least make a head-fake in some other direction, but there was no point. He could not hide an entire army from scrying. The enemy would know where he was going long before he got there. Half of all tactical doctrine on Earth was useless here.

The southern route had one more advantage: it was already mapped. It was the way they had come in the first place. Several wagon trains had already cut through this country, and hence they made good time.

Late the next day they rode down a muddy wagon track, at the end of which they could see the walls of Romsdaal town. They had not stopped at any of the villages, nor had anyone hailed them. The villagers watched them from inside their cottages, though whether that was from caution or the cold was undetermined.

The town, however, was not willing to be ignored. The gates opened at their approach and a man on horseback rode out, in shining blue armor. That his shield was slung on his saddle was their only clue to his peaceful intentions.

Christopher and Istvar rode forward to meet him.

"My cousin," said Istvar, when they were close enough to recognize faces. He galloped ahead and met the man on the road. They clasped arms for a moment, no mean feat when mounted on fractious destriers, and then Istvar returned to Christopher's flank.

"Be at peace, my lord Prophet," the new man declared. "I come not to offer you violence but alliance, if you will have it."

Well, this was easier than Christopher had hoped.

"Yes, of course," he said quickly, before the man could change his mind.

Istvar was not so easily diverted. "Count Armand, though I welcome you like a brother, still I must ask: what of your vows?"

Armand turned his head and spat on the ground. That was enough for Christopher, but apparently the man had more to say. "The King has released us, though no doubt his purple-tongued rat would dispute it. Yet actions speak louder than words."

"What do you mean?" Istvar asked. A fair enough question, given the price Istvar had paid to slip out of his vow.

"Do you not know? My apologies, then. I assumed the wench would keep you better informed. The Vicar of Cannenberry is dead."

Christopher sat up straight. This was ill news indeed. The Vicar had been wise, funny, and a fantastic dinner host.

"He alone responded to the King's command for the clergy of the White to surrender themselves. Yet his trust was not rewarded. The King put him to question at the hands of the torturers."

"That is not strictly illegal," Istvar said.

Christopher boggled at him. The niceties of oath-keeping seemed arcane beyond understanding.

"Ah, but cold-blooded murder is. The Vicar died with the first treatment."

"How so?" Istvar demanded, and Christopher wondered as well. The Vicar, despite being old and frail, had been sixth rank. Tossing him out of a sixth-floor window would have merely annoyed him. What kind of torture could inflict more damage than that and not be meant as execution?

"The torturers assumed the Vicar's rank. Yet he had no tael; his death yielded only the soul of a commoner. A moment on the rack was enough to slay him. By the time they realized he was not faking his distress, he was gone."

Istvar's face twisted into grim triumph. He turned to Christopher in admiration. "For a faith that cannot lie, the White has dissembled more than an army of goblins."

"I don't understand," Christopher said helplessly, and looked back longingly to the rest of the column, where Lalania waited.

"The Vicar atoned," Armand explained. "He surrendered all of his ranks voluntarily, before he answered the King's summons. This was an act of supreme self-sacrifice, for the greater good. His tael still serves the White, albeit reduced. Yet he still held the title of Vicar of Cannenberry, until the Cardinal could confirm his successor. Meanwhile he obeyed the law in every jot and tittle, and the King, through careless malfeasance, did not."

"I didn't even know that was possible," Christopher confessed.

"No doubt the King made the same poor assumption, with the Saint gone." Armand all but chuckled. "Yet obviously the Vicar had a scroll squirreled away, penned by Saint Krellyan in better days. Now county Cannenberry stands safe from rapine and pillage, for its lord has obeyed all law, yet the King has lost his shield by breaking the law."

"A good man is dead," Christopher said, remembering the pleasure of the last time he had sat at the Vicar's table, and the wisdom that he had seen on display there.

"His death was bought at great price," Istvar declared. "He has single-handedly done more for your cause than anyone else in the Kingdom. Before this is over, more good men will die. They can only hope for such glory."

"Why didn't he tell them he wasn't ranked anymore?" Christopher asked, mostly out of despair.

Istvar answered, still smiling in grim admiration. "I suppose, because they did not ask."

26

WALKING ON SUNSHINE

They camped under the walls of a friendly town. Many of Christopher's men had passed through here multiple times, escorting wagons of supplies, and Istvar's men were cousins and brothers. Some of the knights that had ridden in with him had come from Armand's court. They had a little ceremony where they left his army and rejoined Armand's. Until that moment they would have fought against their lord at Istvar's command.

And these were the good guys.

This was why Christopher had to press on to Kingsrock with all haste. He could not bear to kill men who would gladly side with him if only they thought they had a choice. Yet necessity brooked no master. His army had marched hard and fast for several days. They would not rouse tomorrow unless he took spurs to them.

Kingsrock was two more long days of marching, assuming their advance was uncontested. That seemed unlikely. There was a forest just north of Kingsrock that would be perfect for a little ambush. The King's hundred knights could lay in wait, close enough that their unnatural vitality would let them wreak havoc before the rifles brought them down.

They would all die, of course, but they would sell themselves dearly. The goblin knights would not have hesitated to make such an exchange. Human beings might be more circumspect, but there was Torme's lecture to consider. These men might expect to be raised, either by the Gold Apostle or Christopher. They might well commit themselves to a suicidal attack.

Christopher fretted about the possibility through a terribly late breakfast the next morning, while his commanders shrugged it off. It would not change the course of the final battle. After the loss of so many troops, his siege would be weakened; yet without those knights the King could never drive him from the field. Everyone assumed this was all just prelude to a duel between principals, anyway.

Since he was still uncertain he could beat the King in single combat, Christopher was looking for another ending. A siege sounded promising. Assuming no army came to break the siege, time was on his side. The forges of Knockford continued to churn out new weapons. If nothing else, the supply of riflemen would grow.

Looking for a distraction, he decided to needle Uma about the information he had gained without her help. As usual, it was an ill-advised course.

Uma sniffed and looked at him sideways. "Perhaps you will allow us to act in the manner to which we are accustomed in the future. You cannot disrupt our lines of communication and then complain that we are tardy."

For once Lalania stood up to her. "Oh, give it a rest. The Skald didn't tell us because she didn't need to. She could see Count Armand would. She has other commitments for her time, agents who need her advice to escape detection and capture."

"You said something about agents missing their reporting," Christopher recalled. "If somebody dies on my behalf, shouldn't I revive them?"

"If it comes to that, I am sure we will let you know," Lalania said.

Uma put her hand to her mouth, appearing to be shocked. Christopher glared at her theatrics, until Lalania clutched him by the arm. He turned to her, but she was watching Uma with the same look in her eyes.

"My lord," Uma said, sounding as close to contrite as he had ever heard her. "We have been deceived. The Gold Throne sent a small contingent to Cannenberry; we thought naught of it. But Curate Joadan has raised a secret army of mercenaries and stolen a march on us. They have commandeered river barges; they drive them by magic; the Earl of Fram sits in his castle, too far away to intervene. Joadan's forces will be in Knockford by noon."

He leapt to his feet. Around him men stopped what they were doing and stared, like a colony of meerkats looking to a sentinel of danger. It was to no purpose. There was no possibility his army could get out of Romsdaal by nightfall, let alone travel three counties away.

"We have defenses there," Lalania said, trying to put on a brave face. "The militia."

"Knockford is the heart of my army," Christopher answered her. "In more ways than I have told you." Dereth, the smith in charge of his cannon foundry, had needed weeks the last time they had exchanged letters. Christopher could only hope that was down to days. Not that it would matter if the town was destroyed.

"Your secret project." Lalania shook her head. "You need not have bothered. No one would understand the import even if you told them what you were doing."

He paused. "Really? Casting a pair of huge cannon isn't obvious?"

She shrugged. "You have lots of cannons. No one knows why it matters what size they are."

"It matters," he said. Those two guns would not turn a field battle, but that was not what they were for. The walls of Kingsrock were far more impressive than the goblin city. It would require more impressive artillery to defeat them.

A pair of eight-inch Parrott Rifles qualified, an upgrade from the designs he had sketched last year, as Dereth's skill had grown faster than he had dared hope. First deployed during the American Civil War, they were true advances in the field of artillery. They would strike at Kingsrock from a distance of a mile, with an accuracy of a dozen feet. Given scrying as a targeting system, he intended not to just destroy the walls but to actively search out the King and drop explosions on his head. An indirect assault like that probably wouldn't kill the man, but it might well force him to come out and face Christopher. If nothing else, the people around the King would start avoiding him, or the King would spend all of his time hiding underground. Either outcome could only help Christopher.

There were more pertinent issues, though.

"Without powder from Knockford, the guns go silent."

"They cannot have sent too many forces," Lalania said. "Cannenberry only became open to them a few days ago."

"I fear you underestimate the zeal of their commander," Uma said. "He drove through the Undaals with a whip and a sack of gold, gathering every manner of scum in his grasp. Also, knights under a gold banner broke off the north road to Kingsrock and crossed the river yesterday. We must presume they are on the barges too."

"Saddle my horse," Christopher ordered. Two men ran to obey.

Lalania looked up at him with concern. "Even under an endurance spell, Royal cannot travel sixty miles in an hour."

Uma sided with her. "Nor can you fly that fast. Your flight spell will get you there hours after the battle has been joined, possibly after it has been decided, and with no possibility of retreat."

"I'm not flying, exactly." He had learned since he first learned magic. The runes of the spells told him more than just their names now. "I have a new spell."

Lalania reached out from her seat to clasp his hand. "Take me with you, if you can. Of all those here who can turn a battle, yet be spared from this army, I am your best choice."

He grinned at her, because it was true. Not just because of the power of the Lyre of Varelous, but because of the power of her music. She could put heart into ordinary men, to make them stand where they might have run, to fight bravely where they might have cowered. No one in the Kingdom had ever thought much of that power, because no one had ever thought much of the fighting ability of common men.

Pulling her to her feet, he strode out of the mess tent, men scattering in his wake. His commanders met him at his horse.

"Nothing has changed," he told them. "Follow the plan. I'll see you at the foot of Kingsrock or not at all."

"Yes, sir," they chorused. Then they all glared at Lalania, out of jealousy.

Only Karl's stare truly bothered Christopher. Beyond Knockford lay the village of Burseberry, defenseless if the town fell. Karl had a wife and child now, a little infant boy that meant more than the world to him.

"I won't let anything happen to them," he promised Karl. "But I need you here." Of all the people in the army, Karl was the one he could not lose. Only the two of them could be trusted with an army of commoners at the moment, though Gregor was making great strides at understanding.

Cannan was also hard to ignore. "You cannot ride into danger without me," the big man said.

"I don't have the power to take you, too," Christopher answered him. "And I wouldn't, if I could. They don't scry me directly anymore; my rank makes that too hard. Instead, they scry you."

The red knight looked stricken at this betrayal of his mission.

"No, it's okay," Christopher said. "As long as they find you here, they'll assume I'm nearby."

He swung onto his horse and pulled Lalania up behind him.

"Don't worry," he told them all. "Once the King realizes I can do this, he'll wait for us. He'll understand I can flee any encounter as easily as I rush to this one. Kingsrock is the one place neither of us can run from."

"Do what?" Gregor asked.

In answer Christopher grinned and spoke the words of his spell. Wind whistled through the camp. Where it touched him, Lalania, and Royal, it turned them misty white and as insubstantial as a cloud.

The watching crowd leapt back in shock, even his battle-hardened commanders, even Uma the spell-wise, even Karl the impervious.

Then they were entirely of cloud stuff, and the wind snatched them from the ground and hurtled them through the air.

The horse exulted in the experience, breathing clouds of steam and lunging forward. Christopher had forgotten what true speed was. Nothing here went faster than a horse could run, and now he was riding a Jet Ski of wisps and foam. Lalania clung to him, laughing, her grasp insubstantial and yet comfortingly possessive.

This was a spell no one else in the Kingdom could use. Christopher now outranked every spell caster the Kingdom had ever seen, save Krellyan; and the Saint's service to the goddess of healing had denied him these ancillary effects of his high rank.

"What else can you do?" Lalania shouted into his ear, her voice like the whistle of a sharp wind.

"I can call up a satnav map." His laughter boomed like distant thunder. "I can cure genetic abnormalities." He had been wrong about the specific spell to heal Joadan's son, but still right that at the time only the Saint could do it. "I can give life to furniture, for a short while." Awesome, if he ever wanted to recreate the dance number from *Beauty and the Beast*. "And some more ways to kill people." Those were the most useless, to his mind. He already had lots of ways to kill people.

"I don't know what satnav or genetic mean," she called back.

"It doesn't matter," he shouted. "This is the best. This is the only spell that changes things."

The freedom of the Kingdom was now his. The King could fly, but Christopher could fly faster. The two of them could play tag across the sky all week long, and Christopher would always win.

The horse charged through a flock of starlings. The birds passed through Christopher and Lalania with gentle bumps, leaving all parties unharmed, though the starlings screeched in outrage at this trespass on their domain and person.

They cruised over the countryside at tree-top level, for no better reason than it was fun. The closer to the ground, the more sense of speed, and if they struck the occasional branch or leaf, it did not matter. They could pass unharmed through anything that would not harm a cloud.

After a while, though, the road turned due south. Christopher directed the horse higher and left the safe path. Looking at the unbroken carpet of trees, he decided that satnav map would come in handy. The Kingdom was not exactly swimming in landmarks, and he didn't even have a compass. He discovered he couldn't cast spells in this form.

"Hang on," he said and steered Royal down.

Once on the ground, they rematerialized. Christopher got off to cast the new spell, fiddling with the invisible controls. Lalania lounged around, plucking at her lyre, as bored as any girl waiting on her beau to fix his motorbike.

Then they were back in the air and zooming along, an intangible arrow telling him which way to steer. The ground sped by underneath them, but after he startled a flock of sheep he decided to gain some altitude and spare the livestock.

"Gods, what a view," Lalania sang in his ear. "I could get used to this. How long does it last?"

Given his rank and his service to a god of Travel, the answer was perhaps not surprising. "I can keep it up all day."

She hugged him, as hard as their foamy substance allowed. "Why stop? At this speed we could leave it all behind, fly so far before we have to rest that even those cursed Rangers couldn't find us. Then get up in the morning and do it again. We could see the world, Christopher. Not just this stupid little kingdom in this stupid little corner of nowhere."

Everything about that proposition was tempting. Except for the part where he strongly suspected that the rest of the world was just a different set of monsters looking for dinner. He squeezed her hand in sympathy. But already he could see the spire of the church at Knockford. As they closed he saw a dozen horsemen in the field, making a mad dash for the gate. The guards were alert, something he hadn't expected from the soft Church police, and got the gate closed in time. Threats and jeers were exchanged, and then one of the horsemen brought out a crossbow.

So a soldier shot him dead, and the rest ran off to join the horde already darkening the horizon. No more fun and games.

Christopher forced his horse to the street. Men and women cried out at the novelty of a cloud descending, and then shrieked when they saw his ghostly face. Pulling Royal to a halt in front of the church doors, they finished solidifying and slid to the ground. Royal's legs went back to mist and Christopher had to tug on his reins to make him whole again. The horse snorted in disappointment.

"My lord," stammered a white-faced priestess from the doorway.

"Where's the Vicar?" he demanded.

The girl spread her hands in dismay. "Which one?"

What did that mean? "Rana," he said, annoyed.

The girl pointed mutely into the church, and he marched off at double time, Lalania on his heels.

As he climbed the stairs to Rana's office, he felt a tickle in his brain. Her voice filled his mind as he reached for her door handle.

"We are under assault by the Gold Throne. We will hold them off as long as we can, but my town is not a fortress."

"I know," he said, opening the door. "I'm here to help."

Vicar Rana dropped the flaming remains of a scroll. "What trick is this?" she cried, leaping out of her chair and backing up against the wall.

"You just called me," Christopher answered, spreading his hands in a calming motion. "I was already on the way."

She stared at him.

Lalania intervened. "What were her exact words to you?"

Christopher repeated them, and Rana sagged in relief. "Then it must be truly you, if you heard my message."

He had a thought. "Couldn't I have read your mind as you were sending the message?"

Rana laughed weakly. "Only you would argue against your own case. Save your ruminations for later; the enemy is at our door."

"I know," he repeated. "That's why I'm here. Joadan is out there somewhere, with three score of knights and hundreds of mercenaries."

Rana sat down and slumped in her chair. "So little? And yet enough. Then the fault is mine. I should not have played at war like some lordling."

He leaned forward and planted his hands on her desk. "Explain. Quickly."

"I sent the other Vicars and their police to Fram. Sprier and Parnar sent us aid, unasked; I sent them on to Fram as well. The Earl had declared for us, and I despaired of leaving him to fight alone and without healing. I assumed that the enemy must come down the road from Kingsrock, and Fram is squarely in the way. Yet had I kept them all here, I would have kept my town safe."

"I don't think so," Christopher argued. "He would have just brought more. They must know the disposition of your forces. They have more scrying power than we do."

"How is that?" Rana asked. "Do you not have the Cardinal, as well as yourself?"

"Well, yes," he said, squirming with the answer. "But we've been busy." The scrying spell occupied the same rank as the revival spell. He had not yet had a day where he did not have a corpse to raise. He'd left the army with half a dozen for Faren to finish.

On the other hand, the intelligence gained from the spell might well have saved a hundred future corpses. If Rana had acted out of sentimentality, so had he.

Rana eyed him critically. "Why would a mere Curate ride against a Vicar?"

Never mind that Joadan served a god of War and Rana a goddess of Healing. Even a single rank's difference justified the question. "Hmph. He must have a trick up his sleeve." Joadan always did.

"And what trick have you placed up my sleeve in response? A strumpet and a single sword?" Rana flicked at his hands, forcing him to lean away from her desk and stop looming over her.

"A Minstrel and a Saint," he answered.

For the second time in as many minutes, and only for the third time in his experience, Vicar Rana displayed an unfiltered emotion, clasping her penitent hands together in contrition. "Truly? The gods be praised in the our hour of need."

"I'm not as good a saint as Krellyan," he had to qualify. "But I am prepared to send Joadan packing with his tail between his legs."

"Then get thee down to the gate. My son and your digger are marshalling their forces; the strength of your militia will be tried and tested today. I shall don my armor and follow you, but I think healing is the best I can offer to this battle."

Back again they tromped through the halls.

"You're ever so handsome when you're playing the hero," Lalania whispered in his ear.

"Knock it off," he growled back, and the girl they had passed on the way in dropped a pile of papers.

"I'm sorry, my lord," she squeaked.

"Not you," he said. "Never mind. As you were. Carry on." By then he'd gotten out of the doors and into the street.

Johm, master of his engineering works, was there at the head of a column of men with rifles. There was something different about them, and then Christopher recognized it: they were adults. Not the teenagers of his army. Nonetheless, every one of them had served in a draft when they were young. They would not crack like runny eggs just because of a little violence.

"My lord," Johm said, with immense relief.

"Whatever your battle plan was, stick to it," Christopher told him. "I'm going to lounge around, out of sight, until Joadan shows himself. Then I'm going to spank him hard."

"Curate Joadan? Back again despite your express orders? I would pray you do more than spank him, my lord." Johm was already gone, leading his men in a double-march toward the gates before Christopher could reply.

Christopher pulled a man out of the tail end of the column.

"Dereth. What is the status of our little project?"

"All but done, my lord. Just some touch-up with the grindstone to go."

Christopher took the man's rifle away and handed it to Lalania. "Get back and finish. I need you there more than I need you here."

The smith looked dubious, but after a glance at Christopher's face he went.

Next to come down the street was Tom and his platoon.

"Colonel," the young man said, his face bubbling over with a joyful smile.

Half a dozen of Tom's men carried satchels. They were all younger men, with powerful arms.

"Dynamite bombs?" Christopher asked.

"Indeed," Tom said. "For some time now we have all set a bit by for the future, uncertain as it was certain to be. There are three hundred rifles in town, a dozen carbines, and eight cannon sequestered in various nooks and crannies where a visitor might not think to look."

As if to confirm his claim, fire and smoke belched from the church steeple. Somebody had put a two inch gun up there. Christopher laughed; he never would have thought to put artillery in such an exposed position. But what could shoot back? Most spells would not reach from the town walls to the church. Firearms were not only cheaper than magic, they were longer range.

The cannon shot appeared to be a general signal. Gunfire broke out all over town. Tom and his men broke ranks and raced for the wall.

Christopher started casting spells. These days he put up a long-lasting weapon blessing and the energy absorption field as basic precautions.

"My lord." Another one of his people, this time a woman. Fae was dressed to great effect, attractive as always in a tight dress of purple so dark as to be almost black. She walked alone, and yet he knew she represented more firepower than half of Tom's people.

"You look well," he said.

She didn't, actually. She looked a bit green. But he hadn't wanted to say she looked pretty. Best not to encourage her that way.

"I have come to put myself in service of our defense. Though if you are here, perhaps you do not wish me to expose myself to danger." She had a newborn child at home, he knew.

"I don't, actually." She was too important to his industry. "But it might be necessary."

Lalania stepped forward. "There is an alternative. Let me use the wand in your stead. I do not question your courage, Mistress Fae, but I have been on many battlefields, and you have been on none."

Fae was clearly torn. Fear for her personal safety warred with greed, but in the end Fae was a rational person, as all wizards must be if they planned to live very long. Out of her sleeve, she produced a thin stick with a ruby on the end and handed it to Lalania. Stepping in, she whispered the password in the blonde's ear, so close her lips brushed Lalania's ear.

Christopher found himself looking the other way. It was not the sort of image he wanted in his head.

Then she fled back to the relative safety of her shop.

"You can't keep that," Christopher said, to Lalania's triumphant smile. "You're just borrowing it."

"Of course," Lalania said. "I know that."

Her smirk said otherwise, but he didn't have time to argue. "Be careful. They'll have some kind of counterstrike. I don't want to have to revive you."

"You be careful," she shot back. "You may feel like a demigod, but there are sixty lances out there. Any one of them could pin you to the ground, and then the rest would turn you into a pincushion."

He might be superhuman, but shove enough inch-thick poles through his internal organs and he'd die just like anyone else. Probably three or four would suffice.

Screams rose above the din of battle, impressive considering all the gunfire. Christopher took that as a signal that Curate Joadan had unveiled whatever surprise he thought would win him this battle. He went to see what it was.

27

CIRCLE OF RESOLUTION

Christopher stood on the wall and gawked. For a moment he was convinced that Joadan had attacked them with Volkswagen Beetles. Half a dozen rounded, humped creatures of about that size were battering at the wall. Panicked riflemen poured a volley of fire into the things, to no effect, and then were forced to retreat by flights of crossbow quarrels.

One of Tom's men got a nail bomb in among the creatures. The blast blew a leg off, spindly and hooked and hairy, and Christopher realized they were ants. Gigantic ants.

This seemed wildly improbable. And since when were ants bullet-proof? Then he saw Vicar Rana climb onto the wall, ignore a crossbow quarrel that sprouted in her shoulder, and begin to chant.

They were reanimated ants. Renamints? Whatever. The knot of evil was too much for Rana. Her glow died and faded, while the monsters did no more than twitch an antenna in her direction.

So this was Joadan's big surprise. The things probably dragged the barges upriver, crawling on the river bed, hidden from spying eyes and even scrying. And why not? They didn't need to breathe, and they never got tired. Then Joadan used them as siege engines, smashing a hole in the wall. The bulk of his army was hanging off, giving covering fire but not storming the walls, waiting for the breach. Then they would pour in and sweep over a demoralized, exhausted defense. Joadan had known Rana would see their true nature, just as he had known she would be powerless against them. Joadan had calculated to the copper bit what it would take to crush Knockford's defenses.

As surprises went, it was a good one. Christopher would love to have a couple of those in his army. Unfortunately his patron looked rather dismally on trapping souls in dead bodies like demented puppet masters. Presumably this prohibition extended to the souls of ants.

Unless there were human souls in those bodies, which would be even worse. Christopher wasn't really sure how the process worked, but he was sure how to unwork it. He was nearly twice Rana's rank. What for her was an insurmountable defense would be for him a minor hurdle.

He got back on his horse and to the wall just as the entire section went down under the assault. Men ran clear of the zone in a frenzy. The ants crawled over the wreckage, making a ghastly clicking sound, and even Royal shuddered. Then Christopher stood up and chanted.

They were well-made. It took Christopher a few seconds of concentration to destroy each one. But he had plenty of that kind of power, and soon enough they all lay still, like cars abandoned by the side of the road.

Joadan's cavalry was right behind them. With no better options, Christopher drew his sword and kicked his horse forward. The knights had charged with sword and shield rather than lance, expecting a close-quarters battle. This gave him a fighting chance. He met them in the breach, one to many, and laid to with a will.

Some slipped past him, but the main knot would have to break over him to get in. They tried, mightily, their horses lunging at his, their swords raining down on him like hailstones. He paid them back in kind. Thanks to the power of the magic in his sword, it only took one or two blows to send the low-ranked knights to the ground, where horses stomped on them unheedingly. Meanwhile their blows cost him little, as tael healed his body in their sword's passing.

It still wasn't enough. More than a few minutes of this would leave him diced like hash browns in a frying pan. Behind him, Rana's men rallied and pressed forward again. Now that they faced flesh, their bullets bit, and the knights fell back under withering fire. Royal, eager for more, followed. Before Christopher could convince his horse to turn around, he heard strains of music, and the wall rose up behind him, restoring itself.

Joadan's army fell back, rebuffed, until they realized there was still something for them to take their aggression out on. Christopher put his heroic but stupid horse parallel to the wall and told it to run. Royal must have finally grasped that he was outnumbered, because he complied.

Some of the knights were on lighter horses, coursers instead of lumbering destriers. They began to catch up. But by then he had bought enough time, and he and Royal turned to mist.

The enemy swords cut through him without effect, save one. An enchanted blade, it hurt every bit as much as if he'd been solid flesh. He aimed Royal into the air, where swords could not reach him. A flight of crossbow quarrels was no more significant than the starlings had been.

He circled above the battlefield, looking for Joadan. The army milled about, disinclined to force the wall by mundane muscle in the face of gunfire. Joadan had cleverly forgone his golden armor, which would have lit him up like a neon sign, but he could not disguise his competence. Christopher found a knot of order among the enemy mass, and deduced that Joadan had to be at the center of it.

The Gold Curate knew the gig was up. He stood in the saddle and threw a spell at Christopher, trying to undo the magic that made him mist. It failed, as to be expected given their disparate ranks, but it was a good try. Had it succeeded Christopher would have fallen into the midst of the enemy, far from any help.

Christopher would have been annoyed that Joadan's cleverness should be defeated by sheer might, except he was annoyed by another problem. Now that he had found Joadan, what precisely was he to do with him? In mist form his sword would do less than a gnat's bite, nor could he cast spells. Yet to solidify would be suicidal.

He slowed to a gentle wafting, floating over Joadan and pointing down with his sword. Eventually someone got the message, and a cannon round tore into the men below. It missed Joadan, but that didn't matter. The knights were not going to sit around while a ghost called artillery down on them. They shook their heads at Joadan, arguing; when the next cannonball came bouncing through, taking the legs off of two horses, the knights turned and galloped away.

Joadan had to go with them. He wasted no time on idle curses, instead putting spurs to his horse until he led them again. Then he took what remained of his army, a bare thirty knights at this point, and fled.

The Gold Curate left behind a battlefield littered with corpses, not all of them his. Christopher did not know how many dead lay inside Rana's walls, but it hardly mattered. He would not have the time to revive them all. Anger at this senseless waste drove him forward and he paced Joadan, hanging above his head like a doom.

Knights began to disappear from the crowd, discreetly vanishing behind a copse or down a country lane. Joadan shed one or two every mile, until he was down to a brave and loyal four. Then he pulled his group to a stop and waited.

Christopher turned in a circle and finally came down, twenty yards away.

Joadan called out to him. "If you can hear in that form, then hear this. Be done with it. You will get no better odds than this. Come at me if you dare."

He let himself and his horse solidify. The process took a number of seconds, during which Joadan watched without expression.

"These aren't odds," Christopher said, when he was complete. "It is a slaughter. I am a Saint now."

"You took quite a beating back there at the wall. You have exhausted powerful magic to appear here, so soon, in such guise. If this is what fate gives me, I will take it."

"It doesn't have to be," Christopher said. "My third regimental commander used to work for Black Bart. You have options."

Joadan jerked as if he had been stung by one of his gigantic ants.

"To have my mind and will rinsed clean by your magic? To have my nature cut and fit to the box you would lay for it? What a poor excuse for a man I would be if I chose that over mere death!"

Christopher was stung himself. "It's not like that. Dark take it, Joadan, I could make a good man out of you, if only you would let me."

"I am not your plaything!" Joadan screamed in a righteous fury and spurred his horse. Three of his men had couched lances; the fourth rode pillion, to cut off any flanking maneuver. The knot of them charged, and Christopher had little choice.

He called down the tower of flame. Men and horses burned and died. They were no Earls, to turn aside holy fire by the depth of their tael. Out of the charred wreckage, only Joadan emerged. Black and smoking, he strode forward purposefully, his fury unquenched.

Christopher dismounted and went forward to meet him, for the worst of all possible reasons: he was afraid Joadan would kill his horse out of spite.

"Playthings?" he snarled at the younger priest. "Like the toys you've broken on the walls of Knockford?"

"Cut me down," Joadan spat back. "Cut me to ribbons. Sooner or later my bones will find their way to the Gold Apostle. He will invite me back, and I will come. I will leave the luxury of the Tiered City ten thousand times, if it means a chance to bite at your ankle."

"I'll burn your body," Christopher threatened.

They now stood at arm's length, their swords dangling almost forgotten. In this world where death could be undone by magic, where souls could come and go through a revolving door, the only true wound was to the spirit. The only real weapons were words.

"No you won't," Joadan sneered. "You'll cry over my corpse and beg me to change my ways. You cannot imagine having enough pride to own the fate one earns, and so you'll weep your little tears over mine. You disgust me."

"You kiss the hand of a man who tortures children, for no better reason than maintaining your own power!"

"What of it?" Joadan snapped in response. "You've stepped over a thousand broken bodies simply because they were furry. What difference is there between us, save that I can look in a mirror and see what I truly am?"

The enormity of his charge, the unfairness of it all, the sheer thickheaded self-centered stupidity of it, married to the sliver of truth distorted through a mirror darkly, enraged Christopher beyond all reason.

"The difference is this!" he cried out, and called down the tower of flame again, on top of both of them, submitting them both to the cleansing judgment of Heaven, heedless of the outcome.

Joadan's corpse disintegrated into a pile of ashes, his depleted tael no match for the flames a second time.

Christopher stood untouched. He had forgotten he had cast the energy shield.

He sat down on the smoking ground, exhausted with the burden of being himself. He did come close to tears, but only at his own vanity. Eventually the ground cooled enough for his horse to come over and nudge him, bored with the proceedings and the lack of anything to eat.

Joadan's sword and armor were enchanted, as evidenced by their survival. One other blade stood out untouched, possibly the one that had cut him while he was in mist form. He collected these items of treasure. At worst they could be reduced for the tael that powered them.

The process necessarily disturbed the ashes. By the time he was finished, the outlines of the men and animals who had died there were gone, blurred into a circle of charcoal. The wind stirred, blowing a black harvest across the snowy fields.

He slung the plunder on the back of his horse and climbed into the saddle in front of it. With a twitch of the reins he turned Royal to home. Trotting away from the spreading darkness, he and the horse turned white and misty, and blew away on their own wind.

He returned to misery. A squad of hard-faced soldiers stalked the battleground, under the direction of a priestess gone so white and shaking Christopher thought she was about to collapse. As he came to ground and solidness, he watched her stand back from a wounded man moaning on the ground and nod her head tremulously.

One of the soldiers took aim at the helpless man and shot him through the heart.

"Here now," Christopher called, disturbed. He still had healing power left.

The soldier looked up, his face like forged iron. One of Rana's policemen. Christopher wondered how he had ever thought of them as soft.

The man spoke with too much weariness to be insolent, regardless of his words. "If you still have magic, the Lady will need your help inside. We have our own to care for first; only then will we spend magic on the enemy, and only on those who can still be redeemed. Yet there is no reason to let the dregs suffer a needlessly long death, Black though they may be."

The Cardinal had employed the same standard on his prisoners, back in the beginning. Christopher hadn't liked it then, and he didn't like it now. "That's as may be," Christopher said. "But don't shoot any more until I get back to you."

The man looked at him without the slightest trace of concern. "I don't take my orders from you, Lord Prophet. I trust you to respect that."

Christopher had forgotten what defiance looked like. His own army had lost it all. "It's Saint now," he said.

The man raised his eyebrows in appreciation but did not change his stance.

Christopher rode on. The gate was open, and guards waved him through after only a cursory glance.

Rana indeed needed his aid. A young man took him from bed to bed, according to some selective logic only he comprehended. Christopher healed as he was told, until he was drained of every scrap of magic, no matter how small. Because of his rank, that was a considerable amount, but he still couldn't compete with a whole church full of healers.

The one deference they gave his greater rank was that once he was out of magic, they let him leave the hall after only a few mundane bandages. Although that might have more to do with the fact that he saw his young guide redoing every bandage he wrapped, following in his wake without so much as a glance of censure in his direction.

He told himself it was the difference between field work and hospital standards, but he was too happy to get out of it to really care. No one would die without him. He felt no need to inflict his inadequacy on others solely to assuage his own guilt.

Lalania was doing her kind of healing. She was playing to a rapt audience crowded around the chapel steps. Apparently she was composing a ballad on the spot, trying out stanzas and taking the crowd's reaction. She carried them carefully on a tightrope between victorious elation and sober judgment of the carnage of the day.

In the end he found himself in the same inn where he had recruited his first boys. The landlord served him cold, pale lager without a trace of irony.

Tom came and joined him.

"A bloody fine scrap today," he mused over his own drink, a dark ale thick enough to eat with a spoon.

"Indeed," Christopher said.

"It would have been a spot bloodier without your help. I don't know what the Dark those things were, but they were terrifying. They're still lying there, outside the walls. Nobody wants to go near them in case they start moving again."

"Dynamite."

"Pardon?"

Christopher took a long drink. "Dynamite. Enough dynamite would have stopped them. Or cannons, at least the larger ones."

Tom clucked doubtfully. "They moved a mite fast to draw a bead on them with those heavy guns. And they didn't seem inclined to sit around and wait for fuses to burn down."

"What you need to do is put some glue on the dynamite. Attach it to their sides." Like sticky bombs made out of plastique and grease-soaked socks in WWII. And why not? The reanimated ants were effectively tanks.

"A fine bit of craftsmanship to carry out in the heat of battle. Nonetheless I'll look into it, if you think we'll see any more of those."

"I wouldn't know. Where did they even come from?"

Tom considered. "Magic? He took some little ants and cast spells of enlargement on them?"

Christopher stared at the young man. "They can do that? That's a thing people can do?" Size-changing shamans and dragons were one thing, but he had never imagined insectoid warfare on this scale.

"Well," said Tom. "Wizards can do it. I don't know if that accounts for people."

Christopher pretended to chuckle, happy enough for the diversion.

"I do note that you rode in with a golden sword," Tom said, turning serious. "Can we take it to mean the reign of Curate Joadan is over?"

"It is indeed," Christopher agreed morosely. "It didn't have to be. He was smart and principled. He could have been a good man."

"Now my lord, you know I have the highest esteem for your wisdom. But in this, you're as wrong as a cat with three dogs. That was a heart yearning toward darkness with every beat."

With a wave of his hand, Christopher let the issue die unchallenged and changed the topic. "How is Dereth doing?"

"Working like a fiend. I think he thinks you expect him to be finished by morning."

"That would be good," Christopher said.

Tom took stock of him. "Is there something I should know?"

"I suppose you could put it like that. Pack your bags. We march as soon as Dereth's done."

"We, my lord?"

"Every man in this town who holds a rifle holds it in fealty to me."

"Not to put too fine of a point on it, my lord, but we swore to the Lady Rana."

Christopher finished his mug and set it down. "And she to Cardinal Faren, yes? And he to me."

"And you to the King," Tom said carefully.

"There is no king," Christopher said. "There's a murderous bastard with a crown on his head, but that's not the same thing at all."

"Indeed it is not." Tom drained his own mug and thumped it down. "And plenty enough of the boys will be glad to hear it. The ones that won't, well, they'll hold their tongues and do their duty. Nobody wants a rebellion, but nobody with a spine is willing to sit back and let them bury our Saint without a word said crosswise."

"If it is any consolation," Christopher said, not particularly willing to share the news but realizing it would eventually have to come out, "we still have a Saint. Though only half the man Krellyan was."

Tom's grin threatened to split his face. "Once again, my lord, you're as wrong as wrong can be. The Bright Lady save Krellyan's soul, and I loved him like a father; but time's been long past due for a damn good kick in the teeth." He stood up and strode from the room.

Christopher reflected that he should have warned Rana he was stealing her army.

It wasn't the first time he'd stolen from her. She would be used to it by now.

28

DISCORDANT COUNCIL

He stripped Knockford bare, cramming food, tools, and weapons into wagons. Since all the weapons and half the tools were his, few complaints were offered. Senior Palek, armorsmith and loyal opposition, passed by at one point, his face steeled to impassivity. But when he saw Christopher's odd-styled scale armor, his professionalism forced him to sniff in disgust.

It was a rare heartening moment. Vicar Rana had not so much as said "boo" to him. She knew that without him the town would have fallen, and not to noble knights serving the King but to howling mercenary scum who would have torn her town to bloody shreds. The rest of the clergy looked at him like he had two heads: a wonder that was fascinating and terrifying at the same time. The deference wore on Christopher, especially when half the men of the town stood in the street and saluted him.

"Take it all," Rana had told him. "If they see you leaving with it, perhaps they will think there is no reason left to destroy us."

"They might out of spite," he had told her. "I have to leave you a defense."

"Why?" she countered, with brutal logic. "All our efforts would have counted for naught had you not come. Defenses or no, what does it matter, if you are not here?"

In the end he left her another scroll to send to him with. He did not point out to her that he, alone, could not have saved the town, that he needed the power of the militia as well. She was in no mood to hear it.

Penning the scroll cost him half a day, so he had to catch up to his makeshift army, which had marched to the border of Fram without him, safe in the knowledge that the road was clear at least to the town. Lalania smiled saucily when he pulled her up behind him onto Royal. She lasted all of fifty feet before pouting.

"You don't intend to *walk* to Kingsrock, do you?"

"What?" he said. "You want me to burn another sixth-rank spell, just so you don't get dirt in your hair?"

"Oh, please. You enjoyed it as much as I did."

Yet once he cast the spell, she tapped him on the shoulder, signaling that he should delay their launch into the air. He looked around until he spotted the tell-tale. It could only move at a galloping pace. He had to wait until Lalania received her report from the College.

"What news?"

"Good for you, bad for the realm. Estvale has chosen this moment to resume its feud with Wesvale."

He shrugged, astounded at the idiocy of men. "Aren't they both Green?"

"Not for long, I fear. Estvale does not march alone. The Gold army broke off the road to Kingsrock and now marches east, to capture Wesvale in a vise."

Gregor's comment seemed apt enough to repeat. "How can that possibly help them?"

"Wesvale houses the Jade Throne, the center of Green religion in the Kingdom, as much as they can have a center. No doubt the Count of Estvale fancies the Gold Prophet will put him on the seat instead of the current occupant."

Christopher sighed. "Instead, they will arrive late to the battle, after both sides have exhausted themselves, and consume them both."

She beamed with approval. "You're learning!"

"But how does that help the Gold against me?"

Shaking her head, she groaned in disappointment. "And yet so far to go. Come now, my wayward pupil, what word did you just use?"

He used a lot of them, all the time. But of course she meant "consume."

"You're saying the Gold will gain tael from this."

"Indeed," she confirmed. "They will march in with hundreds of common soldiers, and march out with dozens of knights. A good bargain in the best of times; facing you, where their common soldiers have practically no value at all, it is brilliant."

"It gets us to Kingsrock before them."

"So it does. Another battle for them to arrive late to. Why, it's as if they can't learn a thing from their successes."

It was absurd. The two armies fought with such disparate goals as to make their coming together on any given battlefield serendipity rather than strategy.

They caught up to the militia in a fraction of an hour. Then he had to rejoin the mortal coil and travel like any creature of flesh and blood. Lalania perched on top of a wagon and played to a captive audience, who appeared happy to be at her disposal. Christopher rode in front and champed at the bit almost as badly as Royal, but there was no help for it. The Parrott rifles moved like slugs behind teams of eight. They would move even slower if he hadn't had the foresight to rebuild the road from Knockford to Kingsrock last year.

And there was no cause for worry. If the King struck at his main army, the Cardinal would send to him, and he could arrive in half an hour. His two armies were converging on the same spot. The distance between them would shrink to nothing, given the power of his spell.

It was such a lucky break it almost let him forget the fact that he still had to face Treywan in single combat.

Fram Town looked perfectly normal, which Christopher found disconcerting. He had expected the hustle and bustle of a civil war, but, of course, from the perspective of the common people, this was a contest between nobles. Or it had been, until Christopher's three hundred riflemen marched in. The town gaped and gawked, and

Christopher was sure that if he had rifles to spare, he would find hands to grasp them.

As he helped unload wagons and unharness horses, regretting that he had not brought Karl or at least Torme to oversee this chaos, he discovered a batch of priests, priestesses, and clerks. Rana had all but emptied her church, sending him especially the young. She had kept only herself, her police, and staff too old to travel. As if she feared her inability to protect them.

As if she had sent seeds to safekeeping.

He cursed silently. The sooner he laid siege to Kingsrock, the sooner all swords and violence would be drawn there. The men took his mood and rushed to obey. Consequently he could see the relief on their faces when the Earl of Fram's messenger came to claim him for the nobility.

They waited for him in silent rows in the court of the keep. The Earl stood up from his throne at Christopher's approach. In all the years Christopher had passed through the Earl's county, they had never met. In the beginning he had been too small, and in the end too large. After the first goblin war, a lot of people had been careful not to meet him, lest they be forced to take a stance on his unorthodoxies.

The Earl was an older man with graying hair, though still erect and spare of limb. "Well met, Lord Prophet," he said with dignity. "Welcome to my hall."

"It's Saint now," Christopher said, and the crowd stifled a gasp.

"Truly? That bodes well," Fram said with relief. He seemed to think about it for a moment, and then started to lower himself to one knee.

"None of that now," Christopher said, grabbing him by the arm and pulling him back up. "You never knelt to Krellyan. You'll never kneel to me."

"Krellyan did not wear a crown," Fram objected quite reasonably.

"And neither will I."

"You cannot evade your responsibility by a token gesture." The Vicar of Samerhaven strode forward from the crowd. No risk of kneeling here. "If you seek to overthrow a king, you must assume his authority. You will wear a crown in all but name."

"I get that. But it's not going to be the same. I need you all to understand that."

"Not really," said a different voice. The Vicar of Copperton, ever pragmatic. "We are here not out of loyalty to your cause but because we have no choice. The Shadow makes its lunge; we must perforce shield behind our greatest strength. You could be a turnip with eleven ranks and we would kneel to you."

Christopher looked around for friendlier faces. "Sister Banna," he said to a middle-aged woman he recognized as Cannenberry's Prelate. "Are you a Vicar yet?"

"I have the rank," she answered, "thanks to my late lord's generosity. But I do not have the title, and I do not see how I can claim it while my county remains in the hands of the King."

"At least you have a county," Samerhaven said. "He has given mine away."

Christopher ignored the jibe, mostly because it was true and he had no answer. "We're not taking any of them back. Not even Copperton." The town was half a day's travel north from the main highway, a delay he could not afford. "We're going straight to the siege of Kingsrock. The army will be there tomorrow, so we should have a free path. We're carrying a pair of huge cannon that are going to win this battle for us in short order."

Samerhaven narrowed his eyes. "If you smash Kingsrock to rubble, then how shall you rule? And what of the innocents your deviltry will fall upon?"

Christopher gritted his teeth. "I'm going to force Treywan to come out and play."

"To what end? Do you think you can defeat him in sword-craft?"

"I'm not going to be alone," Christopher said, for what seemed the thousandth time. "I've got an entire army with me, every man of which has the ability to hurt him."

"Treywan has an army, too," the Vicar of Copperton said carefully.

"Not really," Christopher said. "We beat three score of knights at Knockford with nothing more than a wooden wall and militiamen. You already know a common man inside stone walls is worth a knight. Now it's time to learn that a common man with a rifle is worth a knight anywhere. And a thousand of them is worth a king."

There were a pair of faces in the crowd looking particularly ill. Fighting men, by their dress, nobles by their bearing.

Christopher looked at both of them and shrugged apologetically.

"Forgive me, my lord," the younger one said. "I did not mean to pull a face. It's just that your words seemed to imply that the profession of knighthood lives or dies by this battle. Please do not hold my misunderstanding against my master, the Count of Parnar, who has dispatched me here for my fighting skills, not my diplomacy."

"I didn't mean to imply that," Christopher said. "The battle is irrelevant. Knighthood is already dead."

The Earl took a step back. "You come to my court to tell me that after you have used my strength for your own ends, you will take it from me with a whistle and a prayer?" The man's hand hung near his sword. Christopher didn't pay it any mind. His hands did the same thing of their own accord these days.

"I'm not taking anything away. You'll still be knights. Your lords will still be rich and respected and powerful. But I don't think anyone will be making new knights. We still need magic, but strength can be made in forges now."

"You dare insult your allies on the eve of battle?" the other knight exclaimed. Presumably he was Sprier's representative.

"I'm not insulting you. I'm telling you the hard facts. The Kingdom would have fallen to the Wild without your swords. Nobody denies what you are owed for the past. But I cannot lead you into the future with a lie. The world I build will be different. It will be better in most ways. But those of you with high rank may not think so. I don't want to tell you this; I don't want to lose you, or even upset you; but I cannot take your oaths under false pretenses."

"Is this how you spoke to the Blue Duke?" Fram muttered. "That explains much."

"Your effrontery is hard to credit." The knight from Sprier tolled like a warning bell.

"It will be easier to credit once you step outside this room and see what I have brought."

"This should come as no surprise," Samerhaven explained to the crowd. "You have seen how only priests, wizards, and bards have gained ranks from his service. Every one of you has heard the tale of Karl Treyeingson, who serves even unto death and yet remains Goodman, never Ser. Saint Christopher has always made his intentions clear, if you would but listen."

"Perhaps it explains why the King moved against him." The knight was fast becoming Christopher's most dubious ally, exceeding even the elf and the dragon.

"The Gold Apostle has always made *his* intentions clear, too, though you would not listen either. You have heard of the peasants we resettled. You have heard of the charges whispered. Who calls out the White for selling arms to monsters while the Gold sells whole *villages?*"

It appeared that Vicar Samerhaven's tongue was equally sharp for everyone. Christopher held his own and let the man have the floor.

"Whispers," Fram growled. "No man's reputation should be brought down from rumors spread by girls in dresses as skimpy as their respect for truth and tradition."

'You desire evidence?" Samerhaven snapped, his face a marble carving of contempt. "You call for proof? My Saint's ashes lie in the ruins of the White Cathedral. What more do you require, Ser? *What more?*"

Only the fact that Vicar Samerhaven carried no weapon prevented immediate bloodshed. Earl Fram's face was so red Christopher thought it would catch fire; Samerhaven's shuddering contempt was ice-cold but not less painful for it. Christopher raised his hands, trying to think of some way to calm the situation.

Lalania chose that moment to strike a few stray notes on her lyre. The entire room turned to look at her, mystified at the breech of protocol more than anything else. She did nothing more, standing idly without remorse.

After a long moment Fram blew out his cheeks, his attention redirected. "Your plan is for naught, anyway. Kingsrock is defended by more than swords. There is magic there to void the efforts of a thousand siege engines. We have all known this, always."

"Oh, my lords," Lalania said with smirk. She strummed a chord and looked down lovingly at the lyre, which until quite recently had lain silent in the King's treasure vault. When she looked up there was triumph in her eyes. "My dear, sweet lords."

Afterward, outside under the cold starlit sky, the knight from Sprier approached him, introducing himself as Ser Conner.

"Please attach my harsh words to my name, rather than my lord's," he said with tight formality.

"Forget it," Christopher said. The man who would speak hard truths could not object to hearing them. "I already have."

"Not just those," Ser Conner said. "These as well. I do not think that I can march my men in your train in good conscience. I beg of you, assign me some other duty or give me leave to go, lest I be forced to an unpleasant decision."

Christopher sighed. At least the man had approached him in private. Had he done so in public, Christopher would have had no choice but to call him out for insubordination.

"Cannenberry," he said after a moment's thought. "No one can fault you for killing thieves and brigands. Take the Vicar down there and restore her rule. Treywan can't deny her that." It was the most neutral act he could imagine.

"Something for swords to do, then?" Conner asked, hard as iron.

"It would be easier with rifles," Christopher answered. "Do you want me to give you some?"

They glared at each other for a while.

Then Ser Conner went and made Christopher like him, merely by being good at his job. "Do you know what we will face? I have a score of lancers, less armored than knights but on quicker steeds. Well suited for chasing troglodytes through the hills, but against traditional forces perhaps not so keen."

"No, sorry, I haven't a clue," Christopher had to admit. "What I can say is Curate Joadan is dead and his knights scattered. The bulk of the Gold Throne's attention seems to be to the east at the moment. My guess is that you'll find nothing but criminals, but if that's not the case, feel free to withdraw until I can offer you more support."

"What of the Witch of the Moors? She holds the southern border."

"I think she's going to be on our side. But at the moment, I don't know. Now that you mention it, though . . . the Lord Wizard of Carrhill has not yet declared, but when he does, he'll declare for me."

"A conspiracy of spell-casters," Conner said, with obvious distaste.

"If only it were only that," Christopher told him.

29

AIR SUPERIORITY

Ser Conner and his men rode out the next morning, going the wrong way. They were headed back to Knockford, to catch the turnoff south to Cannenberry. Vicar Banna rode with them. Nobody questioned this change of plans, despite his having plainly stated he wouldn't be retaking any counties. Karl would have, but then Karl would have made him flog Ser Conner for punishment. Or worse, put him on kitchen duty.

The rest of the army marched east with minimal grumbling. Lalania tried to talk him into scrying. The process sounded remarkably difficult and finicky, so he turned to mist and went back to Knockford to revive a few more corpses instead. He silenced Lalania's objections by the obvious tactic of taking her along for the ride.

The people of the town were bewildered to see him again, so soon after he'd left. No one was used to the freedom of a man with a motorcar. Leaving the spell active felt like leaving the motor running, a constant itch in the back of his mind. He tolerated it, though, because it reminded him he could escape at any moment. So far he had avoided old Pater Svengusta. Despite the fact that he could travel out to the village in literally minutes, he didn't. Facing Treywan's wrath in single combat was a less dreadful prospect than facing Svengusta's grief over the death of the Saint. He wanted Treywan's head in his hands before he had to deal with that pain.

The column camped at the crossroads to Copperton, again having made good time. Tom and Johm had their militia well in hand; the two Vicars and their staff presented no difficulties other than sharp words. Earl Fram had brought only his knights, so their inefficiency was masked by the speed of their mounts, and their lack of supply was solved by Christopher's wagons. He forbore to point this out to them, though. Never let it be said he was without tact.

He still hadn't heard from his other army. The sending spell didn't conflict with anything important, so he reached out to Karl's mind.

"Treywan left a company of archers to die in the woods," came the reply. "Most now march with us. We reach the foot of Kingsrock by . . . ." The message trailed off; Karl was not as economical with his words as the priests. Christopher couldn't imagine any polite way to tell the taciturn young man that truth, though.

It didn't matter. Everything was going to plan.

He did another morning run to Knockford. Rana glared at him this time.

"If you keep coming back, eventually they will seek you here. And the entire point of sending you away was to avoid precisely that."

He pointed mutely at the stacked corpses.

"I can preserve what is left indefinitely," she said. "Turn your eyes to the east."

Since he was there, he revived three more. Lalania bided her time, knowing that tomorrow he would have no excuse to avoid her lessons in spell-craft.

They returned to the column just as it was within sight of the bridge. Christopher was surprised to see it intact, as this was the gateway to the west. Joadan's men must have crossed this bridge on their way to Cannenberry and thus to Knockford.

Instead it seemed to be occupied. Royal perked his ears up for a moment while Christopher stood in the saddle, trying to get a better look.

"Oh, just go see," Lalania said, so he did.

He came down on the other side and solidified, having recognized faces and arms.

"Colonel," Sergeant Kennet snapped out a salute. "It is good to see you again."

"Likewise, Sergeant."

Kennet filled him in. The army should be camped at Kingsrock by now. Kennet and his squad had come to seize the bridge, just in case. Good thinking on Karl's part. Christopher left them to escort the militia and flew ahead to see his army.

The ten miles took him ten minutes, even though it would take his militia column five more hours. Swooping above the plains, he found his army disembarking at the most obvious place: the training grounds where draft regiments waited for their assignments.

He had camped here once, as a first-rank, waiting for a lordly noble to come down and give him orders. Things were arranged somewhat differently this time.

"How often can you do that?" was Karl's greeting. Always to the point.

"All day, if I have to," Christopher answered. "I've got to take you up sometime. It's even better than flying," he added with a grin.

Karl shook his head. "I prefer dull solidity."

"I don't know why. When I'm in mist form swords can't hurt me."

The eyebrows of his general staff all rose at once.

"Well," he amended. "Magic ones can."

They fell again, in unison. Treywan had a magic sword.

"Then other magic must be able to harm you as well," warned Torme. "We may not know what magic that is, but I assure you Sigrath and the Gold Apostle will find it, if it exists."

"Any news?" Christopher asked.

"We were hoping you would bring us some," Gregor said. "The Lady Uma has had no communications for two days. She says the Skald must be occupied."

"I can speak for myself," Uma said sharply.

Christopher looked at her.

"It is as he said," she grumbled.

"Last we heard, the Gold was on its way to Wesvale. How do we know they didn't keep going to Tomestaad?" He would hate to lose the College almost as much as losing Knockford. The College had a library, and he hadn't read all of their books yet.

"Count Tomestaad wields a sharp sword," Earl Istvar answered. "And the Lady is a Curate. Dirty tricks like those they used at Farmark will be to no avail."

"Don't be so sure," Christopher objected, and told them the details of the battle at Knockford.

"Where did he get giant ants from?" Gregor exclaimed.

"I know, right?" Christopher said. "I mean, what the Dark?"

Something about Cannan's stance caught his eye. He followed the man's cue, and looked at Ser D'Kan.

The boy spoke apologetically. "Rumors, my lord. I have heard rumors that Cannan's neatly cropped lands were an ant's idea of paradise. It did not occur to me that anyone meant ants the size of wagons."

"It doesn't matter," Istvar said, with a hint of desperation. "Tomestaad is walled in stone."

"Giant borer beetles," Gregor suggested.

"You're not helping," Disa told him, tugging gently on his arm.

"Let us focus on the here and now," Karl said. "The Parrotts arrive tonight. By morning's light we can begin the siege. Treywan will call for his lyre; the guards will reveal its absence; in a rage he will fly into our camp and cut the Colonel in half."

"Wait," Christopher objected. He didn't like that plan.

"If Treywan comes to us, a thousand bullets will spell his doom," Torme said.

"There are defenses," Karl reminded them. "The shaman Keisari stood against all our rifles."

"Not all," Gregor said. "One got through. And the men were poorer shots then. Most missed on their own. Treywan will have no such grace."

Karl was not convinced. "There is also simple range. Our guns cannot reach a thousand feet into the sky."

"Then he will wait for you there," Cannan said. "Where all can see his challenge but none interfere. You cannot simply ignore him. The morale of your men will demand a response."

Christopher grinned wickedly. "Then he will be breaking the first rule of war. He will be . . . predictable."

Torme chuckled. "This is no duel. Brother Christopher will load up on spells from the safety of our arms, and then strike with the god's own power upon him."

"Treywan will also be cloaked in magic," Uma warned.

"Mmm," Christopher said. "I've got a pretty good track record with dispelling. And I outrank everybody in that city now."

"Your unraveling will not work on permanent enchantments," Uma said. "You cannot deny him flight, or the hardness of his armor, or the sharpness of his sword."

"Or his phenomenal vitality," Istvar reminded him. "Treywan has the lives of thirteen strong warriors to spend."

Christopher was a priest. Despite his eleven ranks, he had half that much.

"I understand. Even if we reduce him to the most basic defenses, it's still going to be a terrible fight. But I don't see any better option. If I don't challenge him, I lose my edge: right now he's trapped in that castle, for fear that I will descend like mist wherever he goes. But if he doesn't fear me, then he'll be free to work mischief anywhere."

"And you do not fear him?" Istvar asked.

"I do, but it's not obvious. So far, I've only gone to places that were full of riflemen," Christopher answered. "So far, neither of us has called the other's bluff."

"Treywan will not call you out tomorrow, either," Cannan said. "He has a priest marching to join him. He'll find a reason to delay for that."

"And you know this how?" Karl asked.

The big man shrugged. "Because it's what I would do."

"Fair enough," Karl said. "Yet now I think the Colonel should rejoin the militia. All of our hopes still ride on the Parrotts."

So he did. Lalania gave him an earful for riding off without her, though curiously he felt as if her heart wasn't in it. She did grill him mercilessly about how long exactly a single casting of the spell would last. Since these were technical details that didn't involve him apologizing, he was happy to discuss it.

The column rolled into camp late at night, traveling long after they should have stopped, solely because no one wanted to quit so close to their destination. Christopher went to bed without qualms, despite what had to come next. The waiting was almost over.

Lalania woke him before dawn.

"Now what?" he grumbled. To his left Cannan moved, instantly aware, his hand on his sword.

"Quietly," she whispered. "No one knows I am here."

He felt a breeze and glanced around. She had cut a slit into his tent. He had sentries, but she had access. She could have just knocked.

"Romsdaal is under attack," she continued, in the same low voice.

"Dark take it," Christopher complained. "How did they march so far north without us knowing?"

"They did not. They marched south."

He sat up, the better to stare at her in the dark.

"The Skald was doing a routine check on your allies. Romsdaal is besieged by goblins and ulvenmen."

That called for a deep breath. And another.

Lalania kept whispering. "Praise the gods we took only their lord and knights. Had we stripped them of footmen, the keep would have already fallen."

"Why are you whispering?" he asked. They should be raising the alarm, not chatting in bed.

"Because I am afraid of what Count Armand will do when he hears."

"He'll leave, obviously."

"Taking how many knights? Just his, or all the Blue? Will he blame you for not having exterminated the goblins? Will he blame you for the ulvenmen? And what of the guns you left with those faithless dogs?"

"What of that faithless elf?" Christopher snarled.

"I presume she is already dead," Lalania answered.

Christopher threw off his blankets. "I can be in Romsdaal in half an hour. I can take Armand with me. We should be able to hold them off until his knights arrive. If they travel light, they can get there before nightfall."

"Two swords against an army? And this time they have the rifles." Lalania sat at the foot of his bed, as immovable as an anchor.

"What else can I do?"

"Accept the inevitable, kill Treywan, and only then march north to punish the goblins once and for all."

"And lose a second town to them? What kind of start to my reign would that be?"

"Technically," she said, "Treywan still reigns. So this one would count against him."

Cannan chuckled darkly.

"If you wanted me to do that," Christopher said to Lalania, "you shouldn't have told me until it was too late."

She looked away and hesitated. When she spoke, her voice was strained. "That was . . . suggested. I overruled the decision."

Christopher was wise to her little games now. "Does the Skald know that she has been overruled?"

Lalania turned to face him again, clutching his hand in hers. "I will not answer that. You cannot hate them, Christopher. They are my sisters. They are the only family I have ever truly known. And they only want what is best for all of us."

"Then why did you tell me?"

She sighed wistfully. "You are so handsome when you play the hero. And like everyone else, I hope you will produce a miracle on demand."

"Okay," Christopher said. "Here's my miracle. Saddle my horse. Rob Tom's men of all the dynamite they have left. Get Armand's knights on the road."

She opened her mouth.

"Go," Christopher ordered her, and turned his attention to getting dressed.

She went.

"You're not going to get yourself dead, are you?" Cannan asked.

"No. I'll never be in sword range of the goblins. A few bullets won't kill me. And the Eldest can try to undo my magic again, if she dares. There's two ranks between now and then."

Count Armand might have been suspicious or even accusatory, but Christopher didn't give him the time.

"I can give you all my horses, or you can give me all of yours. Do you want knights or riflemen to defend your town?"

"Knights with rifles, if it please you," the man answered stiffly. Gregor had been working on them, and over the last three days most of the professional warriors had mastered the basics of black powder weapons. To be fair, it wasn't hard. Dog-men had done it in a day.

They stood in the command tent, still putting on their armor. Pages and soldiers brought bits of metal and strapped them on between bites of breakfast and conversation.

"Fair enough. Take guns from the militia. Take three horses per man. Leave whatever is not necessary and ride hard. Send your second-in-command to lead them. The road is clear, at least."

"My second?"

"You're coming with me," Christopher told him. "Your town will need your moral authority, if nothing else. We should have a respite. They will prefer not to fight during the day."

"And if they do? What magic will you deploy against an army?"

"Not magic," Christopher said. "Doctrine. Specifically, air superiority."

The goblins didn't have anyone who could challenge Christopher in the air. That was not a good position to be in, as they were about to discover.

The sun was still rising when he and the Count marched out to Royal. The horse was loaded with kegs of powder and satchels of dynamite. Christopher clambered aboard and tried to make room on the saddle behind him for Armand.

The Count looked up dubiously. It would necessarily lack a certain amount of dignity.

Lalania bit her lip fetchingly.

"What?" Christopher demanded.

"He doesn't actually need to ride the horse. For that matter, neither do you."

"How could you possibly know this?"

"I . . . experimented. When you left me yesterday, I discovered I could still activate the effect. I actually came up to the camp to make sure everything was alright. I had a bit of a struggle to beat you back to the column so you wouldn't notice."

Armand had a question of his own. "Can we take my horse?"

"No," Christopher said. "I can only take one horse, and I need mine. You'll have to run alongside."

"Don't worry," Lalania told him. "You'll keep up. The spell does the traveling, not you."

Christopher was already chanting. Every second counted. He stayed on the horse, despite her comments. He didn't want to trust to a guide rope while everything was mist.

Armand, to his credit, did no more than make a face while he dissolved into a cloud. Then the wind snatched them up and sent them flying.

They didn't need a map, as they could stick to the road. It was mostly straight, and what little advantage they could gain by leaving it seemed not worth the risk of getting lost. And Christopher preferred to save his spell power for other uses.

The ground flew by underneath them. The flight was no longer enjoyable. Christopher only wished that it were faster, so that they might get there sooner. He had been warned, over and over again, that he could not trust the goblins. Now innocent people were paying the price.

Not the least of whom was Kalani. Facing Treywan with swords in the sky was nothing compared to the terror of telling Alaine that her child was dead. He was amassing a staggering debt of remorse. Getting himself killed might be the less painful option.

Romsdaal was indeed under active assault. As Christopher and Armand flew over the walls, they could see goblins in the woods cutting down trees and making ladders. Meanwhile ulvenmen ran around the empty fields, shooting at anyone stupid enough to put their head above the walls. At this point that was very few of the defenders.

The entire town had sought refuge in the keep, which formed the northernmost point of the town walls. So far the ulvenmen had not looted the town. There was nothing there they particularly wanted. The goblins would be materially enriched, later, but everyone's first concern were the men and women of the town, especially the elderly, who would die easiest and yet provide the same amount of tael.

If not for goblin cruelty and ulvenman hunger, the children could have been safely left in their cribs. They produced no tael.

Armand's people had seen Christopher leave in cloud form. Hence they met his incoming storm with cheers, which turned to sobs of joy when the Count solidified.

Count Armand looked around at his townsmen with surprise to see so few missing. "Praiseworthy quick work, Ser," he said to the aging knight he had left as castellan. One simply did not leave a keep on the border bereft of rank, civil war or no.

"I cannot claim it," the knight answered. "I was warned."

Beside him stood a girl in a poor fitting tunic, her face turned to the ground in shame, white hair spilling over her shoulders in disarray.

"Kalani!" Christopher cried, so relieved he almost fell off his horse. He leapt down instead and strode over to her. "You didn't die."

She looked up at him in anger, unable to form a response. He realized with shock that she was trying not to tell a lie. She settled on an admonition. "You do not understand."

Well, that was true enough.

"What happened?"

"Goblins happened," she said bitterly. "They poisoned Rohkea. Poisoned! The cowardly little wretches. They tempted him with sweets, groveling and flattering like the filthy little liars they are. He was cold and stiff when I found him. Against their deceits my magic had no purchase."

That was terrible and all—Christopher had truly respected the ulvenman leader—but it didn't seem to fully explain the mixed forces currently assaulting the town.

"And . . .?"

Kalani looked around wildly again, then simply skipped ahead in the story. "It was not mere murder, but rebellion. They had suborned a faction; remarkable, as I had not even had factions a few weeks ago. Now the ulvenmen call themselves the masters of the goblins, though we both know how that fiction runs. As soon as I could, I flew south to warn you. I followed your trail, as I knew they soon would. When I found this keep, I had to warn its inhabitants. Praise the luck that Ser Alister took my words to heart."

"I am a bit old," Ser Alister said dryly, "to think that young women appearing naked in my donjon is anything but a harbinger of trouble. When she mentioned the Saint's name, I presumed that valor lay in caution. We brought the craftsmen into the keep and sent the herdsmen south with the animals."

"We didn't pass them on the road," Christopher said, worried.

"Nor should we have," Armand said. "That is the first place an invader would look. They are south and east, in the forest. Assuming we keep these creatures' attention, they should be safe for a few days."

"Oh," Christopher growled, "I'll get their attention alright. Kalani, is the Eldest out there?"

"I think not. I struck at them last night, when they were trying to jump over the walls, and my magic was not disrupted. That gave them pause, and now they're making ladders. I think that they intend a day assault. I think they want the ulvenmen to be able to see me. Your cursed guns are longer range than my spell."

"Struck?" Armand queried.

Ser Alister made a sizzling sound and drew his hand in a ragged line, his eyebrows waggling in appreciation.

Christopher gave up trying to extract the full story from Kalani. He went back to his horse and checked his baggage. The strength of the horse meant it could carry far more weight than he could, and he had a spell in mind that would make use of that.

"Now trust me, old friend," he muttered to the horse. It had taken to the mist spell with nothing but joy. He hoped that extended to less metaphorical aerodynamics.

This new magic caused wisps of clouds to issue from underneath Royal's hooves. The horse looked down in surprise, lifted a hoof, and was disconcerted to see that the smoke still came out. Royal suddenly realized his other hoof was smoking, too, and lifted that one. But the first did not go down, remaining in mid-air, resting on only the pillow of smoke.

"Whoa," Christopher called, and rushed to climb onto his horse before it left him behind.

"What fresh spell is this?" Armand muttered in the background.

Royal strode into the air, treating the smoke beneath his feet like ground. This was not the ease of flight or mist; the animal had to work as hard as climbing a hill. Once they had reached a respectable altitude, Christopher leveled off and let Royal run.

The horse lunged forward. Apparently his ability to be spooked had died a natural death. Christopher was worried now that one day Royal would charge off a cliff, assuming flight was merely a part of his repertoire. But that was a concern for another day.

Turning them both to mist, he streaked out over the ulvenmen, who fired a few desultory shots at his cloud form. The goblins showed a bit more concern, especially once he solidified. He and Royal became flesh and blood again, treading on the tops of the trees.

Christopher reached into a satchel, pulled out a stick of dynamite wrapped in nails, lit it with a match, and tossed it overboard. He got off two more before the first one exploded.

Now he had their full attention.

For the next two hours he played cat and mouse over the woods and fields, switching from mist form to travel quickly and safely, then solidifying to do bombing runs. It was terribly inefficient, as the targets could often run faster than the fuses burnt. Nonetheless he had the advantage. Goblins and ulvenmen died in horrible ways, powerless to affect him. They did not have enough guns or discipline to concentrate their fire and kill his horse instantly, and, given but a few seconds respite, he could heal Royal from whatever wounds they did inflict.

When he finally found the goblin camp, it was deserted, of course. The wagons of supplies and tools lay below him, almost inviting.

He dropped the kegs of powder on the obvious trap, and fled. Behind him smoke rose in a billowing column a hundred feet high.

He returned to a hero's welcome, the keep cheering him as he pulled his lathered horse back into the world of flesh. Royal had spent half the time running on air. He, at least, had earned his accolades. All Christopher had done was murder poor creatures that could not fight back.

"I chased them at least ten miles," he told Armand. "I assume they will be back tonight, but your men should be here by then."

Grooms came forward to care for the horse. Christopher let them, following Armand off the roof and into the donjon.

The Count poured him a glass of wine, which he gratefully accepted. A woman brought a plate of food. While Christopher wolfed it down, the Count watched him appraisingly.

"You have many of the qualities I would seek in a liege," Armand finally said. "You put yourself first in danger and last in luxuries. You wield lethal power with effectiveness but not pleasure. You are kind to animals and women. So, I ask myself: why does every whisper tell me that you will destroy everything I hold dear?"

There was a time Christopher would have protested. Now he understood the depth of his actions. The Count would not forget this. The Count would want to know how to make dynamite of his own. The Count was now on Alaine's list. Simply by saving his life, Christopher had endangered it in a way he could not even credibly explain.

And, of course, Alaine was the least of all their worries. The monsters she fought against would be far less tender with the Count and his people. There was no turning back. It was too late to stop. There was already too much damage done, too many secrets spilled.

"I do what I have to," he said. When he realized it made him sound like Alaine, he growled deep in his throat.

"Pardon?"

"Sorry," Christopher said. "I need to talk to the Lady Kalani. Alone, I am afraid."

Armand retreated graciously. By the time Christopher had finished his meal, Kalani slipped through the door.

"I have to get back," he told her, "so I don't have a lot of time. What is it you're not telling me?"

"It doesn't matter," she said. "It's not your fault. I recognize the extent of my error; I will stay here and see that your people do not suffer for my mistake, until you have a chance to rectify the problem on your own."

"Your fault? I'm the one who spared the goblins. I'm the one who told you to bring the ulvenmen north. I'm the one who let the goblins go outside the wall, after making it all so simple and clear that they couldn't."

"All true," Kalani said, "but I cannot blame you. I should have foreseen these problems."

Christopher sat back. "Are you really so much more exalted than I?"

"No," she said hastily. "I didn't mean it like that."

He raised heavy eyebrows at her.

"I have been trained," she explained. "If I seem condescending, it is only because I have spent more years training than you have been alive. And yet I failed. I have failed you, my teachers, and my tradition. I should have done better by you."

A phrase came to his lips, but he swallowed it.

I am not your plaything.

The words went down bitterly, souring his meal.

"I made my own choices," he said stonily. "I have traditions of my own, which are so foreign to you that I wouldn't know where to start."

She stared at him intently, with her piercingly violet gaze. Then she looked away, but not before he saw the glistening in her eyes.

"I should have known you were no common mortal. Mother was too interested in you. Just another mistake she can throw in my face."

"Then maybe you should treat me like an equal, instead of like a lab rat."

"An equal?" she snapped, turning back to him. "And what of consequence have you ever shared with me? When did you see me as anything but a foolish child?" She quoted his words back to him. "*That could take a while.*" In a credible imitation of his voice, no less. "To have *you* lecture *me* on *time!*"

He stared back at her.

"Okay. I'm from another world. The ancestral plane of man, apparently. I'm the only link to it, I guess?"

She shook her head in mirthless laughter. "Of course. Mother wouldn't roll out of bed for less."

After a few false starts, she gave her own confession. "I died. The ulvenman caught me in a tent and beat it with heavy stones. Then they threw it on a bonfire. None of us come to this plane unprepared, of course. My contingent reincarnation was not disrupted; the fact that I am now trapped in the body of an owl is not even that debilitating, given that I can shapeshift into an elf for most of the day. We all die over here, eventually, and there was never any chance that I would match my mother's record of eight hundred and seventy-three years in her own body, but by the Light! *My very first mission.*"

She turned to back the wall and sobbed softly.

He started to rise, thinking he should hug her or something. She put out a hand to wave him off and collected herself.

"Okay," he said. "Yours is worse."

She laughed through the tears. "I do not agree. I would never want to be in your shoes. I have been raised my whole life on tales of Aelph the Pathmaker. Never once did I aught but pity him."

He shrugged helplessly. "I don't understand half of what you're talking about."

"You are worse," she said. "I don't understand half of what you *do*. You just spent two hours and who knows how much valuable chemistry scattering tael all over the forest floor. Why not just fly out with a chest of gold and dump it in the sea next time?"

That had not occurred to him. He had been so focused on his role as tactical air support that he had completely forgotten why no one here would think of such a strategy. The treasure—the tael in his victims heads—the entire point of fighting and killing—was now in the hands of his enemies, without any hope of recovery. When the goblins had sent their treasure against him, they had at least planned to harvest it after a victory. No doubt their army had been merely waiting for the sounds of gunfire to diminish before following up.

"I just wanted the town to survive."

"Of course," she agreed. "I understand you chose victory over treasure. But do you understand, no one from this world or any connected to it would ever have thought to go about it in quite that way? How did you even conceive of such a wasteful idea?"

Watching WWII movies did not seem like a helpful answer. He shrugged again.

She nodded. "My sentiments exactly."

He stood up. "Now what?"

"I will defend your town because I must, but I am vulnerable. Someone will come and fetch me soon. Perhaps even . . . mother." She caught herself. "Though, to be honest, I doubt there is much danger. You have shown you are willing and capable of holding your territory. The goblins will need time to fully enslave the ulvenmen before they dare threaten you again. I presume before that happens you will deal with your kingly problems and exterminate those treacherous oath-breaking goblins. I will reapply to the Directorate, but I cannot say if they will let me return and try again with the ulvenmen. I am not sure it is viable; I may have missed my window of opportunity."

"Please do," he told her. "I . . . kind of liked them. I mean, aside from the cannibalism."

She looked at him with those violet eyes, and for the first time he could see her age. "They do have much to recommend them, despite their ruinously short lives. I will do my best; but it may be that we shall never see each other again."

So this was goodbye. A pity; there was only one elf he wanted to see the back of, and it wasn't this one.

"Okay." He held out his hand. She took it and let him shake. In response she smiled stiffly and touched her forehead with her index finger in some odd form of a salute.

He went out of the room and up the stairs to the roof. Armand was waiting for him next to a clean and shiny Royal.

"Is this going to be a thing of the future?" the Count asked. "Should I build a barn up here?"

Christopher chuckled. If only he could have a permanent air force. "I've got to get back," he said instead. "Kalani will stay with you for a while. She seems to think the danger is past. Oh—one more thing. According to Lalania, you're still under the spell. If you find yourself turning to mist . . ." He stopped, because Armand's face had gone a sickly color. "Or," he suggested, "I could just take the effect off of you now."

"If you please. As much as I appreciate traveling like the wind, I would prefer not to do it by accident."

On the way back he crossed paths with Armand's knights. He landed long enough to reassure them that there was no immediate danger. They gratefully informed him that they would leave the bulk of his horses in the next village and continue at a more moderate pace on their own.

When he got back to the camp, under the shadow of the spire of Kingsrock, it was hardly past noon.

"No thanks," he said to his quartermaster. "I've already had lunch."

30

DOGFIGHT

They were trying to decide where to dig in. Here, at the mouth of the road that to led to Knockford, or on the eastern side, where the gate led into the city?

"I do not think we can hold both," Karl said. "We have already split our forces enough."

"Surely you see we had no choice," Istvar said, his face darkening.

"There are always choices," Karl replied evenly. "Now we must make another one. We know the Gold Throne is in Wesvale; eventually they will come down the eastern road to relieve Kingsrock."

"Unless they go home first, to resupply or such." Gregor scratched a route out on a map with his finger. "Then they could come up the north road from West Undaal. If we're on the other side of Kingsrock, they could just march right past us and head off to Knockford. Given that we've stripped the guns from the town, I don't think we want that."

"If you do not control the city gates, the garrison can sally any time they like. We will wind up facing both the Gold Throne's army and the royal forces," Earl Istvar pointed out. "We could leave a strong guard on the bridge and invest the gate. Should they bypass us, the bridge can hold until we fall upon them from the rear."

"That would be splitting our forces again," Karl said. "And if they do not hold, then we will arrive to find the enemy fortified on the bridge."

"I thought you had plenty of siege engines," Istvar said.

Christopher grunted. There wouldn't be a bridge left after he used cannons on it.

"So you're suggesting we stay here?" he asked Karl instead.

"On the contrary. I suggest we put all of our forces at the foot of the gates. When the Gold Throne arrives, Treywan will lead a sally out of the gates into our west flank while the Gold attacks the east flank."

"That's good . . . how?"

Karl looked at him, carefully unreadable. "The sally will be down a narrow road. Perforce it will be compromised entirely of nobility, men armored by steel and tael to stand in the thickest part of the battle."

"Still missing the part where that's good," Gregor said.

Christopher knew. "That would be a perfect firing ground. The cannons will make mincemeat out of anything on the road." Karl was engineering a slaughter of the nobility on a grand scale. They would expect their tael, or perhaps a few well-placed spells, to protect them from the usual threats of fireballs and lighting bolts. They would not be prepared for the hailstorm of lead Karl would unleash on them.

Gregor and Torme blanched when understanding dawned. They were fighting men before they were priests. To subject their fellow knights to such a futile death would be harsh indeed.

"It means leaving this road open, though," Christopher objected. He'd just ridden himself silly for the second time to control it. "And fighting on two fronts. Whereas if we camp here, at the crossroads, we can keep them all in front of us."

"Until they use cavalry or magic to flank us," Karl said. "Again."

"More likely Treywan will just line up his knights and let them charge." Istvar looked out over the plain. "He'll trust to the width of his line to exhaust your magic, and the tael of his knights to close the gap. It is what I would do if I were facing common footmen."

The Earl of Fram nodded in agreement, apparently comfortable to let Istvar take the lead in this war council. Cardinal Faren and the Vicars did not attend the strategy meetings. Disa had stopped coming, too. The bards were the only women there.

"He knows the strength of our arms," Torme said. "He will only charge under cover. I would expect a magical darkness."

"Which the Cardinal and I can dispel."

"We cannot count on you," Uma said. "You must not hold any of your magic back when you face the King."

Lalania said nothing, watching him with her face carefully disciplined into neutrality. He knew she was acting again, but he could not guess to what script.

The army spent the rest of the day throwing up bulwarks and entrenchments, making a proper fortified camp. Lalania was saving the lyre for emergencies, so the work was done by muscles instead of magic. The militia earned their keep here, especially since Tom's men were already builders of some note, having built the road they were all fighting over.

Christopher went out to scout around the city, traveling high and fast in mist form. The first he knew of danger was when something tore him off his horse, clutching at his misty form with invisible hands.

Unnatural wind swirled around him, carrying him toward the city. Instinctively he slipped from its grasp. The special favor of a god of Travel was turning out be inordinately lifesaving.

The entity, a creature made entirely of air, howled in rage with literally the voice of the whirlwind. It turned to violence, ripping at him with short, sharp gusts.

He watched fistfuls of mist-stuff dissipate into empty air like the stuffing being beaten out of a teddy bear and felt his tael-fueled vitality evaporating with it. Screaming at his horse, he dove for the ground, triggering the process of solidification. The creature followed, battering at him. He fell the last twenty feet, astonished at how much life force he had lost.

Leaves and grass whirled around him in the funnel of an unnatural tornado the size of a small house. The wind slammed at him with fists of force, knocking him to the ground. But he could cast now. A simple protection spell, and the elemental monster was held at bay. Howling above his head in rage, it tore at the treetops and dumped the branches on his head. His armor saved him from such a petty assault while he poured healing power into himself, restoring what he had lost.

In the distance, he could see the towers of Kingsrock Castle. There he thought he saw the faintest shimmer, perhaps nothing more than a banner flapping in the wind or a page walking past a window. Nonetheless it put ice in his veins.

Above him the unnatural wind swirled and died, the air now still and quiet, the summoning spell expired and the monster with it. He cast another protection spell on his horse and climbed aboard. Soon they were mist again, streaking for the safety of the camp. Nothing stopped them, but then only the wind could catch them at this speed, and the protection spell lasted long enough to get him safely inside his dirt fort.

"Had they the wit or power to send two instead of one, they could have won the war by now," Karl told him after his report. "Stray no more from the camp without escort."

Karl sent orders to the men to beware magical assault. They dug the ammunition pits with care, setting buckets of sand and water everywhere through the camp, and Kennet kept their magic stream-gushing water bottle uncorked and ready to respond. A fire elemental could cause them serious problems.

By silent consent, Karl failed to inform the men of the closeness of their commander's call, though the general staff had to be told. Nonetheless, night fell on an uneasy camp, which still had not fired a shot at the enemy.

"Why didn't the King follow that assault up?" Gregor wanted to know. "Is he really just waiting for that stinking priest?"

"No," Uma answered. "We have learned that the Gold Apostle arrived in the city yesterday. He may even have been the source of the tornado. His army will arrive tomorrow, fresh from the destruction of the Jade Throne. It seems Treywan wishes to contest on the field of blood rather than tael."

Karl's troops kept fortifying, digging trenches and laying stakes, creating traffic hazards to channel approaching troops into killing fields under looming cannons. Despite all that, Christopher felt it was time to begin.

Only one Parrott was ready for action. The other was covered under tarps and suffering some technical fault that no one could quite explain. Christopher didn't care, as one would be enough. He assembled a dozen gunners from his best crews, replacing them in the lines with militiamen. They stood around it now, gazing at the massive engine of destruction, while in the background people pretended to continue working.

Dereth was there, too, looking a little pale. The weapon had not been fully tested. It might fail, or worse, explode.

"Have a little faith," Christopher told him with a grin. "Light her up, boys, and let's see what she can do."

It took two men to lift the squat, pointed cylinder of a projectile and feed it into the gaping breach, behind the twelve-foot barrel hanging over a heavy timber frame bound in iron. A seemingly endless supply of powder followed. The metal alone was worth a fortune, made possible only by the coal-fired forges he had built, the finances he had invented, and the changes to industry he had wrought. Mere chemistry had not built this gun, or even this army.

It took his gunners fifteen minutes of argument and cranking on adjustment gears before they agreed the weapon was ready. They offered him the lanyard.

He declined. His hands had hurled enough explosions to last him a lifetime. Dereth accepted the honor. The smith muttered a silent prayer, glanced up at the city with a flash of hatred so hot Christopher was shocked, and yanked.

The blast knocked them all back, just from the sound of it. Flame leapt twenty feet out of the barrel, a storm cloud of smoke on its heels. The men might have been laughing or crying; he could not tell, temporarily deafened. Massaging his ears, he stared out at the city, trying to spot the projectile on its way. The range was a mile. There was time to look for it.

An explosion in the side of the hill sent rocks tumbling down. The shell had fallen short. His gunners did not apologize, nor did he ask them to. Nobody wanted to overshoot, sending a high explosive to land randomly on the town, like they had in the goblin city. Smoke drifted up from the wound in the side of the mountain while the men swabbed the barrel and reloaded. He could see motion on the distant walls. Perhaps the defenders were jeering.

The next shot took only two minutes to prepare. It struck a tower at the base. Grand and slow, the tower fell over like an old man.

The town was quiet now. Christopher, his hands over his ears, retreated back to his command tent. He didn't worry about the gun crew. If worst came to worst, he could restore their hearing by magic.

All morning the gun fired, once a minute or so. They had to take a break every other hour to let the barrel cool. After lunch his quartermaster, Charles, informed him they'd used half the ammunition they had prepared.

The castle was looking extremely ragged by this point, only one of its five towers still standing, and a huge notch carved out of the northern most wall. Further destruction might be pointless.

And yet the King had not appeared.

"Let's give them a break," Christopher said. "Resume shelling tomorrow. And send to Knockford for more ammunition." A steady drumbeat of terror would be more debilitating than smashing the entire castle in an afternoon.

"Begging your pardon, Colonel, but send to who? The men that make the munitions are all here."

A problem he'd have to solve eventually. But he couldn't send the militia away now, with the main battle unfought. He wanted them to own this victory, not owe it to him.

Late afternoon brought more sour news. Uma reported that the Gold Throne army was straggling into Kingsrock in a panicked and disorderly mob. The Rangers had gotten their revenge, sneaking halfway across the Kingdom to launch an ambush on the rear of the column as it marched east. The entire baggage train was destroyed, with nontrivial losses compounded by the fact that half the army had bolted for the city when the fighting started, leaving the other half to fight a disorganized retreat.

Christopher found himself swearing hard curses. "If only I'd listened to you, Karl. We'd be there, in the way of their retreat, picking them off one by one." Instead, the new troops would be fed and calmed by the King's hand, and tomorrow he'd face two armies where he could have faced one.

"Or, knowing the way was blocked, they may have stood and fought, which could have gone badly for our allies."

Karl was being kind. Far more likely they would have bolted into the woods and simply disappeared.

"Still, your plan would have us halfway to winning, and mine has accomplished nothing. If Treywan doesn't come out, I can't blow up the whole town to force him."

"Now is not the time for tender mercies," Earl Istvar said with a frown.

"It's not that," Christopher explained absently. "We don't have enough ammunition."

Karl shrugged, dismissing the worry. "Once no visible sign of Treywan's authority remains standing, we will force the gates. His soldiers will be disheartened; the people will offer us no resistance. We'll march through the streets and challenge him at the door of his hovel."

"He's cheap," Gregor mused. "He won't want to feed those rascals a day longer than he has to, and they didn't bring any of their own food. Tomorrow is the day. They'll come for us before breakfast."

The morning proved Gregor right. The scouts came riding in, reporting troops issuing out of the city gates and marching down to the plain.

"We could make a mad dash with the cavalry," Gregor suggested. They'd gotten their horses back from Armand the day before. "Bottle them up at the foot of the mountain, shoot like fiends, and then run away when they finally organize enough to make a sortie."

It sounded like a great plan. Christopher looked at Karl, waiting for his opinion.

"I prefer to reserve the strength of our horse, in case they seek to flank us. Or after, when they are retreating, to ride them down rather than let them slip back into the city to fight another day."

"We have plenty of lances," Gregor argued. "We can risk some of the carabineers, just enough to sow confusion, and not incidentally give those footmen a taste of what they'll be marching into."

Karl mulled it over before looking to Christopher for help. Christopher shrugged. "I picked last time, and it sucked. So now it's your turn."

The Earls, Istvar and Fram, watched the exchange with a sense of marvel. Torme and Gregor were past that, though. They just watched Karl to see what he would decide.

"The idea has merit," Karl finally said. "We must be concerned that Treywan will dispatch something to trap them. Remember our rifles are weak against soul-trapped, and the Gold Apostle must have plenty of those."

"Disa can handle those," Gregor said. "You've got the Cardinal and the Vicars now. You don't need her."

Need wasn't what Christopher had in mind. A desire to keep the young woman safe threatened to override his tongue and overrule Karl. Before that happened, he took himself off to the Parrott. Might as well see his mistake through.

The gunners were eager to get started, standing around and shouting at each other at the top of their lungs. Christopher discovered that was the only way they could communicate. He couldn't afford the spell power to fix them today, so he just shouted along with them.

What a difference a day made. Their first shot brought down the last tower, and before they could finish reloading, an armored figure stepped off the distant wall and flew toward them, a long black cloak billowing out behind.

Christopher grinned, even though his stomach was doing flip-flops. This was it, then. He started casting spells, the longest lasting ones first. Strength, sharpness, flight, mist, the energy shield just in case Treywan had brought a little help, and finally the spell that made him into a warrior. In the distance he could hear Royal neighing in outrage. The horse had sensed the coming fight and was angry that he was being left behind.

Christopher had to. Treywan would kill the beast in a single stroke. True, that might be one stroke that didn't land on Christopher, but he couldn't spend the lives of his men and animals that freely. Not yet.

Much to Christopher's consternation, the King flew lower as he flew closer. The people who had gathered around him, Lalania and Torme and the gun crew, began to discreetly disperse, disappearing into the crowd, leaving him alone in a circle of empty ground.

When the King loomed only a hundred feet above the camp, looking properly royal in his gleaming plate mail and flowing black cloak, Torme stood on top of a wagon, sighted down a rifle, and pulled the trigger.

In response, half the camp fired upward, five hundred rifles and a dozen small cannons flinging a wagonload of hot lead at the hovering figure.

In the aftermath, Treywan smiled. Nothing had touched him, not even one tiny pellet.

Christopher didn't waste breath on curses. He threw his most powerful dispel at the King, regretting all the other times he'd begged Marcius for success. This was the one that mattered.

It didn't matter. Heartened by Christopher's act of defiance, the other half of the army let loose to no effect. Treywan threw back his head and laughed.

Some of those guns would have had the weapon blessing on them. Torme and the Vicars would have seen to that. Even the insubstantial ogre magi would have been torn to shreds by the sheer firepower unleashed on the King.

The King, however, spun his great sword in a slow circle, and bellowed down at Christopher. "I know you can fly, little priest. Come up here where everyone can watch me cut you in half."

"Not alone," Christopher muttered, and called out to Marcius for aid. If the god sent him bison this time, there would be harsh words.

Instead a flock of white eagles swooped above Christopher's head. He leapt into the air and charged the King, preceded by his avian retinue. The King snarled, mostly in frustration, and struck at the beasts in great whirling arcs as they swooped on him.

Each bird disintegrated at the savage touch of Treywan's sword. Nonetheless they gave Christopher much-needed cover. He closed with the King and struck, his steel blade charged with magic. The result was less than impressive, but at this point Christopher expected that. The King had a lot of lives to spend.

They traded another set of blows, Christopher drifting around to cut at the King's off-hand side, while the King murdered three more of the birds. Sword-fighting in three dimensions was disconcerting. There was nothing to brace himself against, no ground to judge, no steps to advance or retreat.

The last eagle clutched at the King's helmet, as if trying to pull it off. Christopher lunged, thrusting his blade up under the King's jaw, where it caught on some stray bit of armor and went in only an inch or so, enough to kill an ordinary man but here only a minor drain on tael.

The King ignored both bird and blade and struck Christopher back. It was not like being hit by a large, powerful man with a razor-sharp sledgehammer; it was like being hit by a freight train.

Christopher went spinning in a shower of scales knocked loose, over half his vitality gone in a single strike. Instinctively he swooped and fled. The King dispatched the last bird and gave chase, only yards behind.

They tore across the sky like this, Christopher's army trying not to give voice to their dismay and not entirely succeeding, until the mist spell kicked in. Then Christopher quickly widened the gap, outrunning the King's jeers.

A thousand yards away he stopped and began solidifying. The King came on, growing from a tiny threatening doll to a large and terrifying puppet of menace. Christopher waited out the transformation nervously until he could cast. Three quick spells later, he was whole and hale again. However, his bottle of awesome sauce was empty, the dueling spell expired. He was just a priest again.

A tornado swept up to him from the city. Absentmindedly he cast his protection spell, and the elemental whirled and whined to no effect.

The Cardinal's voice came in his mind: "The Lady Uma says his cloak protects him from our bullets. You must tear it off of him so that we may strike true."

The old man was clearly unnerved. He'd let a word go to waste. Christopher didn't bother to answer. Instead he flew at the King, already triggering the mist.

They clashed in midair, trading immense blows. An elephant would have come apart under the strength of Treywan's attack. Only tael stopped the sword halfway through Christopher's collarbone. As he flew past and ripped the blade out of his body, his flesh knit itself together in its wake. If the King hit an arm or a leg, even tael might not keep it attached.

Though at the moment, Christopher could fight without a leg or two.

Christopher needed healing again. In mist form he returned to his previous position, solidifying over the Parrott and casting. He knew how long he had this time, so he watched the King for clues.

Treywan was tossing something aside in disdain. Silver sparkled in the cold sunlight as the objects fell. Potion vials, full of healing magic. Or they had been before Christopher's dispel.

So it was a contest between Treywan's vitality and Christopher's healing. It was hard to tell how much he had depleted the King, but it was certainly not enough. Trying to pull the man's cloak off, however, would be spending precious seconds in range of that terrible swift sword, and Christopher feared two blows without healing might kill him.

They were too high up for the tower of flame, a ludicrous limitation that annoyed Christopher severely at the moment. The flame came from above; for what possible reason did it have to be exactly forty feet off the ground? Growling in frustration, he let the King close. This time he would spend his velocity in altitude, hoping to let the King overshoot and possibly, gods be willing, even miss.

No such luck. Christopher lunged at the last minute, flipping upside down and falling up. While his blade punched a hole through the King's armor and into his body, the King still caught him with his own sword. More scales went flying; even if Christopher survived this, his armor wouldn't.

Frightfully fast, the King turned and came back. Christopher kept going up, wondering if he dared risk a spell or if he should turn to mist again. Underneath him the King burst into flame, a huge roaring ball of fire that washed over Christopher and flared out at the edge of his energy shield.

It was an odd choice of attack. The King was definitely singed and smoking, while Christopher was wholly untouched. It would require two or three such blasts to wear down his ward, and the King would suffer the worse for it. While Christopher was trying to figure out why and how the King had managed such a trick, Treywan suddenly dropped away, streaking toward the ground.

Christopher's gaze shot past the King, to where Lalania stood in the empty circle of dirt, the wand of fire held high in both hands.

Heartsick in a way that the last few minutes of deadly combat had failed to evoke, he fell after Treywan, willing himself toward the ground at full speed. Lalania lowered her wand, perhaps realizing there was no time left for another fireball. She mouthed something inaudible, touching a necklace at her throat, while Christopher screamed silently at her to run.

Treywan dropped to the ground clumsily. It made no difference. His blade reached out almost negligently and cut the pretty young bard in half from neck to hip, her body falling like broken sacks of lifeless meat.

Twenty feet above the ground, Christopher's magic deserted him utterly. He fell, controlled only by gravity, landing hard on the dirt in a sprawl. Desperately he scrambled to his feet, his armor weighing heavily without magic to make it light.

The King stood in front of him, tall and cruel and unconcerned.

Christopher, blinded by sudden insight, threw himself facedown at the King's feet, tossing his sword away, hugging the dirt for dear life.

Treywan growled without pity. "A bit late for groveling," he said, raising his sword.

Behind him, flame and noise and death. The blast washed over Christopher, tearing at him more fiercely than the tornado. A hot spray landed on his exposed cheek. He reached up and wiped it off, fearful of burning wad or ash or molten lead. His hand came away red.

Something fluttered in the air. A black cloak, floating free to the ground. Christopher raised his head and looked around for the King.

He could only find pieces. A leg, an arm, a chunk of meat and bone that might have been a shoulder. There was a fine red mist over everything. Blood.

Karl staggered out from the ruined tarps that had covered the other Parrott. The canvas was charred and smoking. He kicked spitefully at something round and black lying on the ground. A helmet, still smoking from the heat of the blast.

Karl's eyes swept over the field, lingering only an instant on the sad corpse of the bard. He locked his gaze with Christopher's.

"The King is dead," he croaked. "Long live the Saint."

31

WATERLOO

Christopher sat shaking over the dead girl, unable to tell if his tremors were grief, rage, or relief. The two of them had plotted in secret, telling Christopher nothing, knowing he would have forbidden it if he had known.

They had triple-loaded the Parrott, stuffing it with grapeshot. Lalania had lured the King down with Fae's wand, activating the Skald's null-stone at the last minute, trapping herself in a cage of mundanity when only magic could have saved her. Despite the effects of the anti-magic field, Treywan would still have had his rank; armed only with an ordinary piece of steel, he could still have slain half the army in melee combat. She had pilfered a wealth of magic, all for a plot that could only end in her death.

Karl had pulled the trigger, staking everything on a single shot from a cannon that might well have blown up in his face. If Christopher had not understood at the last minute, he would be dead, too, his body too mangled for the Cardinal's magic to restore. The King was beyond hope; they couldn't find most of his torso. Lalania had run the same risk; Karl would not have given up his shot just because she was in the way.

Now Christopher knelt at Lalania's sides, wondering if his own magic were strong enough to bring her back. Wondering if dying in the radius of the null-stone would block any future revivals.

So many ways it could have all gone wrong. He wanted to beat Karl like a rented mule; he wanted to kiss the man like a drunken Italian.

"I cannot bear to see her like this," Karl muttered, and staggered away. The proximity of the blast had been debilitating.

Cannan was there, watching the King's head with professional suspicion. Cardinal Faren came up to Christopher and gently tugged him to his feet.

"Do not despair, lad. I've fixed worse. But come away now; there is still a battle to be fought."

"What?" Christopher said, amazed.

Torme stood at the edge of the circle and saluted him. "The Gold Apostle presses the attack. No doubt he has told his armies that the King can be revived, if only they can drive us from the field."

"Give me that," Christopher snarled, pointing at the black cloak lying on the ground. While Torme obeyed, Christopher staggered over and pried Treywan's head from its dented helmet. He stumbled out of the range of the null-stone and cast a tiny spell.

The tael drained from Treywan's head, forming a purple tennis ball in his hand. Only a fraction of what had served Treywan, it was still enough to make a Prophet out of a commoner.

Cannan could not repress a cold smile. "Another step closer," the big man muttered.

"You hang onto this," Christopher said, holding it out to him.

"There is no need," Cannan said. "We already know its fate. Until you can bend the laws of heaven on my behalf, there will only ever be one answer."

"There will be bills to pay," Christopher argued back. "We have a battle to fight. Men will die."

Cannan's eyes were as sharp and hard as swords. "I trust our men to kill more than they lose. And you have already sworn not to raise the enemy."

As huge as the ball was, it would be only a down payment on his next rank. Christopher was out of arguments, though. There were few who could be burdened with guarding such a treasure, despite their best intentions. Tael wanted to be consumed, radiating a field of desire. Not to mention that assassins and thieves would risk anything to lay hands on such a prize.

He looked at the Cardinal, who shook his head, his face carefully blank.

"You cannot deny me this much," Christopher said, carving off a chunk and tossing it at the Cardinal. "Lalania's revival, and restoration of her rank." Defeated, Christopher shoved the rest of the ball in his mouth, where it instantly evaporated.

Torme handed him the cloak. "What are you plans, Colonel?"

"I'm going to dishearten the enemy," he answered. "I still have plenty of magic." Outside of the null-stone's sphere, his spells had sprung back to life. He draped the cloak around his neck with his free hand, and Torme stepped forward to fasten it.

Then he was up in the air, guilty and broken-hearted and fiercely, fiercely angry. He flew out over the ramparts to the plain below the city, where companies of halberdiers were laid out like checkerboards, with crossbowmen behind.

They were well disciplined. At his approach, hundreds of quarrels sallied forth to greet him. None came within five feet, which seemed highly unlikely given an archer's training. The cloak would seem to grant immunity to ranged attacks, though it had offered no protection at all from Christopher's sword.

Starting at one end of the enemy formations, he flew in front of the troops at a safe altitude of fifty feet. They jeered and cursed at him while he flew in silence, holding the King's crumpled head by the hair, blood dripping down. As the soldiers understood what they were looking at, they grew silent, though no less angry.

Halfway through his journey, spells lashed out at him, invisible, deduced only from their effects. Though he was solid at the moment, he felt the mist leave him. Someone had dispelled it, but fortunately his flight remained intact. A paralytic spell of immense power followed, binding his muscles like electrified cables. He shrugged it off with a twitch of his shoulders and a silent word to his patron. This was a trick the Gold Apostle should have known better than to try. Perhaps he had hoped Christopher had used up his defenses during the duel.

Christopher ignored these assaults, letting them pass unanswered. He was not here for the Apostle. He wanted these men to know that their cause was lost, that the King was dead beyond any power to restore, that their own deaths would therefore be without meaning. He wanted them to think about running away.

And he wanted an excuse to kill them when they didn't.

A pea-sized pebble of fire rose up from the ground, to burst around him in a house-sized bubble of flame. The enemy had wands of fire, too. Christopher slowed, almost to the end of the line, looking for the source. Another one flew out to envelop him, flaring out on his shield. He was low on spells, but the energy shield was low rank. He renewed it, watching the next fireball come in. At the last moment, he threw the King's head into its path.

Below him, the men groaned in dismay. The fireball burst, and the mortal flesh, deprived of tael and the protection of Christopher's magic, exploded into tiny, black smoking chunks that fell slowly to the ground, wafting in the wind.

The army reacted as one, with a howl of anguish not unlike the ulvenmen when Christopher had been slaughtering them. He turned away and sailed back to his own lines.

Riflemen lined the ramparts, small cannons interspersed among them. An artificial hill had been built out of dirt and logs. Half of the five-inch Napoleons were deployed here, with the rest on either wing. In the center of the camp he could see the Parrotts being wrestled around to face the enemy. They would spend the rest of the battle as howitzers, lobbing shells over the heads of his own men. The rocket launchers sheltered behind the ramparts, not even visible to the enemy on the ground. At the rear of the camp, horsemen stood by their mounts, waiting for the signal. There was a Cardinal in the middle of his camp, an Earl on either flank, and a church's worth of lesser priests scattered throughout the lines.

He turned to review the enemy. Behind their checkerboard of halberds and crossbows was a cloud of armored horsemen, the steel tips of their lances glinting in the sun. Under normal circumstances those knights would simply charge the enemy footmen, trusting to their armor and tael to deal with petty annoyances like crossbows. From this height he could see something else going on. Pairs of figures carrying massive cooking kettles, moving with stilted gaits. They fanned out in front of the enemy lines and began to advance.

A Parrott shell whistled over the field, falling too far behind the lines to do any good. Christopher dropped to the fake hill, where he could see Karl gazing out over the battlefield. Quickly he sketched out the enemy disposition in the dirt, then went back into the air to watch. At only a hundred feet he could still shout commands below while seeing all of the action. This alone was a fantastic tactical advantage. Few commanders could stand on air above the battlefield with so little care.

There were thousands of men fighting today, hundreds of them first rank or higher. The number of wizards was exactly one, with perhaps no more than a dozen priestly spell-casters of significant rank. Muscle and chemistry would rule here, a fact not lost on the enemy.

The cooking kettles being carried by pairs of soul-trapped were now on fire, coughing up a thick black smoke that rolled across the battlefield. Behind them the enemy cautiously followed, hiding in the dark. Bullets began pocking the creatures and the kettles, to little effect.

Christopher swooped forward and chanted, using his power to destroy the animated creatures. Out of sheer reflex the crossbowmen unleashed a futile storm of quarrels. They didn't waste any other spells, though. On the other hand, Christopher was about out of spells, which was unfortunate, as a few towers of flame would not go amiss here.

A Parrott shell fell among the halberdiers, obviating the need for magical destruction. The covering smoke had mostly stopped advancing, so the enemy picked up their pace and marched through it. Christopher retreated back to his lines to watch for the next trick.

And what a trick it was. Stone walls sprang up out of the ground a dozen yards from Christopher's front line. Rather than a useful fortification, it was an obstacle that blocked his lanes of fire. Presumably the enemy had some means to remove it at their convenience.

Below him, Karl issued orders. The Napoleons belched, and the wall shattered in a dozen places. Riflemen began to fire through the gaps. The cannons reloaded and made short work of the wall. Out on the plain, men were falling down and lying still. Christopher prayed that some of them were simply faking it. It would be the rational thing to do. Their crossbowmen released another salvo, still to no effect. The range was too great and the quarrels fell short.

The two ploys had gained the enemy half the distance. Now came their final and greatest trick. Clouds of fog swelled up, as dense as cotton candy, smothering his lines. Somewhere out there, Master Sigrath was burning through an expensive stack of scrolls. Christopher stared, trying to find where the wily rat was hiding. It had to be close.

Below him Karl shouted something about the wall. The fog cloud only reached a dozen yards in the air, but it was enough to blind the whole camp save for Christopher. He stopped looking for the invisible wizard and watched the enemy footmen.

As soon as the first one stepped over the remains of the stone wall, Christopher chopped his hand down to signal Karl. The young veteran paused, his head swaying to some silent metronome. Suddenly he raised his hand and Kennet raised his trumpet. The hand came down, the trumpet blew, and all across the camp artillery men fired the rockets.

They arced over the field, streaks of sparkling red lacing the clouds of white. One passed terribly close to Christopher, and he realized that the cloak was a double boon. He would not die from friendly fire today.

The missiles exploded in the crowds of men. From here they looked like white mushrooms sprouting in a field of purple and gold grass. Both Parrotts threw out shells; the Napoleons fired blindly through the fog, trusting they would find targets at the range they had been primed for.

In the aftermath of the artillery barrage the enemy ran. The footmen fled in any and all directions, as long as it was away from the front, while the knights behind charged straight for the wall of fog, knowing that their only chance lay in breaching the lines where the combat could be hand to hand. Their horses stumbled on the litter of the field: corpses, shattered stone, potholes, and pits dug by bombs. Nonetheless they came on. Christopher shouted a warning, though there was little anyone could do about it.

Yet Karl had found something. His own knights ran forward, on foot, to throw their armored weight into reinforcing the lines. Normally this would be suicide against mounted foes, but lances were fifteen feet long. The battle in the fog would be at five feet.

The carbineers were running forward, too. With their rate of fire, the short range would hardly matter.

At the last minute a fireball streaked forward to the center of the line; incredibly, it did not explode. Instead the fog cleared for thirty feet around where it should have landed. Christopher could see the Cardinal standing in the center, surrounded by a fistful of knights. The old man had dispelled the fireball and taken the fog with it. In the gap, riflemen fired in earnest.

Christopher swooped down to join the fight. The lances were the only thing that had held him at bay, and they were all lying abandoned in the dirt.

WATERLOO   301

The battle was tight and sharp for a while, and then the fog clouds evaporated. Within seconds the surviving knights were casting down their swords, kneeling in the dirt with hands behind their heads. Priests and priestesses swarmed through the suddenly quiet mob, healing friend and foe alike, though only enough to staunch the flow of blood. Soon they were picking their way across the battlefield, saving what they could.

Christopher glared down at the three men he had been rattling swords with a moment ago. "Where is the Gold Apostle?"

"Halfway home, no doubt," one spat. "Would you still be here, in his shoes?"

"I think we both know I would," Christopher answered.

32

CORONATION DAY

Gregor was rustling up knights to enter the city and claim their prize. Christopher wanted to wait until tomorrow, as he had spent every drop of magic healing his men and the enemy. So had Gregor and Istvar and all the other priests in his camp. Consequently his losses were light, only a few dozen slain outright. The enemy knights had fared much worse. As a single bullet would not usually kill a knight, the men tended to shoot anything in armor half a dozen times more than necessary. The enemy foot had suffered the most. Of the thousand men the King had sent to the plain, half remained upon it.

Where they would stay forever. Christopher could not afford to raise so many, even if he had the next year to raise them in. The battle left him wealthy, even after restoring his own men, but not that wealthy.

He would have had tael enough for all of them, even to restore ranks to the fallen enemy knights, if he still had the King's tael on hand instead of in his head. He said as much to the Cardinal.

"Then it is good you do not have it to hand," Faren said quietly. "You still have a realm to subdue. Let us set a precedent here, so that none can later plead confusion."

There would be plenty of subduing. The Gold Apostle had slipped away, as had Master Sigrath. With time and gold both of them could raise new armies, defend them with new magic tricks, and do it all again.

Gregor sat at the head of a column, impatient. "Let us seize the moment," he demanded. "I can knock those city gates down with a feather right now, but delay until tomorrow and we may find them barred by spell-craft."

Christopher looked around to ask Lalania what she thought, then closed his eyes.

"Ride on, Ser," Karl told Gregor. "Let the city know that the Saint spends this night on the battlefield, looking after his wounded. And see to it that there is no looting, no despoiling. We have not come to sack this city but to liberate it." He directed those words more toward Istvar and Fram, who rode just behind Gregor.

"You need not fear my men's discipline," Istvar said stiffly.

The Earl of Fram merely glared, which sort of implied Karl's words needed to be said after all.

The column of horses set off at a gallop. Christopher went to find something to drink. Preferably several somethings. There would be no corpses raised until tomorrow. He could not share Faren's confidence; no one knew what the effect of the null-stone would be. Uma had shrugged it off, unworried, but when he had asked her point-blank if the experiment had ever been performed before, she had to admit it had not.

Trouble did not slip his trail. The commander from Parnar, a baronet, found him at the back of the mess tent, on the edge of a crowd of drunken, deafened, and therefore extremely loud artillerymen.

"My lord," the man shouted. "I would ask a boon of you."

Christopher led the man out to the stables, where he could brush Royal's coat for something to do. Cannan stood by discreetly, watching the Baronet compose himself for a hard speech.

"My lord," the man said, "I would request that you give me your undivided attention."

"Why?" Christopher sighed. "You're just going to ask me to do what I already told you I wouldn't."

There had been eight knights among the friendly casualties. The Baronet had come to demand that their rank be restored. This much was obvious.

"I have been told that you respect words like other men respect swords. Therefore I deploy arguments instead of armies. Consider that you have battles yet to fight, and the morale of the men who serve you will be greatly heartened by the restoration of these few ranks."

"Knights," Christopher corrected. "The morale of the knights. The common men are fine with just being brought back to life."

"And yet you will face many knights, whose spine can only be stiffened if you are seen to reduce men in rank for your own profit. You have won a mighty treasure here today. To squirrel it all away in your own pocket would be unseemly."

This was an argument that had barely even begun. The realm was used to handing out knighthoods to deserving young men for a job well done. Christopher needed such a staggering amount of tael to reach his next rank that he could not support this pyramid of patronage.

"I would prefer not to set a precedent I cannot continue," he told the Baronet, trying to sound hard but succeeding only at sounding weary.

"And yet you already have. Did you not restore the rank of the Ranger when he died in your service?"

A small smile crept to Christopher's lips. The man had done his homework. In sheer point of fact, he had also given Gregor an advanced and therefore expensive knight rank. Had the Baronet led with that thrust, Christopher had a parry prepared: the blue knight had eventually become a priest, after all. But he had simply forgotten about the Ranger.

"Very well," Christopher said. "I shall restore those who lost their only rank of knighthood. So long as you make it clear that I do this for this battle only, and only because of you."

"Me, my lord?"

"I wish to set precedents. You argued your case well. This should be rewarded."

The man knew when to count his winnings. He bowed his head and retreated. Christopher made a mental note never to play poker with the Baronet.

When he was gone, Christopher asked Cannan his opinion. "Did I lose another battle just now?"

The big man shook his head. "It is a hard lord who cannot be dragged even an inch out of his way. No one wants to serve a tower of stone instead of a man."

"True," said a feminine voice. Uma stepped out the shadows, pretending she had just arrived. Christopher could not guess how long she had been there. Not that it mattered. "Small wins will inure them against great losses, like a child's teddy bear holds off the terrors of the infinite night. If you would end knighthood in the realm without stretching a thousand necks, you would do best to proceed slowly."

"Can I?" he asked her.

"For any other, I would say no. The lance has always been our greatest defense against monsters. In the hands of brave men, it can bring down giants. And thus the lords created knights, for the people and the Wild required it, and never mind the blood-price they drew from the common folk. Yet you have given us a weapon that shatters lances like toothpicks, even in the hands of commoners."

"I need . . . so much tael." Christopher sighed again. "I could give you weapons to shatter my cannon. And other things."

"Say no more," Uma shushed him. "If I do not know your secrets, I cannot betray them. And though the King is dead, your true foe still lurks. We can no longer help you there. Our greatest secret, the only trap we could hope to use against them, is secret no more."

"Does it still work?" The null-stone had a limited number of uses.

Uma's lips twisted in bitter irony. "We shall only find out the next time we try."

So it might not have worked against the King. Another risk Lalania had taken.

The horse snuffled at him, telling him to go away and let it sleep. He went to bed, knowing that the morning would tell if the bard had finally run out of luck.

The Cardinal had stitched her body back together with his magic. She lay on a board in the bright morning light, clean and peaceful and so obviously dead.

"I think you should be the one to call her back," Faren told him.

Christopher nodded dumbly. Faren placed a lump of tael on her forehead and stepped away. Christopher recited the words the spell, dreading the vision that it would yield.

In front of him Lalania paused from an elaborate dance, handsome young men melting back into the crowd that filled a vast ballroom of streaked marble. She wore a gown of gossamer threads, moss green and deep-water blue, set off by a line of small emeralds that wrapped from shoulder to opposite thigh.

With a cold shock, Christopher realized the gems marked out the cut that had killed her.

"Lala," he said. "It's time to go."

"Oh my lord, the evening has just begun." She smiled invitingly at him. "Come and have a dance with me."

"I can't." He could not enter the vision. He had no idea what would happen if he tried. At best the spell would be spoiled. At worst he would succeed. And if he could join that unending party with a beautiful young lover who would never age, never feel pain or loss, never lose an iota of the esteem she held him in . . . who would call *him* back?

"You make a poor offer, my lord," she teased. "A lady in my position must choose wisely, for a maiden's heart can only be given once."

This was what he had truly feared. Not that the null-stone would block her return, but that he would fail to win it. Watching the vision drift slowly away was watching her die all over again.

"I will make you any offer you want," he said in desperation.

"Any, my lord? Any at all?" Under batting eyelashes lurked a hunger, hot and raw.

"Anything," he croaked, praying that Marcius would forgive him the lie.

Except, of course, he could not lie here. The spell would not allow it.

"Then a proper kiss seems small enough to ask." With a lovely smirk of triumph she leaned into his arms, her breath warm on his face, her lips with a softness he had forgotten, her tongue like a live thing, close and needful . . .

"Ahem," the Cardinal coughed.

Christopher pulled back, away from where he had knelt over Lalania's corpse.

"Don't stop," she murmured, looking up at him with sleepy eyes.

"You have to rest," he told her. Mercifully she did not argue, merely closing her eyes and sighing. He retreated from the tent, trying to find his bearings in the muddy, cold field.

Faren followed him. Christopher glanced at the Cardinal, expecting rebuke or at least a witty barb. The old man shook his head gently.

"Not today, lad. Today we do what is necessary, and none may gainsay us."

There were more corpses to raise, and hard work it was. Convincing men to crawl back into a world he could barely remember why he stayed in drained his will, fraying his mood like a bad carpet. The Cardinal noticed and gave him a reprieve, letting him turn his attention to the knights. They were, for the most part, prideful and eager to return.

He let his men march into the city first, and not just to take up positions in case there was a trap. He wanted them to claim it, wanted the townspeople to see them claiming it, hoping it might dilute what he knew must come next.

Royal stepped high and lively, glorying in the conquest. The horse strolled down city streets, owning the cobblestones, snorting at the people watching from the sidewalks. At first they were silent, staring at Christopher warily, as if he might suddenly sprout horns or a second head. But as he passed them by, they began to sob and shout his name.

"Saint Christopher!" The cry rose up behind him and overtook his advance. Now the people he passed gave in to their hopes, holding out their hands in a frenzy of need. He had broken the shield that protected them. Whatever its faults and sins, it had kept them safe for twenty years.

"Saint Christopher!" They screamed it like a catechism, a magic phrase that would hold the darkness at bay. That he would be kinder than their last lord was of no weight. That he was bound by a god to goodness meant nothing. All they asked of him was strength.

"Saint Christopher!" The chant roiled the city, twenty thousand voices strong. They might have been enemies a day ago, or even an hour. Now they took his name to their chest like armor. He could not blame them, not after what he had seen in ulvenmen huts and goblin dungeons. The children of Earth hid under the covers from bogeymen; in this world the bogeymen fled in terror from the creatures of the Wild.

Gregor and the Earls waited for him at the castle doors. They had not been opened yet. The knights had slept in the town, not wanting to deny him the honor of claiming his keep. Such as it was. Even from here he could see the holes in the roof.

The first time he had traversed this threshold, he had been in danger of never escaping. Now he realized that fate had claimed him after all. The need of the people lay upon him, more paralytic than any spell, and the favor of the god would not let him slip this grasp.

The people also wouldn't shut up. He gestured impatiently, and the knights fled from the doorway. Gregor yanked the lanyard of a cannon. The gun served a double purpose: it shattered the barred doors while also terrifying the nearest townsmen into a semblance of silence. As the knights returned and pulled the broken doors apart, Christopher spurred his horse into the great hall. It was unlikely that the enemy would have left a trap in such a public place. Although Christopher wasn't about to sit on that throne until it had been through some intense magical inspection.

He dismounted and stood at the head of the hall while his knights squeezed in, crowding around piles of rubble. Treywan had stood here once, rendering judgment. Now that was Christopher's burden. He would have felt a twinge of sympathy, or perhaps even pity, for the role the man had been forced to assume, save for that last terrible dispensation of authority. It might have been an act of war, a blow struck in battle, even plausibly self-defense, but Christopher would not, could not ever forgive Treywan for what he had done to the bard.

Gazing over the crowd, he put all of that anger into his voice, to give it the authority these men craved.

"In the name of the White, I claim this keep, this city, and this throne. Let none mistake mercy for weakness, tolerance for indulgence, restraint for cowardice, at peril of their lives."

"All hail Saint Christopher!" the knights sang out in unison, and Christopher detected in their voices many of the same qualities as in the city streets.

33

AFTERPARTY

The bard Uma walked through the castle with the Lyre of Varelous, singing. Misty figures restored the building at the direction of her voice. In an hour, the donjon was almost as good as new, though it would take more to rebuild the towers. It was sufficient for Christopher to hold court, and hold court he must. There were a thousand details to deal with and still a war to be fought.

The remains of the royal army were first. Christopher offered them a salary and a promise that their lives would be restored if they died fighting for him. In exchange for such unprecedented mercy, they would have to forgo any hope of promotion. The common soldiers fell over themselves to pledge to him. The knights were far more reserved, but in the end only a dozen refused.

He promptly had them locked in the dungeon as prisoners of war. "Treat them well," he told his jailors, who had been their comrades-in-arms only a day ago. "I'll release them after the war is done. But I have no desire to let them go now, only to have to kill them on another battlefield."

Against his will, he sent his militia home. They had jobs to do. He gave each of them a gold piece for their service, which only barely made up for the sting of taking away the rest of their rifles. "If you want more, you'll have to make more," he said, and away they went, grumbling.

He gave the guns to his newly hired crossbowmen. He could afford to arm them without fear that a traitor would take a shot at him, because of the cloak. That was what the King had been waiting on. That was the reason for Master Sigrath's promotion, the secret weapon they had spent so much time and tael crafting.

The cloak was a funny thing to wear; it did not feel entirely there. The cloth existed out of phase with the real world. Normally the enchantment would deflect half of the attacks directed at the wearer. Sigrath had twisted the spell, however, rendering it ineffective at a range of thirty feet or less and fully effective beyond that range. This was a tradeoff most warriors would not care for, as archery was far less dangerous than enchanted swords or dragon claws. The cloak existed solely to defeat Christopher.

It was outrageously expensive, so there was no fear that he would ever face an army of bulletproof warriors. But the lesson was impossible to avoid. Whatever laws of physics he could bend to his will, magic could break. Rulership on Prime was a pyramid of power, with a single high-rank at the top and a narrow base of lower-ranks resting on a bed of common folk. He had thought he could level that construction. Instead, he had made it worse. The base was now wider, as he had replaced the low-rank knights with commoners; but the peak was now higher, as it required ever higher ranks to counter the powerful magic that could render the common men helpless.

He had replaced the entire aristocracy of knighthood with a single priest.

The King's armor was shattered beyond repair, having taken the brunt of the blast. His legendary flying boots had been reduced to burnt leather scraps. So much valuable magic obliterated by the technology of overkill. The King's absurdly large sword had survived, though, thanks to its powerful enchantments. As usual, Christopher tried to give it to Karl, but this time the young veteran just mocked him.

"I have the Parrotts, my lord, and that is sufficient for a man of my rank." Since he had killed a king with one, it was an inarguable point.

Neither Torme nor Gregor wanted it. The blue knight was in fact in the market for a katana like Torme's and Christopher's. It was a symbol of their god, and Gregor apparently felt such details mattered now.

He thought about giving it to Fram or Istvar, but he didn't really want to arm men that he was not entirely certain of, and they didn't expect it. That left one obvious choice, a man who already preferred the large two-handed style.

Cannan held the sword out, admiring it, and shook his head in amazement. "What boy did not dream of wielding this blade? Simply picking it up gives a common man the killing power of a baron. With this I could have hurt the dragon."

As loot went, it wasn't much. There should have been a treasure house of junk to distribute, along with a royal treasury, but the vault was empty of both items and coins. The gargoyles above the door were still intact, so the Gold Apostle had found some way to set them aside while he looted his King's wealth. Or perhaps the King's death had released them from their duty.

"I rule here now," he told the carved figures. "So I can take stuff out of here if I want." Not that there was anything to take.

They remained as still as statues.

"Glad we settled that," Christopher muttered, and told the guards to nail the door shut to avoid accidents. He'd find someplace less contentious to store his gold. Once he had any.

"Nothing for your other faithful retainers?" Uma asked him, all sweetness and light.

"I've got something for them. Rifles, grenades, and cannon."

"Many would see that as a poor gift," she pointed out in that helpful way of hers.

"Not once they remember how many things we still have to kill."

"And we bards?"

Christopher frowned at the lyre in her hands. "You're going to give that back to Lala, right?"

"Of course," she said. "I was only borrowing it."

He spent the next three days fretting over whatever plots the Gold Throne was hatching, but the bards would not let him move from the capital. He could not argue against them; he was unwilling to subject himself to Uma's sharp tongue, and his own went dull and leaden whenever he saw Lalania. The memory of hers robbed him of speech. He wound up avoiding both of them, waiting for time to heal the wound that Lalania had ripped open again, but the women seemed to think he was plotting an escape and called for reinforcements. The Skald herself came to bind him to his throne.

"You must give the realm time to learn the news, and time to react," Friea explained. "As I have come to pay homage to you, so will others. But they cannot fly to your side. And they need time to reflect. Right now they are outraged that you have usurped the King. Given a few days to consider, they will soon be rushing to claim a place in your new court."

"And the ones that don't?"

Friea smiled sadly. "Those are the ones you will have to kill."

She was quickly proven right. The day after her arrival he had two guests: the Lord Wizard of Carrhill and Lady Ariane, the Witch of the Moors. They walked down the long hall together, side by side, to kneel in front of his throne. Last time he had checked, they had nothing but contempt for each other. Now they presented a united front, and the first true challenge to his rule.

"I served your interests," the wizard said, "as instructed. Your people are safe behind my walls."

"I also served," the Lady Ariane continued, "though I had no instruction. My borders were held against your foes, sheltering your Vicar of Cannenberry from the south. Indeed, I hold them still, though daily the threats grow more and more dire."

VERDICT ON CRIMSON FIELDS

"Thank you," Christopher said, and waited for the price.

"We wish to clarify our relationship," Ariane said. "Our old arrangement gave us complete dominion over our lands and our people, with the usual and traditional tax of one quarter of the tael. We understand you have new methods and ideas; we are willing to allow your churches in our towns, your chapels in our villages, and your priests in our courts of law. Your edicts will be uniformly obeyed and your legitimacy shall be respected. In exchange we offer you our personal loyalty and our soldiers to use against the Gold Throne, who remain a puissant and wicked foe."

The throne was made of marble, hard and uncomfortable, as thrones should be. He sat back with a sigh. "You don't seem to understand what happened here," he told them. "This isn't a coup. We didn't trade one ruler for another. We have changed entire forms of government. I appreciate your offer of help, but I don't actually need it. I can conquer the rest of the Kingdom with just what I have."

The wizard seemed taken aback. Lady Ariane, perhaps better schooled in politics, displayed only the affect of cynicism rewarded.

"You would make enemies out of the remaining magic of the Kingdom?" the wizard said, his eyes narrowing.

"No," Christopher said. "I would kill you first."

"You are White! We came here in good faith!" There was fire in the man's eyes. He did not seem to understand. The cold throne Christopher sat on was not moved by outrage.

"You came here uninvited, in the midst of a war. I owe you no guarantees. You are a threat to the realm as it is now constituted. That you thought my color would protect you even while you waded through the field of corpses I laid at the foot of this city makes you too stupid to live."

The outrage turned to hatred, pure and hot. Christopher met it without flinching. He had his fair share to return. The wizard's hands twitched, ever so slightly. In response Lalania shifted her feet from where she stood by the throne, moving a fraction of an inch closer, the null-stone still hanging from her neck. Cannan stood impassively on the other side, his massive sword drawn and resting point-first on the ground. There was no fear the stone would damage the blade; its enchantments were too powerful for that.

Behind the witch and the wizard armored knights rearranged themselves from random clusters to a definite battle line, cutting off any retreat.

"Be at peace, my friend," Lady Ariane murmured, placing her hand on the wizard's arm. "He has prepared a fine surprise for us."

"I am not inconsequential," the wizard snarled. "I have surprises of my own."

"He will nullify our magic and use the excuse of our assault to kill us," she explained in a dry tone. "I prefer not to make his task easier."

The wizard stared at her, slowly realizing she was serious. He was, despite everything, no fool. He shut his mouth and let her do the talking.

"And now what, my lord?" the lady asked. "I confess I do not see a path forward. You dare not let us go, even with an oath of fealty; nor can you slay us for no greater crime than honesty."

"I don't want an oath," Christopher said. "I want something vastly more difficult and binding than that. I want you to *understand*."

He stood up, unable to contain his ideas in repose. They had slumbered there too long. "We still need magic. You still have a place. But that place is not political. There is no reason you should sit in judgment over others. Power is not an adequate justification for authority."

The wizard could not help himself. Half in disgust and half in curiosity, he asked, "Then what is?" It was the first sign Christopher had that he might actually succeed.

"Fairness. It's not just some random theological concept. If you treated the people around you as if they were your equals, as if they could do to you whatever you could do to them, then I wouldn't have to kill you."

"But they are not our equals," the lady said. "As they would be the first to admit. My people have sheltered under my protection for generations. I have presented this face to the world for over a hundred years. They do not understand the forces that drive my actions, nor do they want to. They know only that they have a safe place to raise their children."

"What?" Christopher said. "A hundred years?"

She replied with a diplomatic yet dismissive smile. "I fear you would not understand my motives or my actions any better than they. Which is fair, as I do not understand yours. The ways of power are as different as the professions and the souls of men."

"But understand each other we must," he said. "I need tael; I need all of it, for the best of reasons. I am going to restore a link to the ancestral plane of mankind." He watched them absorb the concept. It rippled out through the crowd like a murky wave, jostling faces and hearts to uncertain effect. The bards stood unmoved; they had already known, of course, since the day Lalania watched him try to go home, and were in any case too disciplined to show an unplanned emotion. His fellow priests displayed grim satisfaction, their suspicions confirmed. Some seemed pleased, such as Gregor and Torme, while the Vicars were resigned to further disruptions of the natural order. Only Cardinal Faren did not react. The old man had different priorities now.

The rest of the crowd wore excitement or incredulity or confusion. The wizards in front of him displayed only indifference.

He kept talking. "Against that, what do you need tael for? Another rank? More magic? To what purpose?"

The wizard shrugged. "To what purpose do you act? What does the plane of man have that we desire?"

"Electronics," Christopher said. "I'll never make a microprocessor here, even if I knew how. Chocolate. Movies. You people don't even know what you're missing."

"How can we need what we cannot understand?" Ariane asked.

"Have you noticed that if people don't eat fresh fruits or vegetables, they get sick? It's because you need vitamin C. You don't know what that is, but you still need it."

"And you know what it is?" she asked.

"Not really," he confessed. "But other people do. They know all sorts of things like that. Where I come from, it's common knowledge."

The hate in the wizard's eyes banked, supplemented by the one thing the man clearly prized over all other emotions: vindication. "Your inaccessible past is explained, if you are from another plane."

"I am," Christopher said. "I'm asking a lot from you, so I'm putting all my cards on the table. We have a chance here to change not just our lives but the lives of everyone. Everywhere."

Lady Ariane shook her head gently. "Like any zealot, you are so enamored of your holy quest it never occurs to you that others will not leap at the chance to join the crusade. Why should we believe, or care, or presume this change would be for the better?"

It was true. He had assumed the desire to reconnect to the home of mankind would be something people just naturally agreed with. He had not considered that the nobility would prefer their primitive riches over the bounty of Earth.

"You don't have to believe," he answered. "Because the common people do. And they matter now."

"My mistake," the wizard said. "I had thought you a pragmatic man, but now I see you are just a priest after all. Do not take it amiss— it serves your cause. I believe you will destroy anything that stands in your way, affiliation be damned. You asked for understanding, and you have it. I understand that I refuse you at the cost of my life. So I shall not refuse you; I will bow to whatever acts of theft you call governance. So long as you leave me enough feathers in my nest that I can flee the inevitable destruction of your madness."

It wasn't exactly what he was looking for. But it was probably more than he deserved.

Lady Ariane tiled her head. "I also agree, under the same terms. Leave me the hope that after you have burned your holy cause to the ground I can still provide for the people I have protected for generations, and I will accede to your changes of the moment."

"And if it doesn't come to that? If I am proved right?" he asked both of them.

"Have I not just bowed my head to cold, hard reality?" the wizard retorted. "Presume I will do the same, should the occasion demand it."

"I take my responsibility to my people as seriously as do you," the witch said. "That will have to suffice. But you have not yet told us what accommodations we must make."

Christopher sat back down, exhausted. "For now, the same thing you already offered. Save that all of the tael must come to the White church."

The cynicism dripping from the wizard's face was so potent Christopher feared for the stone floor.

"You know," Christopher said, "I was sent here by a god to fulfill a mission. Not just to run a swindle."

Lady Ariane smiled sweetly. "Unless the god is swindling you."

He had no answer for that.

34

WINDBOAT DIPLOMACY

The rest of the week was equally unpleasant. The people around him leapt to obey his commands but would not meet his eyes. Difficulties abounded; he had become accustomed to being wealthy and buying people's good will, and now he was struggling to pay his bills. The guardsmen required coin, the city required commerce, and both were in short supply.

Fortunately Karl had been looking ahead. The gold and silver looted from the goblins had never made it to the King's treasury. Now craftsmen hammered day and night to strike new coins, while Christopher handed out contracts for goods from Knockford's forges. Contracts backed by nothing but paper, but for the moment his credit stood. As long as the guardsmen took home their pay the city would carry on pretending everything was fine. That bought him a few weeks at least.

Outside the capital the situation rapidly hardened. Lords chose sides, or created new ones. The druids seemed to have vanished, Copperton was still in Baron Morrison's hands, the goblins remained in their keep, and the Gold Throne marshalled armies and allies every day, aided in no small part by Christopher's wildly unpopular new tax program. Istvar led a delegation to the throne that glinted with so much armor it could easily have been mistaken for a rebellion.

"We worship our own gods," he told Christopher in a booming voice that reached every corner of the hall. "While we recognize common cause with the White, you cannot ask us to set aside our own faith solely for yours."

"It's only temporary," Christopher tried to explain. "Once I can make the link to Earth, things can change."

Istvar put his hands on his hips and stared at Christopher. "Few believe such an event is even possible. Fewer still expect that such an event would result in change that benefits us."

"Who is us?" Christopher asked. "The people? You already know it will help them. The realm? The weapons I can bring over from Earth will be far more powerful than what we have now. Even dragons will fear common men." The dragon's roar had a range denominated in hundreds of yards. Air-to-ground missiles worked in units of miles.

"To be precise," Istvar answered, "the peerage. We have sacrificed much for the safety of our people. Our ways are proven. You ask us to mount a chimera and pray that it serves us instead of eating us."

Christopher cleared his throat and sat a little straighter on his marble throne. "I think my ways have proven themselves."

The Earl was as hard as stone himself. "And yet our faith makes demands on us that rifles cannot satisfy. No more than you do we hold mere power sufficient obeisance to our moral duty."

Cannan's words came back to him. He could not drag these people a mile without giving them an inch. The Earl had, perhaps unwittingly, offered him an out. It would be necessary to take it.

"You know that I intend to replace the peers with priests." It was the best he could do at the moment. The Vicars had run their counties well, their reputation for fairness backed up by truth spells. Plenty of people would be unhappy under such a regime, but not to the point of violence, and any that were he could kill in good conscience. He could manage a kingdom under those conditions. He could not manage under the old way; his own nature would not let him look aside while creatures like Black Bartholomew held the power of life and death over helpless peasants. Treywan's moral flexibility had been, from a purely tactical point of view, somewhat of an advantage in maintaining a feudal system.

Istvar frowned. "You cannot rule a kingdom with four Vicars."

What the man was even now still too diplomatic to say was that Christopher likely could not raise enough Vicars, no matter how much tael he had in his pockets, which as it turned out was quite a lot at the moment. The harvest from the battle had not yielded as much tael as the King, but it was still substantial. Many knights had fallen on the Royalist side. Still, there were always too few candidates for the White. It was not the most popular of affiliations.

Christopher nodded, pretending to surrender to the man's point. "And I cannot fulfill my quest without ruling the Kingdom. I have to spend tael to make tael. I have to make more Vicars. But we both know I can't raise enough White. So here's the deal: I will take your people on board. Agree to rule by my laws, and I will raise up Blue priests. Not knights; never knights. But priests I can do. I said there was still a need for magic, and I meant it."

The Earl paused, staring at him inscrutably. When he spoke again, there was a strain of either respect or aggravation in his voice. The two seemed close enough to be indistinguishable. "It is, let us say . . . *unprecedented* that a Church would do such a thing, even for an allied faith. I am not even sure it is allowed."

That hadn't occurred to Christopher. Marcius hadn't given him a rulebook. True, the Cathedral had been full of books, but he'd never really had time to read them, and now they were all ashes.

He shrugged. If Marcius didn't like it, the god could bloody well show up and say so. "A lot of things I do are unprecedented."

"And how shall we divide this portion?" Istvar asked shrewdly. "Are we to be beggars, living off of your scraps?"

There was one advantage to negotiating with the Blue. They couldn't cheat any more than he could. "Merit. Whenever we have need for a promotion, we'll pick the candidate with the most merit. If that means more Blues than Whites, so be it."

Istvar had the grace to look positively alarmed. "Are you certain your patron will permit this? It does none of us good for you to lose your affiliation."

"I'm not here to make priests or build a Church," Christopher said. "If I can serve the White by cutting off heads, I'm pretty sure I can serve the White by sharing the spoils."

The Earl drew a deep breath. "I find myself in unhappy agreement with that Dark wizard. You believe your holy quest overrides all tradition and decorum. Your single-mindedness will be the glory or the death of us all."

"True," Christopher said. "But at least it will be interesting."

"As much as I appreciate a good adventure, I am not in the habit of dragging hapless commoners along for the ride. They do not ask for novelty, only good weather, stout defense, and a steady hand on the reins of justice."

"They'll be as safe as ever. The only lives at risk are ours. If I fail, if the Gold Throne wins, their conditions will get worse; but that was going to happen anyway."

The Earl lowered his chin. "Do you not see that we could defeat the Gold without turning the realm upside down?"

"No," Christopher said. "That my patron will *not* permit."

The words worked as efficaciously as a magic spell. Istvar bowed his head and spread his hands in defeat. "I cannot ask you to set aside a divine command. I cannot save my people without your help. Perforce I must ride at your heel, at least until divine Forseti grants me another path. Share the spoils fairly with our priests, and our knights will trade lances and rank for rifles. For now."

It was better than the last pledge, but not by much. It brought the remains of the Blue into his court, four more counties, though one was so small it was ruled by a baron. The last easy victory, unfortunately. The Greens would have to be won one at a time, and many of those east of Kingsrock had already taken to flying gold banners, or so the bards told him.

He had to face the Earl again only a few hours later, when his staff met for a strategy meeting. Karl led the discussion with the brusqueness necessary for a young man telling old men what to do. Only Christopher's example allowed the nobles to accept this treatment. He stood and listened without comment until the end of the presentation.

"Alright," he told them once Karl was done. "You've heard our options. Now I want your votes. Starting with you, Lord Istvar."

Not surprisingly, the Blue lords voted for an immediate assault on the goblins. A captain stood in for Tomestaad and Rogenar while Istvar claimed a vote for Count Armand, as all of the Count's men had gone back to Romsdaal. Christopher decided not to challenge the voting arrangements at the moment. The Earl of Fram and the Baronet of Parnar voted to recapture Copperton, as did Gregor and Torme. That left Christopher in the unhappy position of tie-breaker, which was what he had been trying to avoid in the first place. After a moment's consideration, he voted for a strike on West Undaal, as the first step down the long road to Balenar and the Gold Throne.

"That leaves us with no clear path," Istvar objected. "Unless you intend to overrule the advice you just requested."

"It's just for the record," Christopher explained. He resented every step in any direction that did not lead to the source of his problems. "I said we'd vote, and I'll stand by it. We can't do what I want, anyway. The realm will not respect me while my own lands are in rebellion."

"That means you are going after the goblins. Then I must be away," The Earl of Fram declared. "I cannot leave my county undefended while the enemy are on their doorstep." Copperton was between Kingsrock and Fram.

"How reasonable is Ser Morrison?" Christopher asked.

"No more or less than any other," Istvar answered. "Why?"

"He's got what, a company of crossbowmen and dozen knights, right?"

"We believe that to be accurate," Lady Friea said. Christopher would have preferred to hear it from Lalania, but the other lords were clearly more impressed with the Skald's pronouncements.

"Okay, then. We'll do both. Gregor will take his regiment north, with Istvar's knights and both Parrotts. Torme will hold the city with the other two regiments and the new recruits. I'll fly up to Copperton and set Baron Morrison straight."

"Alone?" Istvar asked, his tone trying to remain polite. But then, Istvar hadn't seen what Christopher had done to the goblins while alone.

"I'll take some arguments along. Firstly, that Morrison can't touch me with lances or crossbows. Second, that he is cut off and surrounded. Third, that I have a satchel full of dynamite. I'm hoping after those persuasive facts he'll choose to sit out the rest of the war in a pleasant dungeon."

"And if not?" Istvar asked, still probing.

Christopher met his gaze levelly. "Then I'll do what needs to be done."

"As long as you are skating across the country, a visit to your other allies in the west would not go amiss," Uma offered. "Sprier and Parnar deserve a courtesy call. Camara and Montfort might be won over with a show of power and mercy."

Christopher managed to repress a groan. Lalania noticed and gave him an approving smile. "You need not go unaccompanied. The wind spell will take Cannan and I as well. Seeing the King's sword in your servant's hands will terrify them; seeing the College in your service will reassure them."

"And what of us?" asked the Baronet of Parnar.

Karl answered. "You and the Lord Earl Fram will reinforce Cannenberry. I trust the Witch of the Moors to defend her lands, but a lunge up the river to Knockford is still our greatest danger."

The Baronet stiffened. "I do not intend to spend the war guarding the back door."

While Christopher didn't mind insolence directed at himself, he couldn't allow it to pass unchallenged when aimed at Karl. He opened his mouth to object, but Lalania spoke first.

"You underestimate the danger, Ser. The enemy sent their best magic and most competent commander on that path. With our main forces trapped in Kingsrock they will no doubt try again, with yet more. You will be hard-pressed merely to hold the town, let alone the border."

The man seemed mollified, which made Christopher question his sanity.

Karl continued, as if he had not noticed the insubordination. "The enemy will assume we stall while we secure the west. In truth we must wait for a supply train from Knockford before we can launch a serious offensive. Once it arrives we will choose between east and south; until then our plans must remain deliberately unsettled. My apologies, Lord Istvar, but you will miss the start of the campaign. The goblins will take many weeks to subdue. Which means I can only spare one Parrott."

"I would not ask," Istvar said, "but having seen the goblin keep, even at a distance, animates my tongue. Reducing that block of stone by traditional means would be quite tedious."

"And reduce it you must," Gregor said. "To a pile of rubble, and then break the rocks into gravel."

Those who had seen the place nodded their agreement.

"And the populace?" Istvar asked, piercing Christopher with his gaze.

Christopher took a breath. It wasn't enough, so he took another one. Lalania watched him with carefully hidden sympathy, while Gregor and Torme stared at the ground.

He had to speak. He could not hide from this. He could not pretend the authority was not his. The words had to come from him.

"Let them flee, if they will. If they will not . . . kill them all."

"A harsh judgment," Istvar said carefully, "but fair. No one else in the realm would have extended them a peaceful hand. And yet they chose the sword after all."

"Did they?" Christopher asked bitterly. "The weavers and cabbage sellers, the cobblers and bakers? The little ones, the young and the old, did they vote for their own destruction?"

"Of course they did," Earl Fram growled. "They're goblins. Those bakers would cook your face in a pie and make you serve it to them."

"So would plenty of those who serve the Gold Throne," Lalania said.

"What of it?" the Earl exclaimed. "We're going to stab the lot of them, too."

"Only the ones who raise a weapon against us," she corrected. The rest of the council stood silently.

The Earl finally realized he was on thin ice. "My apologies," he muttered. "I do not follow theology." He managed to imbue the word with a notable amount of disdain.

Christopher could not find any words that would not be either argumentative or self-pitying. In the end he settled for brusque. "You have your orders. The council is dismissed."

The columns would march at the break of dawn, or, in Christopher's case, take flight after a leisurely breakfast. It didn't seem to be a sterling example of his words on fairness. Watching the Earl of Fram's men packing up, he remembered to thank Lalania for her help.

"That was a good line to take with the Baronet," he told her. "I don't know that I could have been that . . . diplomatic."

"You mean, of course, dishonest," she said. "Yet I spoke nothing but the truth. You wonder why Karl has sent so much of the nobility away from the front lines. The answer should be obvious; he sent the men he is most willing to lose. If the Gold Throne makes a serious thrust, those men will buy us a sunset at most."

"A sunset we will need," Karl said, standing nearby. He stepped over and lowered his voice. "At the cost of none of our guns. Do not accuse me of favoritism when my decisions are simply tactical."

Christopher almost smiled at the irony. "Of course not," he agreed. It just so happened that "most expendable" and "nobles" applied to the same group now. Another casualty of gunpowder.

Here came one more. Uma led a nobleman through the crowded courtyard, someone Christopher did not recognize. From the style of his dress, a peer; from the expression on his face, an unhappy one.

"Please forgive the informality," Uma told the man once they had drawn abreast. "Our Lord Saint Christopher demands it of us all."

"Yet he does not stint on his hospitality." Lalania took up his defense. The two girls were suddenly glaring daggers at each other. Christopher saw through it, though. They were like lawyers, preparing to clash on behalf of their clients. Whatever hot words would be said would come from them, allowing their clients to remain polite. Given that the consequences of rudeness often included a fatal duel, this was high service to the realm. Christopher would have appreciated it more if he didn't suspect Uma would use the leverage to sell her client out at the last minute.

But that too would serve the realm, so he held his tongue.

"You call this hospitality?" Uma said, wrinkling her nose at a basket of crusty bread being handed out to the soldiers. Christopher felt she might be carrying the act a little too far.

"I did not come here for the food," the man growled.

"Allow me to present the Count of Easlia," Lalania declared with a little bow. The women had reversed the ordinary course of introductions by each naming the other's companion. They were showing off their value as advisors by demonstrating their knowledge. In this world, names had power and ranks were real, so knowing them mattered.

Christopher still hadn't said anything. The Count stared at him a moment, taking his measure, and then growled some more.

"Not for long, it seems. The Aesir have gone over to you; the Jade Throne has been shattered by the Gold. On every border I am surrounded by enemies who covet my lands. And yet when I ride to the seat of royal power, I hear only that the peerage is to be broken on the wheel. Look me in the face and tell me you will take my son's patrimony."

"Okay," Christopher said, staring the man in the eyes. "I will take your son's patrimony."

The Count's upper lip curled in a sneer, though it could not conceal the appreciation of courage.

"But not your wife's," Lalania said.

This was sufficiently unexpected that it broke up the staring contest. Both men turned to look at their bards.

Uma explained graciously. "My lord's lady wife is a practitioner of the arcane. Saint Christopher's rules allow for magic to still survive in the realm."

"Yet his law still holds," Lalania objected. "All tael will come to Kingsrock, to be parceled out according to merit."

"Merit decided by a priest's measure?" Uma snapped.

"Mistress Fae serves the realm without complaint," Lalania countered.

Since this was far from the truth, Christopher felt the need to intervene.

"I do value magic," he told the Count. "If there are things wizards can do that priests can't, then I'll pay for it," he said, hoping he wouldn't come to regret the words.

"So it's just my sword and my castle you'll take from me."

"There is still employment for your sword," Lalania said. "The Gold Throne betrayed your kin. Surely you will not let that insult pass unanswered."

The Count glared at her. His silence proved her point, though.

"You know I'm going to replace the peers with priests," Christopher said. "That's going to take a while. If you can follow the laws I set down, I can promise you this much: I will replace you only after everyone else."

Shades of Cthulhu; he was promising to eat his loyal servants last.

"That may be a day that never comes," Uma murmured. "Until then you bend the knee only as much as you would have to Treywan, were the Kingdom threatened by dire need. Saint Christopher does not ask for decimation, after all, but merely for a temporary tax adjustment."

"Is this true?" the Count asked Christopher directly. "Is there some danger that requires all of us to grovel like schoolboys?"

Christopher thought of the very frightening Alaine and Lucien, and then of the creatures they were frightened of.

"Yes," he said.

The Count tilted his head back, surprised by the plain and simple answer. After a minute he sighed. "Then I suppose I have little choice. Give me a token that will get the Blue off my back, and tell me how many of my men you require."

Christopher waved a hand at Karl, who had stood by silently through the entire interview. "Major Karl will dispose of your forces. Lady Uma will provide you with documentation. I thank you for your foresight, Ser, and I promise you, one day your people will thank you as well."

The Count nodded ambiguously and let Uma lead him away, followed by Karl.

"Are they all going to be that hard?" Christopher asked Lalania, letting out a deep breath he hadn't realized he'd been holding.

"Dark take it," Lalania muttered.

"What?"

She wrinkled her nose in aggravation. "You're even more handsome when you're being smart."

The rest of the diplomatic tour went somewhat more easily. Christopher solidified in the air above the castle in Copperton while a hundred quaking men pointed crossbows at him. "Go on," he called down. "I wouldn't expect you to surrender without firing a shot." They let fly, quarrels buzzing around him like mad bees, then threw down their bows and fled.

Baron Morrison and a fistful of knights clambered onto the roof, puffing in aggravation. "This is a most undignified way to fight, priest," the Baron shouted. "Come down and face us like the men we are."

"Or I could just stay up here and throw dynamite at you," Christopher shouted back. "It was good enough to kill a king. I think it will do for you."

"We will not bend to mere words," Morrison declared.

Now that the crossbows were dispensed with, the cloud next to him solidified into Cannan. The men below gasped in shock, which turned to dismay when Cannan twirled the great sword.

"Then bend to the royal blade," Cannan told them.

Christopher was amazed that the man could shout and growl at the same time.

On his other side Lalania finished solidifying. He had burned through a lot of spells to put on this little aerial performance.

"Your King is dead, and with it your oath to him. The Saint will take your lands and your position, yet let you keep your rank and your head. We both know it is a better fate than you deserve, Ser. Claim it now or claim a shallow grave in the churchyard you have usurped."

Morrison and his knights threw down their swords in disgust. Christopher swooped down to land among them, unconcerned with possible treachery. Morrison was a baron. That represented a healthy reward of tael, and Christopher needed a lot of tael. A bloodbath would only advance his cause.

The Baron appeared to detect this truth in Christopher's posture. He offered no more provocation. Christopher scanned the common soldiers and picked out a dozen with the brightest affiliations, had them toss the rest into the dungeon, and left them in charge until the Vicar of Copperton and his police force could arrive by horseback.

Then, improbably, they flew on, visiting several other castles, where they received a considerably warmer if equally shocked and befuddled welcome. Lalania was selling the new tax policy as an emergency measure, which made it far more palatable. She was careful not to explain precisely what the emergency was. No doubt the lords assumed that normal rules would return once the war was over.

They wouldn't, of course. Once Christopher had subdued the rest of the country and put another several hundred men into rifle regiments, he could force the peerage to dance like puppets if he wanted to. Only the sheer obviousness of this fact allowed him to leave it unstated.

By the end of the day they were back in Kingsrock, handing Karl lists of reinforcements that were on the march. It was absurd; if Christopher had realized how incredibly potent this ability was, he would have invented cars instead of guns.

35

YOU'RE WELCOME

On Earth, the military campaign would have gone differently. The Gold Apostle would have camped in his distant fortress and let Christopher batter his way through the half dozen castles in the way, bleeding men and materials at every step. Those forts could be held with small forces that would cost the enemy little, while charging Christopher blood and delay by the wagonload. At the end of the march the Apostle would meet his tired troops with fresh armies and supplies. And Christopher would not even have the fortifications to fall back on, having destroyed them by necessity and cannon fire.

This was not Earth. Here, most invaders would slaughter the peasantry, or at least decimate them, gaining rank with every step. Christopher could not do that, but the Gold Apostle would not even willingly surrender the tael of the garrisons. Their lives meant nothing to him, but their deaths were worth much.

A vast host waited for him at the foot of the castle of West Undaal, flying banners of gold and green. Against it marched his own host, gathered over the last two weeks. Istvar's men had returned sooner than expected because the goblin keep was deserted. Apparently they had chosen to take their chances in the Wild.

Consequently his men were confident and ready, militia replaced by crossbowmen turned enthusiastic riflemen, horses rested and eager, knights in freshly polished armor flying blue and green pennants, White priests and priestesses with heads full of spells, and a dozen peers of high rank.

The peers loyal to him stood now in a semicircle in front of him, listening to the council under a smiling morning sun. The witch and the wizard stood with them, as unfriendly as tombs.

Karl was beside him. For once Christopher judged that it was time to bow to noble sensibilities, and the young commoner stood silently. It was enough, for now, that he be here.

"You understand that I want to spare as many lives as I can," Christopher told them all. "We fight not for profit but for the sake of the realm. If they surrender, we will accept. Only the Gold Apostle has to die today."

"If they surrender," the Lord Wizard of Carrhill said in his grave-yard voice from inside his drooping cowl reeking of saffron, "it will only be to bait a trap."

The man was not helping. Christopher didn't think he was trying to.

"Nonetheless, if prudence allows, we will accept."

"Prudence dictates that the sooner your appetite for tael is sated, the sooner we can have our taxes back."

"Nonetheless," Christopher growled.

The witch smiled at the rest of the peers. "I see here great strength of arms. Even absent the Saint's fiery tricks, this would be a battle we might win, were it only mundane. Surely the enemy recognizes this as well, and thus we must conclude it shall be wondrous indeed."

Christopher tried to control his aggravation. "The Cardinal and the Vicars are hidden throughout the army, armed with scrolls. They will attempt to dispel any magic. While it won't work against the Apostle or Sigrath, it should shut down the lesser priests. I'll counter the Apostle. If the two of you block Sigrath, that leaves nothing but soldiers and knights to fight against soldiers and knights and guns."

"Neither of those men are fools, and both are cowards," the wizard said. "They will not contend against such odds without certain hope. I warned you that wizards had surprises. Now perhaps you will see the wisdom of my words."

"Master Carrhill." The Earl of Fram spoke peer to peer. "Can you not provide a surprise of your own?"

"I am not willing to pay the price," the wizard answered. "Nor would the niceties of our good Saint ever allow it. Even Master Sigrath will balk at the cost. Yet the Gold Apostle may well compel him."

"Nor would the niceties of the late King allow it." Surprisingly, it was the witch defending Christopher. "I would not attempt such a thing, under any circumstance. The risk to the entire realm is simply too great."

Christopher could hardly demand that they explain themselves. It was a bit late in the game to admit that he had no idea what the enemy was capable of. On the plain in front of them, troops were already taking up their positions.

"Whatever it is," Christopher said, trying to regain control of the conversation, "we'll deal with it. We've beaten dragons and kings to get here. We'll beat this."

The wizard inclined his head to the other peers, the folds of his cowl rustling softly. "For your sakes we must hope so. Should the battle go against us, I remain confident that the witch and I will be able to make a deal with the victors. You, I am afraid, have no such hope."

He probably thought he was being unhelpful again, but Christopher had read enough Sun Tzu to know that soldiers who dared not retreat would dare anything for victory. "That's right," he agreed, waving at the mundane lords. "You lot and I are in the same boat. You know by now I have never retreated from a battle, regardless of the odds. You know that you and your men will live again, if we win. You know that the Shadow will hunt you like rats if we do not break it here and now, today. You know that the future of all men, everywhere, rides on this victory."

He paused to look each of them in the face. "I will tell you a truth: I can leave. I can take a single step and be safe and sound and home. I can sleep in my own bed tonight. And I tell you another truth: I have not memorized the required spell today."

Drawing his sword and resting it on his shoulder, he swept his other hand out over the castle in the distance and let anger fill his throat. "I'm going to walk down there, kick that door down, and hang that Dark-taken rat from the battlements. What you do is up to you."

Then he turned away and began walking. A lone figure, in scaled armor, muttering prayers as he went. Steadily he put one foot in front of the other. Behind him the peers mounted horses and galloped off to their companies, while the wizard and the witch simply vanished from sight. Around him men stared wide-eyed at his pilgrim's progress, then threw themselves into lines and formations with renewed dispatch.

It was a good mile to the castle gates. The journey would take him at least twenty minutes. If his army hadn't won the battle in that time, it probably wouldn't.

In the distance, the Parrotts barked. Shells screamed overhead and smashed into the castle gates, throwing up showers of wood and stone splinters. Both armies took this as a signal to begin hostilities, shouting and firing weapons even though the range was still too great. The concept of preparatory bombardment was foreign to them. Christopher could have made a strong showing with his aerial tricks, but the risk was too great, and in any case there was little need. He had plenty of cannons and rockets for that.

Christopher did not stop walking when he reached the front of his lines. Instead, the men began to march with him. A tactically unsound maneuver, but still more disciplined than the enemy. His men marched at his controlled pace, keeping formation, firing by rank. Each line paused after shooting to reload, while the line behind marched ahead, stood to arms, and discharged their weapons. The enemy, beginning to feel the stings of death at a ridiculous range, responded with an incoherent charge.

The Parrotts spoke again, this time with the expensive voices of exploding shells. The castle gates disappeared in a blast of flame. Horses pulled ahead of Christopher's slow-marching line, towing field guns with brave crews running alongside. They deployed their weapons in the open, the enemy racing across the plain at them.

Well timed, the guns fired just before Christopher's line swallowed them up. The crews limbered their weapons, preparing to do it again. Strategically, Christopher should have stopped here, forced the enemy to come to him under withering fire. Instinct told him not to. Partly because he hoped the relentless advance would break the enemy's morale and send them fleeing before they were all churned to gristle by the thresher. Partly because he knew that defensive strategy would be what the enemy expected, what they would have prepared for. Partly because he was sick of patience.

When they were close enough for the rockets, all hell broke loose. The world became a deafening, blinding welter of smoke and flame and metal and flesh. In the midst of it, Christopher kept walking. Fireballs began popping around him, one after the other. In their panic, the enemy wasted most of their attacks on him, instead of on his vulnerable men. He had to renew the energy shield several times, but the wands fell silent before he ran out of spells. Perhaps they were empty; more likely, snipers or artillery had found the wielders.

Knights crashed into his line, matched by his own knights rushing forward through the sparse columns of his infantry. Christopher's troops could afford to be loosely formed. Their firepower was great enough that each man could hold his own place on the line, like any hero. After the cavalry charges stalled each other, degenerating into sword fights, the infantry walked among them, shooting knights and horses. Christopher's nobles had spilled gallons of white paint on their shields and armor, creating a mess for the squires to clean up tomorrow. The knights had complained that morning, but now that everything not drenched in white was a target Christopher imagined they were no longer complaining.

Not that he could ask. The noise was too great to shout across the thirty feet of empty space that surrounded him. No one was foolish enough to get within range of the fireballs. The gap was wide enough that a half-dozen knights charged him with lances set. The riflemen on either side shot the horses down. Just when Christopher thought he might have a swordfight on his hands, knights of his own charged past him through the gap, led by his perpetual shadow, Cannan. They left nothing but corpses in their wake.

Then he came to a thicket of halberds. Incredible that there were enough men left to form any resistance; astounding that they charged him with naked rage and unstinting courage. Now he fought against unranked men, cautiously, preserving his tael against their blows, knowing that time was on his side. He had only a few seconds with each foe before somebody shot them.

His riflemen fired on his position indiscriminately. Understanding they could not strike him by accident, they blazed away without hesitation. Another reason no one dared to get within thirty feet.

The enemy fought with a tenaciousness he could not readily explain, especially as they were dying to surprisingly little effect. The combination of knights and guns made Christopher's advance a wall of thorns and fire that ground up mere mundane flesh, while his scattered priests and wizards blocked magical attacks. He did not know what the Gold Apostle had said or done to these men to make them fight so hard, contesting every foot of ground, buying seconds with their lives.

Of course. Buying time. Stalling while the wizard Sigrath prepared his surprise. The King had stalled until Sigrath's magic cloak was ready, and now the Gold Apostle was doing the same. Christopher was beginning to form a very negative opinion of the wizard.

His advance slowed; the gap around him collapsed as men fell on each other, dismounted knights and riflemen mixed in together, shooting and stabbing in swirling violence. He cut through a dozen enemy soldiers before he lost count, but he kept to his leisurely pace. In the confusion he lost track of Cannan, but he was not particularly worried. Neither of them should be in much danger from this phase of the battle.

The smoke lay over everything like a blanket, obscuring the world more than a dozen yards away. Consequently, it was a surprise when the walls of the castle swam into view. The last of the halberdiers fell under rifle fire, leaving him staring at the shattered remains of the gate. No soldiers held the gatehouse, and the battlements were empty. The fortress seemed deserted.

Out of habit he kept walking. A dozen brave men fell in behind him, carbines and grenades at the ready. They passed under the stone arch, stepping over broken wood and iron. The courtyard was as still as death, the din of battle held off by high stone walls.

Bodies littered the ground, men and women, soldiers and servants. All of them were headless. All of them faced away from the keep, as if they had been fleeing the safety of the castle for the madness of the battlefield.

The doors of the keep lay on the ground in front of the great hall. Something had knocked them down—from the inside.

The pressure of men at his back forced Christopher forward. He could hardly stop his advance now, in the face of silence. The men followed him, trapped in his wake. Up the steps of the keep and into the foyer, where light-stones cast dark shadows over more mangled bodies.

Another dozen steps led them into the throne room. Here at last they found their foe. Two men stood in the middle of the hall, surrounded by corpses. The first circle of bodies were bound hand and foot, naked and headless. The second row were soldiers in armor, shepherds to the sacrificial flock, and equally headless.

The living men were easily recognized by their cloaks, one gold and one purple.

"Strike now! There is your target and your reward!" Sigrath's voice quavered, but not enough to stop him from casting a spell. An apple of flame streaked toward Christopher and his men. With a word he unraveled it before it blossomed.

Christopher's men reacted instantly, throwing themselves to the ground seeking cover. Once they realized the spell was blocked, they rose to their knees and began to fire. Sigrath and the Apostle jerked, bullets tearing at their tael-enhanced bodies. Christopher ran forward, his sword high and ready to strike. There was no reason to give the enemy another chance to cast.

Behind him the tempo of the gunfire increased, though the bullets no longer struck at the two men in front of him. A grenade exploded, followed by another. Christopher could not help himself. He glanced over his shoulder as he ran.

A giant figure moved among his men, half-hopping and half-flying on great wings, and trailing a powerful tail that struck like a weapon. Scaled and horned like a beast, twelve feet tall with wings equally wide, it fought on two legs like a man, snatching up his soldiers with heavy claws and swallowing their heads whole, leaving a trail of bloody corpses in its wake. The men stood their ground and fired desperately, uselessly. The creature did not appear to notice the bullets, striding through the grenade blasts without pause. In seconds the battle was over.

The monster glanced up from the last body and stared across the room at Christopher for a hateful, hungry instant. Then it vanished from sight.

In front of him Sigrath was releasing another fireball. Christopher did not have time to counter it, and the blast knocked him off his feet. His energy shield faded away, having done its final duty.

While he was on the ground he had time to think. He cast a simple spell before he stood up.

In front of him, the monster appeared from nothing, discarding its invisibility like a cloak. Huge clawed hands reached for him while the gaping maw of fangs hovered above, eager to be fed.

The claws stopped inches from his body. The maw closed; the creature gazed down at him through solid black eyes with what could only be amusement.

"My lord," Sigrath said urgently. "Undo his ward. Let the demon have him. Quickly!"

"You don't tell me what to do," the Gold Apostle answered languidly.

The demon stepped back and turned to stare at the wizard with the same gaze it had used on Christopher.

Looking down, Christopher could see a diagram inscribed on the floor in colored chalk. The two men stood inside it, careful not to let their arms extend beyond the border or their feet stray on the lines.

The demon glanced at Christopher to make sure he was watching. Then it balled up a huge fist and struck at the wizard so forcefully that Christopher flinched as much as Sigrath. Its blow bounced off an invisible barrier. The message was unmistakable.

"I think it wants me to let it have you," Christopher said. "And frankly, I'm of a mind to agree."

"That will not save you," Sigrath warbled. "As soon as your spell expires, the demon will consume you anyway."

"Perhaps not," the Gold Apostle said. He seemed to find the proceedings amusing. "Saint Christopher may be a better bargainer than you."

"I fed the creature everything you told me to!" Sigrath's outburst was fueled by equal parts of fear and outrage. "I did the ritual just as you said!"

"I was not impugning your demon-binding skills. Those were never in question; no one of your rank could have ever compelled a creature of this power. It was your bargain with me that you should have reconsidered."

"But," Sigrath stammered. "We have no bargain. We both serve the King."

"The King served me. As do you, though you know it not. All of the souls in this kingdom exist at my sufferance. The very realm stands because I choose it, from the lowest beggar to the highest lord. Though it is true no one ever told you this truth, still you should have discerned it on your own. Else what value is that thick head of yours?"

Christopher would have objected, but Sigrath seemed equally shocked by this grandiose claim. He decided to let the wizard argue the case and took a discreet step backward, intent on returning to his army. It would be interesting to see if the demon could shrug off a Parrott as easily as it had a rifle.

The wizard, stung beyond fear, opened his mouth to argue.

The Apostle interrupted. "Nothing. That is what it is worth," he said, and shoved Sigrath out of the circle.

In an instant, the demon snatched up the man and devoured his head. Sigrath didn't even have time to scream.

The corpse landed on the floor with a wet thump, blood gushing out like a broken water balloon. The demon glared at Christopher and then turned its hungry gaze back to the circle.

"I think not," the Gold Apostle said, and his face fell apart.

Christopher stood slack-jawed, stunned with the horror of it. The man's face broke into pieces like a puzzle in reverse, the jaw unfolding into a tentacle, cheeks and ears coming apart into strands and waving in the air. Only the eyes remained, though they too changed, turning yellow and gaining a malevolence so potent it gave even the demon pause.

The Apostle's body stood crowned by a mass of tentacles whose pale color gradually faded to dark greens and grays. The Apostle's voice echoed now directly in Christopher's head, without the need of sound.

"You have been paid with the soul of he who summoned you," it said to the demon, its yellow eyes staring it down. "You may go."

With a low growl the demon raised its wings—and disappeared. Not mere invisibility this time. Air rushed in to fill the sudden absence, marking its true departure.

Christopher stood alone, facing the *hjerne-spica*. Though it was the most terrifying moment of his life, he could not escape the question that burned in his brain.

"How long?" he said. "Have you always been the Apostle?"

"So much cleverer than your fellows. I chose well, that day in the snow. No, Christopher, I have worn many faces in this realm, most of them of no account. I only became the Apostle yesterday, after he had become useless to me."

"Don't call me that," Christopher said. "You don't have the right."

"Don't I? We are old friends, you and I. Twice now I have carried you to a church door, to succor your life where it would have failed. Solicitously I have watched your career, sending you gifts when you needed them most."

Christopher shook off the mysterious hints. It was only trying to confuse him. "You mean traps and assassins. You sent magic items to break my mind and people to kill me."

"And did you not make good use of them? See how your stature has risen! You crawled into our world a beggar and now stride it as a king. All because it served my ends."

"I will never help you," Christopher said. "I will die first."

"You have already died," it pointed out. "And yet still you serve. Today you almost died again. And yet again you live. Do not try my patience, though. This habit of selfless self-sacrifice must end. I cannot make use of tools that break when I am not watching over them."

Christopher still had a sword charged with magic. As horrible as the squid-creature was, it was only normal-sized. Just big enough to make a bowl of calamari.

The thing chuckled. "Not today. I withdraw; but mind you our little chat. We both desire the same event, though admittedly with different outcomes. Should you deliver, you will find me generous, though you do not ask for it. Have I not today given you an even greater victory than your pet dragon?"

Its tentacles moved in hypnotic patterns "But should you fail, you will find your fate far more arduous than simple death. Equally unasked for, I suppose. And yet just as inevitable."

A sound from the entrance of the hall. Christopher reflexively snapped his head around, but it was only Cannan rushing in, backed by a platoon of carabineers and knights.

From in front of him came the distinctive popping sound. He whipped his head around again, but the protective circle stood empty. The thing was gone.

"Search the grounds!" he roared. "Find it!"

He squandered precious time on the futile search. The only surprise his men turned up were the children of the castle servants, hiding in the empty stables. The demon had not touched their bodies with its claws; they yielded no tael. The damage it done to their souls was incalculable, though. His soldiers, hardened men all, retreated from the cries of anguish. These children had watched their parents be destroyed by a creature of nightmare.

When no priestesses appeared to comfort the little ones, Christopher realized the battle still raged outside.

He found an open spot in the courtyard and cast the flight spell. Rising above the castle walls, he could see he was too late. His army was ranging the field far and wide, looking for runaways and hold-outs. The bulk of the enemy—the vast horde that had lined up that morning so grim and proud—lay in broken piles scattered throughout the fields. They had fought without asking quarter, perhaps more terrified of the horror Sigrath was summoning than they were of any death steel and fire could give them.

He had won another fortune. This one tasted far fouler than the dragon's gift. How such a victory could rebound to the *hjerne-spica's* profit eluded him. It must know he would never open a gate without protecting it with a thousand layers of defense. He could not guess the rules of its game. Only the stakes—the fate of Earth and, by extension, all mankind—were clear.

Eventually he found Karl.

"I take it you won your portion of the battle," the young man said.

"Not really," Christopher answered. It was too complicated to explain at the moment.

"We have few prisoners," Karl said. "They babbled about demons. Apparently they were promised that if they died fighting us, they would not be fed to a demon, and their souls would be allowed to go to the Tiered City rather than—wherever demons come from. It was a poor stratagem. They fought bravely but not wisely."

"It wasn't a strategy," Christopher said. "There was a demon. It ate Sigrath and disappeared. Then a *hjerne-spica* ate the Apostle and ran away."

Apparently it wasn't that complicated.

"How unfortunate," Karl said. "A substantial loss of tael. Yet this battle will make you rich again. There were many knights under the enemy banner. The Gold must ever bribe its people to fight for it."

The kettles boiled long into the night.

36

VIEW FROM A THRONE

He sat on the cold marble, no less uncomfortable for the weeks he had occupied it. Unexpectedly, the throne came equipped with a place to keep his sword close at hand. A reminder that in this world kingship was not an exercise of merely political power.

Castles had fallen at the mere approach of his forces, all resistance shattered once word spread that a demon had come and been vanquished. Before long he had only sent representatives, not soldiers, to summon the lords to give their oaths to the new regime. Now the last of his recalcitrant kingdom had finally trickled in. A handful of Ranger Lords stood before him, as stony faced as his throne.

"Our ancestors swore to the throne of Kingsrock," Lord Einar stated. "Our vow was passed from king to king, in lawful descent. That line was broken with your rebellion. We claim our freedom now, as you have claimed freedom for your serfs."

Christopher knew that had nothing to do with it. The Rangers had taken the measure of his soldiers and believed their few companies of forest archers could fight him more successfully than an entire realm of knights.

Unfortunately, he agreed with their assessment. Yet it felt unfair to let them slip out of the yoke of taxation. He was reaching out to Earth for their sake, too.

"I can make you the same deal I made the others. I'll promote druids, if they are worthy, if they agree to my laws, if they serve the Kingdom rather than their religion. But I can't let you stop paying taxes. We need those taxes. All of them."

"No king has ever dared to take all our wealth. None even dared to order us to a decimation. We will kill your tax men like stoats in a rabbit warren. If that fails, then we will simply pack our horses and go. There is a world of Wild out there. We can live in it, even if you can't."

"Please don't," Christopher said. "If you're out there scrabbling in the woods, how will you see how much better I've made things?"

Lord Einar glared at him under dismissive eyebrows. "Your feigned madness cannot camouflage your greed."

"Greed?" Cannan barked. The big knight was standing at his left, as he always did when Christopher was on the throne, but he had never interrupted before.

Now the knight shifted his hands, drawing attention to the sword he bore. A kingly gift, literally, from the man who would not wear a crown.

Cannan filled the silence with his growl. "Do you think I crouch at his feet for a bone? He treads upon the only path that leads to Niona. You'll walk it, or I'll drag you. Either way, you're coming along."

The delegation, which had seemed rock-solid, crumbled and fractured before his eyes. Lord Egil was first to break. His eyes went to the floor. Around him hard men softened in sympathy.

Einar was not a man to surrender while there was still ground underneath his feet. "You have promised to preserve magic. Our Rangers wield magic. It is integral to their function, as you know, having been well served by the lowliest of our knights. Will you leave us, and by extension the whole of the realm, blind and deaf?"

This all could have been avoided. He should have returned D'Kan's body to his people to revive and restore on their own. It was what they had expected, what they would have demanded if he had bothered to ask. Now the precedent was like a thorn in his backside. And the throne was painful enough already.

If he gave in to this, he'd have people banging on his door left and right, explaining the virtues of knighthood all over again. And not without reason. A soldier who took more than one bullet to kill was clearly more valuable than a common man.

In the end, he did what he had to. At least he'd had the sense to challenge the wily druids last, while the mundane lords were still in awe of his implacability.

"I will continue to promote Rangers, but only to the extent that their magic is necessary for their task."

There was enough ambiguity in that statement to start a new war. Einar tipped his head and accepted the territory he'd won. Christopher knew he would be back for more.

The Rangers turned to leave. Christopher leaned into the hard stone, stifling a sigh of misery through sheer willpower. His life was now reduced to these political squabbles, to arguments and tax ledgers, to meting out justice to a world that didn't particularly want or even recognize it. It would be years before he could raise enough tael to finish his mission, perhaps even decades. A time scale he dared not let himself face, lest despair overwhelm.

And, of course, hanging over it all was the threat of the *hjerne-spica*, which could apparently come and go at will throughout his realm, armed with magic he did not understand and plans he could not comprehend. If he progressed too slowly, the monster would kill him horribly; if he went too fast, Alaine would judge the risk too high and kill him just as dead.

Between those pillars of immortal displeasure lay his own raw need. He could not sit on this throne indefinitely without becoming something his wife would not even recognize, let alone desire. At some point he would simply break, step through his own personal gate, and leave all of this behind, forever unreachable. It might even be the wisest thing to do. Exposing Earth to magic would have consequences he could not pretend to imagine.

On the other hand, he could not imagine walking past hospitals for the rest of his life, knowing that he had once held the power to heal any injury, any disease, and let it slip out of his grasp through fear and weakness. Knowing that truth could defeat lies, death could be undone, and the souls of men could be shriven and made pure again. He could no more abandon magic than Gutenberg could have taken a hammer to his printing press.

Lalania, standing on his right, reached out to place her hand above his, where he gripped the obdurate arm of his imprisoning chair. Before he could choose whether to return the gesture or ignore it, she took her hand away.

His salvation entered the great hall, too preoccupied with a sheaf of paper to observe the protocols of court behavior. Johm, come to complain about another drafting error or ambiguous design, ruffling through drawings with a confused frown.

Christopher stood up and went to meet him in the middle of the room, grateful beyond measure for the distraction.

ACKNOWLEDGMENTS

Some people have been waiting ten years for this manuscript. To David, Alex, Dylan, Fletcher, and Josh, I hope it's been worth the while. And my thanks to Kristin, Rene, and Sara, without whom it would have been an eternity. Special thanks to my copyeditor, Sheila, for preventing me from committing lese majesty, among many other literary sins.

ABOUT THE AUTHOR

M. C. Planck is the author of *Sword of the Bright Lady* (World of Prime: Book 1), *Gold Throne in Shadow* (World of Prime: Book 2), and *Judgment at Verdant Court* (World of Prime: Book 3). After a nearly transient childhood, he hitch-hiked across the country and ran out of money in Arizona. So he stayed there for thirty years, raising dogs, getting a degree in philosophy, and founding a scientific instrument company. Having

Author photo by Dennis Creasy

read virtually everything by the old masters of SF&F, he decided he was ready to write. A decade later, with a little help from the Critters online critique group, he was actually ready. He was relieved to find that writing novels is easier than writing software, as a single punctuation error won't cause your audience to explode and die. When he ran out of dogs, he moved to Australia to raise his daughter with kangaroos.